THE BOUND WITCH

IVY ASHER

Copyright © 2021 Ivy Asher

All rights reserved. This book or parts thereof may not be reproduced in any form, stored in any retrieval system, or transmitted in any form by any means—electronic, mechanical, photocopy, recording, or otherwise—without prior written permission of the author, except in cases of a reviewer quoting brief passages in a review.

This is a work of fiction. Names, characters, places, and incidents either are the products of the author's imagination or are used fictitiously. Any resemblance to actual persons, living or dead, businesses, companies, events, or locales is entirely coincidental.

Edited by Polished Perfection

Cover by Book Covers by Seventhstar

For Hooba,

You cuddled through every book. Stuck by me for the late nights and the early mornings. You were my shadow, my source of unconditional love and acceptance, and the best little buddy a girl could ask for.

Until the day we're together again for snuggles, neck scratches, and kiss attacks, you are always in my heart and never far from my mind.

Miss you.

1

The bored hum of fluorescent lights buzzes steadily in my ear. The sound moves around me like a confused bee that's mistaken me for a flower, and I fight the urge to swat it away. My nose tingles with a building sneeze as the overwhelming smell of strong disinfectant fights the underlying scent of decay. Goose bumps crawl across my body, and shock wars with panic as my wide eyes dart around, trying to make sense of what's happening.

I'm not dead. Alive.

Somehow, I'm actually here—naked—and surrounded by refrigerators designed to hold bodies.

Fuck.

I just crawled out of one of them.

My heart—the one that I felt stop beating in my chest just seconds ago—hammers inside of me. The cadence is taunting. Like some schoolyard little shit chanting *naa na-na naa na, you can't catch me* before sprinting away. I press my hands against my body, testing the limits of myself, and look down, needing to confirm with my other senses what my palms feel.

Yep, flesh and blood, just like always...but how?

Moss-green eyes dripping with anguish flash in my mind. Desperate lips pressed softly against my own, and a broken plea to "come back to me" settles like an anchor in my soul.

Rogan.

I know he did this. That somehow, against everything we know about mortality and magic, he brought me back. He saved me. I just wish I knew how it was all possible. I felt the truth in his words when he told me that he and Elon didn't know how they cheated death. I saw the confusion, the pain, and the frustration in his eyes as he revealed what it cost them. How, despite their efforts to figure it out, they still aren't any closer to puzzling together why they're alive when they shouldn't be.

Did the tether do this? Could it be powerful enough to have managed this miracle?

My thoughts drift to Elon, and pain lances through me. I can practically feel him in my arms still, our blood pooling around us as death first claimed him and then came for me. I don't know if he's back from his second brush with death. I have to hope that he is. Could he also be here, in another room maybe, wandering around just as nervous and desperate to figure it all out as I am?

Worried uncertainty builds in my chest, and I press my hand over my heart in an effort to calm myself. My fingers brush over a hard, smooth texture that's unfamiliar, and I look down to discover a scar on the left side of my chest. It's a jagged-edged circle almost the size of my fist. There are small lightning-like lines flaring away in the direction of my shoulder and some angled down toward my sternum. The damage is new, a permanent reminder of what happened to me in that godforsaken church, but it looks as though it's had years to heal.

Astonishment dazes me, and I press my other hand to

my stomach in an effort to root myself here so that I don't float away on the insanity of this moment. I know Rogan and Elon went through this. As far-fetched as it was to believe when Rogan told me, I did. I just never thought I'd experience resurrection firsthand. It should be disorienting, and yet here I am, my mind and body working just as they always have, my memories intact and the rest of me reeling.

My stomach gurgles, but I can't tell if it's hungry or upset. A delicate whoosh of air startles me as the air-conditioning clicks on, working to cool an already chilly room. A faint bang somewhere far away focuses my buoyant and bewildered thoughts. A distant but distinct sound of footfall reaches me, and I flinch at the unexpected noise. Reality comes stomping in like an overexuberant marching band, and fear starts to whirl around me like the spinning flags of a color guard.

I'm alive when it shouldn't be possible, and I need to get the fuck out of here before someone else discovers that too.

Immediately I start looking for a place to hide, but there's nothing else in here beyond the walls, lights, linoleum, and body-fridges. There's no table to hide under, and the tall rectangular windows in the double doors are not going to shield me from anyone's view. The footsteps draw closer, and I debate crawling into the chilled stainless steel slot I just crawled out of. I immediately reject that option. I think I'd rather be discovered at this point than to ever have to crawl back into that fucking thing. I've never had an issue with claustrophobia, but I suspect that might change now. Just one more thing to add to the list of shit I *need* to speak to a professional about.

I rub my temples, my head snapping up just as the footsteps sound like they're right on top of me. Alarm takes over, and unbidden, it calls on my magic. Suddenly, the steps start to fade away, the distance between me and whoever is out there, growing by the second. My magic doesn't calm, and I'm not at all prepared for the massive surge of power that continues to flood me despite the fading threat. I wince against the too full sensation while simultaneously recalling what it felt like for this magic, my magic, to fail. For my abilities to blink out like a dying torch as my body fought against the damage it sustained from Jamie and her spelled bullet.

My breaths become heavy as sensations suddenly assault me. I can feel the heat of the bullet as it tore through me. Smell the gunpowder and blood as it mixed with the musty scent of the stone surrounding me. I clearly see the blade of the ritual knife as it sunk into Elon's chest. Hear a tormented scream as it shreds my throat and ricochets around that cursed church. Jamie's face once again melts in front of me, slowly sloughing off to reveal the demon currently wearing her like she's the outfit of the day.

Terror snakes around me, and I close my eyes and shake my head. *No. I'm not there. It's over now.* But even as I think the reassuring words, I know I'm lying. It's not over. I look around at the greige walls and linoleum of the morgue I'm standing in and realize that it's all just begun.

An anxious shiver brushes up my spine, and I stare at the double doors across from me. My magic surges, ready for the possibility that someone might push through them any minute now and discover my naked ass just standing here. Would they recognize me, know that I should be lying on a cold metal tray just like all the other bodies in here? Or would they think I'm some kind of sicko who snuck in here to do who knows what to the bodies in this room? A shudder courses through me with that thought, and my magic flares, begging for a target, for a threat to go off on.

I don't hear the footsteps anymore. Then again, it's hard to hear anything over the booming pulse in my ears right now. Power starts to overload my system, and several loud bangs explode all around me. I scream, whirling around in search of the danger. I snap my mouth shut, cutting off the shriek that's betraying my location, and find several of the refrigerator doors that were behind me shoved open, the bodies they once contained now on the floor. I can feel my unexpected hold on them, my magic claiming their skeletons, my power permeating their blood.

Shit.

I scramble away from the dead and try to rein in the power pulsing out of me as panic tries to take over. I swear I can feel the absence of their souls. I was magically strong before my showdown with Jamie, but what's happening now is a whole new formidable level. One that I need to get a hold of immediately.

The bodies slide clumsily toward me as I take another step back, and I swallow down the scared squeal that tries to escape. Ragged breaths saw in and out of my lungs, and I attempt to tamp down my racing trepidation. It's two older men and a woman my age. I try not to look at the three naked corpses too closely, not needing any more fodder for nightmares than I already have. But it's hard not to see that some are stiff, others aren't, and all of them have a bluish cast. Thankfully, their eyelids are closed and none of them are looking at me, and yet I feel as though they're judging me for not staying dead like I was supposed to, like they have.

I take another hasty step back, and the magic-animated bodies scoot closer.

"Stop it," I snap at my hands as I watch the dead in horror. "Bad magic!"

I look at the open refrigerator doors that the bodies spilled out of and bite back a whimper. A woman sneaking out of the morgue is hard enough. A woman sneaking out of the morgue with three bodies dragging behind her...yeah, that's definitely going to attract the kind of attention I really can't afford right now. I can sense with my magic that the other fridges in here are empty, and I'm at least grateful that this situation isn't worse. Three magic casualties are more than enough.

The sound of a door slamming makes me jump. I spin back to the double doors behind me, expecting someone to be heading right for me, but there's no one there. Cautiously, I peek through the windows, scanning the darkened room beyond for any signs of life or movement. I hold my breath for one second, then another. Nothing moves and no one comes running in my direction, searching for the source of the blood-curdling scream that just rent the night air. At least I think it's night, who knows.

It feels like forever as I crouch behind the door and stare expectantly into the inky room. I can't imagine that a scream is something commonly heard in a morgue, but no one has come to check on the possible source. Maybe I'm not in some standalone The Dead R Us kind of morgue, but attached to a hospital or somewhere else where my leak of terror isn't so out of place.

An image of the Order's headquarters pops up in my mind along with the reminder that there were lower levels I was forbidden from knowing anything about. Could I be there? I try not to let that thought rock me. Regardless of where I am, I can't stand here forever. I need to find a way out and then find somewhere safe.

I know the watered-down version of what Rogan and Elon went through when their mother, the High Priestess of Witches, discovered they had come back from the dead. I'm acutely aware it's only a matter of time before they come for me, and I'd prefer to be wearing more than a panic attack when they do.

With a deep breath, I shove past my overwhelming dismay and push the door open I'm peering through. I pause for a beat, waiting for something to happen, but other than the whisper of displaced air as the door swings out, everything is quiet.

Warily, I step into the dark. Out of nowhere, a light flickers on, and I slam my hands over my mouth to trap the scream that crawls up my throat. I spin, magic crackling threateningly across my skin, ready for attack or discovery...but the room is empty.

Once again, a thump sounds behind me, and I jump as I turn to see the corpses from the other room have pushed the doors open to follow me. They drag like death mops across the cold floor, and I feel horrible, because there's no way that feels good against their unprotected skin. Then again, they're dead, so truly *nothing* feels good or bad anymore. It's a fucked up doggy pile of death, and I swear my heart can't take much more of all the sudden noises and the fear slamming around inside of my body right now.

Crap.

I harden my resolve and look around as I think through my next move. Standing as still as I can, I take in the new room surrounding me. There are cupboards, counters, scales and other things. Things that, thanks to my years of watching crime shows, now look familiar and conveniently placed for things like autopsies and for the required cleaning up when said autopsies are done.

I spot a phone attached to a wall, and I'm stumbling toward it. I cradle the receiver against my head, and I almost cry when a dial tone chirps in my ear. Tears prick my eyes, and emotion makes my chest heavy as I shakily dial a number and the line starts to ring.

"Hello?" a forlorn voice answers on the third ring, and

my heart leaps into my throat, a tear spilling down my cheek.

I never thought I'd hear his voice again.

"Tad," I whimper, but my cousin's name comes out in a froggy whisper, my voice brittle and dry from disuse.

How long have I been dead?

"Yes?" he asks warily, demanding, "who is this?" as though he barely has the energy to bother.

I try to clear my throat so I sound more like myself, but it only seems to make me sound worse. I swear if I could look into my throat right now, a tumbleweed would go blowing by with a cloud of dust following closely behind.

"Tad, it's Leni," I wheeze, sounding more like Harvey Fierstein than I ever thought possible.

The line is quiet, and I scramble to find something in the room that might help me alleviate the parched desert that's taken over my throat. I spot a sink and scramble toward it.

"I don't know who you are or what you want, but if I ever find out, I will fuck you up," Tad snarls, the pain and venom in his voice stopping me mid-stride.

"Tad," I try again.

"If this is your idea of a joke, Gwen, I won't stop until your entire lineage is cursed beyond recovery. You want to play, bitch? Game on!" he roars, and then the line goes dead.

"Tad..." I cough into the phone, but he's gone.

Fuck!

I rush to turn the faucet on, water steadily flowing into the silver basin as I bend under the tall spout and drink. The cool liquid spills down my throat and starts to work its magic. I chug down more, suddenly so thirsty that it's all I can think about. My stomach gurgles happily and then makes me keenly aware that it would like more than just water in its depths. A bear-like growl courses through my body, the hunger all at once demanding and impatient.

Clearly, my body just remembered that it should be running on more than just crippling fear and anxiety.

I fill my stomach with as much water as it can contain, hoping it will hold off the demand for food a bit longer, and turn the faucet off. I immediately hang the phone up and then try to call Tad again. It goes straight to his voicemail without even ringing. Growling frustratedly, I hang up the call and then try again. And again. But all I get is Tad's annoying voicemail.

Pretty sure the fucker blocked me.

A clang fills the room as I slam the receiver down a little too hard. I search my mind for anyone else I can call, but I come up blank. I thread my fingers through my curls, which are matted and dry. I'm pretty sure someone washed my hair and didn't condition it properly, and that realization creeps me out more than I can say. I look around the room again, viewing it with a rush of unwelcome questions. Is this where I was magically autopsied? Did they cut me open and then clean me up? I search my body for more scars but don't find anything other than the new one on my chest.

Blowing out a deep sigh of relief, my stricken stare once again lands on the jumble of corpses. Shit. I was going to put the bodies back before I got distracted by the phone. I eye the *shadows of death*, and an idea trickles into my seriously messed up mind... Maybe they can help me. It's wrong. So messed up. I immediately start to judge myself as a plan starts to form. But if *I* disappear from the morgue alone, I might as well have a neon sign above my head, flashing to the High Council, *guess who came back from the dead*. But if *all* the bodies were to disappear at the same time, it might take them a little longer to piece it all together. Okay, maybe not *all* the bodies. I can't be greedy. I also don't want to use too much magic and either drain myself or ping onto anyone's radar. But certainly, taking these three would still help. As fucked up as it is to body snatch people, it could buy me some time while the Order or High Council work to solve the mysterious disappearances of the contents of my part of the morgue.

I cringe at my thoughts, a tinge of guilt percolating my gut. As shitty as it is to do this to whoever these people are, I seriously need all the help I can get.

Slap my ass and call me selfish, I guess.

A shiver moves through me, unease pooling in my stomach, and I feel the overwhelming urge to get the fuck out of here. I move to the exit, my steps steadier and stronger from the gallon of water I just gulped down. I gingerly step out into a hall, and more fluorescent lights click on as I make my way through the emptiness in search of an escape point.

I move quickly, ignoring the drag of the bodies behind me as I go. I should feel worse than I do about pulling them along, but I don't want to use more magic and risk alerting people that something's amiss. I don't know how my scream and pulse of magic have so far gone undetected, but I'm not going to push it. Someone could round a corner and slam into me at any moment. The need to get out of here is riding me too hard to care about anything else.

My pace is steady, silent, and I find myself hoping that I'll somehow run into Rogan as I make my way through the windowless building. Did he know I'd come back? I mean, he did ask me to, right? Was that just something whispered in the loss of the moment, or did he mean it? But if he knew, then where is he? Why isn't he waiting nearby to intercept me?

My suspicions begin to harden with each step I take. This has to be the work of the tether, otherwise Rogan would be here. He probably doesn't even know I'm back. I reach for the tether inside of me, but I quickly realize my magic feels like a frenetic mess. It's as though my power is a newborn fawn, all wobbly legs and spastic unsteady moves. There's so much strength to it, but it feels untrustworthy too, like it's not all the way awake and focused yet.

Maybe dying reset things and my magic needs a moment to wipe the sleep from its eyes and deal with the morning breath and bed head before it'll be up and ready to go. I push my power and search for the tether, but all I can seem to really focus on is the hold I have on the bodies behind me. I look over my shoulder to find them following me like obedient baby ducks.

"I'm sorry," I whisper to them.

They don't answer back. Let's hope this c*oming back from the dead* thing isn't a onetime shot, because otherwise I'm probably going to hell next time for this. I pass a door and then back up, reading the sign next to it: Showers. I pause next to the door for a moment, debating. I don't feel any magic, or sense any amulets or protections on anything around me. I don't think I'm at a magical facility, but what the hell do I know? It doesn't make a lot of sense that I'd be at a human morgue either, but wherever I am, I'm not sticking around to ask questions about how I got here and why.

I press my body snatched accomplices against the wall of the hallway and then withdraw my magic. "Stay," I order them, just in case.

Slowly I press against the door to the room marked showers, holding my breath as I look inside. Swanky looking walnut lockers take up two walls. A couple of them have belongings tucked into the cubby above the closed cabinet below, but I don't see any locks on anything. The look of the space is less high school locker room and more something I'd expect to find in the home arena of a revered sports team. I step into the room, moving in the direction of the occupied cubbies, when a trilling whistle fills the air. I freeze. Adrenaline explodes inside of me, and I look around frantically for the source. The light birdsong morphs into a tune I know but can't place, and I realize that someone is in the showers on the other side of the wall to my left, whistling away as they clean up.

Crap.

I hesitate, questioning if I should still try to steal some clothes or get out of here as quickly as possible. My panicked gaze lands on a row of shelves, green stacks folded neatly in columns. I stare at the organized piles for a beat before recognition slaps me across the face.

Scrubs!

As though I'm some cartoon character sneaking around with exaggerated movements, I quietly stalk over, reading the labels on the shelves for the one labeled *small*. As swiftly as a striking viper, I pull down a top and a pair of matching bottoms, quickly pulling them on and listening for anyone who might be headed my way. I look for anything that I can put on my feet, but all I see is a pair of sneakers tucked under a bench. They look entirely too huge to be of much use to me, so I say *fuck it* and opt to head back out barefoot.

The telltale squawk of a shower knob being turned urges me on. I'm out of the locker room and back into the now dark hallway before the water in the showers can so much as stop dripping. Once again, the fluorescent lights above me flick on as I move, but this time I don't flinch in alarm. The hallway ends at a trio of elevators. I press the call button and hold my breath as I watch the numbers count down. I must be in a basement.

The ding of the elevator is alarmingly loud as the steel doors part, revealing an empty carriage. I call the bodies to me, stepping into the stainless car. Cold flesh rests on one of my feet, and I try not to gag. Maybe I should have gotten them scrubs too. No, there's no way I can make what I'm doing better. Naked and dead or dressed and dead, I'm still stealing them.

I make sure all three of my accomplices are in, and then hurriedly start poking the button that closes the doors, while eyeing the panel and the floor options. I scan the carriage for a camera, but I don't see the telltale sign of a red light or a placard telling the rider that they're being recorded. I select *G*, hoping it spills out to a garage. It's probably a safer bet than the lobby or the ten floors listed above it.

It's all I can do not to shush the elevator as it dings loudly again and opens up to an almost empty parking area. Relief whooshes through me as I step over a body and out onto the cold pavement. It's dark outside, but a hint of early morning is lightening the horizon and reigniting my urgency to get as far away from this place as quickly as I can. Rubbing the chill from my arms as I go, I speed walk my ass away from the elevator. My escape partners sweep closely behind me, the light making their pallor even more sickly.

Yep, definitely going to hell if I ever die again and stay dead.

I scan the area for a good place to hide three bodies. I never thought that would be something I would ever think to myself, but alas here we are. Thankfully, it's as though the universe landscaped around this building, knowing I would need hiding places someday. There are plenty of tall bushes that are surrounding several groupings of trees. The clusters of foliage dot the property evenly all around me.

I instruct my magic to relocate my little *death ducklings*, and then I slam a hand over my mouth with shock when my power goes overboard and practically launches the bodies. It's like that attraction at a circus where they shoot someone out of a huge cannon, only so...*so* much worse. In a blink, each of the people I've stolen streaks across the ground into different groupings of brush. I cringe as they settle fully hidden away, whipping my head around to make sure no one is nearby to witness the depravity I've stooped to. I've never felt more selfish and messed up in all my life.

"I don't know who you are, but I will, and I swear just as soon as I can, I will give all three of you the most beautiful funerals ever," I whisper into the chilly morning air. Streaks from the rising sun start to glow brighter as though the universe approves this message, but I still feel like shit. "Headstones!" I whisper yell, my eyes darting here and there, ensuring that I'm still alone. "We're talking the most regal headstones you three have ever seen. The kind of stuff you find in hundred-year-old cemeteries in Europe," I tell them. "Tall, unbreakable, moss-covered even if that's your thing. You want it, you got it," I reassure them as if it somehow makes my theft and fucked up game of hide-and-go-seek okay.

They're dead, Lennox, I remind myself. I mean, what do I expect, that they'll spend their time hiding in the bushes, thinking about how I can make this up to them? I press my palm against my forehead and tuck my guilt away with a sigh.

"Best funerals ever," I promise one last time and then hurry away without trying to look like I'm hurrying. It's easier than I thought it would be to make my way out of the parking garage, hide three bodies, and then scurry away like the cockroach I now am. So easy in fact that I start to question if this isn't some sort of setup.

What if the Order or High Council *do* have me and they're letting me sneak away on purpose so I can lead them to Rogan and Elon? Suspiciously my gaze darts all around as though threats and danger are instantaneously waiting at every corner, but I don't see anyone or anything that makes me feel as though I'm being watched or followed.

I stroll quickly but casually out of the shadow of the

building I'm fleeing from and discover I'm in a city. As clear as that revelation is, none of the surrounding buildings spark any kind of familiarity, and I feel just as lost as ever. I'm definitely not on the block the Order occupies in Chicago, but that's about all I could say for sure. I hasten my steps, hoping I'm not drawing attention to myself. I probably look like some patient escaping from a psych ward, but so far there's been no one around to side-eye me.

My feet pad quickly across the cold ground. Ignoring the small rocks that occasionally prick my soles as I go, I scan everything around me, scared and frantically trying to figure out what to do now. I need to get home, to Rogan, but I have no idea if it's safe or how I'm going to manage it. I have no money, no shoes, no phone or way to get a hold of anyone to come get me. The surrounding skyline is unfamiliar; I could be anywhere, although I'm hoping I'm in the US, based on the fact that I made a phone call to a US number without any issue. I thought that evil church was maybe overseas, but now I'm not so sure. Or maybe they transported me to wherever I am.

Damn, how long have I been dead?

Magic flares out of me uncontrollably as my distress builds. Swearing, I hurry to yank it back. It's as though I'm roping a wild horse and pulling at it with all my might for control. Something strange flares through my chest, a searing heat cutting open my depths like a welding torch. I gasp at the shocking sensation, but my attention flashes away as I suddenly feel the call of magic. Magic that is the very answer I'm looking for.

I close my eyes and thank the stars and my ancestors as incredible power pulses invitingly toward me like a long forgotten friend.

A ley line.

That's it. That's my answer.

I mean, if I can manage not to get myself stuck inside of it, that is. Or accidentally flash myself to some place worse than where I am now. But how hard can it be, right? I *did* pass out the first time I rode one, but I'm way better equipped now.

Totally ready. Badass even.

Who am I kidding, this is probably a horrible idea, but what other options do I really have?

I roll my shoulders as I turn right and move closer to the beckoning power. I'm the Bone Witch. One of two left in the entire world. I've got this.

Hopefully.

Probably.

Ah, moon shits.

2

Concentrating hard, I work to recall the frequency of the first ley line I ever magically tapped into. I conjure the memory of that night with Rogan in the park, and I can once again feel the awe and nerves I felt as he explained how it all worked. The warm, manly scent of mahogany and teak fills my nose, as though Rogan himself is once again standing near me, guiding my thoughts and actions with his smooth, tantalizing voice. I can practically feel the cool grass under my feet as the park I played in as a kid suddenly surrounds me in my mind.

I can recall the way the moon called to me that night, the silvery light caressing my back in warm encouragement.

All at once, the pitch and resonance of the ley line back home takes over my senses. My mind and magic seem to have cataloged the frequency even though I've only tapped into it the one time. It's like reading my grimoire for the first time and realizing that the literal bones of the information are now with me forever.

Magic is fucking cool. I don't know how I could have ever thought otherwise.

Relief washes through me. I know I'm taking a risk even

thinking about riding a line as an inexperienced baby witch, but the familiar call of where I want to go offers me reassurance. It's probably a false sense of security, but hey, beggars can't be choosers at this point. If I want to get away, to stay under the radar as long as possible, this is my best shot.

I start to sense the other frequencies of the lines all around me, my magic now tapping into the grid of magic, all doing their best to tempt me in different directions. I stay honed in on the frequency that leads me home.

Home.

Surprisingly, the thought of that one simple word doesn't conjure the images and memories that it used to. A sparsely decorated one-bedroom apartment isn't what pops into my head. Tad and my Aunt Hillen's house doesn't make an appearance either. No. What *now* occupies my mind is a moss-green gaze, rich brown hair, and the gorgeous face that accompanies a soul that's so much more complex and resolute than I understood before.

Rogan's face is as clear in my mind as my own. I can feel his arms around me, sense the way my body, my magic, called to him from the beginning even though I was doing everything I could to fight it.

I love you.

I pull in a deep breath at the memory of Rogan's unwavering declaration as I lay in his arms, drowning in my own blood, my heart breaking with the realization that I wasn't going to live long enough to bask in what he was saying to me. I shut that line of thought down, refusing to let the pain and trauma of what happened drag me under. The flash of what went down in that church feels like a bucket of ice water to my senses, and I refocus on the task at hand. If I get stuck in a line, it will all be for nothing.

I fill my lungs with the chilled morning air of wherever I am, a car honking somewhere in the distance. I close my eyes and reach out to the ley line running parallel to the massive fountain I'm currently standing next to. A rush of wind sends some of the frigid mist from the massive water feature my way, and I can't help but feel like it's warning me to hurry.

Do they know? Could the High Council and their cronies be hunting me already?

Rogan's voice sounds in my mind, his careful instructions playing back to me *to feel the line and then reach out to it with my magic*. Without another moment of hesitation, I connect to it, opening myself up until the hum and cadence I feel and hear in my chest matches what the line's giving off. A quiet peace crawls through my limbs, and just when I'm about to internally high-five myself for owning this shit, I'm brutally yanked away.

Fuck!

My name unexpectedly rings with warning all around me, as though Rogan is right here admonishing me for getting pulled in. My stomach lurches like I'm on a rollercoaster that's looping around before executing a sudden death drop. Everything is too bright. I'm tingling all over. Sounds and sensations blur and mix in a frantic disorienting way. I grit my teeth and fight to expel everything from my mind except for the frequency of the ley line that runs through the park back home.

Black spots form in my periphery, and the enticing lull of unconsciousness begins to beckon. I shove it away and quickly adjust the frequency of the line radiating through me to the tone of my destination. Just as soon as I do, my body is hooked sideways at what feels like sickening speed. A grunting squeal of a scream rips out of my throat, the force flinging me around so strongly that the sound is torn away before my ears can really register it.

I want to shut down, to turn this feeling off, but I know if

I do, I could get stuck in here or worse. I battle to stay awake and aware, to keep my wits about me. A loud popping threatens to cause my eardrums to explode, and then just as quickly as I was sucked into sound-barrier-breaking speeds, I'm thrust out of them, landing with a dry, pathetic yelp on brittle, unforgiving wood chips.

Ughhhhh, I groan as I lie on my side for a minute taking stock. Surprisingly, I discover that I can breathe, but the rest of me feels very...melty. Like I'm more puddle of goo than person. I lie at the base of a yellow slide and pant awareness back into myself, while also trying to reassure my stomach that there's nothing in it to try and throw up. My body blobs back together like a lava lamp. That's what it feels like anyway as I take a moment to settle and once again feel like *me* against the mulch-covered ground.

It's later morning here in Marblehead, Massachusetts, and the brighter sunlit sky forces me to squint as my eyes adjust. I take another second to be sure any slow-moving lava lamp bits have time to catch up and reattach to me before I move. I definitely don't want to get up too fast and realize that I left a tit in the ley line. Running my hands over my body, I double-check that everything is where it's supposed to be, and then realization dawns.

Holy shit, I really did it. I just rode a ley line.

A smile spreads slowly across my face as pride seeps into my soul. "Wooo hooo!" I scream, and it sounds almost like a battle cry. I shoot up to my feet shockingly fast and steady for what my body just went through. "I fucking did it!" I bellow to the bright overcast sky above me.

An answering high-pitched scream makes me jump and whirl around in alarm. A man decked out in running gear clutches his heart in fear, his eyes wide and focused on me as though I could attack any moment.

"Omg, I'm sorry," I rush to offer. "I didn't mean to scare

you," I add, waving at him limply as though that's all the reassurance he should need that I'm not crazy or a threat. He watches me for a moment and then hesitantly starts to lope away on the wide cement path. I observe that he's not running for his life though, so he probably didn't see me just apparate out of nowhere.

Thank the ancestors for small miracles.

I brush mulch off my stolen scrubs and turn to the parking lot. I pump my fist with excitement, as I find my old Pathfinder still parked where I left it, but I keep my happy *whoop* to myself, not wanting to traumatize any other early morning park goers. Quickly, I jog over to the car and kiss the hood before walking to the gas tank. Popping open the little door there, I pluck my emergency spare key from the magnetic holder attached inside.

I was faintly worried my car might have been towed, figuring some watchful park-going parent would have reported it by now, but I'm in luck. I climb into the driver's seat and pet the steering wheel a couple times as I shove the key into the ignition and hope with everything I have that the old boat starts. I almost cry when the engine turns over and the Pathfinder rumbles to life. I didn't even need to sweet talk it.

My eyes land on a copse of old, time-tested maple trees, and I suddenly recall something I haven't given any thought to since it happened. Someone was watching Rogan and me that night. I could only make out an unfamiliar dark silhouette, but as I stare at the trees that cloaked the watcher in their inky embrace that night, I'm all at once certain it was Jamie.

I grit my teeth against the rush of memories and sensations that overwhelm me just at the thought of her name. The smell of ash and fear hits me first. My very cells seem to vibrate with the memory of what it felt like to be shocked by the magical barrier over and over again. My grip on the steering wheel tightens painfully as I white-knuckle my way through the onslaught.

She's gone, I reassure myself, but that fact doesn't bring the relief I need. The damage she did is irreparable, and there's still a demon that needs to be brought to justice for their part in it all. Uneasiness skitters over me like insects across my skin. The feeling quickly passes, and I do everything I can to pack all the worry and trauma away to be dealt with later.

I'm in gear, pulling out, and then shooting down the road in less time than it takes Hoot to rip a fat one. *Gah, I can't wait to see that stinky little fucker.* I wind my way through the familiar streets of Marblehead, Massachusetts, and a list of all the things I need to do before Hoot and I can be reunited races through my mind.

Before I know it, I'm turning down the street that leads to Hillen and Tad's house. I disconnect the autopilot I clearly activated without realizing it, and swiftly turn down a different road from where I actually want to go. I don't want to risk being spotted just in case their house is somehow being watched. I feel like some two-bit burglar casing the streets, as I casually make my way down a few back roads, looking for an inconspicuous place to park.

I pull over in front of a house that already has a crap ton of cars parked in front of it, my eyes peeled for anything that looks out of the ordinary. My key feels warm in my palm as I pull it from the ignition and grip it tightly in my hand. I jump out, shutting the door as quietly as I can, before crossing the street.

Out of habit, I lace my key between my fingers as I move. I scoff with amusement when I realize what I've done. *Really, Lennox? Keys as a weapon? My whole existence is a weapon now.* I chuckle to myself as I look around at the alleys, blind corners, and obstructed throughways between houses with a new light. *Let* some mugger think I'm prey; my magic has been primed for a fight since I first woke up.

I go from slinking through the familiar neighborhood like I'm up to no good, to strutting like a tomcat on the prowl. Maybe it's arrogant to think I could take on anything right now. Maybe I'm riding some post-resurrection high. I'll have to ask Rogan if he felt like this after he woke up. Either way, I'm feeling confident as fuck right now. You'd think I was some high-paid model walking down a runway in designer duds instead of sporting stolen scrubs and a case of bed head that has to be alarmingly intense at this point.

I wonder if Cardi B would do an anthem for me. She'd be perfect, she's the level of Bad Bitch I'm feeling right now.

I don't spot anything or anyone that would make me think Hillen's house is on any other witch's radar. Still, I cover my tracks as much as possible by opening Mrs. Falcone's gate and making my way through her backyard to the four loose fence planks that separate her green space from my Aunt Hillen's.

The loose boards move aside as though they're helpful bellmen and not the barrier they're supposed to be. I immediately feel less tense as I step onto Hillen's lawn. Shockingly, her garden looks as though it could use a good weeding. I tsk quietly. Grammy Ruby would be appalled. I test the handle of Hillen's large slider, eyeing the kitchen window just in case this doesn't open, but to my relief the glass pane slides smoothly over, and I'm bombarded by the smell of fresh-baked bread, incense, and irises.

Melancholy and loss reach out and slap me hard across the face. The scents wrap around me, immediately reminding me of my dad and his funeral along with the few other times this collection of specific and meaningful smells filled the walls of this house. Sure enough, the counter has warm loaves still in their pans cooling down on racks. I can picture the tears dripping down my aunt's face as she kneaded her sorrow into those loaves, the urge riding her to *do* something, to *control* something in an otherwise completely helpless time.

My throat tightens at the thought that these loaves are for me. I shouldn't be here to smell the sorrow wafting around this kitchen right now, but I am. In a normal world, there's no stealing someone's loss and grief. No matter how much you may want to shoulder that burden for someone else, it's impossible, and yet here I stand in Hillen's kitchen ready to do just that.

"Hillen?" I call out, the shout shattering the sad stillness all around me. "Tad?" I try again, moving further into the house when no one answers.

Uninvited nerves begin to churn in my stomach when the house stays silent.

"Tad? Hillen?" I shout even louder as I turn a corner to the base of the stairs that lead up to the second floor.

Shocked, I stop dead in my tracks when I find Tad is standing in the middle of the stairs in a very wrinkled T-shirt and sweats that look as though he's been living in them for a while. He stares at me, bruising dark circles cradling flat, listless eyes. His light brown hair looks worse than I think even mine does right now. He's pale, haggard as hell, and not in a state I've ever witnessed before.

"Leni?" he rasps in awe, and then it's as though his legs give out, and he sits hard on the stairs, clutching the railing for dear life as agony tears through him.

I rush to him, two stairs at a time, as the sobs take over his body, and he buries his face in the crook of his elbow and cries. I did this to him, and I hate it. The magnitude of his loss is all-consuming, and my own eyes fill with tears as I pull him from the railing to me. He doesn't fight my embrace, and all I can get out between my own wracking wails is that *I'm sorry.* I repeat the two-worded lament over and over again as we drown the stairs in our tears and cling to each other with everything we have.

We stay like that for what feels like an hour. Me apologizing for the pain he's clearly drowning in, and him just clinging to me and purging every ounce of devastation. It's brutal and strangely validating. To know that you're loved that much, to get what he's going through because it would be me in the wrinkled sweats and choking sobs if the roles were reversed.

Hillen doesn't join us, leading me to conclude that she must be out somewhere. I have an itch crawling just under my skin to find her, to make sure she doesn't take another step or live another second with the heartache I know she's feeling. I get why Rogan wouldn't have done anything to possibly give them false hope, but I hate that they've been going through so much for nothing.

"I'm here. I'm back," I reassure Tad, hoping it will help him surface from the grief. Both of our tears have dried up, but there's an echo of a sob still shaking through his chest, and I know he's not all the way free of the toll agony and loss has taken on him.

"Did you bring them? Is that how this works?" he asks, his tone subdued and sadly resolute.

"Bring what?" I ask, confused, leaning down so I can look him in the eye and try to discern what he's saying.

"Ma said there was a reason we hadn't found them yet, that you would get them to one of us when the time was right. Is this some top secret Osteomancer ritual that you only find out about when you're the chosen one?" he asks, his mahogany eyes searching mine. "Is Grammy here?" he presses, suddenly looking around, a spark of hope momentarily chasing away the forlorn look in his gaze.

Grammy? Here?

I stare at Tad, confused for a beat, and then realization kicks in like a donkey kick to the ass.

"Tad, I'm here," I explain, but the illumination of understanding doesn't flick on in his stare. "I came back," I add, trying to make myself clearer.

"I know," he tells me, his eyes welling with emotion. "It's so fucked up seeing you like this, but I'm so glad I can. Will you stay with me...or do we only have so long?" he questions, a hint of desperation settling in his words.

"No, Tad, you're not hearing me," I try, switching tactics from delicate explanation to flashing neon sign of truth. "I'm *not* dead. I'm alive and sitting next to you right now."

Tad leans away from me, his eyes flitting around our surroundings like he's searching for clarity and it's written on the walls and the ceiling. He shakes his head as though he doesn't like the words he's about to speak and turns back to me. "No, Lennox, you died," he tells me, his eyes soft and compassionate as if he's breaking bad news to me. "Rogan told us what happened. How he was too late. Ma decked him."

My eyes widen with shock. "She what?" I demand, half sympathetic to how awful that must have been for Rogan and half wishing I could have been there to watch. I mean, I may love the dude, but he's pulled some slap-worthy moves in the short time we've known each other.

"Not at first, ya know, we were in complete shock. But after Rogan explained what happened, Ma said she wanted to see you, that she couldn't believe it until she saw with her own eyes."

Tad runs his hand down his exhausted face and huffs out a breath that sounds like it carries the weight of the world on it.

"Rogan made a call, and the next thing we knew,

someone in a morgue was videoing us and showing you on a table with a sheet draped over you." Tad's voice cracks with sorrow, but he shakes his head, refusing to give into the ache of anguish now breathing down on him.

"You know how Ma gets, as soon as she accepted what Rogan was saying, she went into Hillen mode. She started working out where to have the funeral. What flowers you would want. Whether or not to have music at the memorial service. She started asking about how to get your remains transferred here, and Rogan got weird. Said she couldn't have them for a while, that they needed to do some tests or something on the magic that kept you from healing."

I close my eyes, knowing exactly how Rogan would have sounded and all the red flags that would have shot up for Tad and Hillen. He would have sounded vague and cagey, and they would have known he was hiding something. They would have thought the worst, and Rogan would have let them to protect his secret...or what he hoped would become *our* secret.

Shit.

I tune back into Tad and what he's saying.

"So, like I said, you're dead. But hey, look on the bright side, from the look of things, you found someone fun to play doctor with on the other side," he points out, gesturing to my stolen scrubs and sounding more like the Tad I know and love. He nudges my shoulder with his. "Does he have wings? Do they do anything besides look hot and make him fly?" he teases, his voice playful and doing a good job of masking an undercurrent of desolation.

"Tad, you seriously think I'm in heaven looking like this?" I demand, fluffing my dry ass curls.

I swear they make a crunching noise.

He looks me over, and there's no hiding the slight cringe he makes.

"I don't know what in the fucked up *Grey's Anatomy* you ghosts get up to, Lentil Soup. I'm not here to judge," he reassures me.

I roll my eyes and give him an obvious once over. "That's probably a good thing, because if you took a good look at the state you're in right now, you might never recover," I taunt on a laugh as I push up to my feet.

"I am in mourning," he counters, swatting my side with a chuckle before following me down the stairs.

"Where are you going?" he asks when I make a beeline for the kitchen.

"I'm starving, and I saw some muffins down here when I came in." I grab the Ziploc bag of baked goods, mentally chanting *please be blueberry, please be blueberry* as I open it up and unabashedly shove one in my mouth. I moan loudly as the flavors hit my tongue.

Yasss! Blueberry for the win!

I close my eyes in pure bliss and pretty much swallow the whole thing in two chews before quickly wolfing another one down. *There. Happy now?* I ask my stomach as I reach for a third muffin.

"Leni, what's going on?" Tad asks, uncertainty ringing in his tone. "I thought I'd be the next in line, but where are the bones? And how are you doing that? Ghosts can't eat. Is this some kind of optical illusion?" he questions, the last part more of a mumbled explanation he's telling himself versus a question actually directed at me.

My mouth is too full to politely yell at him that I'm not dead, so I simply level him with a look of exasperation. Guarding my bag of blueberry treasures, I walk toward him, hip checking him into the fridge as I leave the kitchen. "Can ghosts do that, Tad?" I point out, but it comes out a bit garbled by the muffin in my mouth.

"Rude!" he calls after me before regaining his footing and following close on my heels.

I head down the hall and find myself wrapped up in the warm familiarity of the cream-colored walls and the pictures hung all over of bad school portraits, the Osseous ancestors that came before us, and the silly pictures of family vacations and get-togethers. I gorge myself as I go, wandering into the guest room where I locate the drawer that houses some of my *I'm too drunk or tired to drive home* clothes. Turning to Tad, I take a deep breath and let my eyes grow serious. "I know this is a lot to take in, and I can't even tell you how sorry I am for what you and Hillen have been through since I died, but I need you to listen to me, like really listen, Tad," I tell him, my throat tightening with emotion as he nods his understanding, his gaze confused and clearly trying to make sense of what's happening.

"Rogan told you the truth, I did die. What he didn't tell you is that he knew a way to bring me back. He wasn't sure if it was going to work, which is why he didn't say anything to you or Hillen before." I place both of my hands on Tad's arms so he can feel me, adjusting my position so our eyes are level. "When I say I'm *here*, Tad, I mean that I'm *really* here. I'm flesh and blood, frizzy curls and a beating heart. I'm alive. I'm not a ghost here to deliver the bones. The bones are still mine because I'm *not* dead. Well, not anymore anyway."

I give his biceps a little squeeze, hoping the contact punctuates my point. Tad just stares at me, his eyes unsure but analyzing. He looks like he doesn't know what to believe. I can see that he wants to but that it's just too much to even hope for.

"I swear on Rufio and the epic love you two would have shared if he hadn't died in *Hook*," I tell him, not an ounce of humor in the declaration, because we *never* joke about the great loves of our youth.

Tad's hands shoot up to cover his mouth, a small gasp escaping before he can hide it behind his palms. He shakes his head, like reality is just too much to take in right now. Then all at once, shaking arms wrap around me, tightening to a bone-crushing pressure that grounds my soul and tells me that he finally gets it. He believes.

"Rufio died a hero," Tad sobs after a couple of minutes.

"Bangarang," I confirm, my own tears once again dripping down my face as we hug.

"Even Hook knew he fucked up. He stopped fighting and everything," Tad goes on, hugging me even tighter.

"I mean, he's no Spot Conlon," I counter, picking up on an age-old argument as tranquility settles over me.

Tad scoffs, pulling away to clear the tears from his cheeks and wipe his nose on the inside of his shirt. "Oh please, Rufio would have swept the floor with that Newsie. A slingshot just isn't going to cut it against seasoned sword skills."

"Spot is a *brawler*," I defend for the thousandth time. "That's why all the other Newsies were afraid of him, and don't even start with how he was probably too short for me."

My cousin's eyes are alight with love and happiness as he takes me in, and things suddenly feel right. Like it doesn't matter that the Order could be hunting me as we speak or that maybe Rogan could feel differently about everything now that I'm back. Tad isn't hurting anymore, and that's all that matters to me right now.

"How?" he asks, taking me in, his voice and visage filled with awe and confusion.

I turn to the attached bathroom and set my clothes and the almost empty bag of muffins on the counter. "It's a long story," I warn, turning on the water in the shower before shutting the bathroom door behind me.

"I ain't afraid of a long story, spill the tea...and don't leave out any details," he shouts through the door, and I chuckle.

"Well, it started when a tall, dark, and dickish man of mystery walked into my life..." I begin dramatically, shouting through the door and filling Tad in on every single detail as I step into the shower and wash away the last remnants of death and resurrection from my skin.

3

"Holy shit," Tad exclaims for about the thousandth time.

"I know," I agree, as I scrunch product into my curls and open up the drawer that houses a diffuser attachment.

"Demons are no joke," he warns, as though I didn't just witness that fact firsthand.

"You're preaching to the choir," I shout over the whir of the blow dryer. "I love that you're more concerned with the demon part of that story than the fact that I came back from the dead," I tease.

"Oh, I have every intention of freaking out about that. All in good time, Leno. I'm just trying to process the manageable parts of your story, and demons run screaming to the top of that list."

"Fair enough," I concede with a chuckle.

I probably shouldn't feel so lighthearted right now; the Crone knows my life could turn back into a clusterfuck any second now, but I'm clean, my belly is full, my loved one isn't suffocating on heartache anymore, and I just feel...good. Better than good, really. Power is humming through my veins, and the gnawing unease that's been tugging at me since I woke up is suddenly calm and replaced by determination and relief.

"But how the hell did that bitch get one to cooperate? A demon would gut you nine times out of ten instead of listening to one word of why some no-name ex-witch would have summoned them," Tad states evenly, his observation pulling me from my inner *it's good to be alive* reflection.

I can tell by the way he's staring at the wall that his question is more for him than me.

"Demons don't fuck with Lessers or Mancers unless they *really* have something they want. So, what the hell could Magic-Stripped Barbie have that a demon would want badly enough to get involved in the serious shit show she created?"

Tad's musings reverberate through me like the off-key ring of a damaged bell. A shiver runs through me as I recall the first time I saw Jamie, with demon marks branded all over her and nothing but madness swimming in her eyes. "From the looks of things, whatever she was working with liked to fuck her," I throw out there, shaking my head to clear it of the images and sounds that filled the church when Jamie first summoned her demon.

"Na, that kinda shit is more a play for dominance or a smoke screen when it comes to their kind. They care more about power than pussy or penis."

"How do you know that?" I ask, a little bewildered by his matter-of-fact statement. I flip my head to the other side and start scrunching those curls and drying them as I wait for him to explain where he's getting all his info from.

"Remember that magic adjacent group I told you about, the one that I meet up with?"

I think back to Tad lecturing me on how being tethered to Rogan or anyone else was a very bad thing, and nod my head.

"Yeah, well, the people who grow up and live around you power wielders, they pay attention, take notes, share experiences and knowledge with others like us. Probably more than mancers or other powerful beings realize," he admits. "Just because we aren't ultimately chosen doesn't mean we're any less a part of your world. We grow up knowing about it, affected by it, and we talk."

"Do your friends know about me and Rogan?" I press as I flip my head forward and fluff my hair, thinking through what he said about demons and their motivations.

"No. I like to gossip, but I protect family secrets. You being tethered to the renounced heir of the High Priestess is about as juicy as it fucking gets, and that's before the whole immortal part of your story kicks in," he declares, circling a finger in my direction. "That stays under lock and key as far as I'm concerned. Knowing that kind of shit gets you killed."

Reflexively I cringe, not only from the cold truth in that last statement but also because I keep waiting for Hillen to pop up out of nowhere and get on us about our language. "Is your mom going to be back soon? I keep thinking she's going to walk in and have a conniption, either about the number of times you just said *shit* in the last two minutes or because I'm standing right here, not dead, like she thinks I am."

I turn the diffuser off and put it back in the drawer.

"Fuck, what time is it?" Tad yelps, leaping off the covered toilet and pulling his phone from his pocket to check the time. "Shit, she's going to ream me. I was supposed to pick her up half an hour ago. Fuck my life."

I hear him try to call her, but it goes straight to voicemail.

"Dammit, her phone must be dead. Let's go," he calls over his shoulder as he races out of the bathroom.

"I can't," I call after him, and he spins to look at me

confused. "First off, I don't think the car is the best place to have a *surprise, I'm not dead* reunion with your mom. She's going to freak the fuck out, and it's probably better to do that here, rather than out there," I explain, jerking my chin at the light on the other side of the curtained window in the guest room. "Secondly, I don't know how smart it is for me to be riding around in public like I'm not supposed to be dead. I need to keep that on the DL for, like, ever, or until I talk to Rogan at least."

"Right, yeah, that makes sense," Tad agrees.

"You don't happen to have his number, do you?" I gesture awkwardly to the phone clutched tightly in his palm.

He looks down at it sheepishly. "I did. But...I might have deleted it after the whole *it's my fault she died* thing."

"It wasn't his fault," I argue, uneasy with the thought that Rogan thinks that, let alone wants anyone else to.

"If you say so," he relents easily. "Ma has it. I'll get it from her if she doesn't kill me for forgetting to get her. She only reminded me like a thousand times not to forget."

I wince, knowing he's about to get chewed out within an inch of his life. A pissed Hillen is a Hillen you don't want to fuck with. "Run," I encourage, my tone amused but the look in my eyes dead serious.

Tad gulps audibly, and I can see hesitancy in his face. He doesn't want to leave me. My heart warms, and I swallow back the emotion that climbs into my throat.

"I'll be here when you get back," I reassure him. "I'm not going anywhere."

He blinks away some welling tears and nods, pulling me in for a quick hug before taking off. I can't help but giggle as he sprints down the hallway and out the front door. I fully crack up when the sprinklers turn on just as he sets foot on the lawn. He screams, high pitched and frantic, as he races through the spattering onslaught to where his Prius is parked in the driveway. The car putters away from the house and down the street, and I swear Hillen must be sending some serious bad juju Tad's way—the timing of the sprinklers was entirely too perfect to be a coincidence.

Letting the curtain of the window I'm peeking out fall closed, I head back to the kitchen for some water. Man, resurrection sure makes a girl thirsty. I gulp down two glasses, my thoughts wandering and flitting around the question of what to do now. Instead of reflecting on anything useful, anxiety directs my focus to Rogan.

What will he say when he answers his phone to find me on the other end of the line? We said a lot of things to each other when we both thought I was dying. What if he didn't mean it? What if his words were expressed only to console and ease my suffering and imminent passing? He could hate me for Elon. Even if his brother somehow came back too, I couldn't stop his suffering. I sure as fuck didn't figure out the blood magic loophole fast enough to save him from more pain and death. There could be some harbored resentment for that.

A resigned sigh spills out of me as all kinds of worst-case scenarios flash through my mind. My gut's telling me I'm being an idiot, but that doesn't do much to calm the anxiety and guilt that starts to surge inside of me as all kinds of *what ifs* swirl around my head like a cyclone.

I lean against the counter and try to get a hold of my runaway worries. Logically I know it's stupid to freak out about this. I have bigger worries hanging over my head. This high school *but does he like me* crap needs to fuck off, but instead, it seems to roost in my chest, pecking at me until it's all I can focus on.

A pounding knock comes from the front door, the loud

sound startling. I turn to stride into the living room to see who it might be when I hear the heavy door open.

What the hell?

"Mrs. Osseous? Tad? I'm sorry for barging in. I know I'm the last person you want to see, but we have a situation," a booming voice calls into the house.

I freeze in the entryway of the kitchen when the deep, commanding voice reaches me. My feet and body just up and stop moving as the front door clicks shut and a large frame comes into view. I stop breathing as moss-green eyes land on mine. They widen with stunned confusion, and just like me, he goes still.

One second passes.

He takes me in as though he's trying to understand how I'm standing right in front of him. I can't breathe.

Two seconds go by.

My throat tightens with all the things I want to say. My lips part, readying themselves for the rush of what needs to be explained, but nothing comes out.

Three.

Rogan's eyes fill with tears. He pulls in a shuddering breath, shaking his head as though he dare not believe I'm real. His fists clench. I track the slight movement, my heart tightening at the sign of distress, and then, in four long strides, his mouth is suddenly on mine.

We come together in a desperate explosion of need and disbelief. Fiercely we cling to each other, my body fitting against his as though we were created that way. I gasp at the sudden frenzied contact, and he swallows it down, consuming everything I am and so much more. Rogan drinks me down like I'm everything he needs to survive, and I claim him just as greedily.

He cups my face, his fingers threading through my curls. His kiss is exultant, his tongue composing hymns of moans and needy exclamations with mine. He tastes like the antidote to a poison that's been threatening my very soul. Every doubt, every second thought and what if burns to ashes in the blaze of what ignites between us. It's more than anything I've ever felt before, and all at once, his lips on mine, his body pressing in against me isn't enough.

I need more.

I *need* him.

Heat roars through me as I grab onto his shoulders and pull myself up. Without missing a beat, he reaches down and cups my ass, bringing my face even with his. I take control of our kiss, twining my tongue with his, lacing every stroke, suck, and nip with my building want. I grind my hips against the muscles of his stomach, surprised by the flash of sensation that zips through me from that friction alone.

Well, hello, washboard abs, allow me to introduce you to my very eager clit.

"Lennox," Rogan rumbles as he tries to pull away, but I'm not having it. Whatever needs to be said can be said later, right now all we need is *this*. I answer the question in his tone by crashing my mouth back to his, and he gives into me exactly like I want him to.

He starts to carry me out of the kitchen, and I kiss my way down his jaw to his ear, directing him where to go, between nipping at his lobe and kissing a trail down his neck. His large hands tighten on my ass as he stalks down the hallway to the guest room. I grind against him as he goes, loving the deep moan it elicits as I do.

"We need to talk, I have to tell you—"

"Later," I interrupt breathily. "There will be time later," I reassure him, but it doesn't take much coaxing to keep his focus on the urgent need circulating between us. He carries me into the room, kicking the door closed with his foot, and the next thing I know, my back is pressed against the cool wall, and Rogan is once again kissing the ever-loving fuck out of me.

There's no questioning how badly he needs this too. It's in his taste, in the way he holds me like there's nothing in this world that could ever make him let me go. He rolls his hips up into my spread thighs, his hard length grinding against me tantalizingly, promising me the *more* I'm so desperate for.

I reach over his shoulder and start bunching the fabric of his too soft shirt as I try to pull it up and off. He leans back, pinning me against the wall with his hips, and rips it off with lightning fast speed. Part of me is disappointed; I kind of want to savor the strip tease, but the other part of me, the fiendish part, screams *later, bitch* and then redirects all moisture and focus directly to our vagina.

I pull my shirt off too, reaching for the bralette I have on underneath, but Rogan beats me to it, pulling the fabric down like some savage animal so that my breasts spill out. Without hesitation, he wraps his luscious lips around one of my nipples.

Fuck, that's hot.

I moan as he sucks hard and then flicks his tongue against the sensitive peak. Eagerly, he thrusts up against me again, and I'm both incredibly turned on and pissed that his pants haven't spontaneously combusted yet and freed his dick.

Where's a Circummancer and a little bit of flame when you need it?

I reach down between us and start working on his fly. I'm so lost to how good he feels pressed against me, sucking on me while he taunts my pussy with all that delicious friction he's creating, that I can't do much more than tug on his jeans. Luckily, he quickly gets what I'm after and pulls us away from the wall, setting me on my feet.

My inner fiend sounds the alarm and starts to defiantly slash war paint across her cheeks, clearly unhappy with this turn of events. I focus my gaze on Rogan as he unbuttons his jeans and quickly lowers his zipper, and my hormones immediately stop revolting and catch on to what's about to go down.

Quickly, I rip my bralette over my head and push my leggings down my hips. His *get naked fast* plan is a solid one. My underwear comes off with my leggings, and while Rogan smoothly steps out of his jeans, I have to start hopping around to try and get these clingy fuckers off my feet. With a frustrated growl, I finally manage to free myself, and I've barely regained my balance before Rogan is practically tackling me against the wall again.

I open my mouth to point out that there is in fact a very available bed located in the room we're currently occupying, but when he palms my ass tightly, lifting me up so he can then drag my bare pussy down the length of his deliciously hard, very thick cock, I flip the bird to the bed, because this wall is where it's at.

We both moan in unison as my wet arousal coats his long shaft. I bury my fingers in his dark brown locks as he moves me up and down his steely length, building the anticipation and tormenting me with this titillating contact that's so good and yet still not enough. My breasts are pressed against his warm hard chest, his muscles rippling and undulating against me. I never thought someone's skin smoothed against mine could feel so fucking good. I whimper desperately as he kisses up my neck and sucks on the skin just below my ear.

"What should our safe word be?" he baits, whispering huskily into my ear, his breath tickling and taunting as he slowly parts the lips of my pussy with the tip of his cock.

So close, but not nearly close enough.

I frustratedly clench down against nothing, the need to have him inside of me right now all I can focus on. "Rogan," I plead as I brush my lips against his jaw and try to press down onto his thick waiting length. He holds me tight, not allowing me to move even a centimeter, and I feel a slight whine sneak into my voice as I lick the edge of his jaw and then demand in his ear for him to "fuck me...now."

"That'll do," he growls approvingly, and then with one powerful thrust, he's deep inside of me. We both moan loudly, lost to the exquisite sensation of it all. "Fuck, I've wanted to do that since the first day I met you," he confesses against my lips, his hand tilting my head back until our eyes meet.

I stare into my favorite color of green, thinking about how I almost lost this. I almost didn't see it, didn't let myself see *him,* until it was too late. "I've wanted you to do this from the first time I body checked you. If you hadn't started in on that familiar bullshit, I probably would have convinced you to bend me over the reading table right there and then."

"Mmmmm," he hums as he pulls out of me and then thrusts back in. "I would have fucked you on the reading table, the front counter, I would have taken you against every shelf and surface in that shop. You're the most breathtaking creature I've ever seen. That mouth of yours, your kind heart, and *fuck*, the way you taste and feel, it's been impossible not to want you, Lennox," he tells me, pulling out at the end of each statement and thrusting deeply back inside of me.

I pant against his declarations, an orgasm already building from his raw confessions and the languid assured pace he's setting. His words and sentiments play at my heart while his dick hits all of the right spots that make me weak and pliant.

"Rogan," I beg, his name a prayer on my lips and a plea

for salvation as my orgasm builds, lapping and ebbing with his unhurried movement.

He kisses me deeply, as though he wants to taste his name in my mouth, and I invite him in to drink his fill. Our tongues dance, and my nipples rub against his hard chest as his thick cock moves slowly, deliberately, in and out of my clenching, needy pussy.

I wrap my hand around the back of his neck and desperately start rolling my hips against his. I drive down on him thrust for thrust, picking up the pace hungrily as Rogan swallows down my moans and feeds me his own. We consume each other's desire until it's almost impossible to breathe. Breaking away from his mouth, frantic and panting, I lean my forehead on his muscular shoulder, looking down and watching as he fucks me harder and harder.

He pistons in and out of me, and I stamp his thick cock with wet approval as our skin sings against one another, the rhythm picking up pace with each passing second. I throw my head back, not able to take it anymore, and drop into an orgasm that has me clenching my teeth and curling my toes as the wave of pleasure crests and then crashes through me.

"Fuck, Rogan," I shout out, completely immersed and floating on how incredibly good he feels.

He tightens his hold on me and then surprises the shit out of me when he takes everything up another notch. He grabs my waist and starts to fuck me so hard and so deep, it's all I can do to hold on. I chant his name over and over again as he purges himself of all the brutal emotions he's been drowning in since I died in his arms. Surprisingly, I feel it all in our bond, through the tether.

I can feel his apology for everything that's gone south since we first met. I can sense the "fuck you" to death he's declaring as he loses himself in me despite its best efforts to rob us of this. Regret rings in our bond over his wrong decisions. Hurt and jealousy zip through our connection, but they're quickly followed by profound respect and deep affection.

The possessiveness I feel from him is intense and oddly grounding, but I'm washed away from that emotion as his loss and desolation come for me like a tidal wave. The depth of what he feels for me is so strong and overpowering, and my eyes begin to sting with emotion.

"I'm here," I tell him softly, repeating it over and over again to try and quiet the storm of grief that's crashing through him.

I tighten my hold on his shoulders and fuck him back just as hard as he's fucking me, our tether and bodies saying everything we need. Pure satisfaction and rightness hums through our veins as another climax tingles to life in my core. Rogan reaches between us and pinches my clit, rolling it between his thumb and finger, as he leans back a little and adjusts his position inside of me.

"Now you're just showing off," I tease, but my giggle morphs into a deep groan, and then I'm crying out incoherently as his dick and the new angle he's hitting render me mindless and begging for more.

Fuck.

I knew it would be good with Rogan, but I had no idea it would be life-altering, *there's no going back now* kind of good. I mean, he's easily achieving *do anything for that dick* status, and this is our first damn time. I can't even imagine what it'll be like when he knows my body and everything my inner fiend really loves. At this rate, I'll live the rest of my days as a walking pile of sexed up goo.

Worth it.

Another orgasm slams through me so savagely that I swear I see stars. We're not talking about those Tweety Bird motherfuckers either; I see galaxies as pure pleasure explodes in every cell I possess. Rogan thrusts into me as deeply as he can get, and then he roars out his release, my name filled with worship as it leaves his lips. His body quickly goes slack as waves of bliss ripple through him. I can feel his unadulterated rapture through the tether, and it swirls and mixes with my own, coaxing and extending all of the glorious gratification we're now both floating in.

"Holy shit," I pant against him, running my fingers through his sweat-damp locks.

"You're fucking exquisite," he puffs back, cupping my cheek and kissing me softly.

Moving away from the wall, he walks us over to the bed. He doesn't pull out of me as he sits us both down, with me now straddling his lap. He brushes my curls from my dewy face and runs his gaze over me as though he still needs to make sure I'm really here. His thumbs caress my cheeks tenderly, and he looks me over, his gaze slowly dropping down until it stills on my chest.

At first, I think he's taking inventory of my awesome rack, and I can't help but puff up with pride just a little. I rotate my shoulders just a tad so he can really see the girls at all their best angles. But when I trace his gaze, I realize it's not my tits that have him locked in a staring contest, it's my newest death accessory that's given him pause. His eyes darken slightly as he takes the healed wound in. I can feel the anguish and contrition that swamps him as he studies the edges of the damage that's now a permanent part of my body.

"I'm so sorry, Lennox. This is all my fault," he laments, pressing a palm gently against my chest as though he can magic away the evidence of what happened. "I fucked up so completely. I should have handled things so fucking differently."

My heart soars at his words, all the what ifs and worries

are wiped away and destroyed. He gets it. I see it in his eyes and etched deeply into his gorgeous features. He understands his role in my pain, and that's validating and stokes my hope.

I caress his face, and he closes his eyes, leaning into my touch. My thumb traces over his scar, his long dark eyelashes tickling the pad of my finger as I follow the line of damage Rogan received the first time he died. What he's saying means so much to me, yet at the same time, I don't know what to say in return to his regret and hurt. I don't want to tell him it's okay. We both know some of the shit he pulled wasn't. Even though I get why he did what he did, it doesn't change how it made me feel, how it wounded me.

But even with all of that being true, I got to know him as I spent time with him. Reluctantly, he gave me peeks of what he was like when he let his guard down. In those vulnerable cracks, I could see the funny, kind, gentle, ferociously protective, loyal man that's at the core of who he is. How's a girl just supposed to dismiss that after seeing it? Maybe *these* facets of who he is were more difficult to coax out, but that also made them more precious, and there was no way I was going to be able to resist that. Despite some of the things that have happened between us, Rogan is a good person. A good person who made some bad choices based on shitty, time-sensitive, and incomplete information.

I stare at him, both of us quiet and content to just *be* for a moment. He looks exhausted. It's clear, just like Tad and Hillen, that he's been through some shit in the time I was gone. I think through all the shit we've been up against since he walked through the doors of my shop. I examine all the left turns we took when a little trust and faith could have had us going a different, smoother way. Then again, we ended up here, and everything about what's between us right now feels right, like this is where we were always meant to end up.

Yeah, Rogan fucked up, but so did I.

I spent a lot of time fighting the tether. I was only interested in seeing a future free of it, too focused on how it all happened instead of taking a moment to see what it could mean. I rejected the notion that any part of this binding could be for my good. I closed myself off to the possibility so much that I literally died because of it. Maybe if I hadn't been so hardheaded, I would have realized that Rogan's blood magic was the key to getting out of that church, but it didn't dawn on me until it was too late.

I never want to shut out truth or reality like that again. I never want to be so closed-minded that others suffer around me because of it. Enough is enough. I learned a valuable lesson in that church, and I can see and sense that Rogan feels the exact same way. It's time to open my eyes and see the truth, regardless of how intimidating, final, or scary it might be. I'm a bound witch, and maybe, just maybe, that's a good thing.

4

I take a deep breath, sorting through everything in my mind that Rogan and I need to talk about. There's *so* much it's hard to even know where to begin, but I give my ovaries a good *we got this* and batten down the vulnerable hatches inside of me, because no more avoiding. It's time to accept and deal with what we're up against.

Leaning down so I can bring our eyes even, I ready myself for answers.

"Elon?" I start, his name sticking in my throat like it doesn't want to come out.

I'm not ready, not really, but I must know. I need Rogan to just rip the bandage off and maybe prepare a tourniquet. Hoping feels useless at this point. I want Elon to be okay, but I can't banish the vision of Jamie's dagger plunging into Elon's chest as my rage-filled scream echoes around that forsaken church.

Rogan's fingers are firm on the back of my neck, the grounding touch enough to pull me away from the assault of pain that's welling up. I try to study his face, looking for the answer before he can voice it, but his face is completely unreadable.

He pulls in a hurried breath, like he's preparing to deliver bad news, and my heart sinks. "He's back too," he tells me, emotion cracking through the declaration like the words spilling out of him are still too good to be true. I stare at him as the truth of what we can do sinks in, and then all at once, relief crashes through me so violently that it fractures the weak hope I was clinging to and makes way for a whole new foundation of limitless possibility.

I gasp as the heavy burden of self-blame and guilt immediately lightens, and I drop my face into my hands and let go. Sobs wrack my chest, and tears fill my palms. I knew how much I wanted to hear that Elon was okay, how much I hoped that this would be the answer, but I wasn't prepared for what knowing for sure would feel like.

I cry, and Rogan pulls me closer and wraps himself around me as I do. He anchors me and supports me as everything comes rushing back. I try to fight all of the emotions that are an echo of the fucked up shit that happened the night I died. But instead of winning the battle, I'm forced to succumb to it. It's all so fresh and staggering. I wish I could shut it off, but I can't. I have to get it out. I have to fix the shattered pieces of myself that the trauma of that night took a sledgehammer to.

"It was fucking awful," I profess, the words spilling out of me like I'm an overfull levee. Rogan's quiet as he runs a hand soothingly down my back while holding me tightly to him. "I tried so hard to keep her away from him, to focus on me, but..."

"I know," Rogan comforts, placing light kisses on the back of my hands. "Elon told me what happened. How you..." Emotion bleeds out of his words, and he pauses to try and rein it in. The vehemence leaking to me through the tether has me cracking my fingers so I can look at his face through them. "I fucked up so bad, Lennox. I thought I had to choose, that after everything Elon had been through, he needed to come first no matter what. I didn't want to admit how I was feeling about you. If I did, it felt like I was betraying Elon. I mean, what kind of person finds happiness and hope when his brother is suffering?" he asks, anguish etched in his features.

He shakes his head, ashamed, an indignant scoff sneaking out of his full lips. "I didn't want to make room for you," he admits, bringing his hand to his chest and placing it over his heart. "I didn't want to see that you'd already sunk inside of me so deeply that there wasn't a me without you anymore. It was the wrong time, too fast, too uncertain, but there you were all the same," he tells me, gesturing to his heart.

His last words coax a small smile to one corner of his mouth, but it's gone in a blink.

"That night when you were torn away from me. It was like I was back in that room with my uncle as he tortured Elon and tried to steal his birthright. I lost it completely. I probably would have taken out half the order if Marx hadn't been there to stop me. They brought that Saxon fucker in to search your room for who could have planted the trap, and it hit me like a punch to the gut. You were gone. You were gone, and you didn't know how I felt. I never let you see what you were starting to mean to me.

"I knew wherever that portal was leading, it was going to be bad, and I hated myself for not giving you something to fight for, for failing to show you that *we* were worth fighting for. I'm never going to do that again, Lennox. Never."

Slowly, he pulls my hands from my face, lifting up a corner of the quilt to wipe the tears and snot away.

"I love you, Lennox," he tells me evenly with absolutely no hesitation. "I love you in the way that grows as we grow together. The kind of love worth fighting for, that has me waking up every day grateful and willing to do whatever it takes. I know what you did for Elon, because it's the same thing you did for me. You're the light in the darkness. The stars that guide you home when you're lost. You carry the broken from battle and lift the drowning from the clawing cold that's trying to claim them. *You* slay the demons."

I stare at him, completely dumbfounded. A tear slips silently down his cheek, and I move to catch it, his eyes so intense that he's looking into me rather than looking at me. Warmth pools in my stomach, and my heart races like it's giving its all because Rogan is the finish line.

"You, Lennox Marai Osseous, are *everything*. It scared the shit out of me before, but I'm not scared anymore. I love you. I feel it in my blood, in my bones, in my very soul...and I know you feel it too," he declares assuredly, now wiping the fresh tears from my cheeks.

I kiss Rogan, my lips capturing his fiercely so I can sip on his words and let them soak into me. His raw declaration fills the cracks that mistrust and messed up circumstances chiseled into us, his faith and trust the very mortar we needed to repair and move forward. I know we have a lot ahead of us, that nothing about this is going to be easy, but Rogan is right. We're worth fighting for.

I kiss him so thoroughly, pouring my own silent declarations into the passion once again stoking between us. This is the be-all and end-all kind of love that can only be nurtured with patience and understanding. This is the good shit that takes work and time, but when you truly give it everything you have, it's the epic kind of love that will sustain a soul even in the darkest of times. I don't know how the hell all of this just fell in my lap, but regardless of how long we've known each other or what obstacles may drop in our path, I am *not* letting this go.

Rogan kisses me back just as ferociously, our actions

sealing what words can't. Our tongues rove and explore, eager to spend the rest of forever learning each other as well as we already know ourselves. His hands splay across my back, pressing me into him, and I know I'll never get tired of feeling him like this. Vulnerable and needy. Strong and formidable. Willing to give and take and solidify our bond time and time again.

And I am sooo here for it.

I feel him harden inside of me, and I chuckle at the realization that we haven't even disconnected from round one and we're already sliding into round two. I'm going to have to build a shrine to the sex gods or something, really make sure they know how grateful I am for pitching this dick my way.

"Alright, Rogan Kendrick, let's see what you've got," I challenge, tasting his laughter and feeling his chest vibrate against mine.

His arms tighten around me, and in less time than it takes to say *Blood Witches do it best*, I'm on my back. I release an epic girly squeal and giggle to go with it as he buries his face in my neck. "I meant for our future," I argue, completely full of shit, "but this'll do too," I tease, parroting his sentiment before he took me against the wall.

"You have no idea how much I look forward to fucking that sassy mouth of yours," he growls into my ear as he places a large hand at the small of my back and tilts my hips up.

Oh, hello, new favorite position—I have a feeling I'll be thinking that a lot in the near future.

Rogan grinds into me, his insanely gorgeous body pressing against my clit in a really delicious way that I'm down to explore more of.

"Are you going to say it back?" he asks as he starts to pull out.

I furrow my brow in faux confusion. "What? That I can't wait to fuck your mouth?" I ask, trying to hide the twinkle of mirth in my eyes.

He shakes his head and kisses down my throat, and I wiggle with anticipation, fully expecting some type of retaliation. He nibbles at the spot where my neck meets my shoulder, and I shamelessly lean into the sensations he's creating when there's a peculiar heat that unexpectedly starts to gather at my core.

Did someone just shove a hot pack over my hot pocket?

I look down and find Rogan's devilishly good-looking face watching me, a hint of a smirk dancing on his lips and gleaming in his sultry gaze.

The heat builds even more, and I whimper, not from pain, but because it's making everything very, *very* sensitive.

What the hell?

"Wha...what are you doing?" I demand as I start to writhe and wiggle underneath him. *Fuck*, he feels big. Did he feel that big before? What, does he have *Go, Go Gadget* dick?

"Are you going to say it?" he taunts, and I swear to fuck, if he so much as sneezes, I'm going to come so hard I'm going to need to be resurrected again.

"Are you giving me menopause?" I demand, panting. "Are these hot flashes, because I didn't know they came with a side of *orgasm so good you might just die*."

Rogan laughs, and yep, that does it. I shatter around him so hard that I now know what a meteorite feels like when it slams into the ground and gets obliterated. I'm pretty sure I turn into dust. Rogan must Swiffer me back into a person, because the next thing I know, I'm screaming like one of those porn stars that makes you roll your eyes, because there's no way in hell it's *that good*. And yet, somehow, it's *that fucking good*.

Rogan thrusts shallowly in and out of me as I slam back into my body, the movement the perfect pace to draw out the life-altering release that has me convinced I'm now nothing more than dust bunnies.

"Mmmmm, I see you like the taste of my blood magic," he purrs against my mouth as he nips and flicks his tongue teasingly against my bottom lip. "I was going to wind you up and then let you cool off as punishment, but I like the way you come all over my cock too much to hold out on you," he admits, punctuating the declaration with a sumptuous roll of his hips.

I laugh at his admission, but it comes out sounding more like a dazed sigh. Without warning, heat starts to move in a direct path from between my thighs up to my nipples, and I moan and groan at the same time.

Holy Crone, Maiden, and Mother, I just found what I want to do for the rest of my life.

"You're heating my blood," I accuse, annoyed when the indictment is a blissed out slur of words instead of an outraged challenge.

"Are you going to say it back?" he demands smoothly, a smile in his tone. He emphasizes each word of his question with a pulse of heat starting at my nipples and radiating down into my breasts.

It's like he's sucking on both nipples at the same time, while also pinching them lightly and kneading my breasts to an entirely different rhythm. But none of that is actually happening, because he has one hand at the small of my back and the other is supporting his weight while he moves his cock in and out of me like he hasn't a care in the world.

This motherfucker is going to orgasm me to death, I realize, as he works my body like he knows it better than I do. I debate holding out—I mean, what a way to go—but there's a small spark of vulnerability in his eyes, and the last thing I want him to think is that I don't feel the same way.

"It's just that I never thought it would be possible, you know?" I start, adopting a shy, hesitant mien. Rogan's playful countenance gentles, and his gaze softens with understanding. "With everything that's happened between us, I didn't quite trust what my heart was telling me, but I can't deny it," I admit huskily as I brush hair out of his face and try to breathe through another coalescing orgasm. "I just *might* love you more than your coffee maker," I announce straight-faced. "It's probably too early to tell. We are new to this whole love thing, but the potential is definitely there."

Rogan barks out a laugh, and the loss of his focus gives my nipples and clit a momentary reprieve. I don't know if I'm grateful for that or disappointed.

"You do put out way easier than she does, and make me feel *almost* as good," I add, trying to hide the cheeky smile that wants to break out on my face.

"Almost?" he growls indignantly, and the giggle sneaking out of me quickly morphs into a deep moan as he starts to pick up his pace between my thighs.

"Almost," I repeat, gasping as he nips at my neck, his laughter vibrating through me as happiness fills our bond.

"I won't tell the espresso machine," he whispers conspiratorially in my ear, his deep sexy voice causing need to settle low in my stomach and goose bumps to crawl up my arms. "Your secret's safe with me," he adds, his smile wide, and then he claims my mouth and kisses me *almost* right out of my mind. "I fucking love you, Lennox, now scream my name again," he commands, picking up his pace while heating up every possible erogenous zone I have.

I reach back and grab onto the metal headboard of the bed, trying to ground myself as much as possible as extra heat builds at my nipples, clit, and pussy. Rogan pounds into me, deep and hard, and I start a steady chant of *you can do it, put your back into it*...you know, just to keep that ego in check.

I fight it so hard, but it's a lost cause. I'm mindless and mewling in a matter of seconds. Another one of those dangerous *soul snatching* orgasms starts to tingle and collect in my core, and I don't know if I'm afraid of it or ready to jump in feetfirst.

"You feel so fucking good," Rogan groans, and then he presses my knees back, opening me up even more for him, and starts driving into me even deeper. "Yes, baby, you like that," he hums.

"No, no *baby*," I gasp and then moan as he fucks me senseless.

"Shit, sorry."

"Don't be, I didn't even know I hated it until you just said it and it felt weird," I reassure him, groaning with approval as he picks up his pace again.

"Got it, no babes or babies. How about my honey or sweetie?"

I gag at the suggestions, grabbing on to his arms so he can thrust into me even harder.

"What cutesy name am I supposed to use then?" he asks breathily, trying to playfully pout. It doesn't have the effect he wants because my moans coax out a smug smile instead.

"To be determined," I squeal, but it's all I can get out before I throw my head back and scream his name in complete mind-altering ecstasy.

"Yes, Lennox, that's my girl," he growls, and then he buries himself and comes hard.

We lie there, sweaty and breathless. I feel almost numb with endorphins and bliss from what he just did to me, and a happy sigh sneaks out easily. "You gotta teach me that thing you did with my blood," I tell him drowsily.

"Hand over my secret weapon, just like that?" he scoffs, a

sneaky smile playing on his kiss-swollen lips. "Come now, Osteomancer, you should know me better than that by now."

"Mmmm, true. You do like to play things close to the vest. But I'm a quick study, Kendrick, and I will use my powers for evil," I warn as I wag my eyebrows sinisterly, or at least I think I do, I can't really feel my face.

He kisses me softly and boops my nose. I slap his hand away and laugh. "Oh no, I didn't know you were one of those booper weirdos," I declare, scrunching up my face in disgust. "First the *baby* thing and now this? That's it, I'm outta here," I tease, not even bothering to move to support my faux outrage.

Rogan laughs and tweaks my nipple.

"Ahh, much better," I joke, and we both crack up.

"Come on, let's get cleaned up and talk about fun things like war with the Order and hunting demons." He pushes off the bed, grabbing my hand and forcing me to come with him despite my protesting groans.

"You cannot fuck me into a jelly-like state and then make me talk about your mom. I'm pretty sure there are rules against that," I whine.

He ignores me, pulling me into the bathroom, and starts the shower. "If I could get away with never talking about her again, I'd do it happily, but I don't think we're going to get that lucky," he states, studying me as I rummage through the drawers in search of my shower cap.

I'd normally save this sexy look for later in the relationship, but I already washed and dried my curls earlier. I can't be bothered to do it again so soon. Rogan climbs into the shower and starts to wash off, and I'm struck by the strange intimacy of what we're doing, and even more surprised by the fact that it doesn't actually feel strange at all. I pull my polka-dotted cap on, tucking my curls into it, and just watch him for a moment through the glass of the shower. So much has changed, and yet it all just feels the same somehow, which makes zero sense.

I can't feel like we've done this a million times before, because we never have. We should be in the phase where I sneak off early in the morning to fluff my curls and apply the perfect no-makeup makeup look and then proceed to pretend that I naturally wake up that hot. But no, we're practically at the "poop with the door open while having a conversation" phase, and I both like that and also side-eye it.

"So, what's going on?" I ask, tilting my head and watching raptly as soap suds start to drip down Rogan's abs.

I shake my head to try to snap myself out of my ogling as he turns to rinse himself, subsequently cutting off my view of all his front bits. *Damn*, the dude has an ass you could bounce a quarter off of. I've never felt the urge to bite down on a good piece of ass meat before, but I can now no longer claim that to be true. I turn to the mirror and look myself in the eye. My pupils are huge, and my face looks slightly panicked.

Get a hold of yourself, woman. We've got serious shit breathing down our necks. Now is not the time to daydream about nibbling on some beefy ass cheeks.

"Why do I suddenly feel a lot of frantic concern coming from you?" Rogan asks, and I look up to find his gaze in the mirror.

"What? No!" I squeak out in a rush. He shoots me a look that tells me he's not convinced, and I quickly clear my throat and try again. "It's nothing, and so that we're clear, it's also absolutely rude to spy on my insides."

"Stop projecting them at me then."

I gasp and press my palm to my chest. "I would never," I declare adamantly and fake as fuck. He smiles and shakes his head at me.

"Get in here so I can do other things to your insides. The milkmaid thing you've got going on is working for me," he orders, a sultry smile stretched across his lips.

And here I was thinking that my inner fiend was out of control—this guy is insatiable. I return my stare back to my own reflection in the mirror and roll my eyes. Crap. I do look like a milkmaid. Holding up a defensive hand, I turn around and narrow my eyes at his invitation.

"No more sex. We need to figure things out for real, and we can't do that if I'm trapped on your cock twenty-four seven."

Rogan raises a judgmental eyebrow. "Trapped?"

"You know what I mean," I dismiss. "I woke up in a morgue. I had to sneak out of said morgue. And I'm pretty sure you were announcing some kind of *situation* when you broke into my aunt's house and decided to dick me down."

"Your way with words is truly so eloquent," he counters with a sly mocking smile.

I flip him off. "Seriously though, how long was I out, and what was the situation that had you risking a Hillen beatdown?"

Rogan's playfulness drops away, and as grateful as I am that he's getting back to business, I also hate to see it go.

"You've been dead for thirteen days," he tells me evenly, but his face shows the toll this fact has taken on him.

I feel as though the floor was just yanked out from under my feet. It's like that trick magicians do where they grab the table cloth and pull it out from under a table full of china. Only instead of sitting unmoved and whole like the plates and cups are supposed to, I feel like I'm falling to the ground, destined to shatter at any moment.

Thirteen days.

A lot can happen in thirteen days, and judging by Rogan's face, a lot has.

5

Strong, wet arms pull me into the warm spray of the shower, but I'm still reeling too much to care. Rogan grabs the soap and starts to rub sudsy circles over my skin as I stare at the white subway tile, trying to figure out why the number thirteen is rocking my world so much. I was dead. I came back. These are facts that should shake my foundations. Yet the idea of being gone for almost two weeks is what suddenly tips everything on the *this is too much* scale?

"How?" I ask meekly as Rogan continues to clean me up.

"I don't know," he replies stoically. "You died in my arms, and I just held you, hoping if I did it long enough, that you'd come back. I didn't know if you even could, but I...I couldn't let go. Elon's heart had started, but he wasn't conscious. The Animamancers were happy to take the credit for bringing him back, and I wasn't about to fill anyone in otherwise."

His hands brush gently over my breasts and then start to circle lower. I should feel turned on by the attention, but I'm too shocked to care or to want to stop him and either take over or take things further.

"The first time Elon and I died, we think we were gone for about ten hours. We were told our hearts started again around hour six, and then it took another four or so for us to fully wake up. The second time for Elon was much faster. Only a couple of hours, we estimate, from the time he died to when he was fully conscious again. So I just held you and waited."

He shakes his head, his stare far away and pained. His soapy hands move to my hips, and I watch him methodically scrub every inch of me while he's lost to the torment of what happened thirteen days ago.

"I probably shouldn't have put up such a fight when they tried to take you from me. My parents have eyes everywhere, and I was drawing too much attention to us, but the whole scene was madness anyway. I thought my irrational stubbornness would go unnoticed amongst all the other horrors that were being uncovered in that place."

Rogan's eyes lift to mine with those words, and swimming in them is guilt and dismay.

"All the bodies. All the mancers now nothing more than piles of tainted ash. The state you and Elon were in when we finally broke through the doors." He drops his eyes and, with a small shake of his head, resumes his soapy strokes.

"Elon woke up, and when he saw you...well, it bought us more time. They had set up a med tent outside the church while the Order was processing the scene. That's where we stayed as Elon answered questions. We made other excuses to stick around, but when hour six came and went, and you were still lying on a cot with no heartbeat... Well, as much as we didn't want to accept it, we had to consider the possibility that you might not come back."

I reach down and brush wet locks of hair from Rogan's forehead. He washes between my thighs, but neither one of us are focused on anything else but what he's saying. Anguish mars his features, and I try to imagine what it would have felt like to try to guard his dead body, hoping for a miracle but equally worried about what happens if he gets one. If my heart had started beating in that med tent, it wouldn't have just been his mother's spies witnessing it.

"The Order took you away after the interrogation was over. We tried to argue that we were claiming you on behalf of your family, but we're renounced witches, and the Order wasn't about to honor anything we wanted," he tells me, a growl of frustration tinging his tone. "So Marx stepped in."

I'm surprised to hear this development. Yeah, I figured Marx and other familiar faces from the Order would be hanging around, but Marx isn't in the loop, and I'm surprised he would have gotten involved. I turn to rinse off as Rogan completes his cathartic scrub down and stands up. The knob in the shower squeaks as I turn it to shut the water off, and I get out, grabbing my towel from earlier and handing a fresh one to Rogan from the shelf above the toilet.

"Marx knows now," Rogan states almost hesitantly, and my head snaps up from where I'm drying myself off to find Rogan watching me.

"Holy shit," I exclaim, shocked and at a loss for what to think or feel about that. "How did he take it?"

Rogan rubs the back of his head with the towel and sighs. "He thought we were kidding or that maybe we'd cracked up and lost it from everything that had happened. Elon told him everything from start to finish, and let's just say he stared out the window for a concerningly long time."

"Shit," I commiserate, and Rogan nods.

"Yeah, he didn't take it nearly as well as you did."

"Do you trust him?" I press, suddenly uneasy.

"I do. I wouldn't have told him if we didn't need help watching over you until we were sure you weren't coming back, but that has more to do with not wanting to pull him into this mess than it does about trust."

We get dressed in contemplative silence, which is why I

hear a familiar creak, one that sends my instincts screaming *you are not alone.* The hair on my arms slowly rises, and I throw my palm out to Rogan, indicating that he should stop moving. He does, watching me closely as I strain to listen for any more floor squeaks that will give me a better idea of how many we might be facing.

I want to send my magic pulsing out to detect who or what's going on, but Rogan shakes his head and points to the window. I mouth *doesn't open* at him, and his brow furrows with frustration. Another floorboard squeaks sharply, and this time the sound is followed by an almost inaudible *shh*.

Confusion filters through my dread because I would know that quiet admonition anywhere. She's only spent a good portion of her life shushing me and her rambunctious son. But why is my Aunt Hillen creeping around her own house, and if she is, where the hell is Tad? My fear quickly transfers from me and Rogan to my aunt and my cousin. *Shit*, what if something happened when they were on their way back here?

Without another second of thought, I shove my magic out into the house, terrified that someone else might be with Hillen, someone like an Order member, but all I sense is her. Rogan reaches for me as I pull the door open and run out, but he isn't fast enough to stop me. Frantically I round the corner that leads into the hall where I find a shaking Hillen holding a loaf of bread still in the pan over her head. She screams, which makes me scream, and then she chucks the bread at me with all her might. I flinch, but a hand reaches past me and catches the home-baked missile before it can break my nose.

Hillen's eyes look over my shoulder and narrow with rage. I balk, completely stunned to see my aunt look at *anyone* with such brutal vehemence, but especially Rogan.

"What are you doing in my house?" she snarls at him. "Was I not clear enough before that you aren't welcome here?"

"Hillen," I admonish, taken aback by the venom in her words.

My aunt's furious stare snaps to me, and as though she's seeing me for the first time, her eyes widen with astonishment, and the blood drains from her face.

"Leni?" she chokes out feebly, reaching a hand out for the wall to steady herself as she takes me in. "Honey, is that you?"

I reach for her, and sorrow rips through her features as I fold her up in a tight hug.

Where is Tad?

"It's me, Aunt Hill, it's me. I'm so sorry," I try to reassure her as she quakes in my arms, the sobs slowly building and spilling out of her. "Don't cry, I'm here," I coo as I direct us back toward the living room and the large light blue sofa there.

"He said you were dead," she keens into my shoulder, and I squeeze her even tighter against me. "Said it was his fault, that he didn't protect you," she stammers.

My eyes flash to Rogan, who meets my stare with one filled with contrition before he drops his gaze to the floor, like the onus is too heavy right now for him to bear.

"He was wrong," I tell my aunt, my tone firm as though I'm making this clear not only to her but to Rogan as well. "I did die, but Rogan saved me. He made it so I could come back."

I see questions fill Hillen's teary stare, and seeing her hurt so much makes my eyes sting and my throat grow tight.

Out of nowhere, the front door slams open, and all of us jump. Tad hurries in, grabbing for the knob. "Shit, sorry, it got really windy all of a sudden."

The declaration is innocent, but I find myself looking over at Rogan, wondering if the sudden wind is natural or mancer-made. Like he has the very same concern, he casually moves to the window and peeks out of the closed curtain. I feel his magic flare and start to search as he stares out into the empty street.

So, this is what it feels like to be hunted.

I knew from the moment I was back that I would be eventually, but the reality of it hits me like a charging elephant. I'm not safe, which means I'm also putting Tad and Hillen in danger. My heart picks up, and I try to swallow down the cutting truth. I shouldn't have come here, but I had nowhere else to go.

Rogan spins to me, the look on his face imploring me to calm down. "We're okay," he reassures, but I hear the unspoken *for now* in it all the same.

"What are you doing here?" Tad lobs at Rogan, his curious eyes moving to mine. "Did you suddenly remember his number?"

"Where the hell were you?" Hillen snaps at Tad, and I swear my attention shifts around the living room like I'm watching an intense tennis match. "I had to take a cab, Thaddeus!" she screeches at him.

"Elon is here," Rogan announces, and I swear I get whiplash from how quickly I swivel my focus back to him. "I told him to come here after he searched your shop and your apartment."

Hillen and Tad are quietly arguing, but everything around me goes still and fuzzy as Rogan moves to open the door.

Elon approaches the threshold, his green eyes pensive and anxious as he takes in his younger brother. He looks so much better than the last time I saw him. His cheeks aren't as hollow, and his stare is missing the haunted glaze it always had back in the church. He's clean, his scruffy beard gone, and the olive long-sleeve T-shirt he's wearing hugs his muscles, as do his faded black jeans. He looks healthy, and recovered, and here.

"No sign of anyone at her shop or apartment. Have you heard anything?" Elon asks Rogan as he steps into the house.

I give my aunt a quick squeeze, and then I'm pushing up off of the couch. The movement catches Elon's eye just as his worried gaze moves from Rogan to the other occupants in the living room.

"Oh, thank fuck," Elon proclaims, and then he's opening his arms so I can crash into him and practically strangle him in a hug. "I thought she had you. I thought for sure she'd gotten to you somehow," he confesses, and the relief that fills those words is palpable.

"You're back," I croak out, emotion making it almost impossible to speak.

Geez, coming back from the dead is brutal.

First Tad, then Rogan, and now Hillen and Elon. I should have spread these reunions out; all this crying is going to give me the worst damn headache.

"I'm so sorry," I start to chant to Elon as he squeezes me tighter. "I'm so fucking sorry," I repeat, not sure exactly what my sorrow and apology encompasses.

Is it just that I couldn't stop Jamie, that she killed him because I didn't solve the problem of blood magic fast enough? Or maybe it's because he was taken in the first place, that he endured so much in that church before I showed up and failed to save the day. Fuck, it could be for all the shitty things that have happened to him long before I was ever in the picture. All I know is I wish I could take all the suffering away, and I'm so damn sorry that I'll never be able to.

"Stop that crap," Elon tells me gently. "You have nothing to be sorry for."

"I should have figured it out sooner, maybe if I—"

"What? Had gotten out? Had died first? Maybe if you had what? She was crazy and way more powerful than she should have been. Nothing you could have said or done would have changed that."

I sigh reluctantly, accepting that he's probably right. Doesn't make me feel any less shitty, but I suppose torture and death will do that to you.

Elon pulls back, holding my shoulders as he looks me over. "I can't believe you're actually here. When Marx called about the missing bodies, we thought the worst, but here you are."

"What missing bodies? Lennox, who is this, and for the love of the Maiden, will someone please tell me what is going on?" Hillen demands, her hands cupping her cheeks and her eyes wide with wonder and unshed tears.

I give her a wide smile. "I'll trade all my secrets for a Sloppy Joe," I tell her, love and appreciation spilling out of my words.

She wipes her eyes, and quickly affection replaces bewilderment. "You got it, kid," she agrees warmly, pulling me from Elon's grasp into a strong bear hug before making her way toward the kitchen.

"Make mine an Untidy Joseph, please," Elon calls after her, and the smile that takes over my face is beaming.

Man, it's good to be back.

6

"Hold on, hold on, hold on! You need to go back to the part where you stole three bodies," Tad exclaims, his features animated and his brown eyes sparkling with amusement.

A light breeze frolics in from the open sliding glass door, despite the sun being high up in the sky. I can practically smell fall on the playful wind, and I know the trees will start to change colors and drop leaves soon. The table is full of plates and bowls, their delicious contents all but devoured, and just when I thought I was home free and done with explaining how I woke up and got here, Tad has to go and call me out.

Rude.

I throw my head back in exasperation. Of course he's not going to let me just skim past that part. I swallow down the last bite of my third Sloppy Joe, the dining table silent as everyone waits for me to relive *that* morally gray humiliation. I shoot a glare at Tad, but he's not cowed in the slightest. In fact, I'm pretty sure he giggles before hiding it behind a large gulp of his lemonade.

"First of all, I didn't steal them; they very clearly wanted to come with me," I defend, and Elon barks out a laugh, which he quickly tries to hide in a series of coughs that are not fooling anyone. "Seriously!" I argue, the proclamation just a tinge whiny. "I woke up, and they just came with me. It was like trying to get pet hair off of black pants after you just painted your nails," I explain. "I *told* them to go back to their fridges, but they weren't having it. So I figured what the hell, I'd use the accidental body snatching to my benefit. You totally would have done the same," I accuse, looking over at Rogan, who I discover is fighting a losing battle with a grin.

I groan and roll my eyes.

Jerks.

"And then you hid them in the bushes and rode a ley line to get here?" Hillen asks, repeating that part of my story like she's committing it all to memory.

"This better not go in the Osseous Chronicles," I warn, and her eyes grow just a little too innocent.

"Wait? What are the Osseous Chronicles?" Elon asks, his tone eager and his eyes excited.

"Dude," Tad starts as though that one word says it all. "It's this Osseous family tradition where the relatives who grow up around the Osteomancer document their lives and any other important events for the future family members of the next Osteomancer," Tad explains. "It's a little like your grimoires and things that help pass down the magical information from one mancer to another. The Osseous Chronicles help pass down information that future non-magical relatives might find useful or, you know, super entertaining. You gotta keep the ego of these magic users in check sometimes," he adds with a laugh, and Elon chuckles too like he isn't a magic user himself.

I release an indignant huff. "No documenting anything involving me coming back from the dead; that's just asking for trouble. And in case either of you forgot, I might not be able to die...like ever. Pretty sure that means I'm probably the last in our line, and therefore there's no point passing down my embarrassing stories to anyone," I snark, but the declaration has a sobering effect.

Everyone goes quiet, contemplating the gravity of what I just said.

Well, crap. I totally didn't mean to shit all over that moment.

"How long do you think we have before the High Council knows?" Elon asks, flushing away all hope that this conversation will go back to the laughing and joking that was just going down.

I look over at him, his now serious stare fixed on Rogan.

Rogan sighs and wipes his mouth with the napkin before setting it next to his empty plate. "Honestly, I don't know. Marx said there were people watching the morgue pretty closely up until a couple days ago. I think she called them off, figuring too much time had passed, but you know how she is."

"Sneaky as fuck," Elon mumbles, and Rogan nods his head in agreement.

My eyes snap to Hillen, fully expecting her to admonish them for their language, but she looks lost in thought, consternation heavy in her faraway stare.

"How would your mother even know that this was a possibility?" I ask, looking from one brother to the other as I gesture to my very undead self.

"I don't think she did, but she covers all her bases. *Just in case* is practically her middle name. Plus, she would have noticed that," Elon states, gesturing to the mark on my inner wrist.

I look down at the red lacey circle with the swooping *K* inside of it. I've gotten so used to Rogan's vow being there that I don't even notice it anymore, and I stare at it, wondering why this little mark would be such a big deal.

"She wouldn't know exactly *why* Rogan would have sealed a vow with you, or what it is, but she'd know you mattered enough for him to offer something so sacred. She'd watch to see if he might give you other valuable things too."

My eyes flit to Tad, and he waggles his eyebrows and then discreetly mouths *that D* to me.

I snort out a laugh, which has everyone else turning to see what I find so amusing. My cheeks heat as I shoot Tad and his dirty mind a glare.

"It was an Order morgue, so even if Marx can keep his friend quiet about the missing bodies for a little longer, she's eventually going to have to report it. As soon as Sorrel Adair hears, she'll make a move," Rogan states resolutely.

"That bumps up our timeline," Elon contemplates, and Rogan nods his silent agreement.

"Timeline?" I question, studying the stern planes of both of their faces. They look so alike and yet so different.

"For war," Elon announces, as though it's no big deal.

I choke on the gulp of water I just tried to swallow and fix him with a look that screams *say what now?*

Elon glances at Rogan, confused. "You didn't tell her?"

"I, uh, I mean, we got tied up with other things. I haven't had a chance to catch Lennox up to speed on everything," Rogan confesses, and I swear a hint of red crawls up his neck.

"Catch me up on what?" I press, ignoring his badly veiled reference to the boning that went down earlier.

He better not be pulling that "need to know" shit he was all about before. We sure as hell better be past that crap. A wave of reassurance rolls through our bond, and my sudden frown eases up just a bit.

"I might have declared war on the High Council," he reveals casually.

"Might have?" Tad queries, a sneaky smile on his face.

"As in I definitely could have told my mother that we weren't running anymore and to watch her back," he discloses.

My eyes widen, both impressed and shocked by this revelation. "When did you see her?"

"She came to *check* on Elon when the Order called him into headquarters to answer a few more questions so they could close the case."

"She does like a good ambush," I grumble, and a small smile ticks at Rogan's lips.

"He didn't threaten to stab her with her own femurs, but the sentiment was there," Rogan teases, and it's Elon's turn to choke on his drink.

"Wait, you threatened to stab our mother with her own femurs?" he asks, clearly delighted.

"I'll have to see if we can get the security footage hacked so you can see it; it was incredible," Rogan tells Elon, pride swelling in his voice.

My cheeks heat, and I will the blush creeping into them to fuck off. "I thought her lackeys shut down the camera feed?" I question, brushing off the compliment and the squishy feeling it creates in my belly.

"The Order's feed, yes, but not her own," Elon explains. "The High Priestess studies possible threats against her like a sports team studies gameday footage. She'd have her people recording every second of the interaction so she could watch it back over and over again, examining the syntax, the body language, your reactions, everything really."

A shiver skitters up my spine at what he's saying. I can easily picture it though. The High Priestess in a dark room, rewinding, playing, and pausing a video of me for hours on end. I wouldn't put it past the bitch to be curled up under a blanket made out of happy Labrador skins, looking for the Crone knows what, while eating popcorn popped by the tiny flames of rare baby dragons. The visual is disconcerting as hell, but that definitely fits her vibe.

"But why pick a fight now? Why not fade into the background like you've both been doing since she renounced you? Why the sudden need to stop running and square up?" I ask, concerned. I assumed I was going to have to get used to a life of hiding and constantly looking over my shoulder. This sudden desire to take a stand is surprising as hell.

Elon's eyes settle on Rogan, and he waits for his brother to explain. The room grows quiet as everyone waits for an answer. The silence starts to feel heavy as Rogan seems to debate how to answer that question.

After what feels like forever, he takes a deep breath and turns to me. "Because I had met someone who made me want to run *to* them instead of away...and then I lost her. I was fed up with backing down and fleeing. It was time to make them pay."

My gaze bounces back and forth between his fervent stare, and everything inside of me heats up with his admission. "War was for me?" I clarify, my tone soft and astonished.

We stare at each other, and a profound understanding clicks into place. It's as though every bloodthirsty, eye-for-an-eye strain in my genetic makeup comes to life. My inner cave woman rears her matted head and grunts in approval. My ancient warrior ancestors bang weapons against shields, and I go all doe eyed and swoony.

He was going to go to war for me. I'd died and he was going to burn it all to the ground, fed up and ready to dish out some much deserved retribution.

Well, if that isn't the most romantic damn thing.

I wrap my hands around the back of Rogan's neck and

pull him to me. Our lips meet in a gentle, tender kiss that tells him how sweet and beautiful I think his gesture is. I slip in a little teasing tongue so he knows that my full gratitude will be demonstrated later, and I feel him smile against my mouth in understanding.

I pull back, heat climbing up my neck, not only because I'm wishing we were suddenly alone right now so I could dramatically shove the dishes to the ground and then sit on Rogan's face for a spell, but also because I just made out with him in front of my family.

"Sorry," I mumble, looking around the table to find that Elon and Tad are focused on other parts of the kitchen, both with large smiles on their faces.

Hillen, however, waves a dismissive hand. "Please, it's not like I didn't already put together what the two of you were up to in the guest room," she announces.

My eyes go wide, and Rogan chokes on air, hitting his chest a couple times to try and stave off a coughing fit. Tad snickers and Elon suddenly finds his glass of lemonade *really* interesting.

"The bedding in your den of iniquity isn't going to wash itself though. I expect it to be sorted before you go," she orders, and Rogan and I both answer a contrite *yes, ma'am* at the exact same time.

Tad can't hold in his laugh, and I slap his shoulder with the back of my hand and shoot him a glare, which just makes him laugh harder.

"I was going to fight with the High Council too. What do I get, Lennox?" Elon asks, all faux innocence, his eyes twinkling with merriment.

Without missing a beat, Rogan reaches across the table and flicks his ear.

"Ow," Elon whines, holding his hands up in surrender before rubbing at his reddening helix. "I was joking, no need to piss a circle around her, you animal," he accuses, and Rogan shakes his head, a smile working at his lips and giving him away.

I roll my eyes at the antics, but I also sit back into the easy comfort and levity that encircles this moment. It's such a drastic and welcome change from everything that's happened over the past couple of weeks, and I know this may be our last taste of it until the dust of whatever is going to happen with the High Council and the mystery demon settles.

Aunt Hillen clears her throat and lifts her thoughtful gaze to me. "I had a dream," she announces awkwardly.

I can barely hear her over Tad and Elon's teasing antics and laughter, so I lean closer.

"I had a dream," she repeats louder, and everyone's attention turns to her at the head of the table. She pauses, suddenly unsure, and I can see doubt etched in her features, which has concerns settling in mine. "I didn't think anything of it, you know, because we were grieving, so it would make perfect sense that I'd be dreaming about mom and things, but now I'm not so sure."

"I've been learning a lot about trusting my instincts, even when they don't make much sense," I reassure her, a supportive smile on my face, and she nods and releases a deep sigh.

"Mom came to me in a dream. I was crying. I was looking for you," she starts, her eyes fixing on me and welling with tears that I watch her work to fight back.

I reach out for her hand, and she grips it tightly, like it's more lifeline than comforting gesture.

"I kept looking for you, I was frantic, and then mom was there running her hand over my hair, trying to calm me. I tried to tell her I missed her, that I wished she'd come back, but no matter how hard I tried, I couldn't speak. She looked at me like she understood, and then she said, 'Look for the marks.' I didn't understand what that meant, but she repeated it like I should. 'Look for the marks,' she said again before she kissed me on the head, and then I woke up. I chalked it up to too little sleep and too much heartbreak, but for some reason, ever since we all sat down, I just can't fight the feeling that what she said was never for me, it was for you, Len."

I squeeze her hand once and repeat the statement in my mind a couple of times. I say it out loud, trying to see how it feels in my mouth and if adding my voice to the strange message helps it click, but nothing comes to me. "It's not ringing any bells or setting off any alarms," I tell her, her expectant eyes fixed on me. "But I'll definitely keep that in mind."

Hillen nods and leans back in her chair, and it breaks the air of tension that's crept into the room. All at once, I know that this reunion has found its end and it's time to go.

Rogan clears his throat, shooting me a concerned look before sitting up a little straighter. "I know all of this has been a lot," he starts, his gaze warm and set on my aunt. "I'm sorry I couldn't tell you, but I didn't know for sure, and I didn't want to get your hopes up before I did. I know you and Tad will keep what's happened to yourselves, and I wish that was enough, but it's not," he explains, and I get tense, wondering where the hell Rogan is going with this. "It's not safe for you here," he goes on.

My heart hammers, and a woosh of relief pours out of me at his last declaration. "Not going to lie, I thought you were headed in a *we've told you, so now we have to kill you* direction," I confess as I sag in my chair.

Rogan shoots me an indignant look, the *how could you think that* clear in his eyes.

I shrug. "Listen, I know we're all bonded for life and

crap, and I'm here for it—don't get me wrong—but that doesn't mean I know you through and through, and it doesn't erase some of the sketchy history, even if I can understand why things went down the way they did."

Rogan stares at me, and the atmosphere grows heavy again. "I would never hurt your family, Lennox. And I want you to know that I will never hurt *you* again. We have a lot to figure out, and I know I have a lot to make up for, but I want to be very clear that I will do everything in my power to protect you and the people you love."

"And you'll keep me in the loop?" I press. "No more making decisions without me or living that *it's better to ask for forgiveness than permission* life."

Amusement ticks at the corners of Rogan's lips with my questions. "I'm going to communicate so much you won't even know what to do with yourself. Mistakes were made, but I won't make them again. You will be in all the loops all the time, you have my word."

"Ohh kinky," Tad coos, and Hillen beams her son with a roll.

I laugh at Tad's expense as he rubs at a red spot on his forehead, courtesy of his mom.

"I've never seen so many people use bread as a weapon," Rogan observes, clearly referring to the French bread beatdown I gave Prek before.

"It's a skill; feel free to be jealous," I smirk at him.

"One passed down in the Osseous Chronicles, I'm sure," Rogan teases, and my smirk turns into a dopey smile.

I like playful Rogan.

He reaches out and wraps one of my curls around his finger, his gaze heated and filled with so much promise and conviction it makes my toes curl.

"Will you go to war with me, Lennox?" he asks, his tone sultry and earnest.

I study his face for a moment, everything else around us fading away like we're the only two people left in the world. He cups my face, and I lean into it, relishing the intimate touch and everything we've been through to get here. I press my lips to the palm of his hand and then straighten, ready for whatever is going to come next.

"Lead the way," I assure him, and he nods once, his green eyes filled with fire and determination.

Heigh-ho, heigh-ho, it's off to war we go.

7

Rogan holds the *oh shit* handle so tight that I question whether or not he can even feel his hand still. Clearly, I can be trusted with his secrets and his heart, but driving him safely from my aunt's house to my grandmother's shop is super questionable.

Please, I'm an excellent driver.

I roll down my window and scowl at a driver as I pass him. "Word of advice," I yell at the gray Volvo. "If you're gonna drive in the fast lane, drive fast, jackass!"

"Remember that little part of Elon's instructions about keeping a low profile and not drawing attention to ourselves?" Rogan asks me.

I roll my eyes as I roll up my window. "I'm not screaming *suck my immortal exhaust* at the dude," I defend. "And he really shouldn't be driving that slow in the fast lane, I'm just looking out for him."

Rogan scoffs and looks behind us, offering an apologetic wave.

Traitor.

I gasp in outrage and narrow my eyes at him. "How could you? There will be no apologetic waves," I scold.

"It's a car full of priests," he argues, and I balk as I look in the rearview to see for myself.

Crap, either they're *very* early for Halloween or they're definitely a car full of priests.

I cringe and offer an apology wave of my own. I've already got witches and demons gunning for me, no point adding Hosts of Heaven to that list too. I sigh, slowing down a little and trying to rein in the east coast road rage that's practically a part of my DNA.

I feel edgy as hell.

There's something about saying goodbye to your loved ones as they rush to pack their belongings because they're about to be hurried off into hiding. I know Elon is with them, and right now they shouldn't even be on anyone's radar, but I can't help but feel bad for the buttload of danger I just dropped on their doorstep. Elon promised he'd let them call me as soon as he got them settled in with all the proper protections in place. But the fact that we've gone DEFCON: Cloak-and-dagger makes everything feel entirely more real and threatening.

I mean, technically it was all of that before, but something about losing myself to the throes of passion and then laughing with the people I love over a home-cooked meal made everything feel so manageable.

Late afternoon light and lazy paint-stroke clouds give the familiar streets of my hometown a deceptively relaxed feel. Even so, I can't stop looking around as though the High Priestess herself is going to zip past on a broom, a threatening cackle in her wake, while demanding a taste of the good shit, aka immortality.

"So exactly how are the three of us going to take down the ruling body of all known mancers?" I ask a little too casually as I turn right in the direction of my grandmother's —*dammit*—I mean *my* shop. None of it still feels like it's mine, but Rogan and I did get a solid head start on Demo Day the first time we met, so I really need to stop thinking of it as Grammy Ruby's.

"We expose the corruption," Rogan answers, just as nonchalantly.

"Cool, cool." I look over at him, waiting for him to elaborate, but he doesn't. "Not that I'm doubting that clearly very detailed and, might I add, brilliant plan, but don't most magic users know that the ruling class is corrupt, like don't those things normally go hand in hand in all civilizations? I don't exactly see an angry uprising about it, so..."

"Maybe if we were dealing with run-of-the-mill corruption and degradation, I could see people turning a blind eye, but the High Council has been messing with some serious shit for a very long time. When my mother renounced us, she thought we'd come crawling back, begging for a place at the table we'd been spoon fed from our entire lives. But really, she forced us to see that what we were raised thinking was normal, was everything but."

I nod in understanding, my head bobbing to the rhythm of my blinker as I wait for a green arrow. I think back to what Rogan told me about his childhood. About the abuse Elon survived. I recall learning about how the founding families passed along their magic, how they ensure their lines stay strong and formidable. I can see how being chucked out of that privileged world would be a shock to the system. It's apparent that Sorrel Adair didn't know who her sons were at their core though. They aren't the power-hungry, heartless rulers they were created to be. They are good souls, who recognized evil and decided that would never be their legacy, no matter what the High Council tried to do.

Respect and admiration warm in my chest, and before I know it, our tether is humming with the emotions. Rogan looks over at me, surprise twinkling in his mossy gaze. "What's that for?" he asks, his tone deep and inviting. I practically have to fight off the shiver that wants to crawl through me at that melted milk chocolate timbre.

Come on, body, we can't let him think he's got it like that already. We're still early stages, make him work for it.

"What's *what* for?" I challenge, pretending like I have no idea what he's referring to.

He gives me a knowing smile but doesn't call me out. "Anyway, Elon and I knew that they wouldn't leave us alone forever. We had an inside track on how they played the game, and we were painfully aware of what we were up against. So we started tracking and documenting anything and everything we could against them. We looked into every possible lead. Lines of magic wiped out without warning or provocation. Unsanctioned stripping of power. Blanket immunity for certain families no matter how vile the crimes against fellow mancers. Blackmail. The list goes on and on and on," he explains, and I try to tamp down my anger.

I turn down the block the shop is on, and a warm tingling feeling of welcome washes over me.

"We began to collect what evidence we could. We hacked into our parents' private records and files, worked to gain access to top secret digital records. We've slowly siphoned what we could, and now we'll put it all together and start educating all supernaturals about what's been going on unchecked by the powers that be."

I raise my eyebrows with surprise and shoot an impressed look over at Rogan.

"That's way less *Deathly Hallows and the final magical show down* than I thought this war was going to be," I admit.

Why do I sound pouty about that?

I side-eye myself for a moment, not missing that Rogan seems to be amused by whatever it is that's radiating to him via our tether. I really need to figure out how to mute this thing. A girl does need to rely on her mysterious ways from time to time, although this could come in handy when I'm PMSing and need to send chocolate and comfort food SOSs because I'm too growly to form proper sentences otherwise.

We pull into the parking lot in front of the shop, and a flash of everything that happened the last time I was here courses through my mind. I look to the passenger seat as though Hoot will be right there in all of his unimpressed and stinky glory, and my heart aches a little when I register that it's just Rogan sitting there.

"He's safe at home with Gibson and Tilda, they're all best friends, and as soon as you pick up some stuff, we'll be on our way to see them," Rogan reassures me, reaching out and lacing his fingers with mine.

I offer him a small grateful smile and then turn off the car and step out. Cool air caresses my cheeks as I take in the fig-colored awning and the large front windows that sit on each side of the front door. I run my gaze over The Eye, studying the name of the shop as though looking at it long enough will provide some much needed direction. I pull a deep fortifying breath in, and then I slip the spare key Hillen gave me into the lock and push the door open.

I expect the inside to be a mess. Rogan and I didn't exactly stop to clean up after ourselves before we rushed out of here in search of my grimoire. But it's apparent that Hillen and Tad did some tidying up when they brought my boxes here. My chest tightened when she told me that they had packed up my apartment about a week ago.

I totally get it, no point paying rent when you're dead. Even if I hadn't been murdered, the likelihood that I was going to be moving into the apartment above this shop when I came back from my adventures in magic land was pretty high anyway, so Hillen and Tad were doing me a solid either way.

Boxes are stacked by the front register, labeled in surprising detail even though they were eventually going to find themselves donated. Although this is my *can't stay still* aunt that organized all of this, so really I shouldn't expect anything less. Hillen said they brought some of my stuff here to join what they were clearing out from my Grammy Ruby's place. Then everything was going to those who were less fortunate and needed it.

Rogan comes in behind me, the heat of his body teasing my back. His strong presence practically wraps itself around me, grounding me, and I all at once feel more settled and secure. I step closer to the cardboard stacks, running my finger over the waist-high edge. It's strange that most of my life is packed in so few boxes. I figured there'd be more here.

I guess it makes sense, since my furniture is in storage, waiting for Tad to go through it to see if there's anything he wants to keep. My pictures and other sentimental things are at Hillen's house. These boxes are just clothes, some dishes and cookware, and a collection of other random things that there's no point keeping when the owner is long gone, but it feels good to see them again.

"It's strange to be back here," Rogan observes as he looks around. "So much has changed in such a short amount of time, who would've known," he muses, offering me a small smile as he takes in the righted shelves and swept floors.

"Pretty sure my ancestors did," I tell him as I start to pull boxes down from their stack in search of the ones marked clothing.

"How so?" he queries, taking a box I hand him and setting it aside for me to go through.

"When you applied your best Puss in Boots begging eyes and asked for my help, I was going to say no."

Rogan clutches his chest and shakes his head judgmentally at me. I roll my eyes.

"It's not like you'd exactly endeared yourself to me, barging in and trying to rob me of my choices. There was no way I was getting tangled up in your damage," I tell him, and he snorts out a laugh and raises an enticing eyebrow at me.

"There's no running now," he taunts playfully, and I chuckle.

"There was no running then," I admit on a breathy laugh. "My ancestors legitimately zapped me into accepting. At the time, I thought that's what it must have felt like when I was magic bound to help someone, so I begrudgingly cooperated. But now I know that's not what it was," I go on, searching through the rest of the stack, hoping I'll find a box marked underwear.

Please don't tell me Hillen threw them away. I know it's beyond creepy to donate used underwear, but I promise, this time, I won't judge.

"What was it then?" Rogan asks as he works to restack the boxes I don't need.

"When I'm being called to help someone, it's like this anxious, itchy, *why do I feel like I'm forgetting something* feeling. I feel pulled in a direction and put in that person's path. But with you, it was more a gentle tasing that I'm going to call *fate assistance*," I joke, arcing a hand in the air like I can see the name written in the very atmosphere around us.

"You think we're written in the stars?" Rogan asks, and I can't get a read on just what he might think about that.

I snort incredulously. "I don't know if I'd go that far, maybe my ancestors just thought you were hot," I declare cheekily.

A slow smile stretches across Rogan's gorgeous face, and

he laughs quietly. I start opening the boxes of clothes we've set aside and pulling out things I need.

Hello, leggings.

"Yes!" I scream out like I just won the lottery.

I pull the bag out containing underwear and bras, grabbing a pair from the top to show Rogan, like I'm fully expecting him to be just as excited.

"I prefer you without them," he offers, a flirty twinkle in his eyes as he shrugs shamelessly.

Heat courses through me, but I tsk at him and set the bag aside. I definitely need to keep an eye on it. No *oops, I lost your underwear* is going down on my watch. No sirree. I pack up a box that has a couple months' worth of clothes in it, hoping that will be enough. The plan is to regroup with Elon back at Rogan's and suss out a survival and attack strategy there. Yep, this will have to do.

I hand the box to Rogan to put in the car, shooting him an *I'll be watching you* look so he knows my underwear better not turn up missing, and he just waggles his eyebrows at me, which doesn't leave me feeling reassured at all. I clean up my mess and stand to take in the shop. The scent of incense and my grandmother still permeates the walls, and I hope that will always be the case. I had such big dreams for this place, but now as I stand around looking at everything, it all feels so uncertain.

Will I really ever be able to settle down here? I mean, even if we can survive the evil High Council, how can I stay here when there's the chance that I might never die? I don't even know if we grow old. Am I stuck in this body, with this face, forever?

I look down at myself and shrug; it is a good body and face to have. Why did I never think to ask about this before? Oh yeah, that's right, I didn't know I'd ever come back from the dead. It's been ten years since Rogan and Elon came back for the first time, they both still look pretty good. On the other hand, we *do* scar, so maybe we do age?

I bring a hand up to my chest and press against the mark there. I look outside, ready to ask Rogan about all of this when he walks back in, but he's not there. I squint to make sure I'm not just missing him bending over to load the box into the back of my Pathfinder, but I don't spot his big muscular body through the glass. I hurry to the door to see if maybe he's taking a call or something and has wandered away from the windows, but when I spot a pair of thick, long legs on the ground behind my parked car, fear and panic slam into me like a tidal wave.

How did they find us so fast?

8

Power inundates me with only a speck of a thought. It crackles all around me like dangerous static as I shove it out into my surroundings, searching for attackers. I'm prepared to find cloaked magic users advancing on the shop SWAT-style, or moving to trap us in a grid, but that's not the case. Rogan's magical signature is a steady hum, and I only sense two other mancers nearby. One of which has wards protecting them against the reach of my magic, and the other doesn't.

I prepare my magic to Bone Witch bitch-slap whoever just picked a fight without any protection. I'll deal with the easy target first and then teach the other one a lesson next. I'm just about to let my magic loose on the two mancers on my radar when something confusing happens. The witch I can feel who has no wards or spells protecting them suddenly attacks the other magical presence I sense.

What the hell?

Why would they take out each other?

Without a thought, I call on even more magic, readying myself for whatever is going on, and I shove out the front door. I rush to the right where I can feel the other two magical signatures, and when I round a corner into the narrow alleyway between my shop and the one next to it, I find Marx breathing heavily and standing over the crumpled body of...Prek.

Confusion and relief battle each other in my chest, and I can't seem to find my voice as my eyes dart back and forth between the two of them. Near Prek's hand is a black and brown gun that looks odd. I don't know what's off about it, and apparently my body doesn't care, because just the sight of any kind of gun has me choking on alarm and foreboding.

I'm back in the church, the sound of a gun discharging suddenly reverberating all around me. Pain tears through my chest and then heat as the bullet rips through me, my skin and bones no protection at all. My lungs fill with blood, and I gasp for air, only this time my magic doesn't blink out, instead it flares.

The sensation of hot power pulsing out of me pulls me from the flashback. It's as though a blue hypergiant star has just opened up in my chest, causing flames of magic to consume every inch of me. My shocked gaze lands on Marx's wide eyes, and I can see the fright and surprise in them as he takes a hesitant step closer. He lifts his arms, palms out, and then lowers them slightly, silently communicating that he wants me to calm down.

"Lennox," he calls to me, his voice laced with so much soothing and reassuring power that I want to wrap it around me in hopes that it will help to douse this all-consuming inferno. "Lennox, you're okay, just breathe."

I nod jerkily and focus on pulling air into my lungs. Slowly my chest rises with the smooth intake of a deep breath. It chases away the feeling that I'm drowning in my own blood again.

I survived, I tell myself, blowing the breath out and pulling in another one.

My lungs are clear, my chest is healed, I'm okay.

My raging power starts to calm, and I go from a burning white beacon of magic to a softly glowing ember.

"That's it," Marx tells me, lacing his words with more of his own magic, and I'm immediately grateful he's a Vox Witch and therefore knew exactly how to talk my magic down.

The glow kissing my skin disappears altogether as I continue to breathe through my panic and assure myself that everything is okay. Yeah, Rogan is still lying on the ground, but I'm pretty sure we have Prek to thank for that, and he's currently an unconscious heap too. Marx is here, no one else is closing in on us. It's all okay. The burning hot star in my chest blinks out, and my body relaxes as I finally get my power under control.

I blow out a deep sigh of relief and offer a warm smile to Marx. "What are you doing here?" I ask, my tone friendly but surprised to see him. But Marx's stare is stunned and focused on something behind me. I whirl to see what it is.

Well, shit.

Across the street, a sea of bones floats just over the ground in the massive graveyard. I squeal with panic and start flapping my arms, shooing the bones back to what was supposed to be their final resting place. I look all around as I do, but the few passing cars don't slam on their brakes and run screaming from their cars. I don't spot any pedestrians or anyone else walking slack-mouthed out of the surrounding businesses with their camera phones poised to capture the unexplainable phenomenon. I quickly bury the bones back where they're supposed to be and then awkwardly speed walk away like there's nothing to see here.

With a flick of my wrist, I call both Prek's and Rogan's bodies to me. *I might be getting a little too good at this.* I dismiss that thought as I hold open the door and carefully float Rogan inside. I shove Prek in next, not bothering to be overly careful as I bump him around purposefully. *Oopsie.* Marx quickly follows after, and my anxious eyes flit over everything around us as he disappears into the shop. No one is so much as glancing my way, and I relax a little as I shut the door, lock it, double-check that it's actually locked, and then magically send Prek's and Rogan's bodies through the saffron yellow curtain that separates the main part of the shop from the large room where my Grammy Ruby did her readings.

I set Prek in the high-backed chair Ruby loved to sit in, and lay Rogan out on the table.

"Can you tie him up or secure him somehow?" I ask Marx, who's watching me, oddly quiet, from the doorway.

He nods and gets to it while I check Rogan over. Magic tells me that he's unconscious but otherwise fine. Relief spills out on a sigh, and I reach up and pull a finger-sized dart from his neck. Power pulses at my fingertips as I examine it, but I don't detect any potions or spells. Whatever Prek hit him with seems to be a concoction of the human variety.

I brush hair away from Rogan's face, gently running my fingers over his cheek.

It hits me that I too woke up on this table after meeting Rogan for the first time and being knocked out.

My, my, my, how the tables have turned.

A small smile ticks at the corners of my mouth. He looks way more uncomfortable than I remember feeling, or like he will be when he wakes up. I should probably feel bad about that, but I did tell him he'd rue the day for messing with me, and this day is a ruing.

I debate for a moment trying to speed up the metabolizing of whatever drug is in his system. Now that I know Hemamancers can heat up blood, maybe that would work, but I'm hesitant to try it. I don't want to burn him up from the inside out or cause damage. I could also try to separate the drug itself from his system, but again the theory sounds great, but I don't know how to actually do it.

I open myself up to the tether and the blood magic, willing it to guide my hands like my bone magic has so many other times. I wait for that telltale *knowing* to percolate in my mind, for pure instinct to tell me what to do, but nothing happens. *Okay*, I definitely need to work that out with Rogan when he's awake. No point in both of us having access to the other's abilities if we don't know how to use them when we need to.

I look over to find Marx draping a braided leather necklace around Prek, a small fuchsia pouch hanging from it and resting against the Order member's breast bone.

"What happened?" I finally ask when Marx steps away and starts quickly inspecting his handiwork.

"Siobhan had to report the missing bodies. I tried to get her to hold off just a little longer, but she said *they'd know she waited and that my dick wasn't worth going to prison for.*"

I snort out a laugh, not expecting that overshare, and shrug awkwardly. Marx shoots me a look that very clearly argues this *Siobhan*'s claim, and I hold up my hands, in no position to argue one way or another.

"To be fair, I don't know if any dick is worth going to prison for," I assure him, looking over to Rogan.

I tilt my head in contemplation. I mean, maybe I'd have to spend more time with it to be sure.

"Fuck, this is weird as hell," Marx confesses on a deep exhale. "Rogan and Elon told me what happened to them. It all makes so much sense with what I've seen them put through, but I saw you...die. I watched them shut your eyes and clean you up. You were gone...but here you are." He gestures to where I'm standing less than five feet away from him. "I don't know how to process this. I thought I had. After talking to Rogan, I thought I got it, but I don't know now."

"It was weird for me too, trust me," I reassure him. "You get used to it though," I offer unhelpfully.

He rubs the back of his neck and chuckles at my crappy attempt at comfort.

"For real though, who is Siobhan and why would she wait to report missing bodies? Rogan told me you had a friend who was helping; I'm assuming that's who you're talking about, but you know this fool never paints the whole picture," I tell him, waving a hand at where Rogan is still splayed out on the large circular reading table.

Marx laughs again, and some of the tension and uncertainty drains from his stiff shoulders. I know Rogan and Elon trust him, and I really want to be able to. I feel a little better now that he doesn't look like he's about to freak out.

"Yes, Siobhan's my friend who works at the morgue. She's in charge of processing and discharging bodies that have been claimed for rituals and sacrifices and other things like that. I figured that would be a quiet and discreet place to keep you while we, you know, waited," Marx explains.

"Did she know there was a possibility I could wake up?" I question, wondering if she's now going to be another loose end that could be a threat to us.

"No, definitely not. When she's there, she's normally in her office, making arrangements, not hanging out with the bodies. That part of the Order's morgue doesn't get a lot of activity though. Bodies are held there until Siobhan goes through the request database to see if there's a match between a ceremonial request and what she has on hand. I remembered her saying once that some people wait months and months before they match up with a request. If you were going to wake up, we hoped that would be the best option for it to go undetected."

"Oh," I chirp, processing that information. "The bodies in those fridges were for ceremonies and sacrifices?" I ask, my face scrunched in concern, even though it does help me feel a little bit better about forcing them to help me.

"It's completely voluntary," Marx assures, taking in my judgmental look. "Just like Lessers have organ donation or the option to donate their body to science, mancers can opt in to be used for many different things. Covens all around the world still make sacrifices to different deities or elements. There are ceremonies that require parts of a mancer to be successful. It's really fascinating. I have a great book that deep dives into a ton of great history on it, if you're interested," Marx offers casually.

I make a mental note to pivot from epic funerals and stunning headstones to a kickass sacrifice or something for the three bodies I magic jacked.

"Um, I'm cool, but thanks," I tell Marx, and he just shrugs like I'm missing out. "What happened to the Order though? I thought the High Council had people watching me?" I gesture to Prek, who's still out cold.

"I don't know what he's doing here," Marx declares, toeing Prek's boot and watching for any reaction. "As far as I know, his team was assigned to the file room until the investigation is complete on how portal bones got into your quarters."

My mind snaps back to the owl skull that sucked me into that demon-marked cage and then ultimately helped me break out of it.

"Some undercover Order members were watching the morgue itself, but they stopped about four days ago—we think because too much time had passed," he says with a hint of apology in his tone. I wave it away. "Rogan and Elon had to stay away because we didn't want to draw attention to anything. I was keeping an eye out through Siobhan and a motion sensitive camera I snuck in, but the battery died a couple hours before you must have woken up. I only found out that something had happened, because Siobhan got a notification that the temperature of the holding fridges had gone up. That's only supposed to happen when they're empty, they're magically designed that way. She thought it was a glitch, and I conveniently offered to accompany her while she checked on it. That's when we discovered you and three others were missing."

I nod in understanding, not sure if I'm offended or impressed that he took advantage of his relationship in order to protect me.

"I called Rogan right away, thinking someone must have taken you, and I begged Siobhan to give me a couple hours before she reported the missing bodies."

And alas we come full circle, I muse as all the pieces to the puzzle now fit snugly together.

"I'm assuming you're here to warn Rogan that the Order, and therefore his evil parents, now know that I'm missing," I tell him, and he nods his confirmation. "So now we just need to figure out why *he's* here," I declare, fixing a glare on Prek.

A groan sounds from the table, and I look over to find Rogan stirring.

Perfect timing.

I rush over to him as his eyes start to flit open. "Hey, you're okay," I reassure him as he makes a disgruntled noise and tries to get his bearings. "Prek shot you with a tranquilizer dart," I explain as he looks around, confused. Lush mossy green eyes lock on mine, and whatever bewilderment was floating in them is chased away by sappy affection.

"Hey, you," he coos at me, lifting a hand in the direction

of my nose. I'm pretty sure he's going in for a boop, but his hand drops like it weighs a hundred pounds before he can. "Ow," he grumps when he accidentally slaps himself in the face. Rogan glares at his knuckles but then looks back to me, and a lovesick smile stretches across his face. "You are the most beautiful soul I have ever seen," he tells me, his tone serious and reverent.

A current of tenderness flashes through me, and a fluttering sensation starts low in my stomach.

"I just want to eat you," he goes on, the words slightly slurred.

Oh boy.

"Especially that nose, no, definitely those lips. Your hair drives me beyond the brink of madness. I've never wanted to eat someone just because they're so cute. Not just cute though, like cute in a sexy as fuck kind of way," he announces on a titillating growl that sneaks into my body and settles warmly between my thighs. "Can I eat you?" he asks on an adorable pout, and I cover my mouth with my hand to try and trap in the laughter there. "I mean, not like that," he adds, wagging his eyebrows. It clearly takes way more effort than it should, and he concentrates hard on the movement. "I wouldn't actually eat your gorgeous face, but I would like to dine on that pussy. Table for one," he announces, lifting a hand like he's calling for a waiter.

"Ooookaaayyy," I exclaim loudly, straightening up and trying to fight the blush that's inching into my cheeks.

Marx laughs hard, and Rogan's eyes snap to him. "Heyyyy, buddy," he offers him in greeting, and Marx looks like this is the best thing ever.

Rogan is drugged out of his gourd, and it's better than any *coming out of anesthesia* video I've ever seen online.

He tries to sit up, and I rush to help. Damn, all that muscle is heavy. I grunt as he suddenly stops supporting his own weight, and we almost tip over. Marx hurries over and helps me get him upright on the table.

"You're so damn pretty," Rogan practically shouts, and then his volume must register, because he cringes and brings a finger up to his mouth to say *shhhhh* as though Marx and I are the loud ones.

He turns to his friend. "Isn't she just the most astonishing thing you've ever seen?" he asks Marx, and I chuckle at the weird high pitch to his voice. It has this goofy innocence to it that makes me want to say *awww*, but also makes me want to record it so I can make fun of him about this later. "And it's not just outside, my frrriennnn," Rogan implores, momentarily getting distracted by his finger for some reason. "No, sir, she's stunning on the outside *and* on the inside. Bro, you should see her body!" he whisper yells, and I can't help the twitter that escapes me.

"What?" Rogan suddenly demands. "How dare you," he accuses, as though Marx were the one to suggest checking out my body and not him. "I love you, Marx, but I will kick your ass. I already have to fuck up that wolf, *Saaaxooon*," he announces, mocking the name. "Fucker kissed her twice, bro, twice," he growls as he holds up three fingers. "Never wanted to kill someone so badly in my life, and my parents renounced me! That's fucking legit, man!"

Marx looks over at me and raises a judgmental eyebrow. I roll my eyes. "Puh-lease, your *bro* Rogan wasn't even on my radar at the time," I defend, not able to stop myself from making fun of all the bro-ing.

Rogan's hand shoots up into the air, and he shakes it impatiently like he's waiting to be called on. Marx laughs as he calls on him.

"Not true for six-hundred, Alex," he calls out, like we're suddenly on *Jeopardy*. "I was all over that radar: we kissed in the kitchen, there were talks of a safe word, secrets were told," he counters, and Marx chokes on air at that declaration.

I huff out an exasperated groan that morphs into a chuckle at the end because this is all so ridiculous and yet utterly amusing. We have an unconscious Order member tied up in a chair, and I'm here defending my relationship or the lack thereof when I kissed a lycan twice.

"We *did* kiss in the kitchen, and then you screwed me over at your aunt's cottage. The betrayal negates anything that had been building between us before then. I was well within my rights to kiss Saxon," I justify.

Rogan looks to Marx as though he's waiting for his ruling. Marx shrugs. "She has a point," he concedes, and Rogan groans.

"I *know* she does. Fucking Saxon. Still gonna kick his ass though," he grumbles, all pouty and disgruntled. "But, Lennox," he calls out. "My little bone flower..." He cringes as the endearment slips out of his full lips. "No, that was just weird," he mumbles before continuing on. "You're mine now, right?" he asks, the question both parts boyish and possessive.

"Will someone please shut him up?" a groggy voice groans, and my head snaps to where Prek is tied to my grandmother's favorite chair.

Russet eyes are fixed on me as Prek lifts his head. "Hello, Osteomancer. Correct me if I'm wrong, but aren't you supposed to be dead?"

9

Prek's question settles around me as I eye him. He's still bald, and I wonder if that's a choice or if hair loss forced his hand. The smooth dark skin of his face is clean shaven, his red-brown eyes settled intensely on me. His features don't hint at any kind of emotion as he waits for me to speak.

"Lennox is one of us now, she can't die," Rogan snaps at him belligerently, and it's all I can do not to turn around and cover his mouth with my hand.

Maybe Prek will dismiss anything he says as incoherent ramblings.

"I saw your dead body in the med tent that night," Prek states, his eyes still on me.

And maybe not.

Prek looks from me to Rogan like he's trying to place clues together in order to solve a difficult problem. "One of *us* now?" he repeats.

Rogan chirps out an arrogant, "You know it," and I huff frustratedly.

Inebriated Rogan just went from adorable to a liability real freakin' quick. I turn to Marx. "Can you take him somewhere and sober him up?" I ask, my eyes screaming *get this loose-lipped fucker out of here right now*.

Marx quickly grabs Rogan, pulling an arm over his shoulder, and practically drags him off the table and out of the room.

"What are you doing here, Prek, and why the hell are you picking a fight with us?" I ask, turning away from the doorway and focusing my attention back on the Order member. He seems entirely too calm for someone who woke up tied to a chair. "Are you following Rogan?" I press, knowing that Prek hates him and figuring that's probably the most logical answer.

Life note: start checking for tails whenever you go anywhere.

I watch a debate take place in Prek's eyes. I can see him trying to deduce how to proceed, and it makes me wonder what options he's considering. I've seen him run with *powerful and arrogant*, like that night that he wrecked Rogan's car with the both of us still in it. There's also the *dedicated soldier*, which is what he always was when he watched over me at the Order's headquarters. He was *fair and curious* with me when I called Tad to tell him where I was and that I was okay after Rogan sold me out. And I know he's *driven and ambitious* with a smattering of *petty* mixed in.

Will he try to play me, or will Prek finally reveal who he is at the sum of all of those parts?

He pulls a deep breath in, studying me like the answers might just be written in the planes of my face, and then he exhales, and it's clear in his eyes that a decision has been made. I don't say a word, the need to rush not riding me even though maybe it should.

"Contrary to what Hemamancer Kendrick believes, my world does not revolve around him," Prek declares, and then he sags ever so slightly in the chair. "I wasn't following Rogan, I was following Alvarez."

The name sparks recognition, and I try to put a face to it.

"The Filipino guy on my team who likes to play cards," Prek supplies, and I immediately make the connection.

My brow furrows, and I try to figure out why he would have been here. He was quiet but friendly. He made me tea once. It was amazing, and then he showed me how to shuffle a deck like a pro. He laughed and gave up pretty quickly when I proved to have shitty dexterity. I kicked his ass at Go fish after that though, so I considered us even.

"A couple hours ago, Alvarez got a call and then asked to leave. I don't know why that sequence bothered me, but it did. Maybe it's because the team was under investigation and I was looking for anything and everything that could be a red flag, but I decided to follow him. I discreetly slipped a tracker on him in case he slipped into a line, and then I grabbed a tranq gun for back up."

Prek's explanation washes over me, and I sort through it for any hint of lies or missing key pieces. "And Alvarez led you here?"

"He did. He sat at the bus stop on the other side of the street and just watched this building. I didn't know what to make of it, and then out of nowhere, you pulled up. Alvarez left after about ten minutes, but when Kendrick started carrying boxes to the car, I decided it was time for answers. Either he was stealing or some other fucked up thing was going down, so I stopped him. I thought you were some kind of reflection spell, which is illegal by the way, but now I'm starting to think I'm wrong. How the fuck are you here?" he demands, anger simmering in his words and a hint of hurt ringing in his tone.

This time, the debate goes on in *my* head. Will I lose or gain by telling him the truth? Is it worth the risk?

"How did I not even notice you?" I ask as I think back to pulling up to the shop. There were two Order members right on top of us, and neither Rogan nor I had any idea.

Prek smirks, his arrogant side shining through. "I'm good at what I do, Osteomancer," he tells me silkily.

I raise an eyebrow at that. "I mean, not that good, you are tied to a chair right now," I point out, and he snorts an incredulous laugh.

"Will you tell me what's going on?" he presses, aware of my internal debate.

"Depends," I answer evenly.

"On?"

"If you're in or out?" I provide cryptically, and he huffs out another incredulous laugh. "You have to decide, Prek, because the fact of the matter is, knowing the truth is dangerous. You even seeing me right now puts you on a list of loose ends, and I think we both know that you answer to higher-ups who aren't too fond of loose ends," I tell him, trying to open his eyes without spilling secrets that aren't mine to spill. "If you want answers, decide which side of the fight you're on, because everything is about to come crashing down, and it's them or us, Prek."

I leave him to stew on my ambiguous non-answers and stride to the yellow curtain that separates us from the main part of the shop. I pull it back sharply and find Rogan sitting on the ground with his head in his hands.

"How's it going?" I ask Marx.

"He sang me a rather lovely song, and now I'm pretty sure he's coming down."

I bite back a smile. "Cool, can you get him buckled up in the car, we gotta go...like, now."

"On it," Marx asserts, and then I shut the curtain and look at Prek expectantly.

He studies me for a beat and then nods once. "I'm in."

I stride toward him and lift a hand. The chair beneath him poofs into a cloud of dust, and he falls hard on his ass. He glares at me but pushes the thin rope Marx used to tie him up off his wrists and ankles. Prek stands up, and I will the bone that makes up my Grammy's favorite chair to resume its previous shape.

"Could have warned me?" he grumps, rubbing his ass.

I shoot him a saccharine smile. "Could have not tranqed my boyfriend," I lob back.

As soon as the word *boyfriend* leaves my mouth, it feels wrong. He's more than that, but I doubt Prek cares to understand the nuances of my relationship. He offers a conciliatory nod and then follows me as I quickly move into the main part of the shop.

"Go get in the car, I'll be right there," I order as I move behind the front counter.

I grab a cloth bag and feel for the bone locks that open up the false wall. The smell of patchouli, singed cedar, and warm sugar cookies greets me as my magic connects with the hidden locks, and the wall slides open, like the pocket door it really is. I step into my Grammy's store room, breathing in the remnants of her scent that still fills the stone walls.

Racks and shelves line the walls, filled to the brim with ingredients, old bones, aged potion books, stoppered bottles and sealed jars of anything and probably everything an Osteomancer could ever need.

I infuse magic with what I need and then push that magic out into the cellar-like space, urging it to find what I require. Jars and bottles begin to rotate on shelves like they're being spun on lazy Susans. Bones rumble from the bottom of piles and then climb to the top, and I walk through the room plucking things from their homes and placing them in my bag. I hurry, and when it feels like the room has offered up all the useful contents it contains, I back out of the space.

"Thank you," I whisper to the magic and to my ancestors for good measure.

I guide the door closed, reactivating the magic bones that only my line can sense and unlock, and then I steal one more glance at the shop. I have the strange sense that I'm saying goodbye to it, and as odd as that sensation is, there's a warm peace that washes over me at the same time. I breathe in one last deep inhale of my Grammy, and then I tuck away all the dreams and plans I had for this space, hoping that my instincts are wrong and one day I'll be able to call this magical place home.

"Miss you, Grammy," I murmur. "Pretty sure shit's about to get crazy, so wake up whoever you need to on that side, because I have a feeling I'm going to need all of you watching my back."

I stand as my words ripple away from me, sinking into the ether and, I hope, going to work. I tighten my hold on my bag, and as I stride toward the door, a warm caress of confirmation brushes across my cheek. I close my eyes at the sensation, and I can picture my grandmother next to me, pride shining in her eyes and a stalwart set to her shoulders.

I can feel the *we've got you* in her presence, and emotion wells in my eyes. I swallow it down, nodding gratefully to her, and then without another word or spilled tear, I push out of the door to the shop, lock it, and then dash to the car.

Rogan watches me as I climb in, and I feel support and strength flow from him to me.

"How are you doing?" I inquire cheekily, and he groans slightly, his eyes begging that I take pity on him. Mine glimmer back playfully *not a chance*.

He laugh-grunts and then grabs for the *oh shit* handle as I peel out of my parking space and then race down the avenue. I roll my eyes before looking into the back seat view in my rearview mirror.

"You better be buckled up, boys," I warn, and Prek chuckles as Marx scurries to find his seat belt.

"Why is he here?" Rogan grumbles, nodding to the back seat but refusing to actually make eye contact with Prek.

"He's choosing a side, that's what he's doing," I announce, my eyes finding a pair of russet ones brimming with curiosity in my mirror.

"Lennox," Rogan warns.

"Rogan," I mock-warn back. "I trusted you about Marx, trust me about Prek. If I'm wrong...I'm wrong. I don't see how we'd be any worse off if I am. The High Council already knows, so they're already looking for us, and if he turns out to be a snake, we'll kill him."

"Hey," Prek objects, and Marx chuckles.

I shrug, not sorry at all.

"Watch the road," Rogan grumps as I stare into his eyes and try to get him to see what I see.

I shove reassurance and a whole lot of *trust me* at him through our tether, and a weary sigh greets my ears. A small smile ticks at the corners of my mouth, and I try to tame it before amusement leaks through our connection.

Is it wrong to find joy in his annoyance?

Na.

I take a sharp right without signaling and press on the gas so I can barrel down the empty side road.

"What are you doing?" Rogan demands, his knuckles white and his faith in my driving skills dry as a bone.

"Losing any tails we might have...obviously. If there's one thing I'm learning in this second life, it's that you can never be too careful," I offer matter-of-factly.

Rogan's eyes narrow in warning at my declaration of *second life*, and I huff out an annoyed sigh.

"I don't know if you remember this, but I'm pretty sure *you* let the cat out of the bag when you announced I was part of some *I can't die* club," I point out, and he promptly finds something really interesting just outside of his window.

Yeah, that's what I thought.

Chagrin trickles through the tether to me, and this time I don't even crack the smile that's tickling my lips.

I'm getting so good at this.

I take another series of crazy too fast right turns, making sure I complete a circle before moving erratically in another direction and watching for followers in my rearview mirror the whole time.

"Alright, Prek, you're with us now, so let's get it all out there," I announce, and then everyone in the car is slammed to the left as I jump a curb and turn on squealing tires into a neighborhood. I drop my speed as houses start to flash by, but I've still got my eye out for potential tails.

"It's all fun and games until the human police put you in jail for reckless driving," Rogan mumbles quietly under his breath.

I roll my eyes, but the grump does have a point, so I start scanning my surroundings for followers *and* cops.

"Prek, do you hate Rogan?" I ask bluntly, hoping we can get to the bottom of their issues quickly and then over them just as quickly.

He takes a minute to answer, and I can feel the animosity brewing in Rogan.

"No, I don't *hate* him...I don't trust him. We used to be friendly, respectful, and then the next thing I know, my aunt's dead and so is his uncle. My family wasn't allowed to question it, the Kendrick heirs were renounced, and we were all just supposed to be okay with that and move on."

"And you weren't okay with that?" I dig, still feeling like we're not at the bottom of things yet.

"No, because things didn't make sense. The way all of it was handled screamed that there was more going on here, I just don't know what," Prek admits, and I consider what he's saying.

"It would be very easy for your imagination to run wild, I bet," I tell him, empathy coloring my tone. "I could see a million worst case scenarios that might run through your head. Especially with your profession being what it is. You probably see the worst of witchkind on a regular basis; I can only imagine what you thought might have happened to your aunt. What Rogan and his family were hiding from you."

I'm talking to Prek, but my gaze lands on Rogan. What I'm saying is just as important for him to hear and understand. What happened to Prek's aunt wasn't Rogan or Elon's fault, but Prek doesn't know that. He was fed some bullshit story that never made sense to him and then expected to get over it. That's a solid recipe for resentment if I've ever seen one. It also confirms what I suspected. Prek isn't an angry Order member out for revenge, he's a man who lost someone and would simply like some answers.

Apprehension amps up inside of the car as I loop around to another neighborhood. I feel like I'm walking on a tightrope of tension. If I reveal what really happened and Prek doesn't take it well or believe me, we'll have a serious situation on our hands. Plus, the next time I ask Rogan to *trust my instincts* might not go over so well. I'm risking a lot here for someone I don't really know. I look over at Rogan for a moment. Then again, maybe risking a lot for someone I don't really know is what I'm all about now. I mean, it's worked out well so far.

I take a deep breath and fortify my resolve. "Your aunt

Kyat, she was hooking up with Rogan's uncle Oront, right?" I ask.

"Right," Prek answers, a hint of exasperation in his tone, like he can already guess where I'm going with this.

Pshhh, try again, buddy.

"Oront tried to kill Elon. He didn't want to pass his powers down, so he found some ancient ritual that convinced him that he wouldn't have to if he used it. Rogan tried to stop Oront, but your aunt had to get herself involved and attacked Rogan. Rogan fought Oront off, killing him to protect his brother, but he was hurt badly. He and Elon tried to save themselves using their magic, but in the end, they both died. Rogan didn't murder Kyat, she murdered him. Elon died from the wounds Oront carved into him, and then somehow the magic that was at play that night said *syke* and it brought both Rogan and Elon back from the dead."

I look back at Prek to see if he's getting all of this, and he just looks perplexed. His eyes dart to Rogan as though he's expecting him to start laughing or something, but Rogan is stoic and quiet, and Prek has no choice but to see that I mean every word of what I just said.

"I gotta be honest, you tell that story way better than Rogan does," Marx teases in an effort to lighten the mood, and I shoot him a grateful smile.

"Right," I agree. "Rogan's so doom-and-gloom about it; he wants to draw it out and make you guess. I say it's better to just lay it all out there and hope for the best. Rip off the immortal Band-Aid, so to speak."

I slam on my brakes when I look up and find I'm about to drive through a red light. Rogan grunts as he jerks forward, his hold on the *oh shit* handle so tight that I suspect the handle is coming with us the next time we get out of the car.

"My bad," I declare to the guys. "That one was totally on me."

A bunch of man grumbling fills the car, and I swear I hear Marx mumble something about fighting me in the future for my keys.

Such bitchy little witches.

"Anyway," I sing-song. "Back to what I was saying. The Order found your aunt and three dead bodies. They made her tell them what happened, and then the High Council tied up that loose end by killing her. When Rogan and Elon came back, I'm sure you can only imagine what those power-hungry psychos wanted. It wasn't enough that they rule over and control everything; Rogan and Elon had a shiny new ability, and they wanted it.

"When Rogan and Elon wouldn't give it up, they were punished. Now, I know this all seems like a lot, I get it, but before you go trying to poke holes in the truth or convincing yourself that none of what I'm saying is possible, just remember that you saw me dead in that med tent with your own eyes. And now you're riding in the car and talking with a very alive me."

I zoom into the lot of the park I rode my first solo ley line into this morning. The yellow slide practically waves hello as the setting sun paints the sky in pinks, purples, and oranges that somehow feel like the perfect farewell. I even park in the same empty spot I did before.

The car is quiet as I slip out, the others seemingly content to follow my lead, which is interesting because I have no idea what I'm doing. My back door squeals in protest as I open it and reach for my bag of supplies. Rogan grabs the box of clothes he deposited in here earlier, and then we all trek toward the line.

"Where are we headed?" Marx finally asks when we're close enough that the power is buzzing expectantly all around us. "First, we're going to Rogan's house to rest a little and get cleaned up. Then we're going to use the tracker that Prek put on that dude Alvarez."

Three sets of brows dip with confusion as questions filter into all of the guys' gazes.

"Hear me out," I request, preparing to lay out why I think that's the best plan of action. "The High Council has spies everywhere, but especially in the Order. Alvarez is in the Order. He also got a call and then ended up on a bus stop bench, watching my shop. When he saw us, he probably went to report back. It's probably a safe bet that he's on the High Council's payroll," I explain as my eyes drift over to the spot where I remember someone stood and watched from the first time Rogan and I used this ley line.

"Here's the other part though. Someone put an owl skull in my room that portaled me to a church where Elon and I, as well as a ton of other witches, were murdered. More than likely, it was a member of Prek's team who snuck the skull into my room. They were the only ones besides you, me, and the Major who had access," I declare, my eyes fixed on Rogan's. "Maybe I'm wrong, maybe they're not connected, but Alvarez's split loyalties seem suspicious to me. And if I'm right, it means that psycho bitch Jamie wasn't just working with a demon. It means she was working with the High Council too."

10

The Tennessee sun creeps slowly to bed, and the exit for Sweet Lips is only miles away. From the passenger seat, I stare at the sign announcing the upcoming exit, my head tilted back with exhaustion as Rogan drives us to his place. I'm tempted to check in on Paul and his son. I felt in my bones that he was going to be okay after the reading I gave him, but it might not be bad to stop by and see if there's anything else he needs. I dismiss the curiosity, knowing that my magic isn't being called to do that. Plus, the last thing I want to do is drop any of my trouble at his door, so I don't say anything as the arguing in the car ratchets up a notch.

Since I dropped the whole possible collusion bomb, these three have been going at it. They're not fighting so much as passionately discussing the odds that I could be right or wrong, what either outcome means, pitching other potential scenarios, then playing devil's advocate about everything and starting it all over again when the possibility of peace and quiet gets too close.

Prek hasn't said shit about the whole *could be immortal* thing. He seems more keyed up about the suggestion that any mancer would ever conspire with a demon, let alone a demon using a witch whose line had been stripped of magic. The whole thing is laughable, and Rogan and Marx argue each side of every scenario so thoroughly that I think they've confused themselves at this point.

All I know is that I'm not nearly caffeinated enough for any of this shit. My eyes are scratchy and burning, my body aches, my stomach is pissed that there aren't more fast food options located on the highway in the middle of nowhere Tennessee. The only thing carrying me through right now is the fact that I'm going to see my little buddy Hoot soon, and then I'm going to jump face-first into the nearest bed and sleep off the death.

Dusk deepens all around us as we go, and it's making me even sleepier. I immediately sit up and roll my neck, making myself aware of everything around us.

"Just sleep," Rogan implores me, again. "I can feel your exhaustion; it's okay to crash for a little while," he urges.

I stifle a yawn, as riding the ley line again to get here really drained me, but I can't succumb to the call of sleep just yet.

"I'm fine, it's not too much longer. I don't want anyone sneaking up on us while you three wax on and on and on about witch politics and if there's any major significance to the fact that the skull was an *owl* skull." I fake retch at my words and roll my eyes for good measure.

Rogan reaches over and runs the back of his hand across my cheek. I melt a little inside at the gesture and the way his eyes warm as he looks at me. "It's been a long day," he notes, and I don't know why that simple observation makes me feel like I want to cry.

It *has* been a long day, and I know there are many more to come too. Maybe that's what's stoking my overly emotional reaction, or maybe I'm just tired and hungry. That's never a good combo even on the best of days.

"I was thinking," I start, "before I saw you tranqed on the ground, that it would be good to train each other on one another's magic. It's a little *reading each other's diaries*, but it would probably be beneficial to go through our grimoires too. I know we have a million things we need to do to get ready for what's coming for us, but I think this is important," I tell him, and he caresses my face once more before dropping his hand to mine and threading our fingers.

"I agree," he responds, his tone supportive. "I know my aunt's house is not your favorite place because of what I did there, but I think it would be good to talk to her coven again about everything. When we were there before, we had every intention of severing things between us. Now that things are different, we should try to learn as much as we can."

I swallow down the hesitancy that creeps into my chest at the mention of his aunt's coven. He's right, I know he is, but it feels risky too. "Can we trust her?" I ask, worried that the question might offend him. "She seemed like a lovely person, don't get me wrong, but she's your father's sister. Doesn't she subscribe to the same toxic crap he does?"

Rogan gives my hand a comforting squeeze. "Not at all. My father hasn't talked to her since she was a teenager. She was always all about the old ways and the order of things, and that's clearly not at all what my father was about. I only know about her because my mother used to throw her existence in my father's face whenever they were arguing. She thought Alora was some kind of blemish on my dad's magical line."

I snort incredulously, making it clear just what I think about that, and Rogan lifts an eyebrow in agreement.

"Elon and I met Alora and her coven after we were renounced. It's why we chose to settle in Tennessee—she gifted Elon and me the land our houses are built on. She took us in when nobody else would. She never even asked us what happened, she said she knew our souls were pure and she'd help us in whatever way she could."

Once again, I have to blink back the emotion his words stir in me. I hate that he's had to go through so much, and I'm grateful that at least he and Elon weren't abandoned by everyone. It's nice to know that sometimes good *does* prevail over evil, even though it can be hard to see evidence of that in the world we live in today.

"Love you," I tell him softly.

"Love you," he professes right back.

The car suddenly grows quiet, the steady debate that was just happening behind us stalling as though someone found their mute button.

"Wow, you two jumped right into that quick," Marx observes, his tone teasing but also ringing with a touch of surprise and concern.

"Sure did," I concur, not an ounce of shame or regret in my voice. "The days of too much PDA are on the horizon too, so get ready," I decree with a cheeky smile as I rub my thumb over Rogan's.

"When you know, you know," Rogan agrees casually, like it's really just that simple.

"Well, damn," Marx declares. "I've known the guy for fourteen years, and the first time he's told me he loves me was today."

I crack up at the revelation, and Rogan smiles, amused.

"But then he threatened to kick my ass," he points out, concerned. "Does an *I love you* even count when the person saying it is high as a kite?" he then questions, and I laugh even harder.

"'Ouiser, you know I love ya more 'n my luggage,'" I tease, and then the car goes quiet.

Rogan shoots a puzzled look my way, and I drop my mouth open, shocked and completely scandalized.

"What?" I squeak. "None of you have ever seen *Steel Magnolias*?"

Prek snorts and Marx grunts his dismissal.

"Yeah, Lennox, that's exactly what the three of us do on our time off. Watching old ass chick flicks is most definitely a passion of all of ours," Marx deadpans, and I turn to glare at him.

"First of all, Marx, don't ever let me hear you disrespect the great Dolly Parton again. Second of all, a classic is a classic, and you three would be better men for it. What about *Fried Green Tomatoes*, tell me you've at least seen that one."

Marx snickers, but no one speaks up.

"You're all heathens," I accuse, turning back to face the front, appalled. "Swine," I call back as Prek and Marx start to titter. "My Grammy wouldn't approve a one of ya," I decree, a strange Southern accent popping up like even my voice has declared solidarity with Ouiser and the gang.

Rogan pulls into a long driveway that's dimly lit by solar lights, and the guys start arguing about movies they have seen and think are good. I tune it all out when the *brilliance* of *Rocky* starts to get tossed around. Trees line each side of the drive, and I feel the need to hold my breath until we crest a rise and Rogan's house is suddenly in view.

Just like the first time, welcoming light glows inside and outside, making the palatial modern house feel warm and homey. I run my eyes over the dark gray siding, the gorgeous cedar accents, and all the windows that I now know display gorgeous views from every room in the stunning house. I feel like I'm coming home, which is weird, but I'm going to go ahead and apply the laws of *finders keepers* and just roll with it.

As though Rogan can feel everything I just did, he shoots me a smile so wide and stunning that it makes me forget how to breathe.

Damn, that gorgeous mug he's rocking is potent.

He looks away, his own feelings of relief and happiness flowing over to me, and my involuntary muscles once again remind my brain that we need oxygen. A garage door opens as we drive closer. The frosted glass panes inset in the cedar door are a beautiful combination, and I watch them rise until we're pulling in underneath them.

Prek whistles, impressed, and I smile proudly, even though I had absolutely nothing to do with making this home so damn incredible. What's interesting is that I can feel this house in a way I couldn't before. Now that I'm more open to the tether, I can sense protections, wards, weapons, and even the blessings that are incorporated throughout. I feel it all just like I could feel Elon's house, and it makes me even more awed than I was before.

We all climb out of the car, grabbing my things from the back, and file in one by one. A demon dog bark booms all around us, and both Prek and Marx freeze. The sound of nails on the hardwood rushes toward us, and I set my bag of potions and ingredients down and get on my knees.

Hoot's gray Ewok-looking ass comes scrambling around the corner and squeals with excitement as he barrels right into me. I hug him tight, petting his face and cooing at him loudly as a fluffy corgi comes bouncing at us in Hoot's wake. Rogan grabs the other pup, and I wait excitedly for what I know is coming next. Gibson, Rogan's skunk familiar, prances around the corner, and I hear Prek screech a *fuck no* and then dive into the living room.

I start laughing so hard I almost pee my pants. I can't stop seeing him throw his body out of the way as his voice goes full teenage girl at a boy band concert. Rogan sets Tilda down and picks up Gibson, and Prek proceeds to army crawl behind the couch. Marx is leaning against the wall, grabbing his stomach as laugh tears spill down his cheeks, and I can feel Rogan's smug feelings. I'm sure his thoughts on the matter are somewhere in the range of *payback's a bitch.*

Prek peeks over the couch, still not catching on that the skunk is harmless, and I break into a new fit of giggles at the sight of him. My cheeks and stomach hurt by the time Rogan convinces the Order member that he won't get sprayed. I look down at Hoot and start peppering him with kisses. The normally stoic pooch is clearly excited to see me, and it makes my heart melt.

"Who's a good boy?" I baby talk at him. "It's you, it most certainly is. I missed you so much, buddy," I assure him, sounding like a mix of Scooby-Doo and a Chipette. I cuddle him to my chest again, which is exactly when he rips a fart so loud and lethal that I find myself wanting to dive into the living room, Prek-style, and then army crawl away.

Moon shits, it's bad.

Marx looks over at me like I'm the poop shoot offender, and I flip him the bird while trying to convince my lungs that oxygen is *way* overrated. I put Hoot down and scramble away, pulling my shirt collar above my nose as a secondary offence. Rogan wastes no time in grabbing my hand and pulling me along after him. He knows what's up, and he quickly pulls us both to safety.

Apparently, Marx didn't get the memo though, because he leans down to pet Hoot like the atmosphere around him isn't ripe as hell and dangerous. The moment Marx realizes that he's made a huge mistake, will live rent-free in my mind forever. One minute, Marx is reaching for the adorable little furball that he thinks the rest of us rudely abandoned, and the next, he's inhaling and then seriously wishing he hadn't. He gags and slams back against the wall as though making himself as flat as possible against it will make the reek go away.

Hoot steps closer to him, clearly wanting those pets that

Marx was just offering, and Marx gurgles out a weird combination of groan and squeal before he leaps away. Hoot suddenly thinks this is some kind of game and proceeds to trot after him, a steady stream of toots going off like machine-gun fire in his wake.

Rogan runs to a set of sliders and pulls them open. "Run!" he yells at his friend. "Lose him in the trees, or there's no hope for you," he calls after as Marx books it into the backyard with Hoot, Gibson, and Tilda hot on his trail.

I have no choice but to run to the guest room by now, holding my crotch and bargaining with my pee to not go anywhere until I say it's okay. I'm still cracking up as I slam the door behind me and, in record time, strip down and commandeer the toilet. Laugh-tears drip down my cheeks, and I wipe them from my face, losing it again when I hear Marx scream from somewhere outside.

I love that dog.

After washing up, I head back out to the kitchen where I find Rogan talking to Elon while he makes a sandwich.

"You're back," I announce, surprised, and then Rogan moves over, and I catch sight of my girl.

I gasp. "Oh my god, I've missed you so much," I exclaim and then open my arms and sprint across the massive space.

Rogan looks amused, and Elon looks momentarily confused before he opens his arms, clearly expecting my hug trajectory to take me to him. I run right past him, wrapping the espresso maker up in a bear hug so tight that it communicates how much I've missed her and that I never want to leave her again.

"It's you and me forever, you got that?" I promise her, closing my eyes to revel in the feel of her cool metal outside and the magic all her parts create inside.

"What the hell just happened?" Elon mumbles. "Did I seriously just get pushed aside for the coffee maker?"

"Don't take it personally," Rogan reassures him. "I barely make the cut. Pretty sure she was open to forgiving me because I read the instruction manual and know all its tricks."

"You're not wrong," I confirm, giving him my best puppy dog eyes. "Please make her scream my name," I beg, and Elon chokes on air as Rogan offers me a wide grin and a shake of his head that says *what am I going to do with you.*

He trades me places and starts touching the espresso machine in all the right ways. "Fuck, that's hot," I purr at Rogan, and his eyes turn molten and playful.

"You two are making me uncomfortable," Elon announces evenly, and I turn to him, almost forgetting that he was there.

"How'd everything go? Did Tad and Hillen get settled in okay?" I ask.

As if his name conjured him, Tad walks out from the direction of the stairs, in sweats and ruffled wet hair. Bewilderment crashes through me as I take him in, and then worry inundates me as questions stack up in my mind.

Did something happen when they were going to the safe house? Where's Hillen? Why didn't Elon call to tell us?

"Don't get mad, Len," Tad commands, and my eyes narrow at the instruction.

"Tad, what the hell did you do? You're supposed to be at some safe house I'm not allowed to know about so it can't be tortured out of me!" I shout at him, all thoughts of a coffee-making hot-as-sin Blood Witch fleeing my dirty, dirty thoughts.

"I was," he shouts back. "But then Elon was leaving, and I just couldn't do it."

"Couldn't do it?" I demand, confused.

"No, I lost you once already, and I'm not going to sit

aside and let it happen again. Elon and I already discussed it," he announces as though that makes it all final.

"Oh, you did, did you. You discussed it?" I snarl, aiming a glare at Elon.

Rogan moves toward me, sending me all the calming vibes through our tether, but I shut that shit down. "Elon, it's not safe here," I start, but Tad cuts me off.

"Actually, Lennox, it is. It's safe here inside this house or inside Elon's house. They designed them that way. Elon, Ma, and I all already agreed. I'm staying *in* the house where it's safe. I won't take any unnecessary risks. I will not get in the way, I'll only help where I can while staying completely safe and secure at all times."

I open my mouth to argue. The only problem is I'm struggling to grasp on to anything I can argue about. He's right, Rogan's house and Elon's house are mini bunkers. There's no one getting in here unless we let them in. The plan is to take the fight to the High Council anyway, so there's really no reason at all that Tad couldn't be perfectly fine here.

"What about Hillen?" I counter, raising my eyebrows in a very mature declaration of *there, take that*.

"She's calling the rest of the family we actually care about and getting them to safety. She understood that I needed to be here, and she was fine with it."

I scoff. "Oh please, she was *fine* with it?"

He fidgets for a beat and shrugs. "Okay, *fine* is a stretch. She said, if anything happened to either one of us, that she'd spend the entire afterlife kicking our asses," he admits.

I shake my head. "Quite a mouth on that one these days," I point out, and Tad snorts out a laugh.

"You died and she found her inner sailor."

Tad and I stare at one another for a beat, the rest of the

kitchen quiet, and tension leaks out of the atmosphere. Tad closes the distance and wraps me up in a hug.

"Don't be mad, Supreme Boner," he pleads, his voice soft and filled with love.

"Fine," I concede, hugging him back.

The back door into the kitchen suddenly slams open, and Prek and Marx barrel in, quickly shutting it behind them. They're breathing hard and look ruffled as hell. A scratching sound starts at the door, and Marx flinches and moves further away. Tad and I separate, and it's as though the last dregs of my energy go with him when he does. Rogan moves in closer, a mug of delicious coffee gripped in one hand.

"Come on, let's get you to bed," he encourages, and right in that moment, those seven words might be my favorite sentence ever.

11

I sit up with a gasp, my chest and throat tight. Sweat collects on my brow, and my pajama top clings to my damp back. The air around me feels heavy and thick, and I try to figure out why I just woke up like I was under attack. The room is dark and quiet aside from Rogan's deep, even breaths. My heart hammers in my chest, and I do my best to calm it down before the anxiety racing through my veins wakes him up.

I scan Rogan's room slowly, looking for anything out of place or alarming. I snort quietly at myself—this is the first time I've ever been in his room, so how would I even know? The throw blanket on the large gray reading chair is still in the same place, I think. The large potted plant in the corner looks the same. I look back down at Rogan for a beat, letting the cadence of his smooth sleep-filled breaths ground me.

I push out of the bed slowly, pausing as his hand falls away from my hip. I watch his face, hoping my movement doesn't wake him up. He looked wrecked when we finally climbed into bed, and I know he needs to sleep and recharge as much as I do. Too bad my brain wants to wake me up in a panic for no reason at all.

Maybe I had a nightmare, I think as I sneak into the bathroom for a quick pitstop. I don't recall dreaming about anything though. Rubbing at the scar on my chest, I roll my neck to relieve the tension sitting in my shoulders. I stare at my reflection in the mirror while quietly drying my hands. No parts of me have zombified and started to fall off. I turn around and check my backside to be sure. Everything is accounted for, although I wouldn't have been mad if I had died and come back with perkier boobs, just sayin'.

I tiptoe back into the room and stare at the bed, suddenly no longer tired. I know if I lie back down, I'm just going to toss and turn, and I really don't want to fuck with Rogan's rest. He looks so damn peaceful and serene right now. I want to touch him, see if that tranquility will transfer over, but I don't want to risk waking him up.

I grab a hoodie that's slung over the back of the reading chair and sneak out of Rogan's room as quietly as I can. Pulling the sweatshirt on, I discover that I'm swimming in it, exactly like I love. It falls to mid-thigh like I'm wearing a dress, and it smells like Rogan. Yep, I'm officially confiscating this on a permanent basis.

Yummy smelling softness, welcome to my wardrobe.

I try to be quiet as I sneak into the kitchen and make a cup of tea. The kiss of night all around me is oddly comforting, and the stars are particularly breathtaking out here with less light pollution to get in the way of their shine. Crickets sing songs to me while I stare at the timer on the microwave as it counts down a warning before it will beep obnoxiously and threaten to wake up the house.

Something twines itself in my legs, and I look down to find Gibson going all catlike against my ankles. I try not to go stiff, but old habits are hard as fuck to break. I know he can't spray me, but apparently my body doesn't get the memo as it shoots adrenaline through my system and tries to convince my brain to make a run for it.

I look up as the timer ticks down to two and open the door to my boiling water. After pulling the massive mug out, I drop two bags of chai into the steamy bowl-sized cup. Gibson is just living his best life around my legs, and I laugh, forcing myself to bend over and show him some love.

"Hey, Pepe Le Pew," I whisper at him in my most sophisticated French accent. I stroke the two white stripes down his back, the fur coarser than it looks. "What are you up to, little buddy?" I ask as I give him some good chin scratches.

I giggle to myself as I bond with the skunk. He and Hoot are the perfect bait and switch. People will trust the dog over the skunk, and that's when Hoot will teach them the importance of not judging things solely on their outward appearance. They're beautiful life lessons wrapped up in furry little packages.

Grabbing my tea, I head out to Rogan's back porch. I curl up on a cushioned chair, pulling my legs inside the massive sweatshirt and tucking it securely just under my feet. It's a cool night, and I wonder what winters are like here. The stars twinkle flirtingly down at me, each of them preening and sparkling a *look at me*. The night is so clear I can see the haze of the milky way, and I tilt my head back and feel the light of the moon on my face. I can practically feel the lunar light reinvigorating me. I thought that was a lycan trait the first time I felt it, but now I know it's a witch thing too.

I pull in a long rejuvenating breath and then reach for my tea. I open my eyes and then promptly notice the person sitting a couple chairs away, their body draped in shadows. An alarmed squeal spills out of my lips, and fear rockets through me. I immediately tamp it down when Elon leans forward so that the moonlight can reveal his face.

"Shit, I'm sorry. I didn't want to scare you by saying hi

when you first came out, and then you just looked so content."

"Motherfuck," I grumble as I press a hand to my chest and try to calm my breathing.

I stare back at the house, willing my reaction not to wake up Rogan, and breathe a sigh of relief when I still feel him fast asleep.

"What are you doing out here?" I ask Elon, cringing at my tone when it comes out more accusatory than I intend.

He smiles and leans back into the shadows. "Probably the same thing you are," he declares, and I snort out a laugh and then relax back into the very comfy chair.

"Nightmares?" I question and then take a large slurp of my very hot tea.

Elon snorts. "Sometimes," he confesses on a tired sigh. "Mostly, I just wake up feeling restless and uneasy. It's like something's telling me I'm not safe, but I can't figure out from what."

I nod my understanding, fitting his words with what just happened to me. We both go quiet in contemplation. I cradle my cup and run my gaze around Rogan's property in thought. He has a large backyard, with an extensive garden to the right and dense trees bordering the well-kept grass. I wonder how long it takes to mow back here. Ooh, does Rogan mow shirtless, because I could get on board with Sundays spent sipping on lemonade and ogling. I shake away that thought and focus.

Why am I so scatterbrained lately? Get it together, Lennox.

I think back through what Elon and I were just talking about. *We're not safe,* right, got it. I roll my eyes at myself.

"What is with me not picking up on other people's presences these days?" I question, more to myself than to Elon. "First, I didn't sense Order members watching me at my shop, and now you're just chillin' out here like some predator waiting for prey, and I didn't even register it until it could have been too late," I observe, slightly annoyed and a lot concerned. "Even now when we're talking about serious shit, shit that should take top priority in my mind, I'm sitting here wondering if your brother has a riding lawn mower, and if the answer is yes, will he let me drive it," I admit, and Elon laughs.

"Judging by the finesse in which you handle a car, I'm guessing not," Elon jokes, and I stick my tongue out at him, thoroughly insulted.

"I am a good driver," I defend.

"You're something, that's for sure," he ribs, and I smile into my mug of tea and shake my head at him.

"This is nice," I confess, turning my face to the stars. "I was so focused on trying to get out of that church, I never thought to picture what life could be like if we survived."

"Technically we didn't," Elon jokes, and I huff out a laugh, but the truth in his words brings reality crashing back around me.

"No, we didn't," I agree somberly.

"The feeling off about your senses, like there's a delay or it's hard to focus, that comes with waking up. Rogan and I noticed it the first time, and I definitely experienced it this last time too. It lasts a couple of days," he explains after a long moment of silence where we're both lost in our thoughts. "Does your magic feel slow, like it takes time to tap into it?"

I shake my head. "No, it's the opposite actually, it seems overzealous, but my instincts are definitely off. I could call on my magic before, and it would almost direct me. I could feel all the possibilities in it, and I only needed to choose which one I wanted. Now, it's so damn strong, but the guidance isn't there. I'm nothing but raw power, but I don't feel powerful while trying to wield it. Does that make sense?"

"Do you think that's because of what Jamie did to our line?" he asks speculatively.

"Your guess is as good as mine."

A light breeze dances between the leaves of the trees all around us, and I get lost to the rustling for a moment. I trace the shadowed trunks with my eyes and wonder if I could ever get tired of sitting out here on nights like this. I let loose a contented sigh, just as one of the shadowed trees in the distance moves.

I blink, not sure of what I just saw, when Elon stiffens like he can sense something too. All at once, the chirping crickets all around us stop. Dread prickles up my neck, and alarm bells start ringing in my mind. I shoot up out of my seat, my mug of tea crashing to the ground. It shatters and the noise sounds a million times louder in the menacing quiet that's enveloping us.

"Is it the Order?" I whisper to Elon, but before he can answer, a shrill laugh wraps around me like a noose, and foreboding goose bumps crawl up my arms.

Bile collects at the back of my throat as Jamie's cackle sounds off all around us, and I see the blood drain from Elon's face like he too is hearing a ghost.

I shake my head, my mind trying to deny what I'm hearing, even as the sound drags me against my will back to the night this bitch murdered me.

"She's dead," I croak out loud, for my benefit and for Elon's. "I watched her melt into almost nothing and then get torn apart by shadows," I reassure the both of us, but if that's true, then who is in the woods?

A putrid, tainted presence fills the atmosphere, one I wish I didn't recognize, and I suddenly know exactly what's out there.

"It's her fucking demon," Elon snarls, coming to the same conclusion at the exact same time.

We both take off from the porch at the same instant. Fear pumps through my veins right alongside a seething fury and a crawling need to wipe this being from the face of all realms. Elon and I charge in the direction of the moving shadow that just triggered all of this, as though we're able to home in on the beacon of evil like it's as easy as blinking. Psychotic giggles batter at me from everywhere, and my mind snaps involuntarily to a place of sickening fear. I try to invite my rage to shove out all of the terror that's trying to choke me into inaction.

"I'm not there. She's dead. I'm alive," I shout the words, forcing them out into the starlit night, half reminder, half war cry.

Then the screaming starts. Blood-curdling cries fill the forest all around us. A cold sweat breaks out all over as horrific screams besiege me and Elon. Pain-filled shrieks bounce off the bark of the trees, followed by incoherent keening and pleas for mercy. I can hear the imminent death in all of the cries, and I want to rampage against what was done to these innocent witches at the hands of Jamie and her demon.

"Lennox!" Elon screams from just behind me. He's telling me something, but I feel like I'm lost to the madness all around me.

I call on my magic, and suddenly I feel almost overrun with it. In a raw pulse of power, I shove it out into the trees, looking for the demon who needs to be destroyed once and for all.

"I'm not in a cage now, motherfucker, let's play!" I shout into the trees, abandoning any fear left in me as I close the distance between the house and the forest.

My magic clings to a presence in the woods, and all I can think is, *got ya, motherfucker*. The demon is warded, but I feel the touch of Elon's magic locating it at the same time. Somehow, almost instinctively, our magics work together to create a net. It's not as strong as a grid, but as we both feed more power into it, I know this bastard isn't going anywhere. I can't see where the demon is exactly, but I can feel our magic encasing it as we then start to batter against the fucker's defenses.

I dismiss the flicker of wonder that ignites inside of me when I realize that I'm lambasting this fucker with power, but I'm not tapped into any bones or blood as I do.

"Lennox, don't go into the trees—the protections end there!" Elon yells at me, and it takes a second for his warning to register over the cacophony drubbing at my senses.

Fuck, I'm running into a trap.

I try to stop myself, but I'm sprinting full out, and I'm less than ten feet away from whatever protective barrier Rogan has on his property. Momentum doesn't get on board with the *oh shit* plan, and I trip and skid toward the trees. Stopping inches away from the blood magic blockade, I let out a pained groan of relief that I didn't cross it.

Covered in a few cuts and a whole lot of grass stains, I push back up to my feet. I focus back on the nightmare hiding in the trees and start to pace against the magical barrier separating us. The screaming all at once ceases, and the night once again goes eerily silent except for the sound of Elon's running footfall behind me. I work to catch my breath, an ache in my side from the running and the fall. My eyes dart around frantically, waiting with frigid unease for whatever the demon is going to try next.

"What the fuck does it want?" Elon snarls loudly as he stops at my side. "Why is it just fucking around with us?" he observes, his brow furrowed in both concentration and worry.

"*Kill first, ask questions later* feels like a solid motto for the moment," I lob at him, shoving aside the fetid disquiet that raps at my chest.

I focus everything I can on obliterating this thing once and for all. We can worry about the *why* of all of this later, once we're safe and it's dead. More magic slams against the presence in the woods as Elon and I renew our efforts. I clench my teeth with effort as I throw magic cinder blocks against the demon's weakening defenses.

I taste justice on my tongue as I feel the wards start to give way. I still can't see the battle as it takes place, but in my mind, it looks like bright sparkling light crushing a mass of inky, putrescent darkness in its mighty grasp. Elon and I both pant and strain against the slimy presence that feels like it's taunting us.

I can hear people waking up in the house, and an urgency fills me to destroy this thing before it can get close to the people here I love and care about. I shove more power into my blitz of the demon, and my heart leaps into my throat when I sense a fissure in the demon's wards starting to form.

"We've got you, you piece of shit," Elon growls, and as the crack widens infinitesimally, I know it's all I need. Without a second of hesitation, I brutally shove through the last of the demon's magical shields. I search for a hold, and as soon as I can feel the skeletal structure, I shatter every bone there is. An agonized scream rents through the night, but in its cloying depths, I also hear a taunting snigger that slaps the feeling of victory from my body. The keening declaration of pain echoes all around us, fading quickly before plunging the night back into uneasy silence.

People are rushing out of the house toward us, but all I can do is focus on the man I just killed. Anger and frustration build in me until I'm left standing there seething. I call the bones to me, needing to confirm what my instincts are already screaming at me.

"Fuck!" Elon shouts into the forest, clearly just as pissed as I am.

I know he felt it too. The truth hit just as my magic ordered his death. We both felt the exact second when the demon abandoned the body he was possessing, leaving the mancer behind to inherit a death that was never meant for him.

I bellow out my frustration, tears pricking at my eyes. Once again I've destroyed the witch the demon was wearing, but didn't do fuck all to destroy the demon itself. Elon was right, it was just fucking with us.

I run my fingers through my tangle of curls and try to breathe through the nauseating outrage I feel. My mind whirs and races as I feel the body moving closer to us. It's clear this was a trap, but what was the fucking point of it? The demon brought one witch to face off against us; was it testing our strength? Our preparedness? Our defenses?

I hurry to search the surrounding woods for signs of any other attackers, suddenly worried all of this is somehow a trap within a trap, but I only feel animals.

"What the hell?" Elon asks me, clearly feeling the same level of distress and confusion as I am. I see a slight tremor in his hand as he rubs tiredly at his face, and I know the toll this trip down horror lane took on him. I feel it too.

"I don't fucking know," I confess quietly.

If the Order and the demon are working together, this wouldn't have been the move they'd make, and it makes me question what I was so certain of the day before. The sound of heavy running footsteps reach us, and Rogan and Marx are suddenly there. Rogan grabs for me, his frantic worried stare looking me over and then turning to do the same to Elon.

"What the fuck just happened, are you two okay?" he demands, just as my magic drags the witch I killed into view. The bright moon highlights his face, and recognition launches through me immediately.

Alvarez.

The Order member who was watching me at my shop earlier, the one who had to have planted the owl skull in my room at Order headquarters, lies dead in front of me. Blood tracks out of his ears and nose, his eyes blank and his form disfigured from where I pulverized every bone in his body without a second thought.

"Are there more of them?" Rogan demands, and I don't know if he's talking about demons or Order members. I'm not even sure if it matters; they all want something from us and are intent on taking it whether we like it or not.

Elon tells him no, but I can feel Rogan searching with his magic all the same.

"What the hell?" Marx declares as he works to catch his breath from the sprint down here. "What is this shithead doing here?"

"So much for tracking him down," I mumble, trying hard not to feel defeated and exhausted, but I'm not succeeding.

"Where's Prek?" I ask tiredly when I see that he's not here.

"He's guarding Tad in the house," Rogan reassures me, and my heart relaxes a little with his words.

"What was all that noise though? I thought for sure we were under attack," Marx asks, stepping closer to the body to look it over.

I jut my chin at the dead Order member. "He was a Vox Witch being possessed by a demon with a taste for torture," I explain, still trying to see how any of this makes sense.

Rogan pulls me closer to him, and I feel the worry and

helpless anger rolling off him in waves. My throat tightens, and I shove away the desire to crawl into his arms and crumble. The laugh, the screaming, the defeat, it all settles into my limbs like a weight that suddenly feels too heavy to bear.

Rogan drops his mouth to my ear, as his large hands rub slowly up and down my arms. "I'm here. I've got you now. You're safe."

I lean into him, wanting to drop down into his warm words, but I can't. We're not safe. We might never be. I hear Elon start to explain what happened, but I tune him out. My eyes roam over Alvarez's body as though somehow it holds the key to everything. The key to answers, to safety. I'm missing something here, I know I am, I just can't figure out what.

Think, Lennox, think! What's missing here, what was the point of all of this?

I stare at the body, willing it to tell me what the hell is going on. What was the endgame here? One Vox Witch up against a whole house of much stronger magic users. Why? Everything Tad was telling me about demons had me thinking they're all about aligning with power and making plays for more power. That checks out so far with what I witnessed in the church, but as I look down at the corpse at my feet, I don't see a power grab here. I see a calculated sacrifice.

What's even more frustrating is I had these same questions about Jamie when the same demon was using her. She was covered in so many demon marks she barely looked like a person anymore. I was horrified to think about how every single demonic brand was a contract, some kind of deal between her and the demon. But it still doesn't track that a demon would have chosen someone like Jamie to team up with in the first place. She didn't have an ounce of magic, not a thing other than her cankered soul to trade with. I get that she had a pretty ambitious plan, but there was no guarantee she was ever going to be successful.

What was in it for the demon?

Why take all that risk for someone like Jamie and now Alvarez? Was he a Jamie in the making? Was he part of the team, like Nikki Smelser was before Jamie killed her?

I rub at my temples, a headache forming between my eyes.

Fuck, I'm tired. It's been such a long damn day.

I rest my head against Rogan's chest and sigh in an effort to purge myself from the failure I feel. The house is all lit up, and I can spot Tad and Prek watching us through the living room window. I wonder for a moment if I was wrong. Maybe it's not safe here for Tad. I know he'd hate it, but it might be best for him to go back to the safe house. I could never forgive myself if anything—I pause mid thought as it hits me.

Aunt Hillen's dream.

The message she said was for me from my Grammy Ruby. What did she say? I think back to lunch, sifting through the exhausted haze crashing over me.

Look at the marks.

Hurriedly I bend down and start taking Alvarez's boot off. He's still in his Order uniform, and I find myself doubting that was an accident. It would make sense if we were being set up. I'm not sure why they'd try to smear Rogan and Elon's name; they did that already when they renounced them. I suppose I could be the target, but that feels wrong too. They'd be dumb to draw attention to any of us while they're still trying to steal our secrets.

"Lennox, Love...what are you doing?" Marx asks, a little bewildered.

"I'm looking for his demon mark," I grunt as the laces of Alvarez's boot loosen and I pull it off.

His foot turns to mush in my hands, the bones in his feet destroyed, and it takes me a second to get his sock off. I scan the top of his foot and then the bottom. I know it has to be here somewhere. My eyes land on a brand right above his heel bone, and triumph flares through me. I study the demon mark to be certain, but it looks exactly like Jamie's marks.

Elon bends down next to me and studies it as well. "Anything standing out to you?" he asks, and I shake my head no as I run my gaze over the circle.

It's made up of black shadowy swirls that twine with lines of orange and red flames. It's a symbol that I know will haunt my nightmares for years to come. A shiver of warning threads up my spine, but I refuse to give into the gloom it wants to invite out in me.

"I haven't seen a ton of demon marks in my time," I tell Elon. "But these look like Jamie's did. No idea if that's a good thing or a bad thing."

"I mean, it looks like we're dealing with one demon instead of more. I'll take that as a good thing," he states evenly, but I hear a slight shudder in the casual declaration.

"I'll have Prek come look at everything. He was part of a team that had to hunt a demon when he first joined the Order. He knows more about this stuff than a lot of mancers do," Marx offers, and then he starts jogging toward the house.

Surprise flutters through me at Marx's words, and I tuck them away to talk to Prek about later. I stare at the demon mark for a moment more and then put Alvarez's grotesque foot down. I stand up, huffing out an irritated sigh as I scan the trees surrounding us again. I have no doubt in my mind that setting up Alvarez also meant tying up loose ends. I just wish I knew if those ends belong to the High Council or a rogue demon whose motives are still a frightening mystery.

I know in my bones that we got lucky tonight. We killed a possible threat, but it's clear we're not ready for what could be coming our way. If the High Council had shown up in force tonight, I don't know if any of us would be standing here right now. If the demon had wanted more than to taunt us, I worry we'd be just as fucked. Reality backhanded me brutally tonight, and it's clear we need to step shit up and prepare. Ready or not, they're coming, and no matter what happens...we can't let them win.

12

I lean back against Rogan, resting my cheek against his bicep as we watch Elon work. He shifts me in front of him and wraps his arms around me in a strangely comfortable chokehold-ish cuddle. I settle against him, my back to his front, and he drops a soft kiss to the top of my head as I do. The small but sweetly intimate gesture makes me smile, and I reach up and lace my fingers with his.

Elon types away at the kitchen island, his laptop the most high tech thing I've ever seen. It looks like something out of an end-of-the-world movie that a high up military member hands to the president because it is the case that holds the nuke launch codes. The rest of us are scattered around the kitchen, watching him work with bated breath, but the audience doesn't seem to faze Elon at all.

"We're sure about this?" I whisper to Rogan, and I feel him shake his head and sigh against me.

Okay, maybe this is like the hundredth time I've asked this question since they told me their plan, but it all feels counterintuitive, and I can't help but be a little squirrely about it. Rogan nuzzles me, dragging his nose and scruffy face across the top of my shoulder before moving up my neck, and I can't help but feel a little squirrely about that too.

Moon shits, he feels good.

He nips at the lobe of my ear and then chuckles deeply in my ear when my body betrays me and gets all shivery and goose bumpy in front of him. I had a firm plan to keep his ego in check and not get too melty with all this new contact, but apparently my inner fiend has declared mutiny and is currently making my good sense walk the plank.

"I hear what you're saying, Lennox, we all do, but this *is* the right move. We will be ready for them when they come for us, and this will buy us the time we need to get there," Rogan reassures me for the hundredth time.

I huff a resigned sigh and try to keep my mouth shut.

"Just remind me one more time how does this buy us more time?" I ask, and Prek and Marx both groan.

I flip them both the bird, and Marx pretends to excitedly catch it and put it in his pocket. I laugh at his antics, and the tension in the room drops a notch.

"It buys us time because it forces them to focus on something else other than us for a moment. They'll know we're behind this—our parents will most definitely want to retaliate—but first they'll have to do damage control," Elon explains...again.

"We know we're the underdogs in this situation. We know that we're up against a titan of power when it comes to the High Council as a collective. *This* will help us create a divide and help to possibly level the playing field," Rogan adds, and I nod and try to relax in his arms again.

"I'm just checking that the videos are looped and the bots are ready, and then we can go," Elon announces, and that must mean something to the others in the room, because a sense of relief fills the atmosphere.

"So how many videos do you have?" Tad asks, and I glare at everyone when no one gets annoyed with his question.

"I fed fifty into the program, so it will filter through those, but it will also create new content, based on what gets the most views and if other witches start posting their own claims in addition to ours," Elon answers nonchalantly. "The marriage between the tech and the magic isn't exact, but it will adjust as we go and should get the job done nicely," he adds enthusiastically, pride shining in his voice.

I can't really blame him. If I'd created a program solely designed to rapid-fire all the evidence I'd collected over several years, documenting the corruption, lies, and downright evil behavior of the High Council, I'd be pretty damn proud too.

They've put together their own smear campaign, only this one is nothing but truth and filled with bombs I still don't know how to process. Rogan and Elon are both counting on the fact that the High Council likes to keep secrets even from the other members of the High Council. So, when some of those secrets are revealed, the goal is to help them start to implode from the inside out. They're also hoping that the public outcry these videos will hopefully stoke, will help the crumbling of things by putting a lot of pressure from the outside for justice and reforms.

As nervous as I am to pick this fight after what happened with the demon earlier, I can see their point. I can even enjoy the fact that their parents taught them all about how brutal it can be to be judged in the court of public opinion. This fight is personal, but I also am starting to understand that it also needs to be political and most importantly public. Well, not the part about us and the real reason Rogan and Elon were renounced. But with the shit I learned in the handful of videos I watched, they don't need to spill their own secrets to get a reaction; the mancer population will be frothing for blood and retribution in no time.

Elon taps away for another minute, and then all at once, he closes the laptop and slowly gets up. I watch as he blows out a deep tension-filled breath and looks over to Rogan with a look I can't decipher.

"It's done. Cohen's going to track the program for a bit, make sure everything is filtering to every possible channel and page it can. By this time tomorrow, every mancer who has access to the internet or a TV will know the same things we do about the leaders of our race," he declares, and I offer him a warm supportive smile.

I know this can't be easy on them. They've been preparing for this eventuality for a long time, but planning for something and actually doing it are *very* different things. I can feel that Rogan is relieved but also anxious. He's resigned to win at all costs, but all of this is taking a toll. He and Elon have worked so hard to get where they are now, and in a way, they're destroying all of that in order to take this stand against their parents. It's hard to say what will be left of the life they've fought to build when the rubble of this war is cleared away and the dust finally settles.

Rogan unwraps his hands from around me, squeezing my shoulders once. "I'll go grab my shoes then," he announces, and I step to the side to let him past me. He and Elon head upstairs, clearly wanting to talk about something, and I lean back against the counter and try not to care about what it might be.

"Hey, Lemon Drop," Tad greets as he sidles up next to me.

I snort out a laugh and try not to smile. I worry about his safety, but I have to admit I'm glad he's here.

"Heading out to talk to Prek's demon guy?" he confirms, and I nod, not sure what to expect from today's excursion.

"What's the deal with him anyway? I thought he was an Order soldier through and through. I'm surprised you're trusting him after the whole car accident thing and then getting demon-napped right under his nose. None of that seems worrisome to you?" he presses, dropping his voice so no one else can hear us.

"Do you have a weird vibe about him or something?" I ask, curious.

I know what I think, but I don't want to dismiss anyone else's instincts around me, mostly because I have no idea what I'm doing. *Winging it* doesn't even begin to cover how I'm rolling these days.

"No, he seems fine. I just want to make sure you've got your eyes open just in case."

I give Tad a side hug and sneak a glance at Prek and Marx.

"I thought Prek was the same way too. It was little things I saw when I was with him and his team in Chicago that started to make me wonder," I explain, and Tad leans down to better hear my whisper. "His boss gave him orders to not let me have a phone unless I was being supervised. He didn't follow them, choosing to trust me instead. It was clear he did not like Rogan, but I heard him lecturing his team once about being respectful and keeping any thoughts they had about his presence to themselves. I discreetly asked around about him, and what I got back was that he was good at his job but would never advance the way he deserved because he wasn't enough of a *company man*, if you catch my drift."

Tad nods thoughtfully, his eyes fixed on mine.

"The High Council fed him and his family some bullshit story about what happened to his aunt, but Prek wasn't buying it. He wouldn't stop looking into it, no matter how many dead ends he hit. Rogan told me that, and then when I was digging around the Order because I didn't have anything else to do, I heard the same thing. He didn't trust the High Council. He didn't believe what he was told. It made me think he actually might have a good head on his shoulders."

"I mean, he definitely has that going for him among other things," Tad teases, waggling his eyebrows.

I chuckle and shake my head at him. Leave it to Tad to take the conversation there. I look over at Prek again and shrug.

"He's good-looking," I agree, my tone casual and unaffected.

"Awwww, you're so booed up it's nauseating," Tad taunts, bumping his shoulder with mine.

"Excuse me, weren't you the one insisting I ride that dick for posterity's sake?" I remind him. "You cannot be disgruntled when you were pushing for this from the get-go."

"Fine, fair enough. I'm just jealous anyway. You two have the thing, and I want the thing," he declares wistfully. "But for real, if he fucks with you again, I've already scouted out some excellent places where we can bury him without ever having to worry about him being found. I support your ability to forgive, I am on board too, but I will snatch his soul if things go sideways," he states matter-of-factly.

I laugh and reach up on my tiptoes to kiss his cheek. "I love you. I'm so glad you're here."

Tad hugs me tightly and then moves to the fridge to inspect its contents. "What time do you think you'll be back? Does your man have a crockpot? I'm thinking something hearty and warm is in store for dinner. Especially if you're going to spend the day learning about demons."

"I have no idea, but I give you full permission to go through all the cupboards in search of one," I offer with a cheeky smile and a shrug. "You don't have to cook though; I honestly have no idea what time we'll be back."

He waves me off. "It's fine, I don't have a lot of other things to do around here if you all are gone. Besides, I'm not picking up any interested vibes from this clan of hotties you now run with, so I figure it's time to show off some skills and see if I can reel anything in."

"Got it. So, you want me to text you when we're half an hour away so you can be doing bendy yoga stuff when we get back?" I ask evenly.

He high-fives me. "And this is why you're my people."

"I got you, fam," I announce with a wide grin.

"Spot Conlon is missing out," Tad declares, like the fictional character from my favorite childhood movie is real.

"Damn straight," I agree without missing a beat. "Rogan will do though," I add, as though it's a hardship I'm willing to shoulder.

"True, wish he was hotter though," Tad counters, sarcasm dripping from every syllable.

"We all make sacrifices," I agree solemnly.

"Who's Spot Conlon?" Rogan asks, his broad, well-muscled chest brushing my back as he walks up behind me.

I swallow down the surprised squeak in my chest, and a blush crawls up my neck as I shoot Tad my *don't you dare* eyes. My romantic obsession with a counterfeit Newsie stays between me and Tad.

"Don't worry about it," I chirp a little too airily, and Rogan narrows his eyes at me. "You ready to go?" I ask sweetly, refusing to succumb to the demand for answers I see brewing in his gorgeous green eyes. "Let's do this," I call out to the rest of the kitchen, clapping my hands like I'm some overzealous sports coach.

"Totally threw him off the hunt," Tad chuckles under his breath.

"Nailed it," I sing-song back, tossing him a wink for good measure.

And then I scramble away from Rogan as fast as I can, ignoring all the things I feel in our tether that he wants to do to me to get me talking. Such a filthy slew of emotions that man has.

Yum.

Prek presses a button on a brass panel, and a buzzing sound fills the late afternoon air. I bounce on my heels, trying to rein in my excitement over the fact that we just rode a ley line to freakin' Scotland.

Scotland!

There's a cool drizzle that can't quite make up its mind about whether it wants to be rain or not, sprinkling down on us, and even though I know my hair is going to reject the level of moisture hanging about in the air, I'm so excited I could scream.

We apparated into a line behind something called Tesco. I got from the size of it and the loading docks at the back that it might be a grocery store, but Rogan wouldn't let me go confirm my suspicions. No, instead we walked a short ways away to Fenella Street where we're now standing outside of a stone building, waiting to see if Mr. Muda is going to let us in.

Sadly, I spotted zero kilts on our way here, and I stood next to a group of men talking while we waited at a crosswalk and legitimately thought they were speaking another language until I was able to pick up an English word here and there. To my utter shock, I realized that they were in fact speaking the same language as me, but with a brogue so thick and foreign that I could barely recognize more than three words of what they were saying. Something about a bird, a fanny, and a pint.

Prek presses the buzzer again, and Rogan moves closer to me with the umbrella to make sure I'm fully covered.

"That's very sweet of you, thank you," I tell him warmly.

"Yes, very sweet of you," Marx grumps as he tries to crowd the door to keep from getting wet now that Rogan moved the umbrella so it's only covering us.

"I told you to grab an umbrella," Rogan reminds him, and Marx grunts in response.

"The app said it wasn't going to be raining," Marx defends.

"It's Glasgow, it's pretty much always raining at some point in the day. Should have listened," Elon teases as he holds his own umbrella over him and Prek.

"Maybe he's not home?" Elon observes as Prek buzzes for a third time.

"He's home, he just hates company. He'll give in eventually," Prek reassures us, but I don't feel reassured barging in on a mancer who clearly doesn't want to be disturbed.

If I weren't at a loss for what else to do about the demon situation, I'd tell everyone to let the poor guy be. Unfortunately, this is our one and only lead.

"He's cagey, but this is his job. He just likes to make it clear who's boss before he lets anyone in. It's a power trip," Prek explains, not at all fussed by the fact that we're being ignored by whoever this Mr. Muda is.

Prek explained last night about his first assignment with the Order and how they were tasked with hunting down a demon who was killing affluent mancers in the business district. Prek was on research and paperwork, which is how he ended up learning about Mr. Muda and speaking to him for the first time.

Turns out that the head of an elite family was trying to take out his competition. He was discovered and purged, and the demon was given what he was promised in the contract and sent back to his realm. It all sounded pretty cut and dry until Prek told me that what was promised in the contract was every single one of the Contegomancer's children.

I had gaped at him for a solid minute when he revealed that little tidbit. I also learned that, in the eyes of witch law, if you are under the age of fifteen, you are technically considered property of your parents. As property, you can be traded or sold to anyone, including a demon, in exchange for whatever you want.

I had no idea the rules were that archaic. It still makes me queasy and mad. Apparently, there are lots of loopholes too in the witching world for owning another magic user. Like, for example, forcing someone to become a familiar. While illegal and a prosecutory offence, if you can hide it for five years, you're then home free, because that's the statute of limitations for that particular crime. I might have given Rogan a dead arm when I learned that. I now have every intention of going home and studying the laws, just to be sure I can protect myself in this messed up culture I'm now forever a part of.

Prek buzzes again, and just when I blow out a forlorn sigh, Beast, from *Beauty and the Beast*, snarls a "what!" in that deep, dark, rich way that he does.

A shiver works its way up my back, but not from fear; that damn voice is the stuff of many a red-blooded woman's fantasies, and I'm not ashamed to say I'm one of them. Disney freaking knew what they were doing when they cast that voice.

"Circummancer Orson, Phonomancer Bevit, Osteomancer Kendrick, Hemamancer Kendrick, and Osteomancer Osseous request a formal visit with the Linker," Prek states firmly, and the speaker goes silent.

I try not to fidget as I wait to see what happens now, but

a higher pitched buzzing starts, and Prek reaches for the handle of the door and pulls it open. I guess that's a good sign. Prek does the hand motion that signals the rest of us should go in before him. The guys all look at me in that *ladies first* kind of way, but I swear they're just hoping this guy will be less likely to yell at me than he is at them. Jokes on them though: the Beast always sounded the hottest when he was being all grumpy and bossy, so I'm here for it.

There's only a set of large red double doors in front of us, so I make my way toward them. Just as I get close, one side opens and a very tall, well-defined man stares down at me. From the minute my toffee-colored eyes connect with his silver ones, dread starts to hammer in my chest. I don't know how I know or why Prek would have failed to inform us, but I'm staring into the eyes of a fucking demon, and he looks like he's ready to eat us for lunch.

13

"What the fuck?" Elon growls from behind me, and the entire atmosphere changes in a breath.

Tension skates across my skin as Rogan's consternation and distress bloom in my chest. He doesn't know what's going on, but he can feel my panic. Every single one of us calls on our magic, and I can instantly feel the protections on this demon are strong as fuck.

"I see you've had some recent dealings with my kind," the demon says indifferently, not at all bothered by the fact that each of us is intent on destroying him. "I suppose I should say *half* of my kind since I'm not a *pure blood demon*. Wouldn't want the higher-ups to hear word that I was claiming to be on *their* level."

Uneasy mumbles sound off behind me, and I can feel alarm skittering through the atmosphere like roaches trying to escape light. The demon rolls his silver eyes at the shocked reaction, but the gesture looks odd as his entire eye is silver. There's no distinguishable pupil, nothing that separates an iris from the cornea. Nope, there's only silver, which is framed by long black lashes, coppery brown skin, straight black hair that's longer than mine, luscious lips, and a voice that I'm certain melts the underwear off both women and men in equal measure.

He leans against the frame of the door, his silk robe-slash-smoking-jacket top draping open to show his muscular chest and washboard abs. A delicious V of muscle dips down into a pair of ripped up skinny jeans. He stands there staring at me, bare foot tapping impatiently.

"What?" I ask confused, thrown off by the blasé attitude and the fact that this demon isn't trying to kill us.

"Just the looks then, huh?" he counters, his face radiating faux pity. "I was hoping there was a brain accompanying that gorgeous hair and that sinful face. Better luck next time, I suppose."

"Did you just call me stupid?" I demand, taken aback.

What the hell is going on right now?

Rogan growls, like he's ready to intervene with his fists, but the demon ignores him.

"Doll, you're going to have to catch up quicker than that, or this is going to be a long ass evening. I have a waxing appointment at nine p.m. sharp that I will be attending with or without you here. So, let's get it together, mmmkay?"

He turns to walk back into his flat, and I stare after him, dumbfounded.

Beast is a fucking prick.

I turn back to the group, not sure what to do. "A little warning would have been nice, Prek," I lob, irritated with the jumpstart my heart just got when a demon—correction, half demon—opened the door.

"I didn't know," Prek defends, and I narrow my gaze at him.

"He has silver eyes," Elon counters, like that alone should have given the pompous ass away.

"What? No. He has brown eyes, looks Italian or Spanish, definitely not demonic at all," Prek argues.

Elon and I look at each other, baffled.

"They can't see through my glamour, doll. If the laws are being abided, then you two shouldn't be able to either...interesting," he purrs, his eyes flitting from me to Elon, a hint of curiosity in his quirked brow. "Are you coming in or not, I have better things to do than stand here all day," the demon calls out through his still open door, and I huff out a sigh.

He's an arrogant shit, but he is our only lead.

I move to step into the apartment, but Rogan stops me and instead takes point, striding in first. The rest of us follow in after him, and the door shuts of its own volition behind us, making me jump. The room is a hybrid between a lounge and a library. Walls of books on built-in, dark wood bookcases line the room. The floor is the same rich dark color, and so is the ceiling. Color is sprinkled about the space through the spines of different books and glass antique lamps. Four dark green velvet couches are arranged in a square in the middle of the room, with a large coffee table at the center that's covered in ledgers, chronicles, and volumes of all sorts.

The demon carefully pours water into a tea cup from a tray at his side. After dropping a cube of sugar into the same cup, he starts stirring it, settling in at the corner of one of the couches, not bothering to offer the rest of us anything.

"My name is Muda, as I'm sure your associate has informed you," he announces, jutting his chin in Prek's direction. "Now, how can I be of service?" he continues, his tone making it clear that he'd rather not be of service at all.

"We've had an encounter with a demon—" Rogan states, angling his body so that I'm hidden behind him.

"Yeesss, I gathered that much," Muda croons bitchily, cutting Rogan off.

My temper flares, and I step to the side so that Rogan

isn't blocking me anymore. "Moopa, is it?" I purr, purposely getting his name wrong.

I scrunch my nose at him like I think he's just too adorable for words, as I casually run my finger over a side table. I let disgust flash in my eyes, and then I look down at my hand and pretend to discreetly wipe something off of my finger. There isn't a speck of dust on the table. The whole room is immaculate, but I see Muda's eyes tighten infinitesimally, and I know I've scored one for team *Just the Looks Then*.

"I'm sure a sophisticated half demon like yourself is used to dealing with all types, so I want to cut to the chase and save us the opportunity of watching you get your balls waxed later. Nine p.m. sharp, right?" I confirm on a squealy laugh, like I'm nothing more than a vapid troll who speaks the same level of nasty cunt this fucker does. Prek shoots me a concerned look, but I ignore him. Clearly, these guys don't speak fluent bitch.

Muda raises an eyebrow in a clear invitation to *go on*, so I stride through the copse of male mancers still standing in the entryway and make myself comfortable on the tufted green velvet sofa across from him.

"Now that we've all had a chance to size each other up and find each other desperately wanting," I begin again, eyeing the half demon up and then down before dismissing him entirely and focusing on his home. I catch Rogan doing an excellent job of hiding the amusement I feel through our tether. Marx shoots me a lightning fast wink before I turn away and offer Muda a pitying look that's filled with scathing judgment of his living conditions, as though he's living in a hovel instead of this stunning space that could easily be featured in a magazine. His hand tightens on the spoon he's stirring his tea with.

"I think it's important for you to know that you're staring

at five people who have absolutely nothing to lose. *Nothing*," I repeat sweetly, and Muda moves to set his tea cup down, like this conversation now has his full attention. "There's no doubt that your protections and defenses are strong, and I'm sure from the feel you copped when you first opened the door, that you know what you're up against with us. It would be a good fight, I'm not afraid to say it. You might even win...or, who knows, you might not. *We* are prepared to find out. I'm not so sure that you are though," I tell him calmly, contented to point out these facts. "So, if you're happy to stop fucking around, we can ask some questions, you can provide the answers, and then we'll gladly hop on our brooms and fly away. You can even keep the mean girl shit up—if the worst thing that happens to me today is you calling me stupid, then it's been a good day. Mmmmkay?"

Muda stares at me for a beat, sizing me up as though he didn't see me properly the first time. He sits back and crosses his legs, and that's all the invitation I need.

"If you would be so kind, would you start by please explaining to us why Elon and I can see past your glamour, but the others can't?" I ask, mirroring his position on the couch.

"It was a failsafe woven into the magic of the first Demon and Mancer Accords. If a demon violates said Accords and it negatively impacts a mancer or puts them at risk, they gain the ability to see through glamour and sense when a demonic threat is near. It's a protective measure."

I look to Elon, thinking of earlier when we both just happened to wake up and had the urge to sit outside. I can tell he's thinking the same thing, and I file it away to discuss later.

"Is it safe to say that if we are now seeing through glamour and sensing demonic threats, then the demon that's hunting us isn't supposed to be?"

Muda stills slightly, and if I wasn't so honed in on his body language because I suspected it would tell me more than his snotty mouth, I probably would have missed it.

"Demons and mancers have strict laws that govern our interactions. Hunting is only permissible if you were part of a contract or sold as part of a contract," he declares tightly, and I get the impression that he's choosing his words very wisely.

"And if I was neither of those things, then this demon would be in violation of the Accords, correct?" I press, trying not to get ahead of myself or feel any kind of hope just yet.

"Correct," Muda confirms stiffly.

"What happens, exactly, if the agreements between the two species are disobeyed?" Elon asks, his tone casual, but the gleam in his eyes is ripe with challenge.

Muda clears his throat and smooths his pants in thought for a beat. "*If* the Accords were breached, then the offending side has a set amount of time to correct the infraction. If they are unable to set things right in the allotted time, concessions are made, concessions that will be felt deeply by the offending party."

"And how can we prove that an offence against the Accords has taken place?" Prek questions, moving to sit next to me on the couch.

Rogan releases an annoyed grunt, and I shoot him a look that says *if you snooze, you lose*.

"You file a complaint, and it gets investigated," Muda tells him simply.

I snort out an incredulous laugh, unable to stop myself. If I didn't think this smooth-talking half demon was such a douche, I'd offer him a *good one* with that joke. Muda looks over at me, his eyebrow twitching up in a way that tells me he's back to being unimpressed.

"Wait. Really? That's not your idea of a joke?" I question, now confused and unsure.

"Do I look like the type to jest?" he asks haughtily, and I shoot him a look that says *well, I think you're a joke, does that count?* "There are protocols in place, and technology speeds up the process. My job as Linker is to facilitate a satisfactory outcome for all sides," he declares, as though he's reading lines for a badly written and over-acted play.

I look at Rogan like *this dude can't be serious, right?* I was fully expecting to leave here with vague instructions on how to summon Jamie's demon so that we could try to kill it. I didn't even think we'd get a solid lead on how to kill the fucker, but that didn't mean we weren't going to give it our best shot. Now this uppity bunghole is sitting here telling us, if we file a complaint, the demon police will take care of the problem?

This all feels way too easy, which makes me wonder if this is all some kind of trap. Subtly I start looking around for some sign that a full-blooded demon is lurking in the back room or behind some secret door that leads to a lair below us or something. All I see is books and antiques though.

"Okay, I'll bite," I declare, deciding if this is a trap, it's better to spring it now. I wasn't kidding when I told Muda that we have nothing to lose by going head-to-head with him. "I would like to file a formal complaint," I state firmly, and then suddenly there's a sickening familiar feeling in my gut, and I can feel that I'm being yanked somewhere else.

Son of a bitch.

My panicked eyes meet Rogan's for all of a split second before I'm torn away. Desolation rips through me from the tether, and I can hear Rogan's shouted, "Nooo!" like an echo in my mind as everything around me tilts and blurs.

The sensation of falling overwhelms my senses, and then all at once it stops. Terror crawls up my throat, burning as it rises and robbing me of air. A feral scream sounds off all around me, and it takes me a second to realize it's coming from me. My feet hit solid ground again, but my surroundings are fuzzy, and I scramble back, scared to death that at any moment, I'm going to slam up against a cold stone wall, and then I'll blink and be back inside that horrific church again.

"No, not again. Please, not again," I whimper.

My heart races so fast it feels like it's going to explode, and my body shakes from the overload of adrenaline and dread.

Stupid. I'm so fucking stupid! How is this happening to me again?

I try to tamp down on the self-recrimination so I can focus on wherever this asshole has taken me. I ignore the helplessness I feel, knowing my body will survive another death—Elon is proof of that. I just wish I knew that my mind could withstand another torturous round with the demon and whoever it's possessing. I clamp my mouth closed, and the fearful keening stops. I can break out of this cage, I know I can, I just need to find something to cut my hand open with. I need to bleed.

Why the hell did I trust a demon? I walked right into his home, knowing what he was, and now I'm going to pay the price for that stupidity.

My eyes dart frantically around at my feet, searching when a firm hand grips my elbow. Panicked, I shove every ounce of magic I can at whoever it is. The power slams up against a strong barrier, but I'm too scared and desperate to be deterred, so instead of trying to crash through the barriers, I wrap my will around the protective shell entirely and then shove it and the person inside of it away. I look over in time to see Muda go flying across what now looks like a lobby, and slam hard into a secretary's desk. The female sitting at the sleek setup screams in shock before Muda's body hits her and they both go crashing to the ground.

I stare confused, panting through my panic as a room starts to take shape all around me. Sunlight streams through the walls of windows surrounding me, and I get the distinct impression I'm in a high-rise building. Large, framed artwork decorates the walls, but the images are demonic and gory. Large potted plants take up the corners, and I swear one of them looks like it's eating a bird. A massive dark blue couch sits in what looks like a waiting area, the color of the sofa so rich that I feel like I'm staring into the depths of space directly. The room is frigid, luxuriously decorated, and definitely not the church that haunts me more than I wish it did.

Oh god, please don't let this place be worse.

Muda's mussed up black hair pops up on the other side of the secretary's desk first. He shoots me a scathing look as he scrambles to his feet, and a sheepish realization laps at me. Out of nowhere, a large boom tears through the room, and just when I think I have a grip on my fright, a pair of arched bone-white doors are thrown open and a massive demon stomps out of them.

"What the fuck is going on out here?" it snarls, leveling the entire room with a black glare that makes my blood run cold and my skin prickle with the need to get the hell out of here. "Visha, you know I like to rest my eyes for at least twenty minutes after the masseuse has left. Are you trying to get gutted?" the demon roars, and I flinch from the overwhelming sound of it.

The demon's eyes snap from where Muda and the secretary are scrambling to get back on their feet to me. I stare into enraged black eyes set in a blood red face. The shape of its nose and mouth are eerily animalistic, like it's a lycan whose face is trapped mid-shift. A black crown sits on the demon's head, but as I look at it, I realize they're actually horns that form the shape of a crown. Shoulder-length wavy black hair touches the fabric of an ornate and over-the-top looking suit. I can't tell if that's a uniform of some sort or if it hired Michael Jackson's stylist after the singer died. Four arms, each bent at the elbow, rest on its waist, the posture clearly communicating annoyance, and I try not to stare at them. I'm tempted to think of the demon as a *he,* but there's an androgyny about the being, that makes me unsure either way.

Black eyes take me in with the same level of scrutiny that I was just using, and I feel my magic rise in response.

"Mmmm, as tempting as that show of power is, put your magic away, butterfly. You don't see me walking into your place of business and whipping my dicks out for all to see," the demon commands, its tone even and all at once unbothered.

Dicks?

I'm not at all sure how those things are the same, but I pull back on my magic anyway, surprisingly no longer feeling threatened or under attack.

"My apologies, Sire. I've brought Osteomancer Osseous here to lodge a formal complaint. She caught me by surprise; it won't happen again," Muda rushes to explain, a simpering smile on his face, while he throws me a glare that says *this better not happen again.*

"It sure as hell will if you think you can just yank me around without so much as a heads-up. Priggish demon or not, ask politely next time and maybe you won't get your ass tossed across the room," I snap at the Linker, who simply rolls his eyes like my feelings on the matter are nothing more than an inconvenience to him.

I wonder if his boss would let me get away with tossing him around just one more time.

I eye the other demon speculatively and decide against it. It's *very* tempting though, but I need to ignore the two demons for a moment, now that the immediate danger has passed, and focus on my connection with Rogan and the bombardment of panic, fear, and rage flowing from him to me. I send a wave of calm, comfort, and safety, and am immediately hit with a ripple of relief and promised retribution.

Muda and the other demon are talking, and I focus on what's being said. I catch the tail end of Muda recapping the conversation that occurred between us in his flat in Glasgow, and the other demon is watching me calculatingly. A long black tongue snakes out of his mouth and flicks in my direction, like he's a snake that's scenting me, either that or he's propositioning me for other things. Either way, I fidget uncomfortably, unable to help it.

"Breaking the Accords is a very serious accusation," the other demon points out, rolling its freakishly long tongue back into its mouth. "If you're making a false report, there are consequences, you know."

I look at Muda, suddenly worried that he left that part out, but I quickly shove the apprehension I feel aside. A demon did attack me, threaten me, and then try to come after me again, which according to Muda is against the laws. I square my shoulders and nod my head.

Black eyes drink me in for a beat, and I can feel the demon trying to determine something, but I have no idea what. "Follow me then. I'll take down your statement and have the proper channels look into it."

I'm ushered into a massive office and sat on the other side of an ornate hemlock wood desk. I feel like I'm meeting with the CEO of some massive company instead of meeting with a demon to complain about getting picked on by another demon. The whole exchange is weird, but I suppose bureaucracy prevails in every species.

I shake my head as I look around. "Here I was thinking it was weird when I learned that the High Council had their own offices and penthouses," I mumble as I survey the trinkets displayed on a set of glass shelves. I'm too far away to tell what anything is, but it's not family photos or diplomas at least.

"Guess it only makes sense for demons to have advanced beyond the archaic days of our ancestors' cabins and huts," I go on, returning my attention back to the red demon, who's watching me intently from his leather high-backed chair.

"Not that I know much about demons, really," I hurry to add, realizing that what I just said might've been offensive. "I know that you live in another realm and apparently messing with ours is frowned upon, unless in specific cases and under a clear set of guidelines. Although I just learned that last part today," I announce, like it should be important to the demon staring at me like I'm a fly that just landed on his food. "I have to admit though, so far I find the relationship between demons and witches all a bit confusing and *way* more structured than I thought it would be. As anticlimactic as this whole office experience feels, real talk, I could use a bit more of that in my life, given all the crazy ass shit I've been dealing with lately," I declare as an exhausted chuckle escapes before I shut my ridiculous rambling down.

Really, brain? We just real talked *a four-armed demon?*

Internally, I facepalm and try not to cringe at the word vomit I spewed all over. Nope, I will not let them see me sweat.

"I must say, mancer, the reek of power on you is truly tantalizing," the red demon declares out of nowhere.

"She has a mouth on her too that I suspect you'd find amusing," Muda states evenly, his back to us as he stands off to the side, staring out at the city skyline, like he's already bored with whatever is about to happen even though we haven't even begun.

Black eyes twinkle at me, and I fight the urge to panic or try to run screaming from this office and this demon. "I don't get over to your side of things very often anymore, but if the witches are smelling like you these days, then I will endeavor to make more of an effort."

"They don't," Muda monotones, and I shoot a glare at his back.

"How much for you?" the red demon asks, his face a terrifying wall of seriousness.

I choke on air, not sure what the hell to say to that. "I...um...well..."

"Call me Dyad," the red demon offers, as though my hesitant answer is a result of not knowing his name instead of not knowing what the fuck to say to that inappropriate question.

What in the Crone is going on here?

"Uhh...okay...right...uhhhh...Dyad..." I stammer, scrambling for a way to shut whatever is happening down without creating more problems for myself with any more demons.

I have no idea how we took this turn to *I think not-ville*, but I need to turn this shit around fast. I need the demon I'm already dealing with gone, not a two-for-one deal on trouble.

No. Just...so many nos.

Dyad snaps at Muda, like a douchebag in a restaurant snaps at the server. I cringe at the lack of manners. Muda turns to me, his surly silver eyes gleaming as he huffs out a resigned sigh.

"You should consider this offer carefully, as there is no guarantee that one will be made again," Muda tells me, his tone practiced and bored. "To be in the service of a High

Demon is the highest of accomplishments. You will be offered protection and power, the likes of which you've never even dreamed about. The contract could be platonic. Your services could be rewarded in whatever monetary ways you see fit. Or, if you prefer, your contract could encompass all of the supreme pleasures and delights that a High Demon is capable of offering. You would have a life beyond your wildest dreams."

Muda's eyes are flat as he does his worst to sell me on my options, but Dyad doesn't seem to be bothered by the lack of enthusiasm in the slightest.

"Dyad is a very virile demon possessing both male and female anatomy—some in duplicate. You are guaranteed to have *everything* you need at your disposal to achieve the highest tier of pleasure any being is capable of reaching."

My eyes widen at this declaration, and I suddenly don't know where to look.

This demon is seriously packing two dicks and a vagina in those pants? Do not look, Lennox. Curiosity killed the cat, and it sure as hell might come for an Osteomancer too.

I clear my throat, waiting to see if Muda has anything else he'd like to tell me about the High Demon Dyad, or maybe an escape plan he wants to throw my way, but he stays quiet on both fronts.

Sweat breaks out on my brow as my flighty eyes finally connect with Dyad's black gaze.

Do not gulp, Lennox. There will be no audible gulping to the offer of two dicks, a vagina, four hands, and a whole lotta enslavement.

"Riiightttt," I start, reeling and still trying to figure out how to navigate this insanity. "See what happened was... No...I mean, the thing is...that I am spoken for and not at all for sale," I finally manage to get out, sounding surprisingly and impressively firm.

Maybe too firm, I suddenly worry. Perhaps it would have been better to have gone with *flattered but not in a position to accept*? But it's not like this is some rando hitting on me in the grocery store or at a darkened bar somewhere. No, firm is definitely the way to go. This is a demon trying to buy me for who knows what purposes, and I should be as clear as possible that it's not happening. You know, while trying not to get myself killed.

Fucking hell, I am soooo out of my element right now.

I hold my breath, waiting to see if my refusal is going to have repercussions, but nothing happens. Dyad nods once, shoots Muda a look that makes me think this offer might be revisited at some point in the future, and then the High Demon clicks on a wireless mouse a couple times before returning a professional gaze back to me.

"Shame," he tells me, disappointed.

I swallow down the *you'll get over it* that tries to crawl off my tongue, and stare at him, refusing to drop my gaze and leave any doubt about where I stand on being purchased.

His black eyes deepen, but I can't decipher what that means. "In that case then, why don't you start from the beginning of your encounter with a demon, and we'll see if your complaint has any merit," Dyad croons at me, but I don't miss the hint of a threat in those instructions. "Oh, and *do* tell us everything. We'll discover it all when we investigate, so save yourself any trouble, butterfly, and be forthright from the beginning."

Yep, High Demons clearly aren't a fan of rejection, and judging by the look on this one's face, I might have just made another enemy.

Perfect, just freakin' perfect.

14

"He did what?" Rogan bellows, his rage bouncing around the narrow street and causing other pedestrians to look over or scamper away.

I look around, slightly embarrassed, and hold my hands up to Rogan, indicating that he can be pissed but maybe let's not announce it to the fine residents of Fenella Street, Glasgow.

Fury floats in his green gaze, but he quiets as he tightens his hold around my shoulders. He hasn't stopped occupying every inch of my space since Muda popped us back into his house and then promptly kicked all of us out when the guys tried to attack him. I don't blame them though; that demon really could use a lesson or two in manners.

"I told him no, and he didn't bring it up again, so it's probably fine," I tell Rogan and the others, but Rogan's eyes narrow on me, and if I had to guess, it's because he just felt the trickle of trepidation that I was trying really damn hard to hide from him.

"I thought I knew about demons and what to expect, but I'm starting to think that we have no idea what we're involved in right now," Marx confesses, and I sigh, wishing I didn't agree with every word he just spoke.

"The crux of my demonic education was to stay the fuck away from them. I've never even heard of the Accords," Elon adds.

"I've heard of them," Prek declares. "I'm sure only because it was part of my first case with the Order, but when I tried to pull up any information on what was in them, I could never find anything other than a file of fully redacted text. I pulled Muda's information from an Order sergeant's personal notes. They were scanned into the system from a notebook he kept. They were barely legible, but after staring at them—and a ton of other random documents—trying to piece together information, I saw the name and address sort of just pop out at me."

"You could have warned us," Rogan snaps at Prek reprovingly, and I stiffen.

"If I had any idea that there was anything to warn you about, I would have," Prek barks back, clearly frustrated with all the blame coming his way. "I had no idea the guy was half demon. The title *Linker* was written next to his name, but I never found any information in the Order's databases explaining what that meant. The sergeant who wrote the notes is dead. I thought Muda was simply a knowledgeable 'mancer, not a High Demon Ambassador."

"It's fine," I cut in when Elon opens his mouth probably to argue some more. "It was an honest mistake. Marx is right, none of us have any idea what we're dealing with, and I think it's safe to say that's on purpose. Either way, my complaint is filed. Dyad determined it was valid, and hopefully that means one less threat breathing down our necks."

Mumbles of agreement sound off around me, and we grow quiet as we walk steadily toward the loading docks of Tesco and the ley line that will whisk us far away from here.

The sun has long gone down, and it feels much colder here than I thought it would. It's the kind of chill that slowly gets its clutches around you, and before you know it, you feel as though you'll never be warm again. I shiver and Rogan wraps himself around me even more. I appreciate his efforts to make sure that I'm okay, but he's making it difficult to walk.

I chuckle as we start to trip over each other, and despite how annoyed and angry I can feel that Rogan is, his quiet, warm laughter joins mine.

"Is that it with the demons then? They investigate the demon Jamie was working with, and we'll never have to deal with it again?" Elon asks as he wraps his light jacket even tighter around himself.

"Muda said there will be a trial and that they may or may not require my attendance," I tell him, trying not to cringe as I prepare to tell him the rest.

Rogan stops, pulling me to a stop next to him, and bends down until our eyes are even. I take a deep breath, letting his smell wash over me and the feel of his hands ground me.

"What are you not telling me?" he asks evenly, and I close my eyes and pull in a fortifying breath.

"They gave me a mark," I blurt and then hurry to explain when first confusion and then fury shutter down over Rogan's face. "They said if I'm required to attend the trial, it will summon me. If not, it will simply disappear. Then I'll receive word somehow of the outcome of the trial. Although Muda made it seem that the only possible outcome would be the other demon's death. It appears he broke several laws," I state, and I look past Rogan's newly enraged face to find three more sets of outraged stares.

Crap.

"You have a mark. A mark that can be used to summon you anywhere...like a demon?" Rogan demands, his voice eerily calm, and the timbre of it causes goose bumps to rise on my skin and heat to pool low in my belly.

"On the top of my foot," I concede and watch as Rogan closes his eyes and does his best to calm the storm of rage I feel building through our tether.

"What the actual fuck, Lennox!" Rogan shouts at me, making me jump.

And clearly this asshole needs better calming techniques.

I narrow my eyes at him, pissed that he's dumping his shit on me. I get that he's scared and worried; I know I'd feel the exact same if a demon had stolen him away from me. However, if he thinks I'm going to just stand here and take this, that it's okay for him to behave like this toward me, all because I can feel what's at the heart of his issues through our connection, he's got another thing coming.

"You know what, Rogan?" I snap. "You can just fuck right off. Seriously, off you fuck, because I have hit my limit with this shit. You act like I had all these amazing choices and instead went with the most fucked up one. This is our best shot at getting one more threat off our back, a really fucking serious one at that," I point out.

Fury boils through our connection, and we both stand there seething. Elon tries to get Rogan to leave it alone and start walking again, but Rogan ignores him. Both Marx and Prek look like they wish they had a bowl of popcorn right now.

"You want to be pissed? Go for it. You want to feel scared and helpless? Great, join the club. Rage away if it helps you process things and work through them. But don't you dare forget who I am to you and the kind of treatment and respect that deserves," I yell at him, my heart pounding painfully in my chest as my throat tightens and my eyes sting.

I watch as my words strike him like physical blows, and

he steps back away from me like he's struggling to absorb the impact. I'm reminded of the brutal arguments we've had in the past and am suddenly worried that we might be adding this one to our future. I'm all for the passion and the heat, but I'll never be okay with the disrespect Rogan is dishing out when he behaves this way.

"I am not the dumping ground for your frustration and anger. Figure out a better way," I tell him, my tone soft and quiet.

Pain fills Rogan's gaze, and he drops it to the ground for a beat before lifting it once again to mine. "You're right. I'm sorry. What just happened scared the shit out of me. It was bad enough the first time they ripped you out of my arms," he confesses, his eyes fixed on his hands as though he can still feel me slipping away. "Watching it happen again, I just...I couldn't..." He sighs and rubs a hand over his face. "Knowing they're going to do it again, it's like living through my worst nightmare over and over again," he admits, his voice haunted and his eyes filled with anguish as they connect with mine.

My heart aches at what I see in his face, and I wish I could keep all that pain and worry from settling inside of him.

"Lennox, I know you did the best you could. I'm just afraid for you, for me, for all of us," Rogan explains, and he suddenly looks exhausted. "None of that should be taken out on any of you though. I'm sorry for losing it. None of you deserved that."

I'm taken aback by the immediate apology. The Rogan I know usually takes longer to realize he's being an asshole. Typically, he storms off, needs to brood for a while, followed by some light pouting around, and then *maybe* he'll own his shit and say sorry.

Rogan steps closer to me and cups my face in his palms,

tilting my head until I'm looking up into his repentant eyes. "I know what you are to me, Lennox. I'll do better," he reassures me, kissing me softly and giving me a chance to taste his apology in addition to seeing it written all over his face and hearing it in his earnest words.

I pull him closer, opening up to him and reveling in the searing requisition he's making against my mouth. *This is the passion I want to see and to feel*, I tell him through our bond, filling it with satisfaction and need. His tongue teases mine, and I can almost feel it between my thighs. Heat dips straight down to my clit, and as he wraps his apology around my tongue, and I nip and suck my forgiveness right back, I grow needier and wetter and gain a clearer understanding about why make-up sex is so fucking hot and so fucking important.

I want to climb him right now and demand that he take me against the cool stone of the building on our left. I don't give a shit if I lose an ass cheek to frostbite, it would be well worth it.

A loud and v*ery* obnoxious "awwwwwwww" fills the chilly night all around us, and Rogan and I reluctantly break apart to look over at Marx, who's wearing an overexaggerated look of adoration and delight. "Like, aren't you two just the cutest," he declares in his best teenage girl voice.

"Fuck off," Rogan grunts at him, and Marx chuckles.

"But, like, you totally are," Marx goes on, laughing and refusing to give up the taunt.

"Right?" Elon starts, and I crack a smile, not able to help myself. "I was full on swooning just now. All that emotional growth and concerning commitment to PDA, like for real, for real, talk about romance city," he plays along, nailing *Clueless*'s Cher Horowitz.

I bite back the *as if* that wants to sneak out of my mouth.

Marx reaches out for Elon's hand, and then they start to

skip down the sidewalk together. "I hope we can be lucky enough one day to get mouth-fucked against a building," Marx calls out over his shoulder, throwing me a cheeky wink.

Rogan's stoic demeanor finally cracks, and I catch a smile ticking at his lips.

Elon sighs loudly and dreamily as they make their way hand in hand. "If only we'll be so lucky as to find someone with such an assholic nature as Rogan Kendrick."

I bust out a loud laugh at that, and Rogan rolls his eyes at me before pulling me tighter to his side and tickling my ribs in retaliation. I squeal and wiggle away, tossing him a heated look of challenge before sprinting after Elon and Marx.

"You guys are so fucking weird," I hear Prek declare on a resigned sigh.

I smile even wider as Marx and Elon both coo a high-pitched, dreamy, "Rogan Kendrick," as though he'll be the name they doodle all over their notebooks this year.

Suddenly Rogan takes off after me, and I squeak in surprise and book it in the direction of the ley line. The back of Tesco is empty and quiet, the sound of my running footfall echoing off the pavement and bouncing across the white walls of the back of the building. I can feel the levity in our connection as well as the growl of *challenge accepted* as I hear Rogan gain on me from behind. Before I can make it, he grabs me by the waist and swings me around. I shriek and laugh and weakly try to fight off the attack of kisses he applies to my neck and cheeks. His scruff is tickly, and I make big plans for it when we get home.

"You win, you win," I shout out through peals of laughter as my bladder threatens to ruin the good time we're having.

"Ahh and what do you have for the victor?" he whispers deeply in my ear as he pulls me flush against him.

We're dipped in the shadows of the building behind us, both breathing hard, his chest pressed against mine. I want him so much that slight movement against my peaked nipples is making me wet as fuck. He's hard against my hip, and it's all I can do not to reach down and discreetly say hello. He kisses my neck just below my ear, and I barely bite back a moan. I check for the others, not wanting them to overhear anything I'm about to say. I see that they're further down past the building, over in a patch of grass near the ley line.

With a salacious smile, I thread my fingers through Rogan's hair and pull his ear down to my mouth.

I look around to make sure no one can hear us, and then I saucily whisper, "How about I spend the night riding your cock so hard and so good that you won't be able to stop screaming my name and coming inside my wet pussy." I nip his lobe while my quiet promises sink in, and then I pull away when he groans quietly in approval.

The other guys are all talking animatedly about something, but Rogan only has eyes for me right now. As he runs his gaze over me, his pupils are so big that there's barely any green to his heated stare at all anymore. His breathing is shallow, and he watches me like he's ready to consume me right here and now.

"I vote we leave them here and come back for them later. I can't handle a long car ride home with these two eye-humping each other the whole time," Marx whines, and Elon chuckles as he pulls up the ley line app on his phone.

I blush, feeling bad about making shit awkward, but Rogan makes it so damn hard.

Literally.

Gah, I'm hopeless.

"He's right," I tell Rogan, feeling completely embarrassed. "We shouldn't be allowed to be around people until we learn to behave. We're the couple I always mimed gagging behind to make the other sufferers in the group feel less uncomfortable. How did we go so wrong so fast?" I demand, thoroughly overdramatic. "What have you done to me, Kendrick?"

He laughs, and I can tell by the look on his face there's a sexual innuendo locked and loaded on his masterful tongue. I press a finger to his lips.

"Your brother is right there," I remind him.

He rolls his eyes and sighs against my finger. I take it away tentatively and huff out relief when nothing cringy slips out of his full lips.

Man, I need to get home and in a soundproof room alone with this man STAT.

Elon clicks on a button in the app, and I hear the resonance of the line we're jumping to begin to hum out of his speakers. I listen for a beat, trying to focus on the sound and feel of the line so we can apparate home. Instead, a wide happy smile sneaks across my face as I realize something. Rogan notices and threads our hands together as he leans down.

"That better not be because you're thinking dirty thoughts?" he whispers playfully in my ear.

I swat at his shoulder with my free hand, shaking my head no with a laugh.

"It's nothing really, it's just that we totally rocked our first fight," I tell him, the smile I'm wearing growing impossibly wider.

Rogan's quiet for a beat, and in my periphery, I catch Prek closing his eyes and pulling a deep breath into his lungs. I watch as he silently and almost meditatively aligns his magic with that of the ley line before us. The moment the two frequencies connect and match, it's as though Prek has put himself into hyperdrive, and the ley line grabs a hold of him and his magic and yanks him away. I study the faint trail of light that's left in his wake until it disappears altogether in a matter of seconds. Elon looks around to make sure we're all ready. After the rest of us give him a confirming nod, he exits out of the ley line app on his phone, closes his eyes, and then he too is pulled away into the line.

Rogan watches Elon leave, always looking out for his brother, and then he turns back to me. "We did *rock* our first fight, didn't we," he agrees, teasing me about my word usage, his smile now matching mine.

"We're like *totally* nailing this relationship thing," I rib, my Valley girl accent mocking the one Marx and Elon were just doing.

Marx eyes us and shakes his head, an amused grin stretching across his face. "I'm happy for you, man, but don't forget that you have the car keys. Don't go getting any bright ideas about ditching us and sneaking off with your girl."

I laugh and roll my eyes at him, but Marx misses it as he focuses on the force of power in front of us, and then just like the others, he's there one second and gone the next.

Finally alone, Rogan wastes no time in leaning in for a deep toe-curling kiss.

"Totally nailing it," he agrees, sounding like the turtle from *Finding Nemo*, and before I can crack up, he squeezes my hand and we both match the hum of our magic with that of the line, and it easily pulls us in.

I quickly adjust the resonance of my magic to that of the line I want to travel to and then hold my breath, ready for what comes next. It's far less traumatizing now that I know what to expect. I'm prepared for the stomach lurches and sudden death drops. The tingling sensation isn't alarming anymore, and I know to expect the scrambling of my senses for a beat after the ley line ejects me at my destination.

I can't feel Rogan's hand anymore, but I know he's there. I can feel him through the tether as he goes through his own rollercoaster ride back to Gallywough, Tennessee.

My feet hit pavement, and I only stumble slightly before getting my footing and managing to stay on my feet. I can't see it yet—not until my senses catch up with the fact that I'm once again stationary and they don't need to shut down for protection anymore—but I can picture the parking lot we drove into and the large field next to it. The grass is short and patchy, and tall trees border the clearings and the road that leads up to them. There's a public restroom tucked into the far end of the paved lot, and I decide I should check out the facilities or risk peeing my pants if there's another serious laugh situation on the way home.

Bright light suddenly shocks my senses as my eyesight starts to kick back in. It's as though I can feel the bone-chilling cold of Glasgow as well as the deep kiss of night melt away, and in its place, early evening marked by a mild sun and much warmer temperatures blooms right in front of me.

Surprisingly, I don't feel nauseous or blobby this time around, which is a miracle in its own right.

Man, I'm getting good at this witch shit.

My eyes still work to adjust and focus, and it takes a few seconds more for me to feel Rogan's hand in mine again. His grip is strong, and I give it a quick reassuring squeeze.

We are totally using a ley line to go to Bali when all this war shit is over.

I turn to tell Rogan just that when my ears pop, and all at once I'm bombarded by sounds. Confusion lurches through me, and I look around as though I can make sense of the cacophony I'm hearing, but my eyes haven't adjusted yet.

Screams and booms, shouted orders, and panicked cries surround me.

My hand tightens in Rogan's as fear overwhelms me, and then in a blink, my eyes adjust and all I can see is chaos. Order members are everywhere. They're swarming the empty field and parking lot. I can just make out Rogan's car before visibility is cut off by running bodies. Elon, Prek, and Marx are surrounded, and now soldiers are running at me and Rogan. Warning explodes from me to Rogan through our tether, but before I can do anything more than fill with consternation, I'm hit with a force so strong that it tears me from Rogan's hold.

His angry, terrified shout rings in my ears, and I'm afraid that we'll never stop being torn apart like this. I call on my magic to try and stop the elemental witch who's trying to fling me into the trees. But another gust of wind takes hold of me, only this one quickly drops me hard to my feet in the short grass. The landing is jarring, but nothing hurts and I'm not currently kabobbed on a tree, so I'll take it. I look up to find Prek's russet eyes tracking me maybe twenty feet away and a soldier running up behind him, ready to attack. I shove bone magic out into the mayhem, and when I sense the wards of the woman who's running up on Prek, I shatter them around her, and then without missing a beat, I snap her neck. Prek whirls around to see the woman's body slump to the ground, but there's another soldier quick to take her place, and Prek shoves a hard gust of wind at them, blowing them off their feet and knocking several other attacks out of the way.

Shock rings inside of me, and I look down at my hands.

How the hell did I do that? How did I break through her protections like they were nothing?

Taking advantage of my momentary distraction, someone slams into me hard, and I go bouncing back on my ass. I pull my magic all around me protectively, and the chaos trying to overrun me quiets slightly.

I look around frantically trying to process what the fuck is going on.

How the hell did the Order find us?

Shoving magic away from me again, I search for Rogan, Elon, Marx, and Prek. My power hits other barriers and protections as it goes, but unlike the demons, these barriers feel more like egg shells than the steel walls I've encountered before. Without a second thought, I start to crack the shells, reaching inside and shattering bones as I go. I shove away my alarm and my worry about how I'm doing this, and move as quickly as I can. Fear and instinct drive me as I desperately try to find Rogan and the others.

In my gut, I know this level of power is because of what Jamie did to the Osteomancer line of magic, but I drop-kick that knowledge away. I'll question it all when we're not fighting for our lives.

Order members swarm me like an angry colony of wasps, but I manage to get back on my feet as they bounce off the walls of magic I've erected around myself. I drive the hoard away from me, turning bones into powder, snapping spines, and pulverizing skulls as I go. I should feel sick, but all I feel is enraged. All of these soldiers, sacrificing themselves for a bunch of power-hungry monsters. I don't want this, but the High Council just ripped the choice right out of our hands.

If they're going to attack, then I'm sure as fuck going to defend.

Fighting to move closer to the ley line, I finally feel the others. I force more power out of me to help fortify their defenses and slowly try to get closer to them.

Screams and pain and the sounds of fighting are all I can hear. I taste death and magic in the tainted air. Gray clouds cover the sky, as though they're trying to shield the heavens from such brutality, and bones snap and fracture all around me. I hate that the sound is music to my ears, but each agonized bellow means I'm one step closer to Rogan and the others. More Order members pour out from the trees, and I want to scream in frustration as the numbers keep tilting in their favor no matter what we do.

I search for Rogan in the throng of clambering bodies, desperate to *see* that he's okay, but I can't find him. I can feel his wrath and determination through our bond, and my boost of protective power is helping him, but I don't know how long we can all keep this going. Right now, I feel strong and formidable, but I've never tested the well of my power. As a Source for the Osteomancer line, I know I'm working with more than the average mancer, but I also know it's not infinite.

The call of blood magic sings in my veins, as though it's begging to be called on and put to work. I can feel Rogan fighting though, and I'm worried that if I call on his power, it will fuck him up somehow or leave him vulnerable. Instead, I start collecting large pools of bone magic at my core before sending them out in brutal waves intent on crumbling defenses and destroying every bone in the magic's path. Limbs tilt at odd angles. Bones rip free from skin. Bodies fold into mush as I reduce their osteo matter to pulp. I attack vital organs with shards of a mancer's own skeleton, bodies piling up around me like a defensive wall and a warning to the next attacker who tries to traverse it.

I shove the bodies all around me off to the side, trying to create a barrier of death to stem the flow of soldiers from pouring in on that side. Bellows of rage bleed out into the overcast evening, but still the Order members keep coming. I feel animal bones lying patiently in wait throughout the forest we're surrounded by, and I command them to come to me. I infuse them with the ability to claw, bite, buck, and stab in death, like they would have in life. The rest of the less lethal bone bits, I break into sharpened points, ready to pierce through anything and everything that comes for me and the others.

A fire begins to blaze in the distance, but I ignore the smoke for now, intent on dealing with the more immediate threats. I finally catch sight of Elon, and relief slams through me when I see that he's holding his own, the wake of his devastation almost a match for mine.

A group of soldiers scream as they charge me, their magic battering against my walls of power, frantic and desperate. Before they can even get close to my protective cocoon, I send missiles of antlers through the air and pierce their skulls with them. The group falls dead before their bodies even hit the ground. Marx steps into my view, and hope ricochets through me. If we can get close enough to each other to regroup, maybe I can hold them off long enough to jump the ley line somewhere else.

I press closer to Marx and Elon, gritting my teeth against the effort it's taking me to crush so many protections at once. I try not to let the sheer number of soldiers gunning for us overwhelm me, but a pit in my stomach opens up and alarm crawls over my skin all the same.

I'm so fucking close though. Less than ten feet and Elon, Marx, and I will be together again.

Wildly I start scanning the horde for Rogan again, hoping against hope that he's somewhere close by. Something to the right catches my attention, and my manic gaze lands on a familiar face. He's dressed in an Order uniform, not looking nearly as suave and in control as he did in the crisp cranberry-colored suit that day the High Priestess cornered me in an Order interrogation room. His dark brown hair is disheveled, and he's watching the fight with a disgusted look on his face like he expected our immediate and utter annihilation and doesn't understand how it hasn't happened yet.

I recall that he's a Contegomancer, a very dangerous one, and I switch the direction I'm headed in from trying to get to Marx and Elon to this fucker instead. Maybe if we cut the head off the snake…

I don't get time to finish that thought before the High Council member snaps something to the line of Order members next to him. I follow his tight gaze, and that's when I notice the guns.

Horror and shock explode through me, and I can't even scream a warning to anyone before the deadly cadence of semi-automatic fire erupts everywhere. The line of Order members fires into the bedlam, taking down any moving target with no care to whether it's friend or foe. Bone-white sparks start to burst all over the walls of magic I've encased myself in, and the threatening ping of bullets fills my ears. I whimper, helpless and terrified, as I feel the same metallic assault against the shields I've wrapped around the others. I'm stopping the bullets, but for how long?

Hysteria tries to take over as I reinforce all the barriers I'm holding around everyone. A fervid, stinging power wraps itself around my protective walls of magic and starts battering away at me. It feels acidic and repulsive, and I want to tear my magic away from the contact, but doing so means dropping my barriers. I grit through it, but it gets infinitely worse when that same magic begins to assault the barriers protecting Rogan and the others. The other magic starts to scald me, and I scream with the effort it takes to fight it off, but it's stuck to my power like cloying, corrosive sap, and I can't get it off. More bullets fight to pierce my magic and end this battle, and tears begin to sting my eyes from the pain and the struggle it takes not to give into it.

Fight, Lennox! I snarl at myself, refusing to give up. *Show these fuckers what you're made of.*

Just when I reach into myself again, demanding more power to combat the bullets and the burning of the Contegomancer's magic, something strange happens. My magic suddenly feels wild, like it's trying to jerk free from my control. I struggle to hold onto it when pain erupts in my thigh, and I'm knocked to the ground. I cry out, looking down frantically to find blood pouring out of my quad. I recognize the familiar heat and burning sensation, and I immediately know I've been shot...but how?

My protections were up, I was... I look up, agony welling in my chest as a primal scream rips out of me. I reach for my magic, trying to get my protections back up. Somehow I lost my hold when I got hurt, and now each and every one of them is vulnerable. My terrified eyes find Marx as I rush to get barriers back around him and the others. His eyes widen with shock for a fraction of a second, the sound of gunfire drowning out my soul wrenching plea, and then a bullet rips through his forehead.

15

I watch as the light disappears from Marx's dark brown eyes. Eyes that were filled with laughter and teasing less than thirty minutes ago. Eyes that have continually offered me a warm look of friendship and loyalty since the first time I met him. Eyes that I know with excruciating certainty will never look at any of us again.

Anguish sears through me as I watch Marx's body fall lifeless to the ground. I get my magic walls back up around the others just as the tether between Rogan and me ignites with heartbreak and pain. I can't see him, but I know Rogan's watching his friend fall right before his very eyes.

I was too late.

A soul-shattering lament fills the air, and tears spill down my cheeks as the man I love shatters with loss. I can't breathe, as the shock of what just happened tightens around my chest like a vise. There's a brutal pull on my magic as Rogan taps into more power than just his own, but I do nothing to stop him.

He can drain me dry if it helps him avenge the horror of what just happened. It's the least I can do after fucking up so heinously. I don't know how I'm ever going to forgive myself, let alone ask Rogan to forgive me. Grief claws at my soul, but I try to shove it away. We need to get out of here, or next it will be Prek, and after he's just another body lying on this destroyed field, the High Council will test how many times Elon, Rogan, and I can die, and just how painfully, before one of us gives them anything they want to make it stop.

I feel sick at the thought, and desperation drives me to push back up on my feet. I cry out as I try to put weight on my wounded leg. It hurts like a bitch, but I can at least hobble. Order members slam against my magic-made barriers, their faces contorted in rage and hate as they fight and fail to break through and kill me.

Anger once again begins to boil in my blood, and I scream with violent and vicious fury before shoving feral untamed magic out at every enemy in my way. I limp and watch as they begin to melt from the inside out. I don't know if I'm attacking their bones or their blood or both, I just know I want them dead so I can get to the others and we can run.

Screams and pain dance all around me, but all I can see and feel is Rogan fighting savagely as he tries to purge the grief and rage he's drowning in right now. His green eyes are locked on the Contegomancer, his face promising pain and retribution as the evil High Council member watches back arrogantly from the top of the little hill he's perched on. His smirk is taunting, and I read his lips as he orders the soldiers next to him to reload and fire at will.

Rogan's fighting to get to the High Council member, shattering bones and spilling blood as he slowly makes his way closer. I can feel the Contegomancer focus all his acidic power on Rogan's sluggish advance. I want to scream. I want to rage and avenge Marx. I want to rip every Order member on this field apart with my bare hands, but we need to go. We need to survive. We need to run and prepare so the next time we go head-to-head with the High Council, we crush them once and for all.

I turn, frantically searching for Elon and Prek. I need to get to them and then convince Rogan to get to us so we can get the fuck out of here. More bullets fill the air all around me, ricocheting off my barriers. Instinctively I duck, terrified that somehow a shot will break through like the one that's currently buried in my thigh. Order members go down all around me, and disgust fills me at the careless waste of life.

It's revoltingly clear that the High Council is corrupt beyond hope, but each and every one of the soldiers who are shooting at their own people without question or hesitation deserves to rot in fucking hell. I spot Prek, and my heart leaps until I see that he's carrying Elon's limp body. I think Prek is hurt; he seems to be favoring his right side as he drags Elon closer to the ley line running through the field and parking lot.

I start limping for them, fear burning through me as I make my way, and I steal back some of the magic Rogan is syphoning from me and reinforce the barriers around Prek and Elon. I can't tell if Elon is dead or just unconscious, either way it reinforces the driving need I feel to escape as soon as possible.

"Rogan," I shout in my mind, hoping it somehow gets his attention through the tether, but he doesn't look my way. I shove more of the panic hammering through me at him, but I must weaken my shields when I redirect the magic, because the next thing I know, I'm spinning from the impact of a bullet in my side.

Fire fills my veins as the bullet tears through my stomach and out through my back. A feral scream crawls out of my throat as a new wave of pain assaults me. I press my palms to the wound, and dark red blood slips through the seam of my fingers, all too quickly darkening the front of my shirt and pants. Surprise stifles my thoughts, and I try to shake away the lethargy that's trying to set in.

All I see is bodies. Everywhere. The sun, still hidden in the clouds, dips lower in the sky, and the trees surrounding us blanket the lost with their shadows. Too many vacant glassy eyes stare off at nothing, while others lie on the ground, writhing in pain, injured and calling out for help or their loved ones. Order members run around trying to provide medical assistance to their friends and team members, while other soldiers stay focused on the fact that they're still supposed to be attacking us. It's mass confusion, loss, and bloodshed that will taint this once peaceful place forever.

Tears slip out of my eyes as I look away, not wanting to see the carnage anymore. Rogan's moss-green gaze finally finds mine, and I stagger a little, struggling to stay on my feet. Magic drains out of me, and I fight to call it back, mentally putting a stopper on my source so my protective barriers don't get any weaker. My vision tunnels and then focuses as I try to breathe through the hurt and fear pulsing out of me and dripping to the ground.

Rogan's face crumples with alarm, and he abandons his efforts to get to the High Council member and turns to come to me. In the distance, over his shoulder, I see the Contegomancer's face contort with fury, and he strides off his hill and moves into the fray. Order members rush to get out of his way, parting like a school of fish for a shark.

I refocus my efforts to get to Prek. Elon still isn't moving, and I suspect he's been mortally wounded. My heart clenches at that thought, but he's come back twice now, and I have to believe he will a third time. Prek is almost to where the parking lot pavement meets the field, which is the exact angle the large ley line runs. He turns to see me hobbling after him, and I can see the debate in his eyes, about putting Elon down to come get me.

"Don't you dare," I yell at him.

I don't know if he heard me or just read the manic look in my eye screaming for him to hang onto Rogan's brother at all costs. Gusts of wind start to blow Order members away. Out of nowhere, a sheet of icicles flies through the air like daggers, digging into some witches' barriers or into the witches themselves if their wards are cracked. I realize that Prek is trying to clear a path for me, his elemental magic strong and relieving. I tamp down on the spark of magic envy that ignites in me as another burst of wind allows me to close the distance.

"Thank fuck," Prek sighs as he runs his eyes over me, his gaze fixing on both of my wounds before lifting back up to my face. "Elon was shot through the neck. He's dead, but he'll come back, right?" Prek demands, his tone frenzied and panicked.

I reach out and squeeze his shoulder, offering him a comforting look that I'm pretty sure looks more like a grimace. "He'll come back. Just hold on to him until he does, okay? Your only job from here on out is to watch over him until he's awake again."

Order members surround us, and they renew their attack, sensing that we're within arm's reach of escape. Different branches of magic bombard us, but it's easier to strengthen the one shield now protecting three of us than it was to reinforce separate shields for everyone.

I swallow down the relief that streaks through me now that the three of us are back together again. I want to exalt the fact that I made it here, but we're not nearly out of the woods yet. I look behind me to find Rogan knocking Order members out of his way. Further back behind him, the High Council member is doing the same.

"Can you feel the line, Prek?" I ask, my voice frantic as I watch Rogan pushing to get to us. "I can keep you protected while you apparate the both of you out of here. Is there somewhere safe you can lay low for a bit?"

Prek starts to argue with me, loading his mouth with all the reasons he shouldn't leave us behind, but I silence him with a glare. "Prek, if Rogan and I can't get away, you and Elon will need to get us out. You *have* to go. Is there somewhere safe you can think of? Or a way you can get back to Rogan's house? You'd be safe there."

My gaze pleads for him to listen, and his eyes bounce back and forth between mine for a moment before I see resignation settle into them. He scrubs at his face with a shaky hand and repositions his fireman hold on Elon.

"Yes, I have somewhere we can hide out until we can figure out where to meet," he tells me, and I nod my head, eager to get him and Elon out of here. "You're a good witch, Lennox," he tells me somberly, and I shake my head at him.

"No goodbyes, Prek, you're not getting rid of me that easily," I tease. My smile drops too quickly as battle cries and wounded shouts seem to grow louder. "Tell me when you're ready. I'll drive them back, and you focus on getting the hell out of here," I instruct, and he nods, closing his eyes and pulling in a deep breath.

"Go!" he orders, and I pull out the stopper to my source and shove the magic that's now bleeding out of me at the fuckers in our way. Prek and I push the last handful of feet back to the line, my magic leaving a trail of carnage rippling out away from us as we go.

I watch, panicked, as Prek tries to focus, internally screaming for him to hurry up, and I almost crow in celebration when I see the line take a hold of him and Elon and then fiercely yank them away.

Success rockets through me.

They did it. They got out.

I revel in the peace that washes over me for the briefest of seconds, and then I fold up the relief and happiness coursing through me and chuck it in some far dark recess of my mind as I turn to wait for Rogan. I try to feel for the ley line around me as much as I can, the fighting now background noise as I will myself to jump me and Rogan out of here just as soon as his fingertips touch mine.

It's like watching someone run through three feet of snow when a polar bear is chasing them. The Contegomancer is closing in, and even as quickly as Rogan is moving, I can see he's not moving fast enough. I let go of the hum of the line and focus on the polar bear instead.

My movements are sluggish and jerky. I can feel the effects of blood loss and exhaustion start to kick in. I've been in worse shape though, and I know I still have enough in the tank to get us out of here. With a rabid growl, I clear the enemy from around me, attacking their blood and their bones to ensure I'm buying myself enough time to end this once and for all. Magic pools in my belly as I track the High Council member with my eyes like he's prey.

I can still see him in his swanky suit in the interrogation room at Order headquarters, thinking he's the shit because he runs in high circles that he's deluded himself into believing are untouchable. I would give anything right now to cut him down to size. To make him realize that picking this fight was the biggest mistake of his pitiful, useless life. I want to look in his eyes as understanding dawns that there's no escaping my wrath.

I thrust my pool of magic out. I send every ounce of power I possess, knowing I'll only get one chance. I grit my teeth and wait for the perfect moment, my magic surging and searching for my target. Sweat drips down the back of my neck, and nausea collects in my stomach. Pain pulses out of my wounds, but I try to ignore it all and concentrate.

Five more seconds, Lennox.

You'll have him in four...

I see the moment the Contegomancer senses the rush of power I pushed out into the throng. He smiles as though he knows I'm coming for him, and I feel his acidic crackle through the air as he prepares for my attack.

Three more seconds...

What this asshole will never understand though is that there are far greater forces in this world than vengeance and rage. I could try to kill him. I could give everything I have in an effort to make him pay. It's what he would do, and what he clearly expects of me, but fuck him. I choose love.

Two...

I'll feel his death on my hands another day.

One...

Rogan's bones practically sing to me, begging me to claim them and safeguard them always. I wrap my magic around him, my focus absolute and my will undeniable. All at once, I yank my magic back like it's a rubber band that's been pulled too tight for too long. Rogan is jerked forward, my power in control and calling him to me. He flies toward the line, barreling through Order members brutally, as the Contegomancer realizes what I've done and bellows out an enraged snarl.

Like the body snatcher I'm proving to be, I snatch Rogan from the danger hunting his back and pull him to safety. He's feet away from me when a deranged cackle forces goose bumps up my arms and a shiver to run down my spine. The danger in the sound has me looking back to the Contegomancer, just in time for him to pull the trigger on the gun he's pointing at me.

Everything slows and I can't scream, or move, or react. Every ounce of power I have is focused on pulling Rogan to me. He's feet away, and I risk trying to call the line, hoping somehow we can still prevail.

Rogan slams into me with a pained grunt at the same time the bullet does. I fall back into a ferocious scream of outrage and grief, my lamentation lifted up into the air like a haunting howl as the round pierces the side of my head, and the world and its deep humming all around me cease to exist.

A gasp tears out of me, and I sit up in a dazed panic, trying to make sense of what's going on.

"You're okay, Lennox. I'm here. I've got you," Rogan consoles, his large hand brushing hair out of my face, while his other presses against my shoulder, trying to coax me into lying back down.

Adrenaline hammers through me, and I look around frantically, my brain not processing what it is I'm seeing. Something jostles the mattress I'm lying on, and I bounce up and down as though...

"Are we in a car?" I ask, bewildered, my voice a dusty croak.

Before I can even think about a glass of water, a bottle of it is handed to me. I chug it down, my mouth, throat, and body suddenly desperate. It's gone sooner than I want, but just as a disgruntled whimper starts to sneak out of my mouth, I'm handed another open bottle of water. I drink this one slower, which is to say I drink three quarters of it in two seconds flat and then sip on the remaining fourth like I'm the model of demure and lady-like behavior at all times.

I instantly feel better and more alert now that I'm hydrated. I look around to see that we're in a large Suburban, the back of which is fitted with a mattress and Rogan, and wherever we are, it's dark as pitch outside. I look up to see who's driving, hoping it might be Prek or Elon, but to my surprise, it's Riggs and Viv, the two alphas of the lycan pack near Rogan's house.

Riggs meets my eyes in the rearview mirror, his gaze twinkling with merriment, but he doesn't say anything as Rogan pulls me closer to him, his touch stealing away my focus. I look back at him, puzzled, as I try to piece together how we're here and why.

"What's going on?" I ask, my voice low and careful as I search Rogan's face for any hint of what's going on. "How did we get away?"

Rogan pulls my face to his and rests his forehead against mine, breathing me in for a moment like he needs the touch to ground him just as badly as I do. "You jumped us out of there. I have no idea how you did it. You were dead before we could even hit the ground. One second, I'm feeling you die, and the next we're in the middle of unfamiliar woods with a couple of angry lycans growling at us."

My eyes dart back to Riggs and Viv, and I watch as Riggs reaches over to his mate and threads his fingers with hers, a loving smile stretched wide across his face. I try to shoot Rogan a discreet look, asking if they're officially in the know about what we can do, but as I do, I realize I'm stupid for even questioning it. I *did* just wake up in front of them, and Rogan's not exactly whispering phrases like *you were dead* and *I felt you die*, so my superior deductive reasoning skills are telling me they are officially in the loop.

"Elon and Prek?" I ask, worry percolating in my stomach.

"We're on our way to meet them now," Rogan reassures me.

"Tad?" I add, hoping Rogan has at least called him so he's not pacing around the empty house in his finest yoga gear, stressing.

"My cousin Cohen is picking him up and bringing him here."

I tense at those words, terrified of what could happen if Tad and this Cohen dude somehow walk into an Order trap like we just did. Rogan rubs my arms and drops a kiss to my shoulder.

"They're safe, I promise. Cohen is a force to be reckoned with, and I doubt the High Council will be looking for either of them. They'll be here soon, don't worry."

I want to point out that Rogan also thought the smear campaign against the High Council would buy us time to prepare for a fight with them, but I save the *I told you so* for later when I'm not still reeling over the clusterfuck we barely escaped. I look around again, the darkness outside making it incredibly difficult to get my bearings.

And here I was thinking waking up in a morgue was difficult.

"Where is *here*?" I ask, fixing my disoriented gaze back on Rogan. "How long was I down this time? What's going on?" I add, looking down at myself and then back over to the lycan alphas.

I'm not wearing the clothes I left the house in this morning. My blood-soaked jeans and tee are missing, and in their place is a gray oversized hoodie and a matching pair of sweatpants that I'm more or less swimming in. Rogan releases a sigh, the skin around his eyes tightening, and I immediately want to pull him to me and try to soothe the tension radiating out from every inch of him.

"Did you know there was a ley line that ran up behind

Rigg's pack land?" Rogan asks me, his green eyes astute and careful.

I'm taken aback by the question. "No. I've only been to his pack that one time with you. I never noticed anything."

Rogan nods like he expected this answer, but for some reason, it makes him look even more troubled. I search for his emotions, trying to understand the look on his face, but frustratingly, I run up against a wall.

"The line is apparently unregistered. I didn't even know it was there. The pack uses it for business purposes," Rogan starts to explain, and my brow furrows with confusion.

When I woke up, he said that I had jumped us from the ley line we were being attacked at to somewhere else. Somewhere that happened to have patrolling wolves nearby. My eyes dart around the dark car one more time, seeing our current circumstances in a more concerning light.

Are we in trouble or something? I wonder but then dismiss it. He said we were meeting the others, and I know for a fact he would never put them in danger for any reason, so that can't be it.

"Okay, so I apparated us to a line nobody knows about on pack land," I recap, trying to understand Rogan's obvious worry. "I mean, if you're wondering how I did that, your guess is going to be as good as mine," I tell him, a frantic chuckle spilling out of my mouth. "I was a little busy dying, so I don't know if my magic did the thing it does where it just instinctually guides me to take action. It's been doing a lot of weird things since I woke up, so maybe that's it," I tell him, and when his jaw tightens at my casual declaration, my stomach drops.

He thinks something's up with my magic.

"What aren't you telling me, Rogan?" I ask flatly, and his unsettled gaze snaps to mine.

"What he's hesitant to worry you about, Osteomancer,"

Riggs cuts in to say, "is that the only people who know about the line you rode in on, is my pack and a clan of demons who pay us generously to keep it that way. We've been tossing around all kinds of theories, but I'm dying to know how you did it," Riggs adds excitedly.

Well, shit...that makes two of us.

16

"Wait. But why do demons know about your secret ley line?" I ask, running my fingers through my curls only to snag them on what I'm pretty sure is matted dried blood and a whole nest of tangles.

Distracted, I begin to feel around my skull for an entry and exit wound. With the way my chest is scarred, I know there should be something, and as expected, I find a fingertip-sized circle of smooth healed tissue above the top of my ear, and another at the back of my head about three inches shy of the top. Hopefully, my curls will hide them both.

"We source goods to anyone and everyone," Riggs declares as though that answers my question.

It doesn't, but I get he has a business to run, and it seems part of that business is being cagey about it.

I turn to Rogan and shrug, doing my best to hide my hurt over the fact that he's closed himself off. I tell myself that he probably has a good reason and that reason might not even be me. He just watched his best friend die. Maybe he doesn't want to overwhelm me with that pain and loss.

Unease settles in my stomach, but I try hard not to focus on it.

He has questions in his eyes, and I hate that I have no answers. I'm starting to wonder if I really know anything at all.

"I have no idea what happened," I confess aloud, answering the unspoken *how* floating in his gaze. "I was trying to tap into the line when I died," I go on, as though listing the events out loud might help me hear the answers to all of our questions. "I was desperate to get us out of there and frantic. Maybe when my brain shut down, it tweaked the resonance my magic was focused on, and it just happened to be the pack's line," I provide, not knowing what else to say.

It had to be a fluke. Nothing else makes sense, but I can't shake the feeling that I did something wrong and now everyone is looking at me like I'm not who they thought I was. My heart twinges a little at that thought, and Rogan reaches for me and pulls me into his lap.

He places a tender kiss against my temple and strokes my back. I lean into him, ignoring the upset I feel over the disconnect between us.

"Whatever happened, I'm grateful it did. You saved us. I don't know where we'd be right now if you hadn't," he reassures me.

I sigh warily, suddenly feeling very lost and small and vulnerable. "You still haven't told me where we even are?" I remind him, wishing his words made me feel better, but there's a scratching worry settling just under my skin, and I don't know what to think about anything.

"We're in Utah," Rogan tells me, wrapping his arms around me tighter. "Elon and I have a hidden house here in the mountains that no one knows about."

I pointedly look over to Riggs and Viv.

"We're safe," he assures me, clearly picking up what I'm putting down despite his inability to *feel* it. "Riggs and Viv have been discreet and loyal since Elon and I moved into the area."

Riggs chuckles and Viv offers me a friendly smile over her shoulder. "We always knew something was different about the Kendrick boys," she tells me, wrinkling her nose. "They smell different to us," she admits. "You smell different now too."

Surprise flickers through me at that declaration. I never gave much thought to how I smelled before. I fight the urge to lean down and sniff my arm.

"They didn't seem eager to explain anything to us, so we chalked it up to something that was none of our business. But then one night at an event the brothers both attended, one of our pups very rudely asked them why they smelled different from other witches."

I smile at that. Nothing worse than getting called out on something by a kid. There's no getting around the truth they spill no matter how cringy it may be.

"Elon and I knew then that they were aware we were different, but we still didn't want to bring them into anything that could have put them and their pack in danger. So it just became this unspoken thing between us," Rogan explains, and I can abruptly sense the *until now* floating uncomfortably around the interior of the car.

I can only imagine what they thought when Rogan and I showed up using a line no one is supposed to know about, me with a fatal head wound, and him battle weary and confused as to how we ended up there in the first place.

"Anyway," Riggs barks jovially, breaking the awkward silence that was just building and making me jump. "My brother's pack here helped these boys build their house up here. So when Viv and I discovered that's where you were headed, we thought an escort was in order. I don't get over to Ronan's pack nearly enough, so the timing was perfect."

Riggs's smile is genuine, his kind eyes twinkling with support and care, but there's more there, more to all of this, more that he's not saying. I can feel it, but I'm too overloaded to demand he spit it out. So many questions swirl in my mind, and I feel completely bogged down by them. I'm stuck in a world of magic and chaos so utterly confusing that I don't even know where to start trying to untangle it all.

There's this whole supernatural world that even the supernaturals don't talk about. I've never heard my Grammy say much about demons, other than to steer clear or salt them if you had to. But now I'm learning that they're more wrapped up in the fabric of the mancer world—and now even the lycan world—than I ever thought possible.

I shake away my frustrations and try to pull in some calming breaths. Rogan is still stroking soothing passes down my back, but my ire grows anyway. I thought I was getting past my insecurities of not knowing enough about the world I'm now forever a part of, but now I wonder if I'll ever truly get the many facets, seen and unseen, of this world.

We round a corner, and the darkness all around us changes. Or maybe it's just that my eyes are finally adjusting. Either way, I can now make out the thick trees bordering each side of us as well as the driveway in front of us that leads up to a huge log cabin.

Log mansion? Are those even a thing?

"Wow, Rogan, this is stunning!" Viv coos as she leans forward to take it all in.

Two massive stories with wraparound porches on each level loom down over us. The massive windows all over show lights on inside, and I'm instantly eager to see Elon and Prek and check over them to make sure they're okay.

"Ronan and his crew did a beautiful job," Riggs observes

as they pull into the circular drive in front of the massive house.

"You both are more than welcome to stay," Rogan offers, but Viv waves him off.

"You get settled in. We'll come visit and get the grand tour in a couple days," she states warmly.

"That'll give us some time to make the arrangements that we discussed. We can go over everything then," Riggs adds, and Rogan nods in understanding, not bothering to fill me in on the details they're discussing.

They pull up in front of the house, and Riggs hops out and moves to the back to open the door. Rogan helps me slide out, and as he's climbing out himself, Riggs wraps me up in a tight hug. A squeak of shock escapes me as he does, but after a second, I can't help but feel like his hug is all that's holding me together. My eyes sting, but I blink the emotion from them as Riggs sets me down and offers me a dazzling smile.

"It's all going to be okay," he tells me, confidence and wisdom ringing in his tone. "Even when you can't see how, it *will* all be okay."

I nod, my chest tight with unexpected emotion, and with that, he jumps back into the driver's seat and pulls away. Viv rolls down her window and waves at us as they leave. I wave back, all at once cold and bereft and wishing I believed the advice Riggs just offered.

Rogan walks up the stone path to the front door and turns when he realizes I'm not following him. I study him, and he studies me, both of us silent and distant, and I fucking hate it.

"I know a lot has happened," I start, my voice small amidst the huge house and the dense woods all around us. "We have a lot to figure out, a lot to process."

Rogan steps away from the house and closer to me as I continue.

"If you need space, time to sort out whatever is going on in your head, fine, but blocking me, shutting me out, that fucking hurts, Rogan," I tell him, not wanting to pretend everything is okay for even another second.

He opens his mouth to say something, but the front door opens and Elon comes striding out. He wraps Rogan up in a hug, the brothers taking a moment to reunite, the gratitude and relief palpable in the air. I feel like an interloper watching a deep and meaningful moment, so I quietly try to move around them and make my way toward the house. Elon reaches out and hooks me like I'm a fish, and the next thing I know, he's added me to the hug.

"I was so fucking terrified that you two didn't make it out. When I woke up and Prek told me..." Elon wipes at his eyes, and his words trail away.

"We wouldn't have if Lennox hadn't saved our asses," Rogan tells his older brother, and Elon's arms tighten around us both. "I'm sorry I..." Rogan starts and then stops as though he's trying to figure out how to say what he wants to say. "When Marx fell, I just... All I could see was red. I wanted to kill, to hurt...but I lost sight of what was important," he goes on, his words tight with emotion as though each and every syllable is a struggle.

Pain and grief spill out between the lines of what he's saying, and I hurt for him and for the rest of us. Lights beam past us, and I look up to find another SUV pulling up. It stops at the end of the path, and we all watch as a tall man with ash brown hair and beard climbs out of the driver's seat.

"You got room for one more?" he asks teasingly, and both Elon and Rogan laugh deeply.

The passenger door opens while the driver rounds the

front of the sleek carbon gray SUV, and I see Tad climb out with bags in his hands. His brown eyes find mine, and a huge smile breaks across his face.

"I brought wine!"

I practically leap for him, and Tad doesn't miss a beat when he drops the packages in his grip and catches me. He wraps me up so quickly and fiercely in a *mend your soul* type of hug that I don't know who needed it more, me or him. He squeezes the shit out of me, and then I do what I always do when I finally feel safe after something terrible happens, I allow myself to break and then start bawling my eyes out.

I tip the massive bottle of rosé back and hold my breath as I take several gulps. I lift my eyebrows in contemplation as I swallow them down—maybe this doesn't taste so bad after all—but then my sober tastebuds kick in, reminding me we hate wine, and I lower the bottle and cringe back away from it. Tad reaches for it with gimme hands, and I happily pass it over, my body warm and my mind all kinds of light and fuzzy.

I lean back against the large black apothecary-style vanity, once again admiring the beautiful master bathroom from my vantage point on the floor. The walls and ceiling are a rich walnut color, and beams run across the high vaulted ceiling. The floor is a gray stone and so is the back wall, which might be my favorite part.

There is a gargantuan copper bathtub against that wall, with stairs at the head and foot of the tub that lead to an upper stone deck that allows you to climb down into the tub. But the best part is that the deck also houses a gas fireplace with huge windows above it so you can see the stars. It's a girl's bathtub wet dream, and I didn't even know those existed until I saw this one. The whole space is dark and masculine and dreamy, which makes it the perfect location to get thoroughly pissed with my cousin.

A dry shudder moves through my chest, an echo of the sobbing I stopped doing in trade for the drinking I started instead. It's as though my body is still trying to purge the emotion but my eyes just aren't on board at the moment.

Tad passes the bottle back to me, and I dutifully drink my share. I swear I've never seen a bottle of wine this big with its little feet on the label, but it makes me feel like I shrunk the last time I died and came back to life.

"Can you see my bullet holes?" I ask Tad, brushing hair away from where I felt the scars earlier.

Tad leans closer and squints at me. "Nope, but to be fair, there's one and a half of you right now, and both of them are a skosh fuzzy," he confesses, and I shrug and drop my tangled locks back down. "I need more wine if you're going to talk about head wounds," Tad declares, and I take a few more gulps before passing the bottle back.

"There's something wrong with me," I whine as I throw my head back and bang it on one of the many copper knobs attached to the five hundred drawers the vanity has. I glare at the knob, pissed that it got me again. "We talked about this," I snap at it, giving it the angry mom finger and a withering glare. The knob doesn't even flinch.

Hard ass.

"There is absolutely nothing wrong with you," Tad reassures me as he tries to level me with a chastising gaze. Mostly it looks like he's trying to figure out which *me* to focus on. "I mean other than the ratty hair, *way* too big sweat suit, and the bags your eyes are rocking, but you know what I mean," he adds, and I refocus my withering glare from the knob to Tad.

Rude.

"I don't mean in the *woe is me, existential* kind of way," I correct him, tripping up way more than I should on the word *existential*. "I mean, there is literally something wrong with me, more specifically my magic, which is basically me because I am an Osteomancer, dammit."

"Woot woot!" Tad cheers, like I just said let's do shots instead of my magic is fucked up.

When I don't join in on the cheer, Tad quiets, stares at the bottle of wine in his hand and then shrugs before slamming more of it down.

"Rogan knows, but he's pulling a Rogan and keeping it to himself. Either that or he hates me because I killed Marx," I moan, dropping my head into my hands, only I don't get my hands up fast enough, so I just chin bump my chest.

Ow.

"Wait, you killed someone?" Tad asks, suddenly serious, minus the swaying his body is doing.

"Like, so many someones," I correct, a flash of cracking bones and screaming Order members flashing in my mind before I blink and it's gone. A shiver slithers up my spine, and I reach for the wine. "I couldn't even get his body. I wanted to, but there wasn't enough time or enough magic. I just left him back there like he didn't matter, but he mattered, Tad. He really mattered," I tell him, drowning my words and pain in more gulps of wine.

"Of course he did, Leonardo. You all survived, and that's what Marx would have wanted. He would have been annoyed if you died or got caught trying to get his body. He would have been the first to tell you that was stupid."

I nod at his words, knowing he's right, but it doesn't lessen the guilt. I don't know if anything ever will.

"Were they trying to kill you first?" Tad asks, his head tilted thoughtfully, clearly still stuck on my candid admission to being a murderer.

"Mm-hmmm," I mumble, my mouth full of more wine that I don't like but can't seem to stop drinking.

"Doesn't count then," he assures me, as though there's no way he'll be convinced that I'm a cold-blooded murderer, no matter what I say. "And you didn't kill Marx, Len, they killed him. You did everything you could."

"But he died," I argue, tears welling in my eyes.

"Because of *them*," he repeats, his face softening and his unfocused eyes begging the one and a half mes he sees to hear what he's saying. "I see the way Rogan looks at you, Lennox, and I guarantee you he doesn't think there's a thing wrong with you. Ask him what's up with blocking the tether, give him a chance to explain what's going on with him before you jump to the worst conclusion."

"I will, obviously, but it's not just him. My magic has been weird since I woke up—the first time. Well, and this time. I don't know what it is, but I hate it. I was just feeling good about my place in all of this, really finding my stride as a witch, you know? And then I had to die and everything is all messed up...again."

"If I had a nickel for every time I heard someone complain about dying," Tad teases, *cheers*ing with the now almost empty bottle of rosé. "I'd have three nickels—two for you, and one for Elon," he goes on, laughing deeply at his own joke. "Do you think there are other immortals out there besides you guys?" he asks contemplatively.

I shrug and then realize that's a difficult move to maneuver after too much alcohol. "I mean, probably, there's so much out there in the world that I never knew was there, why not immortals."

"How do we find them?" Tad demands, like they're simply lost.

"Fuck if I know. Maybe I should start carrying around a sword and screaming *there can be only one*. They might stop by for a chat then," I suggest, trying and failing to shrug again, but only one shoulder cooperates.

"I rode a ley line," Tad announces, his eyes suddenly wide.

"Oohhh nice!" I reach for the bottle and finish it off.

"Totally passed out, that hot dude Cohen had to carry me. I woke up in his arms all damsel-like, and I gotta say, I get the appeal."

I crack up, and Tad just nods at me fervently. "You'd totally rock a sword P.S."

"Right? I was just thinking that," I agree.

There's a knock on the door, and both Tad and I turn to stare at it. I realize one of us actually has to say *come in*, and I start cracking up when neither of us do.

Maybe if Rogan had our tether working, he'd know he can open the door, I think smugly, and then Tad shouts *come in*, but it sounds more like *comenuminum*.

Rogan pokes his head in, like he's unsure of what he might find. His eyes land on my face, and I think there's a flash of relief that I'm no longer bawling hysterically. I wouldn't know though because the douche is still blocking me.

"Can I have a word with Lennox?" Rogan asks Tad, opening the door wider and stepping in.

Tad shoots me a look like we just got busted, and Rogan's vibe definitely has a *you're in trouble* feel to it.

"Suuure," Tad agrees, and then he tries to get up.

Rogan scoops down and helps him get to his feet and then holds him there for a moment until Tad gets his swaying under control. He looks down at me and wags his eyebrows.

"I'm tellin' ya, these damsels are on to something," he coos, and I giggle. "I'll go get more wine, be right back," he chirps, heading out into the room.

"I'll bet you five dollars we'll find him passed out on the stairs in five minutes," I tell Rogan, laughing at the visual I just conjured of drunk Tad with carpet lines on his face in the morning.

Rogan moves all the way into the bathroom and shuts the door behind him before looking down at me. I fidget under the weight of his stare, not sure what he's thinking.

"We need to talk," he starts, and everything inside of me plummets into a pit of despair.

Those four words never mean anything good.

17

"Fuck, why do you look like I just kicked your puppy?" Rogan asks, his eyes filled with concern.

"I mean, are you going to? Are you going to kick my puppy, because if you are, can we just wait until tomorrow? It's been a long day. I kind of died and then had a teensy weensy breakdown, and now I'm pretty sure I'm three sheets to the wind, whatever the hell that means..."

Rogan bends down in front of me, his sudden nearness cutting off my rambling. "I think it's Pirate for *drunk*," Rogan tells me, a small smile ticking at the corner of his mouth, and its presence on his face fills me with so much joy that my eyes start to well up.

"Fuck, I love that smile," I declare, blinking back the rush of emotions that just slammed into me.

"I love you," he tells me back, and I stare deeply into his eyes like I'll see all the proof I need in them.

"Do you though? Do you still love me, with everything that's happened?" I ask, hating how uncertain and small I sound.

Come on, you are Lennox Osseous, the freakin' Osteomancer of all Osteomancers, I tell myself, but for some reason, the inner pep talk isn't doing much for me today. Probably because my inner voice is super focused on nachos right about now.

Man, I'm hungry.

Rogan grabs my hands and stands up, trying to pull me up with him. I grumble in protest.

"Nooo. The floor is so comfy, and there's a knob that's been giving me some lip, but I think it's starting to come around to the fact that we were always meant to be friends," I object, and Rogan chuckles.

He gets me to my feet, with minimal help from me, and guides me toward the stairs on the back wall. He sets me down and then turns on the taps to the tub and starts to fill it. Without saying a word, he's back in front of me, pulling at the hem of the huge hoodie I'm wearing, and like the good girl I wish I was, I put my arms up so he can take it off.

I'm completely naked underneath, but any heat I might feel over his undressing me cools when I look down and see the dried blood on my abdomen. A small hole marks the spot to the left of my belly button where I was shot, and I begin to wonder how many scars will mar us inside and out before all of this is over.

Rogan stands me up and pulls my pants down, and then he takes the clothes I was wearing and walks over to the garbage, chucking them inside almost violently. I'm a little taken aback by the level of aggression he just showed those clothes, and I watch him with concern as he comes back to check the temperature of the water.

"Were they talking shit to you or something?" I ask after a beat, too curious to let it go.

I mean, I did almost get in a fight with a drawer knob earlier, who am I to judge a sweatshirt beat down?

An incredulous snort escapes Rogan, and he shakes his head. "When Riggs was alerted that we'd shown up on pack land uninvited, Saxon just so happened to be with him," Rogan starts. "Then, conveniently, *his* house was the closest one to where we were, so I took you there to get you cleaned up. Which is why the both of us have been wearing his clothes since we rode the ley line nearby."

I nod in understanding and try to bite back the amused smile that wants to peek out and play simply because of the annoyance written all over Rogan's face right now.

"Guess that ass kicking will have to wait until next time," I tease, not able to help myself, and Rogan shoots me an unamused look.

Yikes.

"Get in," he orders, jutting his chin at the tub, and I roll my eyes.

"Bossy," I grumble, but I do as I'm told and dip one foot and then the other into the gloriously hot water.

I moan in pure delight as I sink down into the massive egg-shaped copper tub. I swear I could compete for an Olympic medal in this thing.

Hmmm, what would be my stroke?

Rogan grabs some bottles of products from the glass-encased shower and then sits behind me on the step. Out of nowhere, warm water cascades down my hair, and I squeal in surprise. Strong hands encourage me to tilt my head back, and I do as another cup of warm water wets my hair.

"So does Saxon know..." I start.

"No, thank fuck. Your heart was beating by the time they showed up. Riggs helped cover and told him we were taking you to a healer. Saxon was worried, but he didn't question his alpha or me. I told Riggs and Viv the truth after we apparated here. They both swore on their pack that they would never tell a soul unless given explicit permission by us to do so."

I nod and he wets my hair again. Then I hear the top of a

shampoo bottle being popped open, and I realize that Rogan has every intention of washing my hair. I'm surprised but one hundred percent here for it. I close my eyes as the smell of juniper and fig fills my nose, and then Rogan's hands are working through my hair, lathering up the soap and scrubbing all of the blood and dirt out.

I revel in how good this all feels, but it doesn't completely combat the unease that's settled in my chest or the fuzzy head I'm currently battling, although that last one I blame on the wine.

"This is great, don't get me wrong, but it's not going to distract me from the fact that you didn't answer my question," I tell him, and his hands go still in my hair.

"Your question?" he asks, confused.

"Um, yeah, you know that one where I asked you if you still love me despite everything that's happened?" I repeat, not sounding any better as I ask a second time.

"I thought that was rhetorical, sorry," he snarks, and I give him an incredulous snort.

"Of course I still love you, Lennox. You're it for me. Good days or bad, sleep or no sleep, cuddle slut or pouting on the other end of the couch. It's you and me forever."

"I am totally not a pouter," I defend, and he chuckles.

He rinses my hair, and the bath water around me turns murky. I pop the drain and silently beg it to take it all away. Rogan puts conditioner in my hair and then starts to comb it through with a wide-tooth comb. I turn to him, shocked by his hair care knowledge, and quirk an eyebrow. Rogan blushes and I instantly feel even more curious about why the pink is tinging his cheeks.

"I might have looked up how to care for curly hair," he tells me sheepishly, and I find him so damn adorable I almost can't take it. I look at the shampoo and conditioner, and sure enough, they're designed for curly locks.

"But when would you have gotten all of this?" I ask, puzzled.

"The cleaner stocked everything at my request, just in case, when we were in Chicago. After the run-in with my mother, I figured better to be prepared."

My eyes bounce back and forth between his. I'm so touched by this simple yet incredibly thoughtful and sweet thing. Silence stretches between us, and I debate shattering this beautiful moment between us with questions, but I can't wait any longer. I need to know once and for all, or I'm going to scream.

"Rogan, why are you blocking me?" I ask, my voice barely above a whisper. My heart stutters with nerves, terrified that his reasons will shatter the incredible thing we have building between us.

"What? Why would I block you?" he asks, as though my question is ridiculous.

"I don't know, because you're mad at me or hurting or hiding something or you think something's wrong with me but you don't want me to feel it. Take your pick," I tell him, hating that he's making me spell it out like this.

"I'm not," he counters adamantly.

"You're not what? Mad? Hurt? Hiding something from me? Can you answer a question properly? Are you trying to drive me mad so I never get any answers?" I demand, my tone and frustration rising in pitch with each word.

Rogan takes a deep breath and fixes his eyes on mine. "I am not blocking you, Lennox. I'm not any of those other things either," he defends.

"You're not?" I clarify, cautiously.

"No. I'm not," he reassures me, and I don't know what to feel. I reach for the tether, questioning what I know I felt earlier. Maybe I was wrong or confused after just waking up.

I reach the connection that ties me to Rogan and, without a doubt, it's still blocked.

"Then why can't I feel you?" I ask, distress sneaking into my tone.

"It happened when you died. The tether just stopped, and I couldn't feel you either. I figured it would come back, like it did the first time."

My brow furrows with befuddlement. "What do you mean?"

"In the church when you died, the connection blinked out. I didn't feel anything until the morning Marx called to tell me the bodies were missing. I had a flash of fear and panic earlier that day, but I didn't recognize it for what it was, because we hadn't used the tether that much before you died. I only figured it out after I saw you at your aunt's house. I could see what you were feeling written all over your face, and then I matched that to the sensations filtering into me through the tether. I thought it would snap back into place again, just like it did last time," he explains, and I grow even more confounded while not missing the way his face fell when he said Marx's name.

"Why didn't you say something before?" I question, worried.

"I don't know, a lot has happened. I didn't think about it until now. Is that what's been bothering you this whole time? You thought I had purposely shut it down somehow?" he asks, realization dawning in his beautiful green eyes.

"Well...yeah...you never said anything about our connection being affected. I didn't know," I stammer, unsure if I feel upset or relieved over the fact that he's not shutting me out on purpose. I want to talk to him about Marx, tell him how sorry I am for what happened, but it doesn't feel right. He looks too exhausted, too run down, and I don't want to add any more to his plate of things that need to be dealt with tonight.

"Lennox," he starts, my name falling reverently off his lips. His voice is practically a purr, and it does all kinds of things for my fuzzy head and warm body. "I know we're still settling into *us*, but when I say I love you, that you're it for me, I mean it. I shut you out before, and it almost cost me everything. I will never risk that again…never," he reassures me, pressing his forehead to mine, and I can hear the vow in his voice.

I run my wet fingers through his hair and just feel him against me, both of us quiet as we anchor ourselves and recalibrate.

"I don't know what's wrong with our tether, but we'll figure it out. I've already contacted my aunt. Let's see what she has to say before we worry. Okay?" he assures me, a tired yawn sneaking out to punctuate just how worn out he has to feel. "Now, let me finish your hair and then we can go to bed. It's been a long day," he tells me gently, stroking my cheek with his thumb.

I nod, cupping his cheek tenderly for a moment before I turn back around. Rogan combs through my hair in silence and then rinses it with the clean water still pouring from the tap. We trade small smiles and hesitant touches, everything that we've been through in the last twenty-four hours slowly catching up to us.

Rogan kisses me on the shoulder as I work to dry my hair, and disappears into the bedroom to get ready for bed. I scrunch up my curls, staring at myself in the mirror, and start fretting about the tether. What if it doesn't come back? What if every time one of us dies, it damages our connection? I used to want it gone more than anything, but now that it seems to be, the loss feels so much bigger than I ever thought it could.

I abandon my pensive reflection and flick off the lights in the bathroom. Stepping into the master, I find Rogan sitting on the end of the large bed, staring out of the wall of windows at the moon and the incredible expanse of stars. The view is breathtaking, but his eyes are far away, and I can tell he's not really seeing what's in front of him, but lost in something else.

My heart lurches at the deep and profound sadness I see etched in his face. I remind myself that he practically runs himself ragged caring for everyone around him and making sure they're okay. But who does he let in to take care of him?

Today, he lost his friend, the safety of his home, his brother died, and then so did I. He had to open himself up to Riggs and Viv, which I know couldn't have been easy, after all the years he and Elon have spent watching their back and protecting their secret at all costs. And yet, he walked into the bathroom and cleaned *me* up, offered *me* the words I needed to hear, brought *me* the comfort I needed to feel, all while he was quietly breaking inside.

I move to him, and when he registers my presence, he tucks his sorrow back inside himself, ready to give me whatever I may need. I watch the change in his features and his demeanor, the moment he switches from focusing on himself to focusing on me. It makes my heart swell with love and appreciation for how incredibly selfless and loyal he is, but at the same time, I hurt at knowing he never puts himself first...ever.

He looks up at me, his warm calloused hands palming the backs of my thighs while I run my palms over his shoulders. He smiles sweetly at me and then closes his eyes, relishing my touch. His thumb plays with the hem of the fluffy towel I've wrapped around myself, and he leans forward and rests his forehead against my chest. He breathes me in as he rubs soothing lines with his fingertips up and down the backs of my legs.

I trace the scar on his face and massage his temples and neck to help ease the tension that's been collecting for far too long there. I feel him start to relax, and then he sits back and pulls me into his lap. The dark gray towel climbs up my thighs as I straddle him, and he brushes my wet curls from my face as I look down at the gorgeous man I get to call my own.

Damn, my lucky stars do good work.

Rogan looks up at me, and I swear he's thinking the same thing as he coaxes my lips down to his. Flames move through me like every cell in my body is nothing more than kindling for passion and pleasure. I moan into his mouth as our kiss grows deeper, and then I realize that the heat moving through me isn't just metaphorical, but a very real and tangible forest fire in my veins.

I gasp and pull back, but by the time the questions form in my eyes, the heat starts to dissipate, and a knowing smile quirks at the corners of Rogan's lips.

"What was that?" I ask breathily, my head suddenly clearer and my senses sharper.

"I burned the alcohol out of your system. I didn't want you to spend tomorrow hungover and feeling like shit, and I'd like to spend tonight between your thighs."

I full on swoon at that mouth, a blush crawling into my cheeks as I feel him harden beneath me. I smile down at him, and then I kiss him deeply, willing to give him anything and everything he needs. His hands untuck the towel around me, pulling it slowly from my body and then flinging it to the floor. I pull Rogan's shirt off, noticing that he also cleaned up and changed at some point in the night, probably when Tad and I were getting plastered in the bathroom.

His skin feels like heaven against mine, and he runs his huge hands up my back as he wraps his arms around me, pulling me impossibly closer against him. Our kiss turns frenzied, and his hands explore my naked body with wild abandon. His tongue teases mine, flicking and thrusting against mine in a promising show of what his cock will soon be doing inside of me.

I whimper as desperate need builds higher and higher between us, and all at once I need more. It's as though my hands can't get enough of him. My mouth and senses can't consume him as fast as they need to. I have all of him all over me, and I still need more.

I reach down into his sweats and palm his thick cock. Swallowing down his moans and grunts like they're my favorite meal, I stroke him once and then twice before pulling him free of his pants. I lift up on my knees and have him lined up with me in less time than it takes for him to groan my name, the plea in it clear.

I drop down onto him, throwing my head back on a throaty moan so he can hear just how good he feels inside of me. Inch by delicious inch, he fills me up until he's all I ever want to feel. I kiss him deeply as our hips meet, letting him taste just how much I love and admire everything he is, and he drinks me down like I'm water in the desert.

"I need you, Lennox," he begs, his tone revealing everything he's not saying.

Our tether is still closed, but I can sense his need to lose himself in something good, even if it's just for the night. The drive to get lost in pleasure and happiness in order to combat all the horrible, brutal emotions of the day is written all over his face. I can feel it in his hands, in the urgent way he clings to me. It's in the critical pull of his mouth and needy thrust of his hips. It's as though the way we feel when we come together chases all the shadows away for a while. He needs that reprieve as much as he needs his next breath.

So I rock my hips forward, rise up, and give it to him, again and again.

My breasts bounce against his chest as I ride him roughly. There's no holding back, no teasing or drawing it out. I'm going to fuck him until the darkness in his gaze makes way for the light again. Until the ache in his chest feels less insurmountable. I'm going to cry out his name as many times as he needs to hear that he's not alone and never will be again. I'm going to kiss him until all he can taste is my love, and then I'm going to hold him while he breaks, because I know it's coming.

I breathe him in, reveling in the soft pants of *yes* he gasps against the skin of my throat as I work my pussy up and down his cock. He doesn't push for control, needing me to take whatever I want from him at my own pace and in my own time. The thing is, I want everything.

I twist in his arms, climbing off of him for a second until my back is against his chest. I line him up with me again and drop down his thick shaft in a reverse cowgirl position. I lift up and then force him inside of me deeper as I reach for his hands and bring them up to my breasts. He sucks on my neck, pinching and kneading my nipples, and I reach down and circle my clit with my fingers as I bounce on Rogan's dick. Warm tingles start to move through my body toward my core, and I moan at the building orgasm.

"Fuck, you feel so good," he growls in my ear, moving my hand from my clit and replacing it with his own.

I twist my head so I can capture his mouth, and he rescues my tired thighs by thrusting into me at the pace I set. I lean back into him, loving how well he knows my body already, and he grunts as my inner walls begin to tighten as my orgasm draws even nearer. He starts to rub my clit faster, and all it takes is a couple of seconds and I'm exploding around him, his name filling the room as I ride out my bliss.

He cups my pussy with one hand and my boob with the other and then thrusts into me hard, quickly finding his own release. Heat moves in waves throughout my body, and I know it's Rogan drawing out the cloud of pleasure I'm floating in. It's like a massage from the inside out, and it feels so good I can't even talk. I morph into human Jell-O and just melt all over him.

We stay like that for a while, just holding each other, quiet and floating in the peace our bodies just created. He runs a hand absently up and down my arm, and all too soon I begin to feel reality and all of its burdens starting to creep back in. I get up, pulling him with me to clean up in the bathroom. We're quiet as we wipe down and wash up; however, this silence feels different. We're not wading in euphoria and relaxation like we were on the bed, what wraps around us right now feels heavier. We seem to be watching each other in the mirror like we're both checking for cracks that need to be repaired. I dry my hands on a towel and turn to look at him leaning against the vanity.

I smile softly, leaning in to steal one more kiss before conceding to my body's need for sleep. But when I steal his bottom lip between my own and he threads his fingers into my damp curls, he brushes past my new scar, and his entire body freezes. Our kiss stills and his lips pull away as he examines the scar with the pad of a finger, his eyes now fixed on mine. I watch it build in him like we're moving in slow motion. One minute, he's fighting to stay with me in this happy place we're trying to build against all odds, and the next, anguish crashes through him so quickly that it steals both of our breaths away.

He slams a hand to his mouth as though it alone has the power to fight back the sobs, but the tears breach his eyes anyway, and when they do, it shatters the rest of his resolve. Rogan crumbles to the ground, and I go with him, catching his fall and wrapping him up in my legs and arms and my love.

Wild pain-filled sobs pour out of him, and my own tears drip down my face as I try to hold the man I love together despite the world's best efforts to tear him apart. A shroud of mourning and grief wraps around us on the bathroom floor, and I feel him shake against me as he cries. A torrent of torment wracks his body, and it's all I can do to hold him while it takes its toll.

I feel him grieve his friend, his brother, his life, me, and lastly I feel him mourn for himself. So much has been taken from him. He works so hard to rebuild time and time again, and no matter what he does, someone is there to try to steal it all away. It breaks my fucking heart to know what he's gone through, and as I sit there and watch Rogan finally break, I silently promise him and me...never again.

He will get the peace and happiness he deserves, and I don't care what I have to do, I'm going to make sure no one ever fucks with him and the people he loves again.

18

I pull the huge cream cable knit sweater over my head.

Omg, yes, it's even softer than it looks.

I reach for the thick socks I found while snooping through the drawers in the closet and pull them on over the dark blue leggings I found hung up on one side of the closet. Rogan bought me clothes, which is super adorable. He'll probably be annoyed that I'm still wearing his sweater despite the fact that he bought me clothes, but maybe he should stop buying such soft tops, and then I wouldn't have to steal them.

Really, he only has himself to blame.

I rub the sleeve of the sweater against my cheek and sigh. This thing could be made of baby unicorns, and I wouldn't be mad at it—that's how incredible it feels. I tiptoe out of the closet and smile at Rogan, who's still completely passed out. I tried to get all snuggly with him this morning, pressing my booty into him as I *stretched*, but he must have been even more exhausted than I realized, because his dick certainly woke up, but the rest of him didn't.

I kiss the top of his head, not able to help myself, and sneak out of the door. I didn't get to see too much of the house yesterday between my tears and the wine-hazed trip to the bathroom floor, but the bright interior and the huge windows letting in sunlight and birdsong feel amazing. Especially after the horrid fucking day that was yesterday.

I make it down to the kitchen and immediately start hunting for coffee. I find the mugs, the creamer, coffee beans, and all the other frilly fixings for fancy coffee, but where the hell is the machine? I spin around as though the sudden movement is the key to magically revealing the coffee maker, but all it does is teach me that these socks are perfect for sliding around.

My inner ten-year-old is stoked.

"It's built into the wall there, just next to the fridge," a deep voice states out of nowhere. Completely caught off guard, I scream, turn, and in a self-defense move I'm not proud of, I chuck my mug in the direction of the voice.

Shit.

Rogan's cousin, Cohen, catches the cup in midair like this is a usual occurrence for him, and heat crawls up my neck at my completely ridiculous overreaction.

"Moon shits, you scared me," I pant as I press a hand to my chest and bend over to try and calm my fight-or-flight response.

"Moon shits?" he questions on a chuckle.

"It's totally a thing," I reassure him as I catch my breath.

"I've been sitting here the whole time," he points out from the kitchen table that's perfectly well lit, and obvious, and providing no excuses for why I didn't notice him sitting there when I walked in.

This dude must think I'm a psycho. First, I have an emotional breakdown in front of him, and now I attempt to assault him because I'm apparently a wee bit jumpy.

"Are you okay?" I ask him, pointing to the mug. "I'm so sorry," I offer as he strides closer to hand me back my cup.

"Hey, I'll take a flying mug over you crushing my bones or something instead," he teases, and I turn an even darker shade of red.

I mean, it's good I didn't attack him with magic, but what does it say about me that I didn't even think to use it at all? I internally facepalm.

"I'm Cohen, by the way. We didn't get a chance to meet yesterday," he politely tells me, offering me his forearm for a witchy shake hello.

His green eyes are a dark olive, and his skin has a stunning golden undertone. His hair is ash brown, but in the light, I see sun-kissed blond streaks running through it. His beard is shorter this morning than I remember it being. I stare at him for a beat, trying to figure out where I know him from, as his face is strangely familiar. It hits me as I reach for his arm for the traditional witch greeting of grabbing forearms. He's the boy I saw with Rogan in that weird flashback I experienced when we were trying to break that jinx on Tad.

I grab his arm, ready to offer him my name in return, when a tingling sensation moves from him to me. It's as though someone is tickling me with the fuzzy seeds of a dandelion. I chalk it up to static electricity until a familiar face pokes her white, glowing head from around his back, and my eyes widen with shock as I yank my hand back.

What the hell?

I'm pretty sure Osteomancers aren't supposed to see ghosts so freely. That kind of thing is more for the Soul Witches. Which means seeing one is already not normal. The fact that I've seen two is downright strange, but seeing the same ghost twice...that feels like a haunting, and ain't nobody got time for that. Especially not me. There is way too much on my plate to add a clingy ghost to the list of my problems.

"What are you doing here?" I ask the glowy specter, who offers me a warm smile. Or it would be warm if she were still alive. Diem looks exactly like she did the first time I saw her. Her golden blonde hair is straight and falls almost to the small of her back. Her blue eyes are hopeful, and she's wearing all black, which makes me think she was either into the goth scene or more than likely killed at night while she was spying, or meeting someone, or something along those lines.

Diem appeared when I did a reading for her best friend, Colby, back at Order headquarters when I was being kept there for my own safety. It dawns on me that maybe something's wrong with Colby and that's why Diem is here.

"What's going on? Is everything okay?" I press, concern settling in my bones.

Cohen's green-eyed gaze looks bewildered, and he tracks my stare and looks behind him. "Are...are you talking to me?" he asks, eyeing me like I've officially lost it.

I'm confused by the question, and embarrassingly it takes me a little too long to figure out what he's asking.

Crap. He can't see the ghost. Yep, I'm definitely racking up some great first impressions with this guy.

"Sorry, she took me by surprise. I'm talking to a ghost, not you. Don't worry, we've met before, which is why I'm a little stunned to be seeing her again so soon," I announce, shooting Diem a look that says *you better not be haunting me.*

Cohen spins, like he expects to find something behind his back, but there's nothing there, because he can't see her.

"She's actually next to you now," I point out awkwardly.

He side-eyes the space next to him, inching away from it a little before he warily stammers, "Uhh...oh...okay. H-how can you see ghosts? I thought you were an Osteomancer, right?"

Oh yeah, he definitely thinks I'm crazy. He's going to tell

Rogan to run just as soon as he sees him. Jokes on him though; Rogan already knows.

"I am an Osteomancer. I don't usually see ghosts. Although, so far, I've seen this one...twice, but I think that had more to do with the reading I did for her friend than my strange abilities to see souls," I reassure him, but I can see he's not at all reassured.

I cringe and look back at Diem. "Is Colby okay?" I ask her, and she smiles at me before turning her attention back to Cohen. She looks him up and down like the snack he is, and I'm not really sure what to do about that. I'm tempted to tell him that he's currently being checked out by a specter, but judging by the wide eyes and the baby steps he keeps taking from where he thinks the ghost is, I think he may have already hit his limit for weird shit today.

I turn back to Diem.

Okay. Why do I suddenly feel like I'm in an episode of Lassie, only instead of a dog, I'm talking to a ghost? Did Colby fall down the well, girl?

"Are you here about Colby at all, Diem?" I ask, trying to narrow down the reason for her sudden visit.

"What did you just say?" Cohen asks me, his voice suddenly flat and menacing as he takes a step closer.

I blanch at his tone. "I asked the ghost, Diem, if she's here about her best friend. That's who she was with the first time I saw her," I tell him, unease skittering through me at the intense look that's suddenly in his eyes.

"Diem, is that you?" he asks, but he's facing the wrong side. He looks at me, desperation in his countenance now, and it makes me want to step back from him. "What does your ghost look like?"

"Uh...she's tall, blue eyes, long blonde hair...beautiful," I describe.

Cohen closes his eyes, and the quiet anger that was just etched into his features gives way to pain.

"Diem Wembly?" he asks, and Diem smiles next to him.

Well, shit. Diem isn't here about Colby, she's here about Cohen.

"Shit, I'm sorry, Cohen, I didn't realize that you knew her," I explain, my heart aching for him. I don't know if that strange tingle that happened when we met was because Diem was here or if it somehow called her here. Either way, I'm relieved that I'm not being haunted, while also feeling bad because it's clear this whole encounter is digging up some painful shit for Cohen.

"How do you know her...Diem, I mean," I ask, trying to piece together the purpose in all of this. Am I supposed to give Cohen a reading? I don't feel the draw to do that, but Diem's most certainly here for a reason.

"We grew up together. Diem wasn't blood, but she was like a sister," he tells me, and I nod. "Is she really here? Can she hear me?" he looks around frantically, and I place my hand where Diem's face is. His eyes study the space, like he's looking for any sign of her. "I miss you," he tells her, his voice suddenly strangled with emotion. "I'm so sorry about what happened." His eyes grow wide, and his head snaps back in my direction. "Do you know what happened to her? Can she tell me who killed her?" he demands, stepping closer to me, like he's ready to wring it out of me if he has to.

"It doesn't work that way. I don't hear her like I hear you; she spoke to me through the bones when I was reading Colby. But I learned then that she doesn't know who killed her. It was fast and painless though. Her best friend worried about that and asked me to ask her."

"Her best friend?" Cohen asks, like that term being applied to someone else hurts him.

"Uh...yeah...Colby. She's looking into what happened to Diem."

As the words leave my mouth, a knowing suddenly hits me. I haven't read Cohen, and I don't think I'm supposed to either, but I feel strangely certain that he'll play an important role in solving what happened to Diem.

"What's her name again?" Cohen asks, walking back to the kitchen table where he has a laptop that looks similar to Elon's and an open notebook. He picks up the notebook, flips it to a clean page and looks up at me expectantly.

I look over to Diem, seeking her approval. She nods once, and then the white light that comprises her visage and allows me to see her promptly disappears.

"What the hell, she just left," I tell him as I spin just to be sure she's not flashed herself somewhere else in the room.

"What? No. I had questions," Cohen barks out, as though I just opened the door and let the ghost escape on purpose.

"I'm sorry," I offer, but I don't know what he wants me to do.

"Diem!" Cohen calls out. "Diem!" he demands a second time after nothing happens.

He sighs, looking around the kitchen, his eyes suddenly so lost and sad.

"Her name is Colby," I tell him, hoping it can be the lifeline he's clearly in desperate need of. "Colby Trapetti," I repeat, and he starts writing the name down. "I'm not sure where she's living right now. The last I saw her, she was working for the Order in Chicago. However, I wouldn't be surprised if she quit the day I spoke to her," I add. "Oh, and she sometimes shortens her last name to Trapet," I tell him, and his pen stills on the paper.

"Trapetti as in the Trapetti Coven?" he asks, his voice

suddenly dark and filled with all kinds of preconceived notions.

I narrow my gaze at him, suddenly feeling very defensive on Colby's behalf. "Yes, but before you go jumping off the deep end into your judgmental thoughts, Colby doesn't have fuck all to do with her family, and their sins are not hers. Make sure you understand that before you go looking her up. You of all people should know that you can't pick your family," I tell him, offering him a pointed look.

I don't know much about this guy other than he's Rogan and Elon's cousin, he made Tad feel damsely, and that he's the older version of the boy I saw in a vision. The vision was of him and Rogan sneaking out of the house to go fishing when they were kids, then I saw them getting in a fist fight when they were older. I don't know why I saw any of these things. It happened when Rogan and I first used our magic together, so I blame that. I debate giving Cohen the *you will rue the day* speech to really hammer the *don't fuck with Colby* point home, but decide against it.

Footsteps making their way down the stairs reach me, and I turn to find Rogan is up and striding toward me. The steel in my eyes softens as I take him in, and he gives me a slow sensual smile.

"Hey," he offers me in greeting before dropping a soft kiss to my lips.

"Hey," I tell him back, stealing another peck before he pulls away.

"Everything okay?" he asks, looking from me to Cohen and back again.

"Totally," I chirp. "We're just talking about ghosts and how it's bad to judge a book by its cover," I tell him cryptically.

Rogan snorts. "I never got that saying, everyone judges a book by its cover. It's normal."

"Agreed," Cohen adds, shooting me a pointed look.

"Fine, that's not the right comparison anyway. Don't judge a book by its *title* is probably more accurate. You may think you know what you're going to get with a certain title, but you'd be wrong," I announce, throwing that pointed look Cohen just gave me right back at him.

"It sounds like you've been spending too much time at the bookstore," Rogan teases, and I scoff in dramatic outrage.

"There is no such thing as spending *too much time* at a bookstore. How dare you, sir!"

Rogan laughs and looks from me to the empty cup in my hand. "Ah, I know what's going on here: you haven't been properly caffeinated this morning," he declares as though he's figured out a great mystery. "The coffee maker giving you trouble?"

"Bitches, man," I declare on a huff, and he chuckles and takes the mug from me.

"I got it," he reassures me with a wink that threatens to make my panties melt right then and there.

"And this is why I love you," I coo, which earns me a deeper laugh.

"The only reason?" he challenges with a raised brow.

"That thing you do with your tongue is cool too, I guess," I counter casually, punctuating it with a disinterested shrug.

Rogan shakes his head, and I hear Cohen snort before he sits back down at the table and starts typing away on his computer.

"Just cool, I guess," Rogan grumbles quietly, and then out of nowhere my clit, nipples, vagina, *and* asshole, all heat up.

They get so hot that I actually think they might melt my underwear. I squeal and start to wiggle, shooting a glare at Rogan, who's now got a shit-eating grin on his face.

Motherfucking blood magic!

My privates suddenly cool, and I run a finger across my neck in the universal motion of "I'm going to kill you." Rogan just smiles wider and holds up the empty coffee mug.

Crap.

Well played, Kendrick, well played.

"Turn on the TV," Prek barks as he comes stomping down the stairs like his private parts are on fire too.

We all turn to him as he streaks past, headed for the living room and the humongous TV mounted above the large stone fireplace. He searches for a remote but the TV comes to life, and Prek starts watching it like the meaning of life is written across the screen. I look over to find Elon sitting on the arm of the couch with the remote in his hand. I didn't even see him walk in here.

They must have been watching a witch news channel last night, because that's what pops back up on the screen, and there's a man in a suit and tie cheerily announcing the seven day forecast. Rogan sidles up next to me and hands me a full cup of coffee exactly how I like it, and I promptly pay him for his barista skill with a kiss.

"Thank you, Dave, for that fine weather update," a quaffed woman declares in her best news anchor voice. "In other news, the manhunt is still on for former Order Captain Prek Orson. Captain Orson is accused of murdering two other Order members, Private Rick Alvarez and Special Agent Marx Bevit." Marx's picture pops up on the screen next to Alvarez's and Prek's, and I see red.

"Orsin is considered armed and extremely dangerous. If you see him, you are advised to call the local authorities immediately." The woman shifts to a new camera angle and starts in on another story, and the living room is completely silent.

What in the actual fuck.

"Loose ends, that's what you told me, right, Lennox? That the High Council was good at tying up loose ends?" he demands, thrusting his hand toward the TV like I don't already see what's on it. "Is my family in danger?" he asks, as though he didn't ever consider it until now.

"No, they'll run your name through the mud, make it so your own family wouldn't help you if you turned to them," Rogan tells him evenly.

I set my coffee down, unable to enjoy even one sip, and start to pace. Prek takes the remote from Elon and changes the channel to another witch news show. Within five minutes, they're sharing the same bullshit report about Prek being a cold-blooded murderer.

"It's everywhere. My cousin messaged me to ask me what's going on. That's how I fucking found out that the High Council just framed me for not one but two murders. How do they even know Alvarez is dead?" Prek asks, his voice strangled with anger and outrage.

I feel like shit, like I pulled him into all of this, but what choice did I have? He wanted the truth, and this is the truth. This is a perfect example of the fucked up shit that the High Council has been pulling for entirely too long. I look over at Rogan, hoping he can do or say something that will help, but instead I catch the tail end of a look he's giving Elon and Cohen. He shakes his head as though he's answering a question.

"It's the perfect nail in the coffin, Rogan, not to mention I literally died to catch the footage. People are pissed. Our other video campaigns are working, but if we show them this video, it could tip things in our favor," Elon argues.

"What video?" Prek and I both ask at the same time.

I step closer to Rogan as he runs his fingers through his hair frustratedly. "Elon took video of what happened yesterday," he tells me, and it takes me a minute to realize what he's saying.

"You have a video of the Order attacking us?" I ask, turning to Rogan's brother, completely shocked.

"Better," he counters. "I have video of the Order murdering Marx and of High Council member Bordow commanding soldiers to fire on other living and wounded soldiers.

"Holy shit," I mumble, completely taken aback.

"You have to post that, and not just to clear my name, but because it's the most damning piece of evidence anyone has ever gotten on the Order. People deserve to know the truth," Prek growls, and as much as I agree with him, I also feel torn. I don't want to see a non-stop loop of Marx being killed. It was bad enough the first time.

"It could blow up in our faces though," Rogan argues. "You know how they work," he tells Elon and Cohen. "They might have footage of the fact that they were fighting us, and they could flip this on us somehow. Paint us to be the aggressors, and then instead of people being against the High Council, they could turn on us," Rogan counters.

"Maybe before, yeah, but they jumped the gun by trying to tie up loose ends with Prek. His face is on every news channel being cycled through every five minutes. They're building a story to make him the bad guy, and we know it will get more and more convoluted as time goes on. But *we* have video evidence showing he's not the killer at all," Cohen points out.

"With the other videos circulating, Marx's death would be one more push of proof that people are looking for. Plus, this just happened. The High Council can't sweep it under the rug like some of the older claims. This shows that they're *still* doing everything they're denying. Prek is right, people need to see that," Elon adds.

Rogan huffs out a sigh, and I rub his back. "I get that, I'm not disagreeing with you, I'm just trying to plan for all the contingencies. They will find a way to make this our fault, and we need to be prepared before they do."

"Not if we take them out before they can counterstrike. And this could make the people mad enough that they'd actually help us do it. I can cut the stuff with Marx out if it's too much, but they need to see all the other times Bordow ordered soldiers to shoot into the battle," Elon tells his brother emphatically.

Tad comes stumbling into the living room, looking worse for wear and not expecting to see the whole group gathered here. "What happened?" he grunts, looking around confused.

The news anchor on the TV starts reporting about Prek again, and Tad goes still watching it. Rogan looks at Prek for a moment, clearly debating what the right move is.

"No," he states warily. "Don't cut the stuff with Marx out. Prek deserves to have his name cleared, and Marx would want what happened to him to count for something. Fuck the High Council, and fuck their constant stream of lies," Rogan growls and then gives Cohen and Elon the nod of approval they're looking for.

They quickly jump up, ready for action.

"We should wait to post though," I call after them as they hurry back toward the kitchen. Elon turns back to me, his eyebrow raised in question. "Let them spend most of the day digging a hole for themselves. Like Cohen said, they'll start adding details and making themselves look worse. Once they do, that's when we should post the truth," I tell him, and he nods in agreement and hurries off to get to work.

"Are you going to be okay?" I ask Prek, knowing that this has to feel awful.

Prek turns off the TV and chucks the remote at the couch hard. With a growl, he strides over to the front door, throws it open and stomps out. I debate going after him to make sure he's okay, but Tad shoots up off the couch.

"I got him," he calls over his shoulder, and then he heads out, shutting the door behind him.

I sigh and rub at my face with my hands. There's just never an end to the bullshit. Rogan pulls me back against him, and I go willingly.

"I know it's hard, but Elon's right," I tell Rogan as he wraps his arms around me. "This might be the thing that tips the scales, and we need that now more than ever," I admit, hating how true it is. I know that video footage is going to be brutal for Rogan, for all of us, but we need all the help we can get. "Is it too late to go back to bed?" I ask, and his deep chuckle vibrates through me.

"If only there wasn't a war to fight," Rogan declares, but it makes my face fall.

"I don't want to be the Debbie Downer here, I really don't, but how the hell are we going to win a war when we couldn't even win the battle?" I point out to Rogan.

He turns me in his arms, his eyes soft and his touch gentle. "We just have to figure out how to outsmart them, out fight them, out manipulate them, and hit 'em where it hurts," he tells me confidently.

I shake my head, but I can't fight the smile that sneaks across my face. "Oh, is that all?" I tease, and he nods as though it's that easy.

The doorbell rings and we both look over at the front door.

"But..." Rogan starts as he moves to answer it. "First, we have to fix our magic."

19

I stir the coffee in my cup, the spoon obnoxiously loud in the quiet room, and I barely stop myself from shushing it. Alora, Rogan's aunt, looks at me, her smile polite, but there's a tightness to her gaze that wasn't there the first time I met her. She's still immaculately put together and would give any old Hollywood leading lady a run for their money. Today, she's draped in a deep royal blue sweater with a long cowl neck, and her leather pants fit like a second skin. She has boots on with a vicious-looking spiked heel, and finger waves in her raven black hair.

Alora's husband, Dave, looks happy and carefree to her right, and her wife, Harmony, has a contemplative gaze that bounces around the long table we're sitting at in the formal living room. Harmony runs a hand over her light blonde, slicked back, ballerina bun. It's the second time she's done it, and I categorize it as a nervous gesture. I want to offer her some reassurance, but I have no idea what's made her uneasy in the first place, so I'm pretty much shit out of luck until someone starts talking.

Alora, however, doesn't seem to be in any rush. Her dark gray eyes track Rogan in the kitchen as he fills three tea cups with water straight from a whistling kettle. He sets them carefully on a tray with a plate of cookies and any other tea-making necessities his three guests may require. He starts to carry the tray over to where we're seated, and I return my gaze to the three witches sitting on the other side of the table.

When Rogan told me that he had contacted his aunt about our tether, I had assumed we'd get a phone call or perhaps an email. I didn't expect that they'd drop everything to come here and speak to us in person. The fact that they did makes me even more nervous for whatever is going on with the tether—that and there's a palpable strain at this table, and it's making me fidgety as hell.

Rogan doles out teacups and saucers and then sits next to me as his aunts and uncle make themselves the perfect cuppa. He drops a hand to my thigh and gives it a little squeeze. Unfortunately because our tether is broken and we've never been in a position like this before, I can't tell if the thigh squeeze is an attempt at reassurance or a signal to buckle up because shit's going to get bumpy.

A smile ticks at Dave's mouth across from me, and I once again debate whether or not he can read my mind. I'm tempted to think about a bunch of obscure amusing crap and then gauge his response to it in order to see if I can test this *mind reader* theory once and for all. But this conversation is important, so I probably shouldn't be reciting Ali Wong bits in my mind while it's happening, just to see if he'll laugh.

"I want to thank you for coming out to see us on such short notice," Rogan tells them, and they each smile at him warmly.

Then all of a sudden, his Aunt Alora drops her smile and levels him with a look that makes even Rogan squirm. "Rogan, we're absolutely delighted to be here and that you called us for help. We hope you know that we will always be here for you whenever you need it. With that being said, what happened in our home the last time you visited was unacceptable."

Rogan drops his head as though it's suddenly heavy with shame, and it isn't until Alora looks at me that I realize the unacceptable thing that happened was Rogan betraying me. She turns to me and squares her shoulders.

"Osteomancer Osseous, we know this kind of apology requires much more than just words, but we hope you will accept them along with our most heartfelt and deepest apologies for what occurred when you last visited our home. Had we known what was going to happen, we would have protected you at all cost. You were an invited guest under our roof, and that is not something I or my coven takes lightly. We would like to extend to you the same vow of protection my coven has offered our nephews. We hope that you know that you are always welcome in our home and among us, and we will ensure your safety and comfort at all times when you are in our presence or under our roof in the future."

The three witches stare at me, their eyes filled with apology and regret and hope that I'll find it in my heart to forgive them. My instinct is to tell them it's fine and that it wasn't their fault, because it wasn't. But there's a deeper code here, something more rooted in the times of our ancestors, when covens relied on allies and made deals or traded provisions or goods with one another.

So I give the ardent apology the care and thoughtful attention it deserves. I consider Alora's words on behalf of not just her but her coven. Walking into this, I didn't feel the need for an apology. I didn't hold them responsible, I still don't, but the fact that they do, touches me.

I offer Alora a warm smile, and her shoulders immediately relax a little, some of the tension bleeding out of them immediately. "Thank you. I don't blame you or your coven for what happened. It all worked out for the best, but it means a lot to me to know that I'll be welcome and safe with you and your coven in the future. I appreciate that more than you know. You all are always welcome at my house too, same rules apply. Well, when I have a house, that is. I'm sort of in between residences at the moment, and then there's this whole war, but you know what I mean," I tell them, internally facepalming when I start to nervously ramble.

So close, Lennox. So damn close to owning the whole mature Osteomancer vibe.

The smiles that cross the faces of the three witches across from me are blinding. Just like that, all the anxiety and nerves in the room dissipate, and everyone takes a deep relaxing breath.

"Excellent," Dave announces, looking around at all of us with a delighted grin. "Now, what seems to be the issue with your tether?" he asks as he folds his hands in front of him like he's eager to solve our problem.

Alora grabs a large satchel from the floor and begins to pull things out of it. She sets a large stone bowl on the table. Next to that, she adds glass bottles of various liquids and herbs, a stem of thorns, a thin wooden spoon, and a pile of crisp white rags. When it seems the bag is finally empty, Harmony takes it and hangs it from the back of her chair while she and Alora organize the small apothecary shop they just unpacked.

Rogan clears his throat and reaches over to take my hand. Instead of the gesture helping me to relax, it hypes up my anxiety instead. "I know we've never gone into details about what happened with me and Elon and why we were renounced, but in order to explain what's going on, I'm going to need to," he starts, a pointed look fixed on his Aunt Alora.

"No need, Rogan, I've known from the beginning what happened. You mattered more to me than your ability, and therefore I never felt the need to discuss it," Alora declares, and Rogan nods like this doesn't surprise him.

I look to Dave, who gives me a cheeky wink, and my suspicions deepen. Rogan made it seem like his aunt wasn't big into details about his story, mine, or even ours, but I don't think that's the case at all. I think her mind reading husband gives her an inside look at things, and because of that, she's never really had to pry.

"Right, well, to put it simply, when Lennox first died, our tether did too. When she came back, it returned as well. However this last time, the tether hasn't snapped back into place like before. We're hoping you can help us figure out what happened."

They nod and Alora's eyes grow speculative.

"Tethers are a very strong and yet very fragile connection. While in place and healthy, it combines magic, strengthens it, gives each participant access to the other's emotions and sometimes even thoughts. A tether is designed to fortify and bolster our power when used and nurtured correctly," Harmony explains, and Rogan and I both nod our understanding.

"The fact that the tether came back after the first death, is a testament to how strong it must have been. But I suspect it didn't return after the second time because the magic doesn't work that way," Alora adds.

"When magic dies, which happens when there isn't a genetic relative to carry on the line, the promises and vows connected to that magic die as well. Now obviously your situation is different, the magic doesn't move on, because it's still tied to you, knowing somehow that you will come back.

But I suspect the tether is simply behaving like a tether would when part of the connection passes away," Dave states evenly and simply.

"So it's gone?" I ask, surprised by how sad and worried this makes me feel. "I mean, I still feel it, at least I think I do, it's just not working like it normally does," I explain awkwardly.

"We can absolutely test your magic and confirm one way or another. The fact that you can still feel the tether is a good sign, but regardless of what the tests tell us, there are solutions and things you can do to repair or strengthen a tether, so I don't want either of you to worry, but first let's see what we're dealing with," Alora tells us, her tone positive and reassuring, and I immediately feel like I can take a deep breath.

Okay, this is good. They can help us fix this, and we can go back to the way things were.

Alora starts to pour things into the large stone bowl, and I'm transfixed by her steady hand and the knowledgeable gleam in her eye. I've never seen a Soul Witch work, and I'm fascinated to see what she does and why. Vials are unstoppered, and drops of this and that are mixed into what I'm pretty sure is moon water—or at least that's what the bottle says. I try to track the other ingredients and link them back with what I know about them, but Alora moves so fast I eventually give up and just enjoy the show.

She reaches out her hand, palm up, and Rogan must have done whatever this is before, because he immediately places his large hand in hers, also palm up. I watch as Alora reaches for the stem of thorns and, with practiced ease, flicks it down against the pad of Rogan's finger. He turns his hand, and three drops of blood make it into the stone bowl before he flips his palm back over.

Alora then pierces his palm with the thorns, giving him

a small scratch this time on the meaty part of his hand where his thumb connects. This time, only one drop of blood is added to join the others. With that, Rogan pulls his hand back, and all three Soul Witches then lean over the bowl, whispering an incantation about revelation, power, dispersal and guidance from the earth mother as well as The Mother, who is often mentioned in reference to fertility, abundance, and growth.

"Ahh, yes, the blood magic is incredibly strong, look how it consumes the pomegranate seed," Dave points out, gesturing for me to look into the bowl and see what he's saying.

I do, and I'm surprised to see Rogan's blood, as well as other things, appearing separate within the contents of the bowl. It's like looking at droplets of oil in water.

"This white substance is bone milk," Dave explains. "See how it's being pulled closer by the blood. It shows there's a draw there, a connection, but it's weak, just like you were saying it felt like.

"That's cool," I exclaim, watching the blood float in the middle of the bowl.

"The ivy stem leans toward Rogan's essence too, you'll notice, and that's because there's traces of soul magic in his line even though Rogan isn't a carrier of that magic," Harmony tells me, and sure enough, the little vine twitches like it wants to go to Rogan's blood but is playing hard to get.

"We can see that Rogan is wise and pure of heart, because the lavender oil circles the blood," Alora declares. "Coriander seeds float at the top, which is an indication of long life," she adds, and both Rogan and I snort at that. "I don't see anything that would make me think the tether is damaged beyond repair," she adds, and then she grabs the wooden spoon and scoops out Rogan's blood and spoons it into an empty glass container, like that's that.

Alora extends her hand again, and this time I know it's my turn. I place my hand in hers, watching as she grabs the other end of the stem of thorns and flicks it down against my pointer finger. I'm surprised that it doesn't hurt. I'm also surprised by Alora's lightning fast hands; she moves the stem so quickly and accurately that only the tip of one thorn catches me. I don't have soul magic, but I suddenly want to learn how she did that without pricking herself too.

Like the observant witch I've been, I turn my hand and let three drops of blood plop into the moon water. Then Alora scratches my palm, and I add one more drop into the mix. Once again, we all lean over the bowl to see what happens.

My blood immediately soaks up all the bone milk, and the pomegranate seed zips toward my essence next. There's a small branch that looks like it's two twigs that have been twisted together, and for some reason, that rises from the bottom of the bowl. It touches my blood, and then strangely, the blood starts to swirl in the middle of the moon water like it's creating a mini tornado. Everything in the bowl zips into the center, and gasps ring out all around me.

I look up, confused, and three sets of wide, shocked eyes take me in carefully.

"What happened?" I ask, but it's more of a panicked squawk than anything else.

"Oh honey, I was just about to ask you the same thing," Harmony coos at me, and my brow furrows at the sympathy I see in her face.

"How is that possible?" Rogan asks, his eyes suddenly haunted, and Alora looks from him to me.

"What?" I demand again, and her dark gray eyes soften.

She leans forward, her gaze suddenly filled with warm concern as she stacks her hands in front of her demurely.

"You have demon markers in your blood, Lennox."

20

"I what?" I snap, completely taken aback by Alora's declaration.

"It's okay, Lennox, there's no need to panic, just calm down and we'll figure this out," Rogan tells me softly, and I glare at him.

"Name one time telling someone to calm down actually worked. Just one," I challenge, and Rogan thinks for a minute and then shrugs. "Fine, freak out all you want," he says instead, and if I wasn't in the process of doing just that, I might have laughed.

"You have demon markers in your blood," Alora repeats as though I'm dense. "I can see they aren't the foundation to your power, which shows me that it's not genetically inherited. I've never seen it before, but at some point, it looks as though demon magic was bonded to your own."

"H-how...how do you know?" I stammer, not sure where to even begin trying to process what she's saying.

"These two branches are hawthorn and hazel," Dave starts, pointing to the twisted twigs now in the center of my blood tornado. "These represent the foundation of all magic, which was originally bestowed upon us by the Fae.

With mancer magic, these branches always stay on the bottom of the bowl. Demon magic will wrap around the branches, and mixed magic...will do this," he tells me, gesturing to the bowl.

I stare at the swirling contents, my mind feeling like it's doing the exact same thing in my head.

Demon markers in my blood?

Demon magic bonded to mine.

How the fuck?

And then it hits me.

Jamie's demonic chant fills my mind as she used magic that wasn't her own to try and steal power from the other Osteomancers. I can suddenly feel the painful jolt of magic as it transferred from the dead witch on Jamie's altar...to me.

A sinking feeling crawls into my stomach, and for the first time since I woke up to find the tether broken, I'm glad Rogan can't feel what I'm feeling. Desolation and anger war in my chest, and I don't know if I want to scream or cry.

"That fucking, demon cock sucking, trifling, thirsty, magic whore!" I snarl, and the room goes quiet.

Crap. I did not mean to say that out loud.

Rogan looks over at me, his eyes filled with devastation as he reads my face. He knows what happened in that church. *I* thankfully never had to tell him, but I know Elon provided him with the graphic details. He takes one look at me, and I see the moment he realizes what happened, and then I also see the moment that he blames himself for it.

Rogan shoots out of his chair and swipes the tray of cookies and other tea fixings off the table. It goes shattering against the window, cracking the pane with a loud boom. Alora, Dave, and Harmony all shoot to their feet, concern and shock written all over each of their faces.

So much for being calm.

Elon, Prek, Tad, and Cohen come running into the

kitchen like we're under attack. They look from Rogan to the Soul Witches to me still sitting in the chair, not sure what to do, and unease and aggression settles thickly in the air.

"What happened?" Elon demands, and Tad moves closer to me.

"What fucking happened is that my selfish bullshit let that human stain, Jamie, fuck with Lennox's magic," Rogan snarls, and the others' faces blanch.

"What?" Tad snaps, turning to me as though he knows Rogan is too lost in his guilt and anger to get details from.

I blow out a deep breath, suddenly feeling less out of control now that Rogan is feral enough for both of us. "It seems when Jamie was using her demon's magic to try and steal power from the other Osteomancers, either she or it somehow fused demon magic with that power and..." I trail off, feeling weird saying it out loud.

"And then that magic transferred to you because you were the source," Elon finishes, and my eyes flick to him, and I nod in confirmation.

"Fuck," Cohen exclaims, crossing his arms over his chest, his gaze looking far more distressed than I thought it would, given our heated exchange earlier.

"But what does that mean?" Tad demands, looking from me to Rogan.

Rogan doesn't say anything but looks over at Alora and her mates. All eyes in the room shift to the three Soul Witches too, and Dave steps forward, his hands raised as though he's trying to calm a volatile and dangerous situation. The look on Rogan's face tells me Dave has the right idea.

"Obviously, no one wants to have their magic altered in such a violating and traumatic way," he starts, and I flinch, unable to help myself, because he's not wrong.

Rogan runs his hands through his hair, and I want to reach out and offer him some comfort, but I'm not positive my legs will work right now.

"With that said, however, these changes do not have to be a bad thing. We'll need to do more research before we have exact answers, but ultimately magic is magic. We all have what the Fae bestowed on our ancestors, just in varying branches and dilutions. Right now, all we can tell is that Lennox's magic is closer to that of the Original Source before the magic was broken up into separate lines for safekeeping. Some of that will be because there are only two Osteomancers left in the world, and the magic of that line is now extremely condensed. The other part of that will be because demon magic in its nature is wilder and harder to control. It's more reminiscent of Fae magic at its purest, and therefore Lennox's power will have similar qualities or markers," Dave explains.

His words seem to be the drop of calm everyone needs, but *I* don't feel any better. Is this why my magic has been acting weird? Is this why I can now do things I couldn't before? Is this the reason why I connect with my magic differently and feel more than just bones and blood when I'm wielding it?

I think back to what happened right before Marx was killed. How it felt like my magic was suddenly this wild thing and I barely had a hold of it. Dave's words describe exactly how it felt, unruly, turbulent, and so fucking strong.

Without saying a word, Elon moves to the other side of the table and starts to clean up the shattered tea set and tray.

"I'll go get some plywood for the window," Cohen announces, and Prek declares that he'll go with him.

Tad looks at me as though he's reading my thoughts on

my forehead. I meet his eyes, and he gives me his best *well, shit* look, and I crack a small smile.

Well, shit is exactly right.

Some of the tension bleeds out of me, and Tad strides over and pulls me into a big hug. I soak up his calm affection and smile at him after he kisses the top of my head and pulls away. My smile doesn't reach my eyes though, and Tad gives me a look that says *meet me for wine on the bathroom floor later.*

"I just want to check one thing before we leave to go research what we've learned here today," Alora announces, and then she reaches for the glass container that has Rogan's blood in it and drops it into the bowl.

I'm not sure what they're looking for, but each of them stares down intensely, clearly waiting for something pivotal to happen. I look down and see that my blood is darker than Rogan's. My little tornado is still going strong, and Rogan's blood seems to swim around it as though contemplating its reaction to my blood's volatile display. All at once, Rogan's blood zips toward mine as though it were simply looking for the perfect opening, and then the two essences seem to dance with each other, spinning and chasing, and winding round one another until the darker blood and the lighter blood dissolve into one another and simply become one.

I look up to find colossal grins on each of the Soul Witches' faces. Alora looks up at me, her eyes filled with so much joy and affection.

"You two are a beautiful match. I've never seen anything like it." Tears fill her eyes, and she looks over to her wife and then her husband. They all reach for each other's hands and smile lovingly at one another before turning back to me and Rogan. "We know a thing or two about tethers and bonds, and love and matches. So trust us when we say, your bond is one for the ages."

I look at Rogan, and he turns to me. I'm floored by the look I see in his eyes, his moss-green gaze telling me loud and clear that he already knew that. Worry falls to the background as I let Alora and her mates' words sink in. A small smile creeps across my lips, and I can't deny, one for the ages feels about right.

Alora and the others start to pack up, and a tinge of panic moves through me. Is that it? *P.S. you have demon magic, but you and your boyfriend make a cute couple, so you should be good?*

"But how do we fix it?" I hurry to ask, worried they're going to disappear before Rogan and I get the answer to the question that brought them here in the first place. "How do we repair the tether?"

Harmony grins and smooths down the front of her black V-neck sweater. "You just re-tether yourselves. It's good to do it annually anyway; we've always done it on our anniversary," she tells us before giving Alora and Dave a sweet smile.

"It's best if you're as connected as you can be when you recite the incantation, both emotionally and physically, if you catch my meaning," Alora adds, and it takes me a second.

Sex?

Did Rogan's aunt just tell us to be having sex when we try to reawaken the tether?

Alora waggles her eyebrows at me, making certain we're on the same page, and I try so damn hard not to blush.

Oh god, never let her do that again.

"We just re-tether ourselves? That's it?" Rogan confirms as though he too didn't think it would be that easy.

"That's it, just recite the incantation with purpose and commitment to it, and you'll be all set," his aunt chirps, placing the last of the vials in her bag.

She reaches out for Rogan's arm, and he offers it to her and escorts her back to the front door.

"Bye, Elon, it was lovely to see you again. We're sorry we can't stay longer, but given the circumstances, it's best to get as much information as we can as quickly as we can about the bonded demon magic and what Lennox can expect to deal with down the road," Alora calls over her shoulder.

Elon sets his dust pan and hand broom down and walks over to us to disperse hugs and kisses. "We'll see you soon, I'm sure," he reassures them, and they all nod and move to head out.

Dave offers me his arm, and I take it awkwardly. Gradually we make our way to the entryway, and Dave is silent until we've almost reached the door. Slowly he leans toward me. "For the record, he does look at you with all the overwhelming love and respect and affection that I look at my wife with. Oh, and Ali Wong is hilarious, I wouldn't have minded the extra entertainment."

His smile is wide and knowing as he straightens up, pats my hand once, and then unfolds his arm from mine and moves to his wife and her wife. It takes me a moment to realize what he said, but shock and excitement rocket through me when I do.

Holy shit. I was right. Dave can read minds.

I easily recall my plan to try and catch him reacting to my thoughts on Ali Wong's jokes. But it takes me a minute to figure out what he meant by the first thing he told me. I watch the Soul Witches hug Rogan and wave goodbye to me. As they file out the front door, it suddenly dawns on me. When I first met them, Dave escorted Rogan and me into the gorgeous room with the night sky and constellations painted all over. I remember watching the way Dave looked at Alora and wishing I had someone who would look at me with such raw devotion and pure love. My eyes sting as I make the connection, and Dave shoots me a wink over his shoulder before the door is shut, and Rogan turns around to take me in.

And just like Dave said, it's there.

Despite my newfound demon blood or the crazy magic that's currently spinning in my veins. Regardless of how heinous my morning breath can be or my unhealthy addiction to coffee and grilled cheese sandwiches. My cuddle slut ways when I'm tired and the fact that I'm a nighttime farter don't matter one little bit. Because I can see it as plain as day in Rogan's gaze, just like I could in Dave's when he looked at Alora.

Rogan loves the ever-loving shit out of me, and don't I just love the ever-loving shit out of him right back.

His face is concerned, but it banks with heat as he closes the distance in two strides. I'm up and over his shoulder in less time than it takes me to squeal, and then Rogan is marching through the living room, past the kitchen, up the stairs, and into our room. He throws me on the bed like the caveman he is, and all I can say is that I am here for it.

He reaches behind him and with one hand, whips his sweater over his head in that way hot guys know how to do, and I swear I moan just from that action alone. His smile turns predatory, and suddenly my mind is pumping the brakes...hard. Rogan isn't just feeling feisty and in need of some one-on-one time with my vagina. He's ready to snap that tether back in place like it's no big deal. If I hadn't just found out that my magic has demon magic bonded to it, I would be all for it, but now I'm not so certain.

Rogan reaches for my leg and pulls off first one thick sock and then the other.

Damn, why is that so hot?

And then he grabs my leggings and pulls them off my legs.

"Rogan, wait," I pant as I scramble back on the bed to try and get away from him. He leaps for me like he's fucking Tarzan or something, and I scream way too excitedly for someone who's trying to get him to calm down and listen.

He wraps his big arms around my waist and pulls me to him, crushing his lips to mine in a kiss so searing my ancestors' toes would curl. I kiss him back just as fiercely, because how can I not, but when his hand skims under his sweater that I'm wearing to cup my breast, reality crashes down on me, and I know we need to talk first.

"Rogan, hold up, we need to think about this," I tell him, moaning and almost changing my mind when he rolls my nipple between his thumb and forefinger.

I shake my head, trying to clear it of the barrage of lusty thoughts that just avalanched through me, and slap his hand away. "Seriously, the demon magic thing is huge, and we need to talk about that before we just jump back into a tether like it's no big deal," I tell him breathily, putting space between us so he can't distract me with, well, pretty much everything about him, because *yum*.

"It's not a big deal. I love you, you love me, the tether felt right between us, and I know you want it back just as badly as I do," he tells me, and the matter-of-fact declarations melt my heart a little.

"I do love you, which is why I want us to really think about what we're doing instead of jumping in with both feet and potentially fucking something up."

"Fucking what up?" Rogan grumbles, offended.

"Oh, I don't know, like your magic for starters. Right now, mine is the only one acting all crazy, but if we jump back into a tether, mine is going to affect yours too. We don't even know what the long-term ramifications are of what Jamie did. Shouldn't we wait and get more information from your aunt and maybe a few other trusted sources before we make a decision this big?" I ask him sincerely.

"No," he counters simply. "I don't care what the long-term ramifications are. Our tether worked when you woke up the first time, and your magic didn't fuck with mine then. What makes you think it's going to start doing something crazy now? In fact, Dave said that it was more powerful and potent, not that it was dangerous, so I don't see the hesitation here," Rogan argues, and I roll my eyes.

"You are purposefully trying to be obtuse, Rogan Kendrick," I accuse. "I'm not saying the tether is off the table, I'm just saying maybe we should be sure that everything is in working order before you do something that one day you could regret."

"I am sure," he growls back, but it's the sexy kind, not the scary kind, and I try not to let him see how it affects me. "And when it comes to you, there's no such thing as regrets. Now come here so I can kiss you until you're dripping, and then bend you over and fuck you until you can't see straight, and then we can make love to one another while we tether our souls together again the right way, the way we should have done the first time," he purrs, and I huff out a sigh.

Fuck. Why does he have to make this so damn hard?

My foot starts to heat, and I roll my eyes at him. "Cut it out, I don't have a foot fetish, so you're barking up the wrong tree," I tell him as I try to figure out how to make him stop and think about what he's doing.

"Good to know," he grumbles dismissively. "Tell me what you *do* like then so I can start there, because I'm done arguing. I love you. I don't care what's mixed in your magic. I wouldn't even care if yours suddenly consumed mine and left me powerless. I love you, that means every single part of you. I know we'll figure this all out together, but I miss feeling you inside of my soul. I can't help feeling like a piece of me is missing, and I want it back, Lennox. I want *you* back right where you're always meant to stay," he pleads with me, his hand pressed against his heart as his eyes are filled with heat and beseeching.

My foot grows even hotter, distracting me from his incredible heartfelt words. "Seriously, Rogan, stop it. Messing with my blood isn't going to win you any favors. I hear what you're saying, and I want it too. I *miss* you too, I just want to make sure you know what you could be getting into before we jump in feetfirst again," I plead with him.

"Lennox, I'm all in, feet or otherwise," he counters, but just then the heat from my foot shoots up into my leg.

Out of nowhere, I feel it everywhere. My eyes widen with shock when I realize I've made a mistake. It wasn't Rogan messing with my blood.

It was the demon mark summoning me.

"Fuck," I gasp when the tugging sensation starts in my stomach. "Don't freak out," I hurriedly tell Rogan as I feel the magical hook sink into me and start to pull me away. "I love you, I'll be right back!" I shout at him as I go, but all I hear is a furious roar.

Shit, please let me be right back.

21

Bones crunch under my feet as I drop barefoot into a dimly lit cavernous room. The air is thick and stale, the walls and floor a smooth blue marble with black veining, and bones...bones are spread out as far as the eye can see. My magic prickles with their presence, greeting them like old friends, but my pulse races, and anxious butterflies flutter in my stomach furiously.

I look down to see that one of my heels has crushed a horn that was attached to a skull. I step away from it warily and survey the thick layer of osseous matter all around me. I'm surrounded by all shapes and sizes of skulls and skeletons, some with tails, others with horns, wing bones are scattered here and there, and the one thing each and every one of them has in common is that they're all demon bones.

Is that a dragon skeleton?

Unease creeps up my back as I look around me. Why am I here? Why bring me to a room filled with demon remains? Is Jamie's demon here already? Is he about to join these piles of bones, or am I?

I run my gaze over the flickering sconces on the walls. The chamber is long and empty, well, except for me and the bones, and an ominous warning curls around my shoulders like a needy cat. I should feel some sense of relief standing in a room filled with the very thing that fuels and guides my magic, but I don't.

Maybe it's the fact that I'm currently only donning Rogan's sweater, my bra and underwear, and a circumspect disposition. Or maybe my apprehension comes from the fact that the mark Dyad gave me was supposed to summon me for a trial. I look around as though maybe I missed something. There's a raised rostrum with what appears to be three lecterns placed on it, but there's no one here but me.

"Hello?" I call out, my shaky voice bouncing back at me from the walls.

The sound must displace a pile of bones, as they start to cascade down, and the sudden noise and movement has me whirling around in fear, expecting someone or something to pop out at me. I watch the bones fall down the little slope they were once perched on, reaching out with my magic to make sure there's nothing living beneath the dusty layers all around me. I don't feel anything living, but I do feel a heavy patina of death on every inch of this place.

Fuck.

I don't know what I'm doing here, but it's impossible not to get the impression that whatever the reason is, it's bad. Do they know about the demon magic now saturating my blood? Am I in trouble for having it?

I shake my head as I search the walls and ceiling for a door or seam that would hint at a way to escape. It would be just my luck that having demon magic when you're not actually a demon is considered an offence punishable by death.

A whooshing sound startles me, and all at once, the air around me is disturbed and displaced. I call on dragon ribs for weapons, ready for whatever is coming, or at least trying to look like I am.

Fake it until you make it, right?

Dyad drops down a couple feet next to me. Dust plumes all around him as he does, but not a spec dares to settle on his immaculate clothing, red skin, or long black hair, as though the dust itself is unwilling to risk the demon's wrath. The crown his horns form on his head makes him look even more regal and menacing in this light, and it makes me wonder if he actually is some kind of demon ruler. He mentioned he was a High Demon before, and I thought I knew what that meant, but now I wonder.

A woman, or rather female demon, rises up out of the ground next to Dyad, like she's a blooming plant. Instead of leaves and petals unfurling in the dim light of the space, petite milky-white limbs unfold, as does floor-length straight snow-white hair. Her face is beautiful and young, her ivory eyes lacking a pupil or any other color at all.

A grunt sounds behind me, and I turn to see a man in a gray tweed three-piece suit. He looks completely human, with light skin and short light brown hair. He smooths his suit jacket down and then looks up. I immediately take back the human designation as his glowing red eyes meet mine. He dismisses me with barely a glance, focusing his attention instead on Dyad.

"Is this the accuser?" Red Eyes asks, and his voice sounds more like the deep rumble of an earthquake than it does a voice.

"It is," Dyad confirms, not bothering to look at me either.

"Let's set up so the accused can arrive and we can get this over with," the red-eyed man-demon instructs, his tone bored and his face disinterested.

I stand there, not sure what to do. No one is addressing me, and despite my thoughts to the contrary, this *is* where the trial is going to be. A shiver moves over me as I wait and watch the three demons make their way to the platform.

They step up, Dyad grunting like his body objects to the movement, and it makes me wonder how old he is. I have no idea how long demons live, and I make a note to look into it another time.

There must be a bench or something behind the raised lecterns, because the demons sit behind them, and all of a sudden they look like three judges who are now presiding over the room. Well, minus the judges' robes and if the courtroom were a marble-encased boneyard, that is.

The sconces brighten on the wall as though someone finally found the dimmer switch and flicked it up, exposing the dark recesses of the massive room. Flickers of flame no longer make the shadows all around me dance, but seeing the magnitude of death all around me more clearly doesn't make me feel better at all. Goose bumps prick at my skin, and I don't know if it's from the bleak vibe or the fact that it's cold in here. I can't see my breath, but I feel my warmth leaching out of me, and it's all I can do not to wrap my arms around myself.

"State your name," the white-haired demon demands.

I look around, wondering who she's talking to.

"Are you deaf? I said state your name," she snaps at me, and I balk.

"Lennox Marai Osseous," I tell her, vacillating between nervous and annoyed.

"You will address me as Cozen," the white demon states. "Him as Gremory," she says, gesturing to the man-demon in tweed. "And since you filed the complaint with Dyad, you should know him already."

I nod at the names and pronouns mentioned, and Cozen continues.

"You are here accusing Count Botis the Murk of violating the Accords, is that correct?" she asks as though she's in a hurry to get this over with.

Count who? The Murk what?

"Uhhh...I don't...I don't know," I admit, looking to Dyad for help. His fixed stare on me is blank.

"You don't know if Botis violated the laws between our kinds?" she asks, clearly pissed.

Fucking hell. Someone woke up on the wrong side of hell this morning.

"I don't know the demon's name," I tell her, trying to bite back a wince at her sudden fury. "I only know what it looks like. I have no idea if Botis and the demon hunting me are the same."

Gremory snaps a finger, and out of thin air, a glass-walled cage appears to the left of me. Inside is a huge demon that seems to be wrapped in writhing shadows. I see short black flames instead of hair, and the impression of massive muscles and nudity, but the roiling darkness over its skin blurs the demon somehow. I can see it but can't focus on it enough to make the details of its body clearer. That is until it turns to me, and I see its eyes.

Every muscle in my body locks with terror. Frigid fear skitters through me like a thousand rats, and my palms start to sweat as alarm settles in my chest. The memory of agonized screams fills my ears as the demon's full onyx lips smile threateningly at me. I suddenly feel like I'm being consumed by cold fire, like I'm a lowly moth being dragged closer toward deadly flames against my will. The demon's bright orange eyes have a pupil that's slit like a goat's, and it looks me up and down lasciviously before licking its lips with a long obscene black tongue.

"Hello, Leni, it's nice to see you again."

I pale as the voice that plagued my dying breaths tries to wrap around me like a noose of shadows. Horror clamps around my chest, and my breathing picks up despite my efforts to keep it even. I turn away to look at the three higher demons who are in charge of this trial, and silently repeat a mantra I used to chant when I was a kid and afraid of the monsters under my bed.

If I can't see them, they can't see me. If I can't see them, they can't see me.

The only problem is I don't have covers to pull over my head and hide under right now, and I really fucking wish I did. I want to move away from the glass cage, worried that the walls aren't strong enough to contain something so heinous, but I stay where I am partly because I don't want to show fear and partly because I'm too terrified to make my legs work. I try to swallow, but my throat feels dry as fuck.

"Is this the demon you're accusing?" Gremory asks, his face still the epitome of *over it*.

"Y-yes," I stammer, hating how fucking weak I sound, but I'm standing next to something that haunts my nightmares, and as much as I hate it, there's not a lot I can do about the wobble in my voice. Hopefully, this will go quickly, they'll kill this fucker, and I can go home and rest easier knowing Count Botis the Murk's bones are down here rotting until they're dust.

"And you attest that you have no contract with this demon and that you are not owned by anyone who does?" Cozen demands.

"Yes," I announce, glad at least that I didn't stutter that time.

Cozen turns her bored white eyes to the demon next to me and surveys him. I look up at Dyad, trying to get a feel for what's going to happen, but his black eyes are also on the Count. The title *count* makes me nervous. I don't know if it has the same standing with demons as it does with humans, but I don't like the idea of this demon's position affording him special favors or sway, especially when that special favor could be my death. Or my attempted death.

Fuck, what are they going to do to me when they realize I can't die?

I immediately shut down the horrid options that flash through my mind with that question, and tell myself it'll be fine.

This is a trial.

I have solid evidence.

Everything is going to be okay.

My heart hammers harder in my chest, and I swear I can hear the rapid beat echoing quietly around the marble room.

"How do you plea, Botis?" Dyad asks, and I think I see a glare in his eyes.

"Not guilty, of course," Botis purrs, the sound more akin to nails on a chalkboard, and I wince, which makes the orange-eyed demon laugh.

I shake my head, feeling like I'm going to cry and trying to tamp it down with everything in me. All the demons in the room turn to me expectantly.

You can do this, Lennox. Just lay out the facts plain and simple.

"This demon helped kidnap and kill Osteomancers in an effort to steal their magic. I was taken and saw with my own eyes the possession and ritual the demon participated in to illegally steal magic that never belonged to him or the human he was working with. He killed that human and then possessed a new one and then showed up where I was staying for no other reason than to fuck with me. I don't have a contract with him. I don't owe him anything, and yet he won't leave me alone, which is a violation of the Accords. Also, the fact that I can sense him and the danger he tries to put me in, further supports that he broke the Accords? My understanding is that's a failsafe worked into the agreement, so I would like to point that out as more evidence that he broke the law," I declare, looking at Dyad, who told me that's how the failsafe worked.

"The sensing him in your realm is an element of proof, but if we're going to sentence a Count to death for violating the Accords, we're going to need more proof than your good eyesight," Gremory snaps.

I balk, not sure what to think about that. I just gave him my other proof. *Was that not enough?*

The three demons ruling over this trial all turn to Botis as though this is some fucked up tennis match and it's his turn to serve.

"I *did* have a contract, and Leni here is collateral from that *sanctioned agreement*. I would also like to claim damages because this little cunt interfered with my contract and cost me the agreed upon return," he argues, and my stomach drops.

He can't be serious. Damages?

My head snaps to the three demons at his words, and I reel when each of them looks thoughtful. Are they really considering what he's saying? He didn't even provide any proof. Is his *claim* more important than my evidence? Panic starts to layer in my chest, and I immediately wonder what the hell I've gotten myself into. I thought this would be the best avenue for dealing with the demon, but now I'm terrified I've somehow dug a bigger hole for myself.

"Interfered how?" Dyad demands, only this time the glare he's wearing is for me.

Shit, what have I done?

"She killed a soul that belonged to me, which kept me from collecting the agreed upon terms," Botis states bored, and rage fires through me.

"That is a lie," I yell, suddenly afraid they'll believe anything and everything this monster says. "I never killed Jamie, he did. And the agreed upon terms was magic that didn't belong to either of them. You can't have a contract with someone promising you magic that they don't own," I argue, hoping like hell I'm right.

Out of nowhere, Botis charges his glass cage. "Don't you dare speak over me," he snarls, and I scramble back, too afraid to even scream. Thank fuck the glass holds as he slams into it. His sharp-tipped teeth gnash as though he's wishing he was chewing on my bones right now, and his orange eyes are filled with unhinged rage as they track my every move.

"It would have been my fucking magic if you hadn't gotten involved. You fucked up what should have been mine, and I'll take it from you one way or another," he bellows, the force of his words escaping his enclosure and blowing curls out of my face. I feel like I'm seconds away from being torn apart.

"Silence," Dyad shouts, and even though I can still see Botis ranting inside the glass enclosure, I can't hear him anymore.

"Is what the witch said true? You were using a human to kill Osteomancers in order to take their magic?" Cozen demands, and I notice that she conjures a glass orb that looks like it has some kind of vapor trapped inside and sets it in front of her.

Botis eyes the orb and then sneers at her. "Yes," he admits, almost begrudgingly, and the orb glows white.

"Then the witch is correct, you can't have a contract promising magic that doesn't belong to you or the person the contract's with," Gremory declares, and suddenly there's a gavel in his hand. "Trying to steal what never belonged to you or the being you're in contract with is a violation of our laws."

I hold my breath, too stunned to believe that this could actually be it. Did I pull it off? Did I prove my case?

Gremory holds up the gavel. "As the High Demon Council presiding over this trial, we find you—"

"Wait!" Botis screams so loudly that I swear the glass around him rattles. "I'm not done," he growls more quietly, now that Gremory is silent. "The contract I'm talking about wasn't with the human. It was with the High Council."

A loud whooshing sound fills the room, and dread pools inside of me as Botis's declaration rings around the room, and other people suddenly appear. I turn around slowly, and my eyes meet a kelly-green stare framed by dark lashes and a beautiful oval face. Long pitch black hair falls past her shoulders, and the white streak at the front looks elegant as always. She's in a pant suit that matches her eyes, and there's a gold pentagram broach that's pinned to the lapel.

Just like the first time I met Rogan's mother, Sorrel Adair, the High Priestess of Witches, stands behind her husband the High Priest, and her Council member, Bordow, the Contegomancer who murdered Marx.

Sirens blare in my brain, and it's all I can do not to scream.

I knew it. I fucking knew it. I didn't know how or why Sorrel Adair would be messing with demons, but I felt in my bones that her hand was in this somehow. I thought it was Jamie who could possibly be working with the High Council, but it was the demon. Botis is the connection, not her.

Fuck my life and fuck Sorrel Adair.

I want to rage and scream and wipe her evil presence from the face of all realms, but I need to keep control. I need to figure out how to beat this bitch at her own game.

"What the hell is going on? You have not been summoned here," Dyad growls, and the High Priestess fixes him with a smile so saccharine it makes my skin crawl.

"Oh," she chirps in faux surprise. "It seems you started without us. Shame really, you know the Accords allow for a mancer representative to be present at all trials," she declares sweetly.

"Mancer representatives never attend these trials because they can't be bothered, and you know it," Gremory states irritably.

"Well, then it's your lucky day, because we'll be sitting in on this one," Sorrel declares as though somehow she's running the show.

My gut twists, and I realize she probably has been. Maybe I didn't see it up close and personal, but she's been pulling strings and forcing our hand the entire time. Anger battles with the overwhelming desire to puke, but I press them both back and level Gremory with a frustrated look.

I don't know what the hell is going on right now, but shit just went from bad to fucking catastrophic real quick, and I'm getting the very distinct impression I am fucked.

"Do all demons bow so easily to the High Council?" I challenge, hoping somehow it will focus the High Demon's anger on Sorrel and not me for calling him out. "One demon says he has a contract with them, and now you're pretending like she's simply sitting in on a trial and not the reason why we're having one?" I accuse, both pissed and terrified in equal measure.

How the hell does this bitch have so much power? She just saunters in like she owns this place and they all let her. Fuck, maybe she does own this place. What the hell do I even know anymore?

My brain whirs as I try to figure out all the angles of what the fuck is going down right now. I know I've walked into a trap, that's obvious, but I have no idea how wide the net is. I don't know how she's going to do it, but I have no doubt in my mind that this is all about getting to her sons, and what's worse is I don't know if I can stop it.

I reach for the tether instinctively, wanting to call Rogan

and warn him, but my heart plummets through my chest when I feel that it's still closed.

Fuck. Fuck. Fuck.

The High Priestess just showed her hand, and I can't even warn Rogan and Elon that she's coming for them. I can feel her stare on the back of my head like hot lasers, but I ignore it as I try to see a way out of this mess.

"Is that true, Adair? Do you confirm that you have a contract with Botis?" Cozen asks, and I swear the white demon suddenly looks ashen.

High heels click on the marble floor, a stiff breeze removing bones from the High Priestess's path. She passes me without so much as a glance and moves to step in front of Botis's glass prison.

She takes in the three High Demons seated behind the lecterns and then turns to wink at Botis. Fear rips through my entire body as she turns back to Cozen with a haughty look.

"Yes, I do have a contract with Botis the Murk," Sorrel Adair finally confesses, and everything in me wants to explode and implode at the same time.

Rogan's dad, the High Priest, walks confidently past me to join his wife, but I don't focus on him, as I fully freak the fuck out. I have to get out of here, but I have no idea how. This trial was pure bullshit, I was never going to win, and she's here to make sure of it. I try not to think of all the ways I could be used against Rogan or what Sorrel will do when she finally gets what she wants. If these demons think she won't come for them and their power, they're as stupid as I am for not seeing this was a trap.

Suddenly I see Bordow in my periphery. I watch as the asshole blows a mocking kiss at me, and abruptly I'm back in the clearing, grass sticking to my knees, bones calling to my magic, and death thick on the back of my tongue as I watch a bullet pierce the forehead of my friend. I blink and Marx's face is gone, but Bordow is still there arrogantly striding past me. Something vicious and animalistic takes over. I stop caring about where I am and what they'll do to me if I give into the drive to hurt this murdering motherfucker. I suddenly want to kill them all, and what do I have to lose? I'm fucked either way.

One second, rage is climbing up my throat so fast that I can't even breathe, and then the next, my fist is connecting with Bordow's face so hard that I feel his cheek and jaw shatter. Sorrel's head snaps in my direction, and I'm suddenly being thrown back by a brutal breeze. It slams me into the blue marble wall so hard that if I hadn't just called on magic to fortify my bones, the hit would have broken far more than just my back and skull.

I call on the bones in the room while also looking for a line or something that might get me out of here. Everything feels as though it's moving in fast forward, and I watch Bordow fall to the ground, clutching his face, as I slide down the wall and tap into all the bones in this room. I can hear yelling and see the three demons rising up out of their seats to try and regain control of the chaos. I will the demon bones all around me to sharpen, ready to put up the fight of my life, but out of nowhere, water somehow fills my airway. My eyes go wide and I lose my focus, my magic snapping back to me like it's a hand that was just slapped for being naughty.

I try to cough, but nothing I do clears the water enough to let oxygen in. I clutch my throat, scratching at the skin as I drown from the inside out. Frantically I look around for help, and bright orange goat eyes find mine as I fall to my side, desperate and begging for air. Black dots start to cloud my vision, but I can still see both the demon and the High

Priestess smiling at me as they stand there and watch me die.

I glare defiantly at Rogan's mother, fucking Circummancer and her elemental magic. Water spills into my lungs, and my body does everything it can to expel it, to no avail. I see Bordow kneeling on the ground, clutching his face, and satisfaction blooms in my chest.

That one's for you, Marx.

22

I feel like I'm going to shatter my own vertebrae from the force it takes to try and purge water from my lungs. I hack and gag and gasp, bent over and dizzy as Dyad slams his large red hand against my back.

"You will stop right now, or I fucking vow I will hold you in contempt for the maximum sentence outlined in the Accords," Gremory bellows at the High Priestess, and with a huff like someone just took away her favorite toy, Sorrel Adair stops using her magic on me.

The water immediately evaporates from my chest and throat, and I choke on air as I try to pull it into me. I gulp down huge greedy swallows of oxygen and try to fight the residual panic coursing through me that I'm not pulling air in fast enough. Dyad bends over me, blocking the rest of the room from my line of sight, which is probably a good thing, because I'm shaky as hell from what the High Priestess just did to me, and water isn't even her strongest element.

Fucking hell.

Despair and anger war inside of me, and I try to get a hold of all my runaway emotions so I can shove them behind a hard mask of anger. I rub at my throat, and Dyad looks me over as I desperately try to figure out how to win against someone who's never lost before. I feel like I'm playing chess against a fucking Grandmaster and all I know how to do is play checkers. Every time I get close to yelling *king me*, this bitch is over here cackling *checkmate*.

"I don't give a shit who you are," Cozen screeches behind me. "You are not here under the capacity of the High Priestess of Witches, you are a witness in a trial, and you will stand there and shut the fuck up until one of us asks you a question. Am I clear?" she snaps at Sorrel, and I decide I like the white-haired demon.

"The same goes for you, Osteomancer, keep your magic to yourself and obey the rules of this court or face the consequences," she snaps at me.

And...it seems I spoke too soon.

Dyad moves away from me now that I'm once again breathing, and I catch the frigid glare Cozen is aiming at me. I debate the merit of pointing out that I didn't use my magic to assault Bordow, I used my fist, but I figure it's best to just stay quiet at this point. I nod instead, standing up and walking slowly and shakily back to where I was before Rogan's evil bitch of a mother sent me flying.

I observe Bordow standing on the far side of Botis's cage, still clutching his face, but my attempts to escape or *take everyone in this room out while trying* just failed miserably, and all I can focus on is what's coming. Sorrel Adair is going to tighten the noose and then use me as bait to catch her sons. I know it.

"Now, if we're done fucking around, let's get back to the point of this trial," Cozen snaps, as though everything that just happened was a mild inconvenience and not evidence that this entire thing is a fucking sham.

I stare at the three High Demons presiding over this shit show and wonder if they all have contracts with the High Council too. They start to discuss something between themselves, but I can't make out a word of it. Looking to my left, I find Botis staring at me hungrily, and it makes my blood run cold. All I can see is Jamie summoning him, and his shadows bending her over an altar stained with countless witches' blood, as he fucked her and branded another contract into her skin.

I shove away the visual and try to think through the dread that's starting to weigh me down. If Botis's end goal wasn't Jamie, but Sorrel, what would the High Priestess want in order to make that deal? I shake my head at that stupid question. She would want what she's always wanted: Elon and Rogan's secret.

I do my best to ignore the demon who's still watching me like he's making a list of all the things he's going to do to me when he gets out of that cage, and turn my attention to Sorrel, who's focused on the arguing High Demons.

Jamie was clearly the cover. The High Council stole her magic, then dangled a carrot of power, set her up with the demon, and let her loose to kidnap Elon and the others. I'm sure she was hoping that Rogan would trade the information his parents wanted for his brother's safe return, or she hoped Elon would break from the torture and give it up himself. Sorrel wouldn't have cared if the demon made a side deal with Jamie for the magic, because the end goal for Sorrel Adair was something more important to her...immortality.

My thoughts swirl around in my head, and I try to lay them all out in front of me in an effort to make sense of all of this, but they don't seem to fit together quite right yet. The thing that I can't figure out is what my part was in all of this. Was I really just collateral damage, one more string to pull to get Rogan to do what she wanted?

"Enough," Dyad snaps at the two other demons next to him. "This is a simple matter of whether Count Botis the Murk violated the Accords. The presence of members of the High Council shouldn't fucking matter, because the trial is Botis's, not theirs. This is still within our remit, and that's fucking final," Dyad declares, and Cozen and Gremory both close their mouths and swallow whatever was left of their arguments.

I watch them, confused, but I don't miss the satisfied look on the High Priestess's face, and it makes my skin crawl.

"Botis," Dyad barks, "explain how your actions are covered in your contract with the High Council, and do it quickly. I've had enough of all the bullshit."

The murdering Contegomancer, Bordow, and Rogan's dad move behind Botis's glass cage as though they're trying to move out of the way. Sorrel stands at the front, her control over the situation clear, and Botis is as close to me as the back corner of his glass walls will allow him to be.

Fucking creeper.

"I contracted with these three members of the High Council to capture, detain, and then hand over Elon Kendrick and Rogan Kendrick. I bartered for the High Council members' souls and magic upon death and for the branch of Osteomancer magic to be held as collateral until the three promised souls were collected," Botis declares evenly, and the three High Demons all look shocked as fuck.

"Are you seriously telling me that the High Priest and Priestess of Witches sold you their souls and magic, all so that you would kidnap their sons?" Gremory demands, utterly flabbergasted.

I stare at Sorrel, confused. Why go through all that trouble just to take Rogan and Elon? Why the huge, convoluted ruse just to...and then I realize why. The High Priestess of Witches doesn't get her hands dirty. She needed someone not just to steal Elon and Rogan, but to fucking torture them until they broke. Who better to do that than a demon? Of course she sold her soul; she knows as soon as she gets what she wants from her sons, she'll never have to fulfill her end of the bargain because she'll never die.

Disgust overflows into every inch of me. What kind of mother—fuck that, she was never worthy of that title—what kind of person is capable of such loathsome atrocities against another person, let alone someone related to you by blood?

"Yes, that is my contract," Botis replies smugly.

Gremory looks at the High Priestess like he still doesn't believe it. "He's telling the truth," she informs him, looking just as pleased as Botis does.

"Fine, she has a contract with him, but Rogan and Elon are not minors, they're adult mancers. This bitch doesn't own them. What she wants doesn't override their rights under witch law or the Accords," I point out, remembering Prek's first demon case and how shocked I was that the man traded his children to a demon.

Prek explained that there is a death loophole that allows a demon to kill as part of their contract as long as there aren't any relatives to file a complaint about the death, but Elon and Rogan can't die and they absolutely can file a complaint about being kidnapped and having their rights violated.

"Well, little Osteomancer, I am Witch Law, but even if that weren't the case, I do own Elon and Rogan, and I can do whatever I damn well please with them, including trade them to a demon if I want to," she coos at me, and bile and rage crawl up my throat. "In fact, the both of them are key components to this case, and I request that they be summoned here to join us."

My heart turns to lead and crashes down through my body like a runaway elevator.

No.

They can't come here. She'll get exactly what she wants if they do.

Sorrel observes the alarm etched all over my face, and she smiles. I flounder, trying to figure out how to stop this.

"No," I shout out, and the High Demons turn to me. "They have nothing to do with this and shouldn't be here. This is between me and Botis, not between this piece of shit and the sons she's trying to have tortured," I plead.

"We have no way of summoning them last minute unless either of them has a contract we can use—do they?" Gremory asks, his red eyes boring into the High Priestess.

"Why, yes, actually," she answers sweetly, and her response sends me reeling.

Elon and Rogan don't have demon marks, what the hell is she talking about?

"If you check the inside wrist of the Osteomancer there, you'll find a vow that connects her to Rogan. He'll be able to confirm ownership, and this trial can be done once and for all," she declares haughtily, and everything inside of me is lost to panic.

No, no, no, no.

She can't do that.

I can't let her trick them into trapping Rogan down here too.

"I take it back," I yell, my declaration echoing off the walls and bones all around me. The terror and panic in my tone slaps me around like it's a prized fighter and I'm an amateur. "I take back my complaint. Do whatever the hell you want to punish me, but I'm done with this. I'm not going to keep playing into this fucking monster's hands," I snarl at the High Demons, tears welling in my eyes.

I reach for the tether again, but I can't feel or send anything. *Fuck.* I don't know if they're going to put me in demon jail or give me to Botis. I'm not even sure which of those options might be worse or if there's something else they do to people who make false claims.

Will Rogan ever know what happened to me? Will he ever forgive me for not coming back like I promised?

My throat grows tight with emotion, but I square my shoulders and promise myself I'll get through whatever it is they're going to do to me. I know Sorrel won't give up, that she'll keep going at Rogan and Elon, but I can only hope that this will buy them time and they'll be ready for her when she comes for them again.

"It doesn't work that way, Osteomancer," Cozen informs me, and I swear I see a hint of empathy gleaming in her white eyes. "Once the trial has started, it doesn't stop unless the accused is found guilty or not guilty. You can't end it simply because you want to, and you can't retract the statements that you've already made to the court."

"So find him not guilty then. Send me on my way, and the next time that fucker shows up anywhere near me, I'll kill him and whoever sent him," I seethe at the white demon, desperation crawling up my throat and strangling my words. "Please," I finally break and beg. "Please," I say again, pleading for her to help me keep the man I love away from this evil.

She drops her eyes from mine, and it's as though she's reached into my chest and ripped all the hope away.

Sorrel chuckles quietly, like my pain is the funniest thing she's seen in a while. "I really should thank you, Lennox," she chirps at me, her eyes filled with nothing but cruelty. "You made all of this far easier than even I could have hoped for."

The rage that's been festering inside of me since I first

laid eyes on her boils over. Bones snap up around me at my order, ready and waiting to be told where to stab, bludgeon, and maim. But before I can so much as breathe in her direction, glass walls slam down all around me. Shock and then fury tsunami through me, and I scream as I pound on the glass cage.

"You fucking bitch! You leave them alone, you power-hungry whore!" I bellow at the top of my lungs as impotent tears drip down my face. I bang on the glass so hard my hands start to bruise, and try as I might, I can't use my magic in here.

Dyad steps down from the dais and walks over to me. Without warning, I'm slammed against the glass wall in front of me, and my hand is forced out of the glass as though there's a perfectly designed hatch to hold my arm in place. I scream and thrash as I try to pull Rogan's vow mark back into the safety of the cage. I even try to break my own arm in order to regain control of the limb, but nothing works.

Dyad does something to my mark, and I feel a jolt of power rush through it. "You fucking liar," I snarl at him. "You set me up, I know you did," I screech, my face and features the epitome of madness as I try everything I can not to let this happen, but I was fucked before I ever even got here.

Sobs wrack my body, and I cry even harder as a whooshing sound fills this godforsaken room, and then out of nowhere, Rogan is suddenly there, and I know I've failed miserably.

He looks around confused, and then like I'm a beacon that's calling him, moss-green eyes land on mine. He pales as he sees my face, and then fury quickly takes over, and he sprints toward me. I look over to see his mother watching him like the prize she thinks he is, and I feel sick.

A loud boom sounds off all around me, and I see Rogan

punching the glass to try to get to me. I run to the back side of the cage and press my palms against the glass to make him stop.

"What the fuck is going on?" he bellows, turning his attention from me to the three demons at the front of the massive room.

"Osteomancer Osseous is only in there because she violated the rules of this court by trying to attack someone...again. The sooner you tell us what we need to know, the sooner this trial will end and the sooner she will be let out," Gremory tells him, his tone clipped and exasperated.

"Let her out and I'll answer your questions," Rogan tries to bargain, but Gremory just glares at him.

I stare at Rogan, willing him to feel how sorry I am for bringing him here. I know what his mom has planned for him, and like a fucking idiot, I walked in here and basically handed him over on a silver platter. Anguish washes through me, and I press my palm to his as he focuses on Gremory and darts suspicious looks at his mother.

I'm sure he's trying to figure out what the hell is going on, but his perfect poker face is locked down tight now, and I know he won't let it crack for anything.

"Sorrel Adair has claimed she owns you and your brother, is this true?" Dyad asks. I stare at Rogan, waiting for him to laugh or sneer or do anything other than what he does, which is nothing. From this close, I see a slight tightening around his eyes, and it's all I need to see to know we've lost.

Tears drip steadily down my eyes as Sorrel turns to her son expectantly. "Come now, Rogan, tell the High Demon all about how you swore fealty to me," she orders him, a greedy glint in her kelly-green eyes.

I shake my head as though it will erase the truth of what

she just said, but Rogan pulls in a deep breath and squares his gaze on her.

"I was barely eighteen," he argues, and she tilts her head mockingly at him.

"Still counts," she purrs.

"I'm a renounced witch, how the fuck does that still count?" he snarls at her, and she steps closer to him.

"Because I say it does," she counters, all pretense of sweetness gone.

Her words strike right through like a lightning bolt of *holy shit*, and I push away from the back corner of my cage and rush to the front. I slam a battered palm against the glass to pull the High Demons' attention back to me.

"He may have sworn fealty to her, but I never have," I yell at them, my heart hammering desperately inside my chest for this to somehow work. "She may own him, but she doesn't own me, which means she contracted with Botis for magic that she had no right to. Just like Jamie did," I point out.

"Nice try, Osteomancer, but when Rogan tethered the two of you, *his* fealty became *yours*," she snaps at me, clearly ready to be done with this and off with her prize.

I go still as her words batter around my mind. I study each and every syllable, every breath between the words of her statement, trying to see if there could be some other interpretation. But I don't see one, and a small flicker of hope sparks in my chest because...I think I've got her. My eyes sharpen as I look around the room warily, worried that somehow the truth I just stumbled across will be ripped out of my desperate clutches and stomped to pieces on the ground in front of me, but no one is paying me any attention. No one knows that I just found the key.

Holy fucking shit, I think I've got her.

"Is that true?" I ask, my voice dry and my heart racing as I try to sound as feeble and small as I can. "If Rogan bound me to him, then his fealty is my fealty?" I demand, and the High Demons all turn to me.

"Yes," Cozen replies, and I've never wanted to hug a word so hard in my fucking life.

Hope and a trill of triumph builds in my chest, but I lock it all away as I nod my acceptance at what Cozen just confirmed. "Then I would like to point out that Rogan didn't tether me to him, *I* tethered him to *me*. So in that case, *my* fealty is *his*, and I'd like to make it crystal fucking clear that I have none," I inform them, my tone lethal and my eyes fixed on Rogan's mother.

Her mask cracks slightly, not enough to drop the confident smile from her face, but I see her dart a look back to her husband, and it's all I can do not to crow out my victory. Rogan and I aren't owned by anyone but each other, and that means the High Priestess of Witches promised things to a demon that she wasn't allowed to barter with, and in turn they both violated the Accords.

King me, bitch.

"Is that true?" Dyad asks Rogan.

"Yes," Rogan affirms, a hint of astonishment clear in his tone. "I initially formed a familiar bond, but it was Lennox who established the tether, not the other way around. A Soul Witch could confirm it for you," he tells them, but all the demons turn to the orb in front of Cozen, and when it glows white, they nod their head like that's all the proof they need.

The room is quiet for a beat, like no one knows what to do with this unexpected twist, and then all at once the High Demons start to argue with each other, and Botis starts to pace in his cage. His orange eyes bounce from the High

Priestess to the High Demons, rage frothing at his full lips as he worries the floor with his feet.

I try to hear what they're arguing about, but it's all a jumble of whispers, and I can't identify any words or sentences. I work hard to rein in my fervent hope and see how Sorrel could try to counter this. I try to see the loopholes in the facts like I know she's doing right now.

My hands are shaky with adrenaline, and when I look over at Rogan, I see that he's staring at his mother with so much hate and vehemence it makes the hair on my arms rise in warning, but what really pisses me off is that she's staring right back at him, and I can practically see the declaration in her kelly-green eyes that no matter what happens, he belongs to her.

Botis snarls menacingly, and it snaps Sorrel out of her staring contest. She says something to the demon—I don't catch it—but it was something condescending by the look on her face, and Botis redirects all the creepy obsession and silent promises of pain that he was aiming at me, and focuses it all on the High Priestess.

The High Demons stop discussing amongst themselves, and I hold my breath as I wait to see what they'll say. Silence fills the marble boneyard, and all I can hear is the boom of my pulse in my ears. Out of nowhere, I blink and the glass case all around me disappears.

I gasp, and more adrenaline fires through me when I look up and once again find that the High Demon Gremory has a gavel in his hand.

"This High Demon Council finds the contract between Count Botis the Murk and the High Council of Witches...invalid," Gremory announces, his rumbling earthquake tone forcing me to not only hear his words but feel them as they move through the room. "As such," he continues, "Botis is found guilty of violating the Accords."

My head snaps in the direction of Jamie's demon as he bellows out his objection. "You fucking cunt, you did this, you slippery viper. If you think you're safe, you have another thing coming! I own your soul, you stupid whore," he snarls at the High Priestess as he attacks the front of his cage with nothing but pure rage and fury. "I was tricked! I demand the contract be reviewed!" Botis screams, but the gavel is already slamming down against the wood of the lectern.

Botis's furious threats and demands morph into visceral feral screams as blue flames erupt inside his glass cage. He attacks the glass barrier with renewed ferocity, and I can feel the ground shaking with each hit against the barrier separating his madness from us.

"I'm going to rip you all to pieces and bathe in your innards. I am Count Botis the Murk, you cannot sentence me to death," he rages as the flames grow taller. He screams and snarls as the shadows coating him fade away against the flames. He starts to attack every wall of his enclosure, and then the blue fire is so high that it's all I can see anymore.

I breathe through the panic that crashes through me. It's the justice he deserves, but his visceral keening as he dies takes me back to the church, and I feel achy with terror as the memories breathe threateningly down my neck. Strong arms wrap around me, pulling me in tightly, and Rogan presses my face to his chest as he discreetly covers my ears to help block the sound.

"You did it, Lennox. You won. He's gone and he's never coming back," Rogan chants quietly to me to help drown out the noise of my brutal memories. I'm surprised to hear such confidence in his voice, like he always knew this would be the case, he never even doubted I might not pull it off.

I shake my head, reeling and in shock over what just happened. It all feels so surreal. I thought for sure it was over, and then it wasn't.

Did I really just figure out how to climb out of that trap?

I know in the long run, this win doesn't mean shit. Sorrel is just going to keep coming for us until we find some way to beat her, but we'll at least live to see another day, have more time to plan for the next attack, and we'll be together. I hug Rogan so hard he grunts from the impact. I feel him press a kiss to the top of my head, and I vow that as soon as we get home, I'm reactivating this tether no matter what. Not being able to reach him was the worst fucking feeling, and I will never let it happen again.

The screams stop, but I can hear the flames still crackling as they finish the rest of Botis off. Out of nowhere, a flash of familiar icy pain moves through me. My gasp is hidden in Rogan's chest, and as he feels my muscles tighten and strain from the sudden assault, he holds me protectively closer.

"What's wrong, Lennox? What just happened?" he asks distraughtly, and I can feel him scanning the room for the source of this attack. I shake my head against his chest, but it's all I can do until the icy clutches of agony start to abate.

Deep breaths, Lennox, this is not your first rodeo, it'll be over soon. Just breathe.

Dyad stands behind the lectern, his crown of horns making him appear regal and superior. I want to punch him for it. His black eyes take in everyone in the room, and he lifts his chin haughtily. "I officially call the trial of Count Botis the Murk to an end," he announces, and I look up through the pain to see the High Council members all together again and glaring up at the demons. "I warn the other parties present, specifically the three High Council members, that they are facing future charges for their role in today's events. I also warn that Botis's next in line will inherit all open contracts, and that their legal bargains with him are still active contracts."

I watch the three High Council members' reactions to Dyad's declaration. I expect to find fear or apprehension or at the least a slight bit of concern, but Sorrel once again looks smug, like she knows something the rest of us don't, and it makes my stomach churn with vicious anxiety.

The pain in my body starts to recede, and I relax in Rogan's arms. He breathes out a sigh of relief and drops his lips to my ear so no one else can hear.

"What just happened, are you okay?"

I nod against his chest and whisper back, "It was a transference of power," I explain, confusion percolating through me, because I thought Elon and I were the only Osteomancers left, and Elon can't transfer power to me because he can't die.

And then it dawns on me.

I look down at my feet, parts of them still stinging from the power I just absorbed. Shock makes me freeze, and my eyes widen as a new shot of adrenaline courses through me. I stare dumbfoundedly at the demon marks now decorating my skin. I trace the lacey circles with my eyes, identifying a mark with the letter *A* in it, one with a *K*, and the last one contains a *B*. Unlike my vow mark with Rogan, the demon marks are black, and I know without a shadow of doubt what just happened.

Holy moon shits.

That wasn't a transference of magic from an Osteomancer, that was a transference from the fucking demon, Botis.

Which means...

My head snaps up just as Dyad stops talking and Gremory prepares to pound his gavel again and end this trial once and for all.

I step forward, but Rogan keeps an arm draped over my

shoulder protectively. "Wait," I cry out before the gavel can meet the dark wood of the lectern.

Gremory groans, looking thoroughly pissed. And the High Priestess's shrewd eyes narrow at me.

"What the fuck is it now?" Gremory snaps, but I'm too fucking shocked and excited by what I just discovered to let it get to me.

"You said that the next in line inherited their contracts, is that correct?" I ask, gesturing to the High Council members, who have already turned to leave.

"Yes, now fuck off already," he growls, raising the gavel again.

"Sorry, just a couple more questions," I rush to add, and he shoots me a glare that threatens to burn me alive if I don't shut the fuck up.

I'm not cowed.

"Each of the High Council members lied in their contracts with Botis and then also violated the Accords; isn't that going to be dealt with?" I demand, and Rogan gives me a warning squeeze around my shoulders as Dyad also shoots me a glare.

"Yes, we've already established that the consequences will be determined by Botis's next in line. The heir can decide if they want to call in the contracts early or simply assign a penalty," Dyad announces, annoyed.

"Either way, that has nothing to do with you, Osteomancer," the High Priestess snaps. "Are we done here?" she demands, already skirting Botis's bones to leave. "And before you get too excited, I've already ensured that Botis was the last of his line," Sorrel tells me, a vicious smirk painted on her face. I can practically see the wheels turning in her mind as she already starts to plot and plan her next move.

My smile grows wider, and victory sings in my veins as I

look up at the three High Demons. "Then, as Botis's next in line and the new owner of the High Council members' contracts, I'd like to call in *my* contracts early," I inform them evenly, my head high and my heart screaming with excitement.

That's checkmate, you evil cunt.

23

Outrage and shock bombard me from all angles. And maybe it's all this new demon magic that I just inherited, but I'm feeling smug as fuck.

"What the hell are you talking about?" Dyad snarls.

Sorrel looks at me as though I've lost my mind. "That's not possible," she declares dismissively.

Rogan just looks at me, stunned, his gaze dropping to my feet as he makes the same connection I just did.

The High Priestess sneers at me as though she's calling what she thinks is my bluff. I don't say anything, perfectly happy to let her think she's about to walk out of here. The Crone knows, Sorrel Adair has fucked with me enough times for me to appreciate the importance of dangling the carrot and then snatching it away at the last possible moment.

Unfortunately for them, the carrot I'm dangling is their souls, and there's absolutely zero chance that they'll be leaving anywhere with those anymore. The High Priestess doesn't get that yet, but she will. Soon.

She turns on her heel and motions for the other two to

follow her as she tries to leave. I turn calmly to Dyad, my eyes icy and commanding.

"I am Botis's next in line. His transference of power occurred at the precise moment he died. If you don't believe me, check, I don't care," I tell him evenly. "But I suggest you stop them from leaving," I add, gesturing to the High Council members, "or I'll personally hold you responsible for allowing three souls that I own to escape," I threaten, eyeing the High Demons, officially done with all the bullshit.

They wanted to play when I was just a lowly Osteomancer, let's see how well they do with a level playing field.

Dyad debates for all of two seconds. Oddly, I feel the moment Sorrel and the others call on whatever magic brought them here. It's not a ley line, but close. I didn't feel it before, but I certainly do now. Interesting.

"Stop!" Dyad orders, and the High Priestess extends a murderous look at him for the command.

"You can't be serious. What? Do High Demons now entertain every impossible and ridiculous claim that crosses their paths these days? Maybe you have time to waste, but I certainly don't," she snaps at him, and I can't help but smile when a strand of white hair falls in her face.

Awww, is the High Priestess feeling a little flustered?

Rogan watches everything with a stoic, guarded expression, and I wish more than anything I could feel what he's feeling right now.

"If you make one more move to leave after you've been ordered to stay, I will consider it an act of war. Think very carefully, High Priestess, about whether you have time to deal with *that*," Dyad snarks, and if I didn't hate his guts, I'd be offering him an *oh snap*.

Sorrel practically snarls and pushes the errant strand of hair out of her face with such force I'm surprised she doesn't just rip the traitorous thing from her scalp altogether. I look over at Rogan's dad, whose name I can never remember, and wonder if the man ever talks or reacts to anything. I suspect his wife might have had him lobotomized at some point, but who the fuck knows. Bordow, however, looks like he has a better understanding of the severity of the situation. His olive skin is waxy, and his eyes dart around the room like he's waiting for the shadows to come and eat him.

"You have exactly five minutes to make it very clear why you're detaining us, or *I* will consider this an act of war," the High Priestess barks as she marches back over to stand in front of Botis's bones.

Dyad looks over to Gremory and then to Cozen and nods. Gremory disappears without a word, and Sorrel grumbles something under her breath. I've never seen her so out of sorts, and I look over to Rogan to see what he thinks about it. He slips me a sly wink and then moves closer to me so that his arm is brushing mine, and I bite back the smile that wants to sneak across my face.

I pull in a deep breath and try to put my game face on as Cozen's haunting white eyes fix on me and she looks me over. Her gaze stops on my feet, and instead of seeing shock in her gaze, I think I see...satisfaction.

"What exactly makes you think you are Botis's heir?" she asks me, her eyes alight with the answer already.

"Something happened when Botis kidnapped and tried to kill me. I don't know what exactly it was, but it bonded his magic with mine." The orb in front of Cozen blinks white, and I'm a little surprised, although maybe I shouldn't be.

I *technically* have an idea of how Botis accidentally bonded his magic to mine, but I'm not lying when I say I don't know *exactly* how it happened. Either way, the details of *that* will get locked in the vault next to my *hey, guess what, I can't die* secret.

"When he was executed just now, I felt the transference. And if that's not enough...look at the marks," I tell everyone, holding one foot out and then the other for everyone to see.

Internally I thank my Grammy for giving my Aunt Hillen a heads-up to "look at the marks."

Sorrel and Bordow both look over, which is exactly when the High Priestess once again thinks she's off the hook. I shrug at her.

"If you don't believe me, then look at your marks," I tell her simply, one eyebrow lifted in challenge.

The High Priestess looks down at her high-heel-booted feet, and for a second, I think she's actually going to take her bootie off. Instead, she glares at the Contegomancer until Bordow begins to unlace his shoe.

Rogan laces his fingers in mine and squeezes once as we both watch the Contegomancer slip off his shoe and pull off his sock. He stares at the mark on the top of his foot, and I see his shoulders slump in defeat.

"What?" Sorrel stammers, staring at the new pattern of Bordow's mark as though it's a cobra ready to strike at any moment. "How?" she demands on a haunted whisper, her green eyes snapping up to mine. Her gaze quickly morphs from denial to bewilderment to outrage.

The High Priestess calls power to her so fast I feel it create a vacuum of magic all around her, her eyes alight with the fire she's calling on, and Rogan and I both ready ourselves for an attack. She opens her mouth to screech something at us, but before she can so much as blow a plume of smoke in our direction, a glass cage slams down all around them, trapping the High Council members in there and cutting off Sorrel's access to her magic.

I jump a little as the cage slams down on top of them, and then I try to brush it off as nothing when I feel Rogan chuckling at my expense next to me.

"This is an act of war, do you hear me?" Sorrel shouts at Dyad, her voice slightly muffled by the glass encasing her. "Let me out right this minute!" she screams even louder.

She paces inside the glass like an animal, and I can see her calculating and twisting things and trying to figure a way out. I should feel bad for her; I was just in her shoes, terrified and trying to figure out a way to save Rogan and Elon, but all she's doing is looking for a way to save herself. She can rot in that glass cage for all I care.

I feel a strange pull on that magical source that feels similar to a ley line, the one Sorrel tapped into earlier when she was trying to leave. I want to ask what it is, but Gremory appears back in the bone room, and he's accompanied by three other demons. One looks strikingly like a praying mantis with a long human-like face, and the other two demons look like people-sized versions of a bright yellow tarsier monkey. Their eyes are huge and dart around the room frantically in a way that makes me nervous.

All the demons start discussing things amongst themselves again, and this time I don't even try to listen.

"You okay?" Rogan leans in to ask me, and I nod.

"Yeah, I just wish this was all over already. My nerves are shot to shit," I tell him, and he nods with understanding. "Are you okay?" I turn to him to ask, looking him over for any signs that what's happening is taking a bigger toll on him than I realized.

Technically, there are two people in the cage to our left who are the reason Rogan and Elon even exist. I wouldn't blame him if this turned out to be harder than he realized.

"I'm fine, I keep waiting for her to find a way out of this," he admits with a hollow laugh. "She's been hunting me and Elon for so long now I don't even know if I believe this is it. I doubt I'll even believe she's dead when she actually is. I'm afraid to get too hopeful."

"I know exactly what you mean, and I haven't even been dealing with her nearly as long as you have. It's going to take time to deal with everything. There's a lot to unpack and process," I agree, and Rogan pulls me in for a hug.

I burrow in against him, relishing his warmth and strength. I thought for a while there I was never going to feel his arms around me again, and now I want to be sure that I never take this for granted, not even for a second.

"Do you not want me to kill them?" I ask quietly, not looking Rogan in the eye so that he feels he has the space and support to answer this question however he wants to.

He sighs and kisses the top of my head. "I hate that they're forcing you to make this decision. I wish all of this wasn't on your shoulders, but as brutal as it sounds, they need to die," he tells me with firm conviction. "There isn't a redeeming quality in any of them, and the world will be far better off without them than it would with them."

I nod my agreement and look up at him. I offer what comfort I can in a soft smile and a gaze filled with respect and admiration.

"Should I request that Elon be allowed to witness this?" I press.

Rogan runs his fingers through my hair in thought. "He probably won't like me deciding for him, but he's seen enough horrible things in life. I don't see the point in adding more to that, especially not for monsters like them," he tells me, gesturing to the glass cage, and I look over to see Rogan's mother is watching us.

Unease skitters over my skin, and I can tell by the manic twinkle in her eyes that she has a plan.

Oh goodie...not.

"Lennox Osseous," Dyad calls, and I look up at the collection of demons by the dais. "In order to confirm your claim, Julius will test your magic," he tells me, gesturing to the praying mantis demon. "Once that's established, the twins will then review your contract for the souls."

"Fine with me," I tell him, and he studies me as though he's looking for how I'm tricking them right now.

Jokes on you, bud, no tricks up my oversized sleeves.

Julius scurries closer to me, and I try not to flinch away from him as he does. He indicates for me to extend my arm, and when I do, he gives me a small scratch. He collects a small amount of blood and then scrapes it into a vial where he promptly starts to shake it, and then all eyes are on him as he analyzes it with nothing more than his own two eyes.

"Rogan Kendrick, you will let me out of this cage right now, do you hear me?" Sorrel suddenly snaps out of nowhere, and fury instantly boils in my blood.

I hear Rogan scoff next to me like he finds her efforts amusing, but I don't find anything funny about it. This bitch hired a fucking demon to torture secrets out of her own children, and now she wants to order one around like she has any right to play the mom card.

I whirl on her. "If you know what is good for you, you will never speak to him again. Do not say his name, in fact don't even look at him. I don't have to make your death painless, let's be very fucking clear about that," I growl at her.

She glares at me but doesn't say another word to him.

"The claim is valid," Julius announces, and then just like that, he disappears.

The High Demons all look at me again like I'm some sort of freak of nature. They're not wrong, but still it's rude. Sorrel and Bordow start to argue venomously, but I'm distracted from their catfight when a leather reclining chair appears behind me out of nowhere. I squeal in surprise when there's suddenly a giant yellow tarsier monkey in my face, pushing me down into the chair. My feet go flying up with a shriek when someone pulls the reclining lever without warning, and Rogan chuckles but doesn't leave my side. I wrangle in my fight-or-flight instinct and barely stop myself from giving the man I love the bird for laughing at my expense, damn handsy monkeys. The yellow tarsier demons stare at my feet intently, and I try very hard not to fidget.

"Uhhh, what are you doing?" I ask them after a couple of minutes of weird ass staring at my marks.

"We're reading your contract, Countess," one of the demons squeaks.

Countess?

I'm taken aback by the title, but I suppose it makes sense. I look over to Rogan and wag my eyebrows at him. "I think I found a cutesy couple pet name that doesn't make me cringe," I inform him, and he chuckles and rolls his eyes.

"Does that mean I'll have to go by the Count?" he asks, appalled.

"Please," I scoff. "You haven't earned that title. Go get your own demon magic," I challenge, and he cracks up. "You think I have a castle somewhere in the UK that comes with this title?" I ask thoughtfully.

"No, but I have a stinky dog and a stinkless skunk back home who will be happy to see you, if that entices you to move into my place," he counters, and I crack up.

"Throw in coffee and orgasms whenever I want them, and you, sir, have yourself a deal," I tell him, and his smile melts my damn heart.

"Done," he agrees, and what do you know, our smiles match.

"I want to speak to the High Demons alone," Sorrel demands. "I have reason to believe that this witch is tricking you, and if you'll just give me a moment, I can prove it."

"The contracts are valid," the twins squeak, and I'm

suddenly flung forward out of the chair and back on to my feet.

Fucking hell, why do I feel like a demon-led NASCAR pit crew just came at me?

Rogan catches me and keeps me from face planting, and I offer him a grateful smile.

"I said I want to speak to the High Demons alone," Sorrel screeches, and the High Demons all look at me for a response. "Don't look at her, I'm speaking to you. I'm the fucking High Priestess of—"

"You're the fucking High Priestess of nothing," I bellow at her, and she flinches with shock. "What do you not understand about the fact that I own your useless soul? I watched a psychopath, that you created by the way, torture your son, and he whined a hell of a lot less than you. Shut the hell up and die with some dignity, you fucking coward," I snap, fed up with the entitled commands and delusional rants.

"Countess, would you like us to silence the cage?" one of the yellow twins asks me.

"Oh, I can do that?" I ask, surprised and a little embarrassed.

I didn't know I could choose the mute option.

I turn to Rogan. "I think I've reached the hangry part of my cycle," I admit, and he laughs.

"Good to know, but on the plus side, only one more phase and it's cuddle slut time," he announces as though we're almost home free.

"We have silenced the cage and will keep it that way until the procedure is over. Would you like to be present for the soul retrieval or simply informed when it's complete?" the yellow twins query in unison, as though we're not talking about snatching souls like it's no big deal.

First bodies and now souls. Oh dear, I think I'm escalating.

I shake my head at myself. What is this world even doing to me?

I think about what Rogan said about Elon and having seen enough bad things in life. I look over at him, and he nods in the way that tells me he's good to do whatever I want to do.

The glass of the cage rattles slightly as Sorrel pounds on it furiously. She screams and snarls, her eyes full of hate and her face contorted with rage. Venom pours out of her mouth, and I'm grateful I can't hear the vitriol being spewed at me right now. My eyes land on the Contegomancer, Bordow. His face is swollen, and bruises are starting to mottle the skin of his cheek and jaw from where I hit him. He looks resigned but completely unremorseful as he turns to say something to Rogan's dad. The High Priest doesn't respond; he just stares blankly at a pile of bones as though they have all the answers. Maybe they do, I know how much a pouch of bones changed my life for the better.

I take a deep breath and then let it out slowly, turning away from the evil in the cage once and for all.

"Just let me know when it's done," I tell the twins, and then, as easy as blinking, they disappear, taking the glass cage with them.

"How do you know they'll do it?" Rogan asks, eyeing the cage's former spot warily.

"Look at the marks," I tell him simply. "If my marks disappear, then the contract is fulfilled. If they don't, I'll know something is up," I tell him, and he considers that.

"Seems like a solid system," he agrees after a beat. "Where to now?"

I smile at him sweetly as I feel for the magic that everyone keeps using to get in and out of here. "Let's go home."

24

I yawn and lean back against Rogan as he lazily plays with my hair. He wraps a strong arm around my chest, and I tuck the soft as fuck blanket around me a little tighter, feeling all kinds of warm and cozy, and relishing that fact.

I seriously need to ask Rogan where he gets all this soft crap from.

"Just tell me one more time what happened when you told her you owned her contract?" Elon asks, and he just looks so damn adorable and peaceful as he does.

"She didn't believe it at first. She tried to throw her weight around, but it wasn't until Lennox stuck out her foot and told her to '*look at the marks*' and Bordow looked at his mark, that's when she started to stammer *what* and then *how,* and then she called on her magic, trying to get all threatening, so the other demons locked them up in a cage," Rogan recounts, and I stare bleary eyed at the fire crackling in the fireplace and try hard not to think about anything.

Elon laughs at the cage part, and for whatever reason, it makes me want to laugh too.

"Fitting that the efforts she went to in order to lock me and Rogan in a cage, is what ultimately led her to dying in one. If that's not a slice of justice, I don't know what is," Elon declares, his laugh now slightly hollow.

My heart tightens as I watch him get lost in thought for a moment, and I can only wonder at the demons darkening his door right now. I know none of this is easy for him or for Rogan, but I also know the rest of us will do everything we can to protect them.

I look over at Prek and Tad on the couch, and I can hear Cohen upstairs packing so he can head out. I think his hurry has something to do with Diem and maybe wanting to track down Colby, but I don't ask him. If any of them need anything from me, they'll track me down.

"Anyway, after the demon checked my blood and confirmed I had demon magic, they read through the details of the contracts. Did you guys know that the contract between a demon and someone else is actually written in the demon mark itself? Then the shape made by the lines in a contract is based on the demon's magical signature and the other person's magical signature. Cool, right?" I tell them, but no one seems to be as into it as I am—I blame the demon magic.

"I think it's cool," Rogan whispers in my ear, and I smile widely at him and then settle in against his chest again.

"Man, I wish I could have been there," Elon sighs, staring wistfully at the high ceiling, like he's picturing every word that we're saying.

"I'm pretty sure I shit my panties at least five times before they pulled Rogan down, and I honestly thought that was it for all of us. It was brutal, so don't let the semi-happy ending fool you," I reassure him, and he offers me a soft, understanding grin.

"Semi-happy?" Prek asks, looking from Tad to me.

I make a mental note to ask Tad about that. I swear I've

caught both of them staring all moony-eyed when the other one isn't looking.

"She's grumpy because before they would let us leave, the High Demon Cozen insisted that Lennox had to come train with her twice a week until she mastered her demon magic," Rogan teases, and I scoff like a petulant teenager.

"I hate school, and I'm a super busy person, so it's just really inconvenient," I whine, and everyone chuckles at my expense.

"I can't believe it's over," Elon states pensively, and we all kind of float on that thought for a moment.

"There's still a lot of political moves to be made in the next year as the mancer community recovers. Our smear campaign did its job, which is great, but it's going to take a lot of time to bounce back and rebuild from the level of corruption that was uncovered. The news says the High Council high-rise was pretty fucked up after that angry mob got done with it. Reports are saying that Sorrel and her two right-hand men are on the run, which will embolden some of their supporters," Rogan points out.

"Good, let it embolden them. Makes it easier to cut them out like the cancers they are. People have their eyes open now, and they're not going to tolerate the same crap as before. There will be elections and hopefully a lot of changes in the near future. And of course, we'll all be there to try to steer things in the right direction," Elon declares.

"Well, not us, we're still renounced. Once a renounced witch, always a renounced witch," Rogan states like he's reciting a famous slogan.

"You don't think they'll lift it?" Tad asks, confused.

"No, we'd have to tell them what really happened, and there's no chance in hell I'm risking that information. Between that and keeping a lid on how Lennox got demon magic, we've got plenty of secrets to protect, which means we stick to the shadows and keep our noses out of things," Rogan tells him, a tired chuckle punctuating his words.

"Fair point," Tad concedes, sneaking a quick look over at Prek.

Yep. There's definitely something going on there.

Another bone-tingling yawn takes over me, and I feel Rogan laugh against my back. I'm enjoying the catch-up session as we all wind down and try to decompress, but I'm so tired I feel like I could sleep for a week. And now that we don't have a war to fight, I'm really hoping I can.

"What did Riggs say when you called him to tell him the war was off?" Elon asks Rogan.

"He was oddly bummed out," he admits with a deep laugh. "Several of the packs were ready to go balls to the wall against the High Council. Riggs said leave it to Lennox to steal everyone's thunder."

I laugh and shake my head. "You know what they say: no balls, no babies," I declare, pretending to be all macho and savior-like.

"What? Who says that?" Prek demands, looking at me like I've lost it.

"Wait. You want babies?" Elon adds, a cheeky smirk on his face.

I blush and immediately start panicking. "What? No. I didn't say anything about me wanting babies, it's a saying," I defend.

"That is definitely *not* a saying," Tad taunts, totally calling me out.

"I mean, if you want us involved in discussing such an important decision, just say so. You don't have to make up a saying and make things all awkward," Elon jokes.

I flip everyone the bird and then turn to Rogan. "I didn't say shit about wanting babies," I reassure him, and he shrugs, not bothering to hide the amused glint in his eyes.

I get up off the couch and shoot everyone a glare. "I am going to bed, and each and every one of you can fuck right off. Also, I would just like to point out that in the future, when I save all of your asses, you can thank me with soft clothes and blankets and your undying love and devotion."

"Naturally," Tad scoffs like that's already a done deal, and I give him a wink before abandoning them all and fleeing for the comfort of a hot shower and a soft bed.

"I'm going too," Rogan announces, which is peppered by a series of sniggers.

We make it to the bottom of the stairs, and then Prek yells, "Don't forget: no balls, no babies!"

Laughter erupts from the living room, and I bury my face in my hands in total mortification.

"And just when I was starting to like that guy," I grumble, my cheeks on fire. "I swear that's a saying," I tell Rogan over my shoulder, and he just laughs and swats my ass as I start up the stairs. "I'm not even close to thinking about kids, okay? I want you to know that, just in case you're silently screaming inside and freaking out."

"I'm not," he tells me evenly, but I don't miss the mirth twinkling in his eyes.

"Good, because neither am I."

"Yeah, you just said that," he points out, and a cheeky smile slinks slowly across his face.

"I don't even think I want kids. Plus, the whole immortal thing, that doesn't exactly work as a parent. Plus, we just won a war, and we're still getting to know each other."

"I thought you weren't thinking about it," Rogan teases.

"I'm not, obviously. I'm absolutely *not* thinking about it."

"Noted," he states, grabbing onto my hips when we get to the top of the stairs and holding on to me as we make our way to the room. "Go start the shower, and I'll meet you in there. There's something I have to do real quick," he tells me, and I nod on a yawn.

I get the water molten and then strip down and step under the spray. I stand there and let the hot water melt away the worst of my fears and worries and all of the stress and concern still clinging to my skin. I wash and condition my hair and then scrub my body until it's almost raw. I watch as the soap sluffs off me, bubbles and water dripping down my feet and swirling toward the drain.

I look down at my now demon-mark-free skin, thinking of the three souls that are currently locked away in a demon vault that I really hope in my heart looks like Gringotts. *I mean, there were dragon bones in that trial room, so the chances are...honestly, still pretty low, but a girl's gotta dream.* I trace the smooth skin of my feet with my eyes and feel a profound sense of solace. The demon marks disappeared shortly after we got back, and as painful as it was to have them transferred to me, I only felt a brush of soothing cold when they vanished. Knowing that the contracts were fulfilled, that Sorrel, her husband, and Bordow were finally dead, and their souls forever mine...well, it ranks up there with some of the best feelings I've ever felt.

So much has happened and all so incredibly fast. I'm on my third attempt to process it all when Rogan finally joins me. He steps in behind me, and I'm reminded of the insane level of attraction I felt the first time his body was pressed up against mine like this. I turn around so that my nipples can skim the hard planes of his torso as we simply stand together, our bodies caressing the other's as we just breathe in and out.

I watch him soap up his hair and body, reveling in the intimacy and the fact that I'm totally perving out. If someone would have told me when we first met that we'd eventually get here, I'd have said sign me the fuck up. Even if they had warned me about all the awful, scary, traumatic shit I'd have to go through to be standing here ogling this man, knowing he's mine, I wouldn't have hesitated for a second. I also would have never admitted any of this to anyone for any reason, but it doesn't matter because all the shit happened and now I'm here, eye-fucking the love of my life.

"If you keep looking at me that way, we're never going to make it out of the shower, and I had big plans for when we got out of the shower," Rogan purrs at me.

I shamelessly watch as the water flows freely down his hard chest, past his cut abs, dips into his yummy Adonis belt, and then drips off his hardening cock.

"Looking at you like what?" I tease, my eyes languidly sliding up his body, pausing on his lips and then rising to meet his eyes.

"Like a demon who wants my soul," he tells me, and I immediately scrunch my nose in rejection of that suggestion. "Too soon?" he asks.

"Way too fucking soon," I agree on a laugh. "You have to stick to that romance novel shit and say something like *you're looking at me like you want to eat me*," I encourage.

He rinses off and shakes his head, a deep chuckle rumbling out of him and settling deep in my belly.

"Well then, come over here so I can eat you."

You don't have to ask me twice. Bon appetit.

I jump at him without missing a beat, but I don't anticipate how slippery the water has made us, and we both almost go down. I'm screaming and then laughing as Rogan almost pulls a muscle trying to keep me from killing us both. Wouldn't that be a story: Remember that time we both died because I leapt without thinking in the shower?

Never leap without thinking in the shower.

That's going up there with "never date a man with two first names" and "always trust the bones."

I cling to Rogan's neck, terrified and completely amused. "That's my bad," I offer him as he grunts and readjusts my body against his. "Let's just move this to the bedroom like you originally planned," I tell him, eyeing the wood beam above us and promising myself that one day I'll hold on to it while I ride Rogan's face.

"That might be best, you know, for safety reasons," he ribs as he reaches behind us and turns the water off.

My smile is huge as I slide down Rogan's body to grab a towel and dry off. He watches me like he can't get enough of me, and it's making me feel fucking amazing.

"I gotta say," I tell him as I hurry to put product in my hair so it doesn't frizz out, "this whole hero worship thing you've got going on is working for me," I razz, throwing in an eyebrow waggle for good measure.

He barks out a loud long laugh that I feel keenly between my thighs.

"I take it back, that gorgeous laugh is now what's doing it for me," I amend, and he stalks toward me in that way that makes me want to get all squealy.

"You fucking do it for me, Lennox," he declares simply, and I feel the passion in those words all the way down to my toes.

"Let's get our tether on!" I announce, so ready to get our connection back to where it's supposed to be.

Rogan laughs hard again, closing the distance between us and pulling me out of the bathroom. "Get our tether on?" he questions, and I cringe.

"Yeah, it sounded cooler in theory," I admit, following after him and getting wet just at the thought of all the orgasms I know are about to go down.

We clear the bathroom doorway, and Rogan steps aside

to reveal a room covered in lit candles. White pillar candles in all shapes and sizes dot every surface except the bed and floor, while the huge windows reflect the flickers of candlelight, and it makes it look like we're completely surrounded by warm, incandescent light.

"It's gorgeous," I gasp, loving the effort and the ambiance it creates.

He reaches for something, and the next thing I know, he's handing me a warm cup of coffee. My face lights up with even more excitement, and I take a huge sip. It's exactly how I like it, and I groan with pleasure.

"You are nailing this," I purr at him, warming my hand on the mug as I gulp half of it down.

Gotta get properly caffeinated for the plans that are forming in my mind right now.

"Are you still going to try and talk me into waiting on the whole tether thing?" he snarks, and I roll my eyes.

"Maybe my *tether on* wasn't clear enough, but no. Absolutely no waiting. Let's do this. Give me that dick!"

Rogan laughs and takes a sip of my coffee before putting the mug down on a side table. "It's like listening to poetry spill from your luscious lips," he quips, and I laugh.

Rogan swallows my joy down with a kiss, and my mirth quickly morphs into moans. He cups my face, stroking my cheeks with his thumbs as he nips and teases and plunders my mouth with such passion and skill that I'm immediately aching and needy all over because of it.

"I love you," he whispers against my mouth as he starts to kiss across my jaw and down my neck.

"I love you," I exclaim back as he finds a sweet spot just under my jaw.

Rogan leans down and wraps his lips around my nipple, and I bow into him. My body bends and sways nearer of its own volition, and I can't get enough of the delicious way his mouth feels as he sucks and flicks his tongue against the sensitive peak.

I run my fingers through his hair, watching him take me into his mouth and loving how much it turns me on. He releases my nipple with a pop and moves to pay the other one equal attention. I roll my hips against him, feeling the tip of his cock press in against me, and I suddenly need to wrap my lips around it and hear him moan my name.

I cup his face and lift it to mine for a deep kiss that leaves us both panting, and then I drop down in front of him and wrap my mouth around the head of his cock. Rogan groans deeply and tries to pull me away, but I am not having it. I slap his interfering hands away, and he laughs and gives in. I wrap my hand around the base of his shaft and work him in and out of my mouth in time with the strokes of my hand.

"Fuck that feels so good," he encourages. "Yes, just like that. God, that fucking mouth might be the end of me."

He wraps his hands in my hair, pushing it away from my face so he can watch his dick pumping in and out of my mouth. His moss-green eyes are filled with need, and I take him as deeply as I can, loving the way he tastes and feels down my throat and the way he groans my name as I swallow him down.

"Don't make me come, fuck," he warns. "No, I want to come in that pussy," he announces as he pulls out of my mouth and backs away from me like I'm dangerous.

I sit there on my knees, licking the taste of him off my lips and watching him with eyes so hungry and worked up that he could probably make me come with only a deep laugh and a dirty thought aimed in my direction. I crawl up on the bed and turn to lie on my back. He watches me with just as much need as he tries to calm his dick down. Slowly, purposefully, I spread my legs. I reach down and run a finger down the slit of my wet folds.

"Then come in my pussy, Rogan," I order, and the next thing I know, his gorgeous face is between my thighs.

I moan but resist the urge to close my eyes and lean back into the sensations he's coaxing out of me. No. This time, I want to watch him feast. I want to watch him circle my clit with the tip of his tongue and then lap at it like a cat does cream. I want to see him suck me into his mouth, bobbing his head around my clit as he works his lips and tongue against it. His eyes meet mine as he licks up my seam and then drops to shove that long thick tongue in my dripping pussy. I love the way my desire shines around his mouth, and the way he devours me like there's nothing better than the taste of need on his tongue or the heated groans he elicits when he sucks on my clit and slips two long fingers inside of me.

I whimper as he fingers the perfect spot inside of me, while he works his mouth and tongue against my clit. I force myself to watch and gasp and then beg for more as I get so fucking close, my muscles tightening in preparation. Then he fingers me harder, and I'm lost to the twitches and rolls and shouts of his name as he wrings wave after wave of pleasure from me.

My clit heats as he drips soft kisses, and I wiggle and fight the overload of sensation, but he pins my hips and shows me why I'm now ruined for anyone else but him.

"Yes, Rogan, you feel so fucking good," I encourage as he warms my blood, making me even more pliant and ready, and this time when his fingers start to play in my pussy, I'm gone again in only two strokes.

I pull his face from between my thighs, begging him to give me what we both want. I kiss him hard and deep, mewling and panting as he lines his cock up perfectly, and in one deep thrust we're both gasping each other's names.

"I fucking love you," I sigh as he settles deeply between my thighs.

He kisses down my neck and pulls out slowly before rolling his hips back in. I groan and run my nails tantalizingly up his back.

"Fuck me, Rogan, god, I need you to fuck me so bad," I beg as he slowly rocks back out and then in again.

He kisses me hard, pistoning inside of me just as hard and swallowing down my moan of approval.

"Is that what you need, or do you need me to fuck you harder?" he taunts, and I'm a mewling, encouraging mess as he starts to do just that.

"Yes, fuck yes," I exhale, and then my eyes meet his as he gives me exactly what I need.

I've never stared into someone's eyes before as they fucked me, something about it was far too weird and intimate to me, but as Rogan thrusts in and out of me faster and harder until my entire body is singing his name, it's made all the better because I can see so much while he does. I'm swimming in a moss-green pool of molten heat and need and love and affection. I feel his admiration and respect, his want and desire, and he can see all of mine.

He fucks me hard, working my body like only he can, while we look into one another and connect in every possible way. He lifts me off my back, never losing his rhythm in and out of my pussy, until I'm straddling his lap and we're both meeting each other thrust for thrust.

"Are you ready?" he asks against my mouth.

I nod, feeling another orgasm start to build. "Do it, please," I beg, and he smiles and starts thrusting even harder like he's trying to time both of our orgasms with the tether itself.

"*Tedas ruk shaw aus forin ve Lennox Marai Osseous. Ise hiruse ou fooiq tork shin iei.*"

Warmth licks through my body, and I can feel Rogan's magic pulling at mine playfully. I smile as I start to feel parts of him that I've missed so much it makes my eyes well with emotion.

"Please, I need you," he begs as he wipes a stray tear from my cheek, and I look into him as deeply as I can while his body fills mine in every possible way.

"*Tedas ruk shaw aus forin ve Rogan*...Shit, what is your middle name?" I ask, realizing that I have no idea what it is.

Rogan laughs, and it almost sends me over the edge. "It's Arlo," he tells me, and I chuckle. "I think it means 'between two hills' or something stupid," he adds, and I start to laugh harder.

"I mean, accurate," I point out, gesturing to the fact that my tits are bouncing around him right now.

He laughs even harder, and while the sound of his happiness echoes around the room, I look into his eyes and start again.

"*Tedas ruk shaw aus forin ve Rogan Arlo Kendrick. Ise hiruse ou fooiq tork shin iei.*"

Power swarms both of us, but unlike the first time we did this while we were fighting each other in every possible way, the tether sinks into both of us like an anchor gently floating to the bottom of the sea. He snaps into place inside of me exactly like he's supposed to, and I feel like I can breathe for the first time since I came back to life...the second time.

Rogan kisses me fiercely, and I claim his mouth right back. Pleasure slams through me, both mine and his, and it's all so incredibly overwhelming that we both scream out at the same time as ecstasy wraps around us. We come so hard that all we see is light, all we feel is each other, and all we are is this...just like we were always meant to be.

We fall over, a tangle of limbs, orgasms, magic, and bliss. We pant through everything that just happened, and I don't think it's possible for my smile to get any wider. I feel a giddy excitement in Rogan that gives me pause, and I look over at his sappy face and laugh.

"What are you up to, Rogan Kendrick?" I demand. "You're not fooling me now that I can feel you once again," I remind him, and his happiness flares so brightly in my chest I can't breathe. It's the most profound and beautiful thing to feel, and I immediately well up with tears again.

"Don't cry, my little Bound Witch, I have a present for you," he croons, and I laugh through my happy tears and pull him in for a long slow kiss.

"Is it your dick again, because if it is, I'm here for it, but also lets get more coffee first," I announce, feeling sleep's siren song already in my limbs.

He chuckles and rolls off the bed to get something from the closet, and I sit up and do my best not to pass the fuck out while I wait for him. He comes back with a black box that's too big to be a ring but too small to be anything else I can think of. Rogan's eagerness is catching, and I'm practically bouncing with anticipation as he crawls back into bed and places the box in my waiting palm.

"I got this for you because it was the first time I saw you smile with such pure joy and happiness, and I knew right then and there that I was a goner," he tells me, and I immediately wonder what the hell is in the box. "Open it," he encourages.

I untie the ribbon and slide it off the box, and then I carefully separate the top from the bottom, exhilaration coursing through me and mixing with Rogan's nervous excitement. I stare at what's inside, completely dumbfounded and stunned. My eyes immediately well up again as I pick up the small jackalope antler from the box and set it in my palm.

Tears drip down my face, the significance of this moment and everything we've been through suddenly overwhelming in all the best ways. I kiss Rogan so fiercely it's as though I tattoo myself all over him and then let him do the same right back. I pepper him with kisses as we fall back on the bed, careful not to hurt my newfound most-prized possession.

"Omg, my ancestors are going to be so damn excited when I induct this little guy into the pouch of bones," I squeal as we wrap ourselves around each other and just be. I sigh, still shaking my head at the incredible treasure in my palm. "Giving me presents is going to be so impossible from here on out, because nothing could possibly top this," I tell him. "So well fucking done, but also good luck."

Rogan laughs and tucks me into his side. He sighs deeply and shoots me a panty melting smile. "I was going to teach you how to make the espresso maker cum next," he teases, and I moan in approval.

"Probably shouldn't though," I advise casually. "What would I need you for then?" He plucks my jackalope antler from my hand and sets it on the side table, and then I'm squealing and laughing as Rogan Kendrick reminds me of all the reasons I love him...and also love screaming his name.

I can't believe this all started with a purple pouch of bones and a world I never wanted to be a part of. Who knew between the bones, the blood, the deaths, and the love, that I would find everything I was looking for and so much more?

My name is Countess Lennox Marai Osseous, and I don't even know what the hell I am anymore. What I do know is that I hated magic until I learned how to make some of my own. Then I discovered that love truly is the greatest magic of all. Now I'm tethered to the man of my dreams, surrounded by family and friends who I would die for—and have—and I wouldn't want it any other way...moon shits and all.

ALSO BY IVY ASHER

Dark Shifter Romance Standalone
The Savage Spirit of Seneca Rain

Rabid

Paranormal Romance RH
The Sentinel World

The Lost Sentinel Series

The Lost and the Chosen

Awakened and Betrayed

The Marked and the Broken

Found and Forged

Shadowed Wings Series

The Hidden

The Avowed

The Reclamation

More in the Sentinel World coming soon.

Hellgate Guardian Series

Grave Mistakes

Grave Consequences

Grave Decisions

Grave Signs

Shifter Romantic Comedy Standalone

Conveniently Convicted

Dystopian Romantic Comedy Standalone RH

April's Fools

Urban Fantasy Romance

THE OSSEOUS CHRONICLES

The Bone Witch

The Blood Witch

The Bound Witch

ABOUT THE AUTHOR

Ivy Asher is addicted to chai, swearing, and laughing a lot—but not in a creepy, laughing alone kind of way. She loves the snow, books, and her family of two humans, and two fur-babies. She has worlds and characters just floating around in her head, and she's lucky enough to be surrounded by amazing people who support that kind of crazy.

Join Ivy Asher's Reader Group and follow her on Instagram and BookBub for updates on your favorite series and upcoming releases!!!

- facebook.com/IvyAsherBooks
- instagram.com/ivy.asher
- amazon.com/author/ivyasher
- bookbub.com/profile/ivy-asher

Printed in Great Britain
by Amazon

HIS SECRET

THE HUNTER BROTHERS BOOK 4

M. S. PARKER

BELMONTE PUBLISHING, LLC

This book is a work of fiction. The names, characters, places and incidents are products of the writer's imagination or have been used fictitiously and are not to be construed as real. Any resemblance to persons, living or dead, actual events, locales or organizations is entirely coincidental.

Copyright © 2018 Belmonte Publishing LLC

Published by Belmonte Publishing LLC

READING ORDER

Thank you so much for reading His Secret, the last book in the Hunter Brothers series. All books in the series can be read stand-alone, but if you'd like to read the complete series, I recommend reading them in this order:

1. His Obsession
2. His Control
3. His Hunger
4. His Secret

PROLOGUE

Manfred

I took my seat behind my desk and waited for Bartholomew Constantine to get settled. We met two weeks ago when I'd originally gone to him about investigating what had happened to my son, daughter-in-law, and granddaughter, but for this meeting, I'd asked him to come here. Olive had gone shopping with her sister, and I didn't quite trust our new nanny to keep my grandsons out of trouble all on her own. She was sweet, but those four could rattle anyone.

Maybe I should have hired someone like Bartholomew. He was ex-military, getting a medical discharge after six years of service. Even if I hadn't done a thorough background check, the left sleeve hanging empty below the elbow would've told me the reason. My contacts had given me the details. He'd taken a sniper's bullet, the shot shattering his left elbow and nearly tearing the bottom of his arm off. Because he'd been rescuing another soldier at the time, he was given a medal, but he didn't talk about it.

"Mr. Hunter," Bartholomew began, "I brought some papers with me."

He pushed a manila envelope across the table, and I picked it up. As I opened it and began looking through the contents, he explained what I was seeing.

"I managed to get a copy of the accident report," he said. "There were no skid marks."

I was an intelligent person, but I wasn't going to make assumptions about what something did or didn't mean. I needed facts. Solid facts that I could take to a prosecutor. I wasn't going to bring this all up again after things were just starting to settle down. The boys still missed their parents and sister, of course, but I'd begun to see moments where they reminded me of the grandsons I'd known before.

"What does that mean?" I asked as I skimmed the paper in my hand. "No skid marks."

"It means your son either didn't attempt to stop the car when it went off the road, or he couldn't stop."

I looked up, eyes narrowing. "Are you suggesting that my son *intentionally* didn't stop the car? That he *wanted* to crash?"

"I'm saying what the possible interpretations of the facts could be," he said mildly.

I had to hand it to him. I'd been dealing with people my whole life. Politicians. Other businessmen. I was known for having a steel spine and an iron will. People didn't push me around. They did what I told them to do. And they sure as hell didn't stand there, with passive looks on their faces while they told me what I *didn't* want to hear.

But just because I respected it didn't mean I liked it.

"My son wouldn't do that," I said, the bitter words tearing from my throat.

Bartholomew held up a hand. "I tend to believe that too. I'm just telling you all the ways the evidence can be interpreted."

"You said it could also mean that he wasn't able to stop." I went back to the explanation I could handle, no matter how horrible that option was.

Bartholomew nodded. "The two most likely scenarios are that either his brakes failed, or something happened to him that kept him from being able to do it."

"Either of those could be benign or malicious, correct?" I was starting to see where he was going with this.

"Right. The brakes could have malfunctioned, either from normal wear and tear or from something faulty."

"Or someone could have cut the lines."

Bartholomew's grim expression told me I was right. "Same with him not being able to stop. He could have passed out, had a seizure, a heart attack. Any number of things."

"But he could've been drugged too."

The PI sighed. "Yes. And now you see my problem."

I did. "A lot of possible reasons to chase down."

He shifted in his seat and pulled on his jacket. "A lot of possibilities, and not enough answers."

I frowned. "What do you mean by that?"

"The car was too damaged for the police to determine if there were any issues with the brake lines."

I leaned back in my chair. "Which means we can't know if the brakes failed, or for what reason."

"Correct," he said. "I did check with the car manufacturer, and there've been no recalls, no reports of brake issues with that make and model." He gestured toward the envelope. "I have an official letter from them."

I pulled it out and skimmed it. My company didn't make cars, but I knew a form letter when I saw one. It was put together well, though, providing the specific information that Bartholomew needed. Unfortunately, it didn't help me know what happened to my son.

"I have a paper in there for you to sign," he said. "It'll release your son's medical records."

"Why do you need those?"

"To determine if he had any pre-existing conditions that might have caused him to pass out."

I opened my mouth to tell him that I knew my son's medical history, but then I remembered that Chester had been thirty-one when he died. By the time I'd been thirty, my father hadn't known much about what was going on with my health. I liked to think that I paid more attention to my son than my father had to me, but Chester had been an adult, with his own family and his own life.

"All right." I flipped through the papers and pulled out the release form. "And if there's nothing in his files?"

For the first time, he looked nervous, like there was something he had to say but didn't want to say it.

"Just say it," I said mildly.

"There was no autopsy..." he paused, letting that settle in, "which means there's no way to do a drug test or check to see if anything physical happened to him."

It was my fault. I'd been the one who'd pushed for no autopsy. Olive had been frantic when she'd realized what they wanted to do, and I hadn't been able to bear upsetting her even more. I'd thought I was doing the right thing.

One thing I had to ask, even without the ability to back it up with physical evidence.

"Do you think my son used drugs?"

If Chester's name was smeared because of what I'd done, I'd never forgive myself.

"No," Bartholomew said. "I don't. But it would've been better if we had a toxicology report to back me up. If legal action needs to be taken, any decent defense attorney will come up with a dozen different ways to put the blame on your son."

"His medical records can help with that, right?"

"Some," Bartholomew said. "Without a history of drug and

alcohol abuse, getting a jury to believe that a good family man with a solid job completely changed his behavior in the middle of the day with his family in the car would be difficult." He paused for a moment, tapping his fingers on the arm of the chair. "Without an autopsy, it also becomes difficult to prove that someone else may have given him something that caused him to crash."

I took a deep breath and let it out slowly. "What does this mean as a whole? Where do things stand?"

"Honestly, Mr. Hunter, we're at a bit of a dead end. No one saw the actual wreck, but evidence supports that they were the only car on the road. I'll look at the medical records and talk to his doctor, but after that, I don't have any other leads."

I leaned back in my chair, folding my hands in front of me. "Nothing?"

"There's only one other thing I can think of, but you're not going to like it."

I raised an eyebrow. "What is it?"

"The kids," he said. "Your grandsons might have heard things at home that they don't even realize could be important. They might know if their father was arguing with someone, or if he was worried."

I was shaking my head before he'd even finished. "They're just starting to get back some sort of normalcy. They don't need to be thinking about what happened."

"The thing is," he said quietly. "Blake was there. He saw everything. He's the only eyewitness we have."

I stood. "He's four years old. I'm not going to let you ask him if he saw his parents and sister die."

Bartholomew stood as well and held out a hand. "I'll continue to pursue whatever leads I can find, and if you change your mind about allowing me to talk to the boys, please give me a call."

I shook his hand and thanked him, but as he left, I knew it

was over.

I'd keep him on the case, no matter the cost, but I had to put this behind me. I needed to find my own closure and not let it rely on whether the PI was able to find definitive answers. Besides, I had a family to take care of.

"Grandfather!" Jax came running into the office. "Blake's trying to break his cast again!"

Case in point. I had a feeling my youngest grandson was going to continue to be difficult, no matter how old he was.

ONE
BLAKE

Twenty-Four Years Later...

I HATED PEOPLE.

Not really. I just hated having to deal with them. Like the woman on the other end of the phone who was insisting that I owed money for a physical therapy session I'd had two years ago after I'd strained my shoulder.

"Mr. Hunter, I'm looking at your account right now."

Her voice had that sort of sickly-sweet tone that reminded me of the girls back in Boston who used to follow my brothers around. They thought all they had to do was bat their lashes and toss their hair, and guys would do whatever they wanted.

"I understand that," I said, gritting my teeth. "But *I'm* looking at my paperwork right now, and it says that I'd already paid my deductible in its entirety."

"It doesn't matter what some papers say," she countered. "It matters what your account shows."

"Because computers never make errors."

Unless I was working on making something, I wasn't a

patient person, but I tried to be reasonable when it came to dealing with people...until they said or did something stupid. Then, all bets were off.

"Would you like to make the payment by credit or debit card?"

I closed my eyes. "I'm not paying it because I don't owe it."

"Yes, you do."

That was it. She was talking to me like I was a child or an idiot, and if there was one thing I hated worse than people, it was people who patronized me.

"I'd like to speak to your supervisor."

I could almost hear her smile. "My supervisor's not available right now."

"Bullshit."

"Sir, if you're going to use that sort of language–"

And I was done.

"I'll be handing my paperwork over to my lawyer. Your supervisor can call him." I rattled off a number and then ended the call.

Was it rude of me to hang up on her? Maybe. Did I care? No.

I had more important things to do.

I pulled on my coat and stepped outside. Mid-March outside of Rawlins, Wyoming, was always cold and dry. This morning, it was also sunny, and I tipped my head back, closing my eyes and simply enjoying the warmth. I didn't hate everything in the world, even though it seemed like it a lot of the time. I loved *this*. Being outside. Alone.

When I was a teenager, I'd heard once that there were more cows in Wyoming than there were people. From that moment, I'd had a goal in mind. A place of my own in Wyoming.

I breathed in the fresh air and then let it out slowly...then frowned.

I wasn't a happy person. I knew that. But here, on my ranch, doing what I loved doing, without anyone telling me how I should be or act, I'd been more or less content. Then Grandfather died, and I'd gone back to Boston for the first time in three years. Something about being there again had left me restless.

"Dammit," I muttered as I set off on my usual morning walk.

I needed to get back to normal. My normal. That meant checking my property as I did every morning, rain or shine, sun or snow. Once I was done with that, I'd get some lunch, then head to my workshop. I was behind thanks to the time I'd wasted back East.

I felt a stab of guilt at the thought. Grandfather and I had butted heads constantly, and my brothers pissed me off to no end, but me not wanting to spend time with them didn't translate to wanting them dead. It was one thing to choose not to talk to them. It was something else entirely to know that choice wasn't there anymore.

A gust of wind sent dirt against my face, and I wiped at my eyes, blinking away grit and tears. Tears from the dirt, not from emotions. I didn't cry. Not because I hadn't loved my grandfather, but because I *didn't* cry. I hadn't since I was little.

Both of my horses neighed at me when I walked into the barn, and the sound helped me push back the thoughts of the past. I'd thought I had put all of that behind me years ago, but Grandfather's funeral and those stupid rules he'd made about my brothers and I reconciling had brought everything back to the surface.

I'd taken Shane out yesterday, so I passed by his stall and went into Annie's. She was a gorgeous roan, large for a mare, which was good since I wasn't exactly a small guy. I planned on breeding her and Shane in another year. They didn't have the sort of pedigrees that won awards or races, but I was confident that they'd produce a beautiful colt.

"Hey, girl," I said softly as I moved around her.

I didn't talk much to people, but I liked talking to the horses.

They didn't talk back, and they didn't care what I said. I could tell them everything and anything and nothing. And if I didn't want to speak, I didn't have to.

She danced a bit, like she always did when she first got outside, but she settled after a few minutes, and I swung myself up into the saddle. "All right, Annie, let's get started."

I went down the drive first, swinging around when I got to the road. One of the things that'd attracted me to this place was that it was on a dirt road off a paved road and off a highway. I couldn't see a single building from any of the property lines. I didn't know who owned the land bordering mine on any side, and that was fine with me. I didn't care who they were, as long as they left me alone.

I let myself fall into the familiar rhythm of riding, let my mind wander as I scanned the perimeter. I didn't raise animals, so I didn't really need to check fences and that sort of thing, but I did it anyway. Maintenance was always better than having to rebuild something.

Besides, this entire place was mine. I'd bought it myself, with money I'd *earned*. I hadn't touched my trust fund or anything else that had come from my family. Even during high school, I'd done apprenticeships with the best tradesmen in both woodworking and blacksmithing. By the time I was twenty, I'd started taking on jobs of my own. By twenty-two, I'd been making a decent living. Now, at twenty-eight, I owned a multi-million-dollar ranch and had enough in my bank account that I could probably go a decade without working if I didn't spend crazy.

It didn't matter if no one else came here to see what I'd accomplished. I knew, and I was damn proud of it.

"Hello, there!"

The shout caught me off-guard, and Annie reared, throwing me back in the saddle.

Shit.

TWO
BREA

I hummed as I looked at myself in the mirror. I'd chopped off more than eight inches of raven-black curls two weeks ago, and it was still strange seeing myself without it. I'd had long hair my whole life.

I knew what my mother, Blair, would say. I was manifesting my choice to live as a responsible adult by cutting off the hair I saw as a symbol of my childhood.

She'd planned to go into psychology before she'd met my dad, and while she'd never pursued it after they'd begun their whirlwind romance, she'd always loved to use what she remembered from her high school courses to make those sorts of pronouncements.

I'd gotten my hair and dusky complexion from her, and my dark eyes from my father. Both were smart, impulsive, and all about living life to the fullest. They'd been good parents, if unconventional. I knew that neither of them understood why I'd chosen to not completely embrace their way of doing things, but at least they accepted that it was my life and my choice to make.

I fastened my favorite necklace and straightened the wooden pendant. It was an infinity symbol carved into a round piece of ash, hung from a hemp choker. My parents had brought it back for me from a trip they'd taken when I was thirteen. I couldn't remember exactly where they'd gone, but it'd been one of the times I'd stayed home. Well, wherever home happened to be at the time. I was pretty sure it had been a yurt in South America somewhere at that time. I remembered them leaving me with some twenty-something girl they'd both been seeing. She'd been around a few months, and we'd called her Rain – original, right? – but I doubted that was her actual name. Most of the twenty-somethings they picked up to join them went by things like Rainbow and Butterfly or Khaki and Apache.

"Don't dwell on the troubles of the past," I said to my reflection. "Focus on a positive future."

I wasn't saying it because I had some awful past I was trying to get over, but rather because everyone had some sort of baggage in their past that they could keep thinking about until it kept them from moving forward. A bad test, a missed appointment, a lost job, a broken relationship. I found that reminding myself to keep focused on the present and the future helped me reach the goals I set for myself.

My apartment was directly above my store, which meant I didn't have far to go to begin my work day. I carried my container of homemade trail mix and a glass of water downstairs and set it next to my laptop. I liked to think I was a good balance between being a complete Luddite and being entirely dependent on technology.

I did my usual rounds to double-check that nothing had been disturbed in the night. I didn't think anyone would ever bother to break in here, but the occasional rodent had been known to sneak inside and wreak havoc with some of my products.

Nothing looked out of place this morning though. I loved the way my storage room slash work room smelled. Lavender and sage and various citrus scents, mixing with ones that were harder to distinguish under the stronger ones. I knew them all, through sight, touch, smell, and taste.

I paused at my work table, lightly touching the stone mortar bowl and pestle I'd been given by Galina, the mentor I'd become close to while studying in the UK. We kept in touch even though it'd been nearly three years since I'd last seen her. She was as much responsible for *Grow 'n Heal* as the money I'd inherited when I'd turned twenty-one. More so, in my opinion, since Kevin's parents were dead, and Blair's parents hadn't approved or supported my decision to forgo college and essentially pick a vocation that I could learn through hands-on experience and assisting others like me. Not that I'd really heard much about it since I rarely had the opportunity to see them.

I pushed aside the negative feelings that thinking about my grandparents brought up. I'd never really had a relationship with them, and I didn't plan on changing that any time soon. They'd never forgiven my mother for running away with my father.

Anyway, I didn't need their approval. My shop was doing well. Rawlins, Wyoming was far from a large city, but I'd built a good reputation in just two years and I did a decent business. My online orders made up the majority of my profit – yet another reason why I made sure I was up on the latest technology. I probably could have done away with most of my online presence if I'd moved to a bigger city, but I didn't want to leave Rawlins. I'd chosen it on purpose, after all.

It was the one place I'd lived that actually felt like home. Both of my parents had been here with me, and they hadn't been bringing all sorts of other partners through the house. Granted, it had all been because Blair had needed some recovery time after having caught malaria while she and Kevin had been in some South American country. Kevin had wanted to write a book on their experiences, and they'd both decided that the atmosphere out West was the most conducive to health and creativity. He'd gotten halfway through it before getting bored. Not that it surprised me. That was how things went with him.

I loved my parents, and I knew they loved me, but they'd never quite understood why I didn't think having parents in an open relationship who insisted I call them by their first name and travel around the world was the greatest thing.

I made my way back to the front of the store and flipped around my sign to say that I was open. The sun was finally out, and I took a moment to step outside. My dress was a bit thin for mid-March, but I let myself enjoy the combination of scents that I'd always associated with Rawlins at this time of year. A hint of spring with that sharp edge of snow.

Wind gusted down the street, and I shivered, goosebumps prickling my skin. I stayed out a moment longer, waving at Mr. Kendrick who owned the barbershop across the street. He came out every morning to sweep or shovel the bit of sidewalk in front of his store. He'd done it when I was here as a kid too, and he'd seemed ancient even then. When I'd first moved back here, I'd asked him if I could help him in the mornings, but he'd insisted that he'd be out here rain or shine every day until he keeled over of a heart attack.

I had a bad feeling that, one day, he was going to do just that. At least his grandson Benji had joined him a few months ago. Maybe he'd be able to convince Mr. Kendrick to take it easy.

I'd take them over some tea later and see how they were doing. Maybe I'd mix up some of my granola bars too. I used local honey, just like I bought any local produce or grains that were available in the area. While my shop was more about herbal supplements and homeopathic remedies, I liked to have healthy snack options around too. I sold a decent amount of them, but they were mostly on hand, so I could snack throughout the day and not feel guilty.

I headed to my in-shop worktable and my less-sentimental mortar bowl and pestle. I needed to grind up some spices to put into the custom-made tea pouches I stocked, and I always left those to do during the workday since they didn't require the sort of precise measuring that the more medicinal ones did.

By mid-morning, I'd finished everything except the ginger I was saving for last. When I was done with it, I'd brew a pot and take it across the street, then head over to the bakery for a few of their homemade poppy seed rolls.

My phone buzzed just as I was setting out the new supplies, and I headed over to the counter to check it.

A message from Blair. I swiped the screen.

Brea, darling, we have some exciting news we'd like to share in person. Please meet us this evening for dinner.

Dinner? Today? I frowned at the phone. The last I'd heard from them, they'd been living in Vermont with one of Kevin's old philosophy professor buddies.

Are you flying me out?

After a moment, Blair's response came back. *I'm sorry, dear, we must have forgotten to tell you that we were in Rawlins.*

In Rawlins? Since when? I blew out a breath and reminded myself not to be frustrated. She'd tell me everything, eventually. She just took her time getting there.

We'll explain over dinner. Meet us at six o'clock.

The address was outside of Rawlins, but nowhere near Vermont. What in the world was going on?

THREE
BLAKE

"Whoa! Easy, girl!" It only took me a second to react, and I ignored the underlying problem while I got Annie under control. She wasn't an excitable horse usually, but I couldn't blame her when she was startled like that.

As soon as she was calm enough for me to dismount, I jumped off, catching her reins so she wouldn't go wandering. Only when I was sure Annie was safe did I turn toward the idiots who'd spooked her in the first place.

"What the fuck?!" Normally, I didn't curse or snap at total strangers unless they did something like, well, like they'd just done. What sort of moron didn't know they shouldn't come sneaking onto someone's property and scare a horse someone was riding?

Then I got a good look at them and realized what the first problem was.

These two were not farmers or ranchers. I'd been around both enough for the past few years to tell the difference between people who worked their asses off for a living and rich people who liked to play at life.

These two were in the rich category.

The man had the sort of tanned, leathery skin that a lot of men got from working long hours outside, but my gut told me he'd probably gotten it more from lounging on beaches than wrangling cattle. His hair was silver, and his eyes were hidden behind a pair of sunglasses I knew were worth at least a few hundred dollars.

My oldest brother, Jax, had a pair by the same designer.

The woman was shorter than him and younger, but the way she clung to his arm told me she wasn't his daughter. Both were wearing the sort of clothes that looked like they could have been straight out of a hippie commune, if they hadn't been more expensive than my horses.

"I'm so sorry," the man said, giving me one of those toothy grins I'd always hated. "I didn't mean to startle your horse. Blair and I were just so eager to come over here and finally meet you, I guess my excitement just got the best of me."

I kept glaring at them both; waiting for them to say something that made sense.

"I'm Blair McCormick," the woman said, leaning forward as she held out a hand. "I'm Kevin's partner."

I considered not shaking her hand and blaming it on the fact that my hands were sweating inside my riding gloves, but then I reminded myself that I didn't have any reason to be extra polite. I yanked off my glove and shook her hand, then turned to the man.

"Nice to meet you," he said as he shook my hand, "Mr...?"

"Blake," I said reluctantly. "Just Blake. You two shouldn't be trespassing out here. You could end up on the business end of a shotgun or get torn up by a guard dog."

The two exchanged a look I couldn't read and then turned back to me with nearly identical smiles. Creepy smiles, if I was being honest.

Were they on something?

"We're not here to trespass," Kevin said. "We're neighbors."

I waited for the punchline. When it didn't come, I took a closer look at where we were. I was near the front of my property again, and I could see the car now, a shiny red muscle car that told me Kevin was still doing the mid-life crisis thing. It sat at the end of my driveway, which meant they had to have just pulled in when they saw me coming and decided to park there.

"Technically," I said, "you are trespassing. This is my property."

Neither one of them seemed to care that I was being rude.

Blair beamed at me like I'd given them a warm welcome. "We've just been so excited to come meet you, and this was the first time we'd seen you since we've come out here, so we thought we'd just seize the day, you know?"

Shit. She was one of those sunshiny happy people.

"You bought one of the ranches?" I needed to figure out which one, so I could avoid it at all costs. Not that I'd ever been a neighbor-visiting person. I just had a bad feeling that these two would be the sort who'd 'pop over' now and again, and I wanted to make sure I had some sort of warning system in place to keep *this* from happening ever again.

Security cameras. I needed more security cameras.

"We did," Kevin said. "We actually used to live in Rawlins years ago, so when we decided to retire, there was only one place either of us wanted to go. There's no better place for communing with nature, and the harmony here has always been magnificent."

Yeah, he was one of those.

"We just want you to know that we're sending good vibes out to all of our neighbors, wishing you, health and happiness." Blair reached out but stopped before she touched me.

Smart move.

I doubted they'd like to hear that the way they could make me happy was by getting back into their car and getting the hell off my property.

"Thanks," I said gruffly. "I have work to do."

"You are so lucky," Kevin said. "To live in a beautiful place like this. To spend your days in such a paradise. The blue skies, and the sun, and the trees, and all of it. To be in tune with the world around you."

I didn't bother telling him that I hadn't grown up here. It wasn't any of his damn business, and I never intended on being in a position where it *was* their business.

I just waited.

I'd learned years ago that if I wanted out of a situation or conversation, a great way to do it was to be quiet and wait. Not quiet like my brother Cai. His quiet was calm and all that sort of shit. My quiet...my silence had always felt like I was just waiting for everything to blow up. Like I was in some sort of pressure cooker or something equally hostile.

So, I didn't say a word.

"Was this your family land?" Blair looked around like she expected to see generations of my family suddenly riding up. "I can see how amazing it would be to hand something like this down through generations."

I finally saw something real on her face, but it didn't interest me enough to ask about it. These two were driving me nuts.

"Anyway," Kevin continued, "we wanted to make sure you knew you were welcome to come over to our retreat any time. I'm sure all of this can block your chi, and everyone wants a little time to meditate, am I right?"

"Oh, and if you happen to see anyone wandering onto your property, don't be alarmed. We're going to encourage our guests to explore, and we never know where our life path will take us—"

I was tired of waiting for them to figure out I didn't want them here.

"You came over to introduce yourselves. Consider yourselves introduced. You know where you parked."

If it annoyed them, neither of them showed it. In fact, if anything, their smiles grew wider.

"Of course, of course," Kevin said with that obnoxiously patronizing tone that my brothers always used with me.

Big. Mistake.

"Look," I said, "I don't give a fuck what you're doing over there. Go back to your retreat or whatever and stay off my land."

I turned my back on them and headed toward the barn. I would've preferred to ride, but I didn't trust them not to spook Annie again.

Idiots.

FOUR

BREA

I turned off at the ranch exit Blair had given me and frowned as the car bounced a little. I rarely drove, and this was just one of the many reasons why. I wasn't the sort of person who thought everyone everywhere could completely stop using vehicles, but I like to cut my carbon footprint down as much as possible.

It was absolutely beautiful out here, I thought as I found the driveway Blair had described. If I hadn't wanted to live close enough to my shop to walk, I would've loved to have gotten a place like this. Maybe, if I could expand, I'd be able to…

I pushed the thought aside. I wasn't looking to become a businesswoman. I owned a business, sure, but that wasn't the same thing. I was happy with where my life was right now, and I was going to be happy and content.

Before I went any further down that path, I came around a line of trees – planted in too straight a line to have been natural – and saw a massive ranch house that seemed to be in the process of being converted into something else. I couldn't quite tell what, or how much work was left to do, but I had a feeling whatever it was, it was the reason I was here.

"Brea!" Blair was hurrying toward me before I'd made it two steps toward the front door.

No matter how strange my relationship with my parents was, there was still something comforting about seeing those familiar features, the long flowing skirt, and fuzzy cardigan.

"Hi," I said, wrapping my arms around my mother. The familiar scent of cloves and cinnamon enveloped me. She'd worn these little sachets for as long as I could remember, and even though we'd never stayed in one place for long, that smell to me had been home.

"You cut your hair," she said as she took a step back and let Kevin come forward to give me a hug.

"I did," I said with a smile.

My parents might not have been the most conventional when it came to marriage and family, or even the most observant about things, but I'd never doubted their love for me.

"You look lovely, as always," she said, linking her arm through my father's.

"You two look good," I said as I followed them up the gravel path to the front door.

"Thank you," Blair said, moving ahead of Kevin to open the door. "The aura around this place is amazing. I feel refreshed just breathing in the air."

I wasn't into the whole aura thing, but I got how she felt about the air. I meant to ask them what they were doing here, but as soon as I stepped inside, I lost track of any questions I had.

We were in a rustic lobby with soft lighting and the sort of old-fashioned iron fixtures that must've cost a pretty penny. The rugs were done in various Native American patterns, and I didn't doubt they were authentic. Similar blankets hung on the walls instead of artwork. It wasn't, however, until I smelled the incense Blair and Kevin always burned that I realized they weren't simply visiting.

"What's going on?" I asked.

"The dining area is in here," Blair said, gesturing to our right.

It was definitely an *area* and not a *room*. The table could easily fit more than a dozen people, though at this moment it was only set for three. I moved to the far seat and waited until my parents joined me before looking at them expectantly. Instead of answering me, however, Kevin opened a bottle of wine and filled all three of the wine glasses.

"A toast." He held his glass up high. "To a bright and glorious future. May we all reach our maximum potential and make this world a better place."

I only took a sip of the tart beverage. I generally preferred beer, but my parents always liked to toast with wine.

"We bought it," Blair announced.

"Bought what?" I was pretty sure I knew what she meant, but I'd learned to not assume. Blair and Kevin didn't always follow the most logical progressions and making them spell things out was a good way to avoid misunderstandings.

"The ranch." She beamed. "Kevin and I have decided that we want to settle down."

I stared at her. That couldn't mean what I thought it meant. "'Settle down'?" I echoed.

"We're not young anymore," Kevin said, and for the first time, I noticed the lines that had grown deeper around his eyes.

I often forgot how much older he was than Blair. He was forty when I was born while Blair had been only nineteen. My grandparents were only four and five years older than him. One of the many reasons they hadn't approved of the relationship.

"I'm just surprised," I said, gripping the glass in my hands. "I know how much you love to travel, but even if I'd pictured you guys buying a place, I never would've thought it'd be here. You're both so social. I would've thought you'd go back to one of the communes you liked."

"We thought about it," Kevin said, "but in the end, we decided that we wanted to be closer to you."

Blair reached over and put her hand over mine. "We've missed you."

I smiled, a rush of warmth washing over me. "I've missed you guys too."

It was the truth. I was used to them being absent, but that didn't mean I didn't want them to be around more.

We ate in silence for a few minutes before I asked one of the many questions that had been bouncing around in my head since I'd gotten my mother's text. "Not that I don't think the place is gorgeous, but I must ask, why here? There are plenty of houses in Rawlins you could have bought."

"That's the other part of what we wanted to talk to you about," Kevin said, exchanging a look with Blair. "You know we've never liked the idea of retirement, so this isn't only going to be our home. We've converted it into a retreat."

Blair picked up the explanation, excitement lighting up her face. "It's going to be amazing. We both saw so many people in the corporate world and in those high social circles completely burn themselves out trying to do everything at once. Think of how much better it would be if they had somewhere they could go to relax."

"We're going to offer all organic meals," Kevin continued, "with options for vegans or specialty diets. We'll have organic facials, wraps, mud treatments, hot stone massages."

My parents were opening a...spa?

Blair took over again. "Of course, all of these will be amenities offered, but if guests simply want time and space away from the hustle and bustle of the world, that's an option as well. We have rooms here in the main house, but there are some wonderful cabins we'll be renovating as well."

Cabins? It took me a minute to realize they meant the quarters where ranch hands would normally have lived. They would be easy enough to convert into more traditional cabins, I supposed.

"Blair and I will be offering seminars on simplifying one's life, living holistically, the benefits of rejecting societal constraints."

"Nothing will be required, of course," Blair said. "Guests will be encouraged to commune with nature and find their own life's path wherever it may take them."

"That's great," I said sincerely. I was happy for them and glad that they were going to be living nearby, but now I was also a little relieved that they hadn't decided to put the retreat in Rawlins itself. I had a feeling I'd be coaxed into becoming a part of the retreat if I was too close.

"You haven't even heard the best part yet," Blair said. "We converted the front parlor into a shop for you and turned the room behind it into a bedroom suite." She clapped her hands together. "So, it'll be just like your place now."

Oh.

"That's a great offer." I chose my words carefully. "But I like my apartment and my shop in town. I do most of my business online, but I do have regulars who probably might not feel comfortable coming out to a retreat to buy things. Plus, I own the building, and I'm not sure I'd be able to find someone to buy or rent it."

It was all true, but I didn't give them the underlying reason why I didn't want to drop everything and move my store out here. With the singular exception of the time we'd lived here before, my parents had never stuck to anything for more than a few months. It wasn't only the appeal of traveling that had kept them on the move all these years. Short things like hiking the Grand Canyon or meeting indigenous tribes in South America, those generally got done, but when it came to anything that was a longer commitment, they simply didn't have the staying power.

Once, when I was around fifteen, they'd decided they wanted to live off the land in northern Canada. We spent more time getting to the cabin they'd rented than we did actually living there. When I was eight, they became involved with an organization that fought for land preservation. It was a great cause, but after a couple months of nothing more than a handful of single-day protests, they decided their time and energy was better spent with a group trying to save the rainforests. They always meant well, and they were always sincere in their passions.

But they had the attention spans of toddlers most of the time.

If I moved my shop here, I might make decent sales for a while, but once they got bored, I'd end up having to move right back into Rawlins, and I'd most likely lose the base I'd carefully built up over the last two years.

"It's open to negotiation," Kevin said with a smile. "Maybe we can come to a compromise. We really would love for you to be a part of this."

I took another sip of my wine. When my father said things like that, I remembered he hadn't always been the man I knew. Most of the time, I forgot that he'd been a businessman for years before he and Blair met. He came from old New York City money and had been groomed to take over the family business. I wasn't sure what that business had been since he didn't have it anymore.

He'd gotten an MBA, married a woman from the right family, and then after his parents died, took over the company entirely. Then, when he was thirty-four, something happened, and he'd decided that wasn't the life he wanted. He'd sold all his shares in the company, gave his wife a generous settlement in exchange for an uncontested divorce – which she was more than happy to do – and then walked away from all of it. He still had plenty of money, which was how we'd been able to travel so much, but he'd never deliberately flaunted it.

"What would you think about having a shop here that's open once or twice a week?" Blair asked, her brows raised in hopeful expectation. "The room in the back can be yours whenever you come out to visit, and you can set the store hours however you want. If you need some help to hire someone for your shop in town, we're more than happy to do it."

"I can handle hiring someone part-time," I said.

I'd never been busy enough to consider it before, but I could get someone to take care of things two days a week while I came out here, especially since it wouldn't be permanent. If I wasn't making anything out here, I could close the store without my parents feeling like I didn't want to work with them, and if it did well, then I'd stay until they got bored and left again. If they got through more than six months, I'd consider it a miracle.

"Does that mean you'll do it?" Blair asked.

I smiled at her. "It does. We can work through scheduling when I bring in some inventory. Does that sound good?"

"It sounds wonderful," Blair said. "Now, let me go get the dessert I made. It's something new. Kale chips and fruit dip."

As she walked away, I made a mental note to suggest that they hire a cook to feed guests. Health food, junk food, organic or not, it wouldn't matter. Blair only knew how to make two or three meals, and everything else was an experiment that usually failed. Kevin knew enough that he didn't go hungry, but for large groups of people, a cook would be best.

A glance at Kevin told me he was thinking the same thing. At least we were one hundred percent on the same page when it came to that.

FIVE

BLAKE

As much as I may have looked like the sort of guy who liked to live off the grid, I liked my electronics. Mostly because they meant I could usually have supplies delivered to me rather than going into Rawlins for them. It was a nice enough town, but still...people.

I'd put it off for as long as possible, but now I had things that I could only get in town. Or, at least, things that I preferred to get from local sources. I wasn't so much of an antisocial bastard that I wouldn't support locals, even if they didn't deliver.

When it came to lumber, there was only one place to go here. McPherson's. Wyatt McPherson was from one of the founding families of Rawlins, and in some places, I knew that would've meant he could pretty much do what he wanted. Hell, my family hadn't been one of Boston's founding families, but we'd had enough money that my brothers and I had gotten away with more than we should have. Wyatt wasn't like that though. He and his huge family were as down to earth as anyone.

If I liked people, I would've liked them.

I pulled my truck up to the loading dock and saw that Wyatt already had my order stacked and ready to go. By the time I was up on the dock, Wyatt and his two oldest kids – Lucinda and Scott – were waiting.

"Good morning, Blake." His voice was as gruff as ever, but he was smiling.

"Morning, Wyatt."

We'd both come to an unspoken agreement when we'd first met that we'd be on a first-name basis even though he was probably close to Grandfather's age.

"Lucinda. Scott." I nodded at them, and they nodded back.

"Let's get him loaded up," Wyatt said. As his kids moved to do just that, Wyatt turned to me. "Mind if I ask what all that's for?"

I stuck my hands in my pockets to keep from grabbing a couple two-by-fours. I'd done that the first time I'd ordered from McPherson's, only to have Wyatt reprimand me. I'd thought it was some bullshit about customers not getting their hands dirty, but then he'd explained to me that his business insurance would have a fit if a customer got hurt. I didn't like standing around while other people did work, but I understood respecting a person's business.

"I got a customer who wants me to build him a rowboat."

Wyatt gave me a sideways look and reached into his pocket for his cigarettes.

"I thought you quit," I said as he lit one.

"I thought people usually bought their boats already made," he countered.

I shrugged. "This guy wants it to look like he built it himself for his girlfriend. Supposed to be some sort of romantic gesture to his girl."

Wyatt snorted, then took a drag on his cigarette. "Damn fools."

"Tell me about it," I muttered.

"Still don't have a girl, huh?"

I rolled my eyes. "I'm not going out with your granddaughter."

He snorted again. "You think you're too good for my family?"

"I think your granddaughter is eighteen, and I'm twenty-eight."

"Dad are you trying to set Jessie up with someone a decade older than her?" Scott asked. "I thought we talked about this."

"You'd rather she gets serious with that college boy she brought home for Christmas? Damn city boy."

It was Scott's turn to roll his eyes, but he didn't argue. Wyatt wasn't really trying to set me up with Jessie. It was just our thing. How we passed the time while the truck was loaded so I didn't feel guilty for not helping.

"You're just making a rowboat?" Wyatt asked. "Damn big boat."

I barked a laugh. "Yeah, well, this guy doesn't want some SS *Minnow*. He's got it in his head that if he has this fancy boat, she's going to accept his proposal."

"Women don't care about that," Wyatt said. "Well, they might care, but it won't change the answer. Ask 'em simple or ask 'em expensive, if they're going to say yes, that's what it'll be, no matter the where or how."

Now it was my turn to give him a sideways look. That was the most I'd heard him say at one go. "You trying to give me dating advice?"

"I'm just saying that when I asked my Nancy, I just asked her. Didn't need a fancy ring or anything like that."

"The way Mom tells it," Lucinda said, "you didn't actually *ask* her at all. You basically *told* her you two were getting married."

Wyatt shrugged and took another drag on his cigarette. "Point is, she still said yes. And we've been married forty-seven years."

Forty-seven years.

I couldn't imagine being with someone that long. Grandfather and Grandma Olive had made it that far. Mom and Dad probably would have too if...

Nope.

Not going there.

"All set," Scott said, dusting off his hands.

"Thanks." I shook hands all around this time, then reached into my pocket and pulled out several folded bills. I handed them over and then headed back to my truck.

I had non-perishables delivered, but when I wanted fresh produce, I went to *The Peach and Plum Market*. It wasn't really the season for anything fresh, but I'd rather get it here than somewhere else. The only drawback was the usual cashier had a thing for me and hadn't accepted that I wasn't interested.

I picked up a basket and went straight for what I needed. A couple apples, pears, carrots, a few other things here and there. The place wasn't busy for a Friday afternoon, but I still avoided eye contact with anyone who happened to walk by. Most people in Rawlins knew who I was – well, the reclusive blacksmith part of me anyway – but if I looked at anyone, they'd still try to talk to me. Best to keep moving.

"Hi, Blake."

"Morning," I mumbled. I didn't look up from the things I was putting on the conveyer belt.

"Trish," she said in that same bubbly voice. "It's Trish."

I grunted. If I said I remembered her, she'd read too much into it. If I said I didn't, she'd be upset. Better a noncommittal response.

"I think it's going to snow again," she continued. "It doesn't seem fair, does it? That it's almost spring and it's still snowing. I can't wait until I get out of here and go somewhere that is warm all the time. Nashville is my first choice. I'm going to be a singer."

She paused, and I knew if I looked up, I'd see an expectant light in those blue eyes. It was the same one I always saw when I came here. She was bound and determined to get my attention.

Which meant I had to ignore her.

I used my card while she packed up my food, then left without looking at her once. Trish was a pretty enough woman, but I wasn't going there. Aside from the fact that I had a feeling she'd be clingy, she wasn't discreet. I didn't need the whole damn town in my personal life.

I set my groceries in the passenger's seat and then leaned back against my truck. Trish was probably right about the snow. I could feel it in the air. It shouldn't be a storm, but I didn't want to risk running out of anything, so I took a minute to think over everything I had to pick up, as well as what I had at home.

I wasn't really looking anywhere specific when I was thinking, but then a flash of something caught my eye. I'd seen the shop before, I knew. I had to have seen it since it was right across from the barber where I get my hair cut, but somehow it had never really registered in my mind. Then my brain processed the name: *Grow 'n Heal*.

Now I remembered. A couple years ago, some of the men had been talking about it when I'd been getting a haircut. According to Palmer Griffith who owned a cattle ranch on the other side of town, when he'd first seen the young woman moving in, he'd thought she was opening a nursery – a *plant* nursery – because she'd had all sorts of plants in pots, but no cut flowers. But when Palmer and his wife Cleo had gone over to see what the new shop had to offer, they saw it was a little...different.

Potted plants, sure, but most of them weren't the normal sorts of flowers. There were some lilies, roses, tulips, that sort of thing, but most of the plants were ones they didn't recognize. And then they'd seen that plants weren't all that was being sold.

Teas. Potpourri. Decorative dried arrangements. And a

whole section of what Palmer called 'New Age crap.' Herbal remedies, supplements, that sort of thing.

I got the point of vitamins in general, but I thought people put far too much faith in them. I didn't believe a person could go pick a weed, eat it, and suddenly their memory would improve. Tea was for drinking, and maybe it'd help with a sore throat, but that was the extent of its 'medicinal powers.'

"New Age fluff," I said with a sigh. I pushed myself off the truck, shaking my head. The things people would believe.

That glint of light came again, and this time, I recognized it as the sunlight reflecting off the chain holding up the open / closed sign. Someone was flipping it over to say it was closed. I caught a glimpse of a flowered skirt, but nothing else. I supposed it was the young woman who owned the place. I didn't know if I'd ever seen her before, or if I'd even heard her name, but I didn't really care.

Someone like her, into all that flower power free love shit, wasn't someone I'd be interested in talking to, so there was no point in meeting her.

SIX
BREA

Lamb Woodall.

Her name was actually *Lamb*. Not a nickname. Not short for something. Her parents had named her Lamb.

I made a mental note to thank my parents for giving me the sort of unique name that I had. I supposed Lamb could like her name, but I wouldn't have wanted to be named after an animal, and certainly not an animal that was known for being fuzzy and timid.

I raised my head to watch her for a bit. I'd been looking over her résumé while she acquainted herself with the store so that when we sat down to the interview, both of us could ask questions. The last thing I wanted to do was hire someone who thought this was a florist shop. When I'd first opened, I'd had a lot of people come in, thinking that's what the shop was. I needed someone who understood that, while I did sell plants, the point of *Grow 'n Heal* was a function beyond simple beauty. Though many of my plants were beautiful.

Lamb took the lid off one of the jars and sniffed delicately. Fitting, I supposed since she was delicate. Barely over five feet and with fine features, she was the definition of the word. I felt huge next to her.

Damn. She even sneezed delicately.

"Lamb," I said. When she didn't respond, I tried again. "Lamb!"

She turned around, those long henna-red curls knocking a tin of tea to the floor. She flushed, pale skin going blotchy, and immediately bent to pick up the tea...and bumped into a display, nearly knocking it over.

"It's okay," I said. "Just leave it. We can pick it up later."

She gave me a concerned look, and I smiled at her. I'd been a little worried about possibly hiring someone more than a decade older than me, but Lamb not only looked like she was younger, she acted like it too. Not immature, necessarily, but rather...inexperienced in some way.

"Miss Chaise, I'm sorry. I just get clumsy when I'm nervous."

"It's okay," I said again. "There's nothing to be nervous about. And it's just Brea, not Miss Chaise."

"Oh, I'm sorry, Miss–I mean, Brea."

I gestured to the chair across from me. "Why don't you have a seat and tell me a little about yourself, and why you want to work here. And be honest. It's all right to say that this is the only place hiring right now."

She let loose an odd giggle that made her seem even younger. The strange thing was, I didn't get the impression from her that it was something she put on. Whoever she was right now was who she was all the time.

"That's not why I want to work here," she said. "I don't even know who else is hiring. I just walked by here and saw that you were looking for someone and I had to come in because I just love this place."

I leaned back in my seat. "I don't think I've ever seen you in here before."

"No." She shook her head, blood rushing to her cheeks again. "I've been going through the website and trying to learn as much as I can...so I can impress you...fudge-icicle."

I blinked. An inventive take on that pseudo-curse that I'd never heard before.

"Lamb," I said, "why don't you just tell me about why you want to work here and why you think you'd be a good employee."

Not like I had much in the way of other options since the only other applicant I'd gotten was Adam Freeman who'd ogled me the entire time, but I still wasn't going to hire someone who didn't have a clue about what I did here. The fact that she'd been looking at the website gave me a little hope at least.

"I've always been interested in plants and healing and how they can offer all sorts of benefits that people don't realize. I've done a lot of research. Like all the ways mint is useful, like aiding in digestion, and how willow bark can help lower fevers and is a natural painkiller. I've read tons of books about homeopathic remedies and supplements."

She did her homework. That was good.

"I don't require you to actually make any of the salves or blends, but you'd be welcome to watch me and learn," I said. "Most of the time, you'd be here by yourself, selling the things that are ready-made. If someone came in with a specific question, I'd expect you to call me if you didn't know something with one hundred percent certainty."

"Of course." Her head bobbed up and down. "I really want to learn."

"Good," I said with a smile. "Do you mind if I ask a couple questions?"

"Please." She folded her hands on her lap.

"What would *Ranunculus ficaria* be used for?" I went with something obscure to see just how deep she'd gone with her research.

She frowned. "I don't think I've heard of that one."

"It's usually called pilewort."

Her forehead furrowed as she thought. "I don't know it."

"That's okay," I said. "It's a bit of an obscure one. When you look at a lot of the labels, I'll have the Latin name, as well as the common name."

"What does pilewort do?"

Good, she was curious about the answer rather than remaining ignorant about it.

"It can be made into a salve to help with hemorrhoids."

"Oh." She blushed.

"Any of the books you see, you're more than welcome to read. I encourage you to at least look through some of the remedy ones to familiarize yourself as much as possible. Things in here are usually slow. That's a good way to stay busy but still be doing something work-related. And if you want to buy any of them, you get a thirty-five percent discount."

"That's wonderful," she said.

"Is there anything else you want to tell me?"

She nodded. "What about rituals?"

And there it was. The other common misconception about my store. I tried not to sigh.

Her blue-green eyes widened. "I know there are all sorts of plants used in cleansing rituals, protection, things like that. I know you wouldn't do anything dark. I'm very interested in learning how to cleanse auras."

I forced a smile. "That's not what I do here. If someone wants to buy plants to use in something like that, they're more than welcome to, but I don't put together anything for rituals. What a person believes is their business, and I make a point to stay neutral. The supplements and homeopathic remedies I offer are science based."

"Of course," she said, color leaving her face as quickly as it had rushed in before. "I didn't mean to offend you."

"You didn't," I said honestly. "I want you to ask questions. It's how I learned, and if you're interested in more than simply running a cash register, it's how you'll learn too."

"Does this mean I have the job?"

She wasn't a bad sort of person. I could handle a little dotty. I had lived with Blair and Kevin, after all. For nearly a full month when I was thirteen, Blair had color-coded her wardrobe to influence the weather by sending positive color vibrations out into the universe, and around the same time, Kevin had started off each morning standing on his head to encourage toxins to leave his body.

"It does." I held out my hand, but Lamb squealed and ran around the table to hug me.

"Thank you so much," she gushed. "You won't regret it, I promise."

I hoped not. "Why don't you come in Monday morning and we'll start going over things."

She nodded, hugged me again, and then practically danced out of the shop. I stood at the door and watched her go, unable to stop a smile. She really was a sweet person.

As I started to turn away, movement caught my eye. The man's back was to me, but even from across the street, I could sense how much power was in that body. At five-and-a-half feet tall, I was a little over average height, but the man I saw was easily three or four inches above six feet, with broad shoulders and muscles that his flannel shirt couldn't disguise. He had light brown hair that looked like it could use a trim, and as he turned to get into his truck, I saw enough scruff to tell me that he hadn't shaved in a day or two.

Then I recognized the strong jaw and scowl. Blake Hunter. He'd already been living on a ranch outside the town when I arrived here, but I'd only seen him a handful of times since then, and I'd never spoken to him. The people in Rawlins talked about him on occasion, but I'd gotten the impression that other than the fact that he kept to himself, there really wasn't much in the way of gossip when it came to him. Most of what I'd heard was about how he was gruff and sometimes rude, but that most people wrote it off as him just being eccentric and anti-social. There was, however, some talk among people of the female persuasion that he'd occasionally hook up with someone in town. He must've picked discreet women because no one I'd ever heard talking about it had been with him, but the rumors were there.

He was handsome enough, I supposed, but I didn't understand people who seemed so angry all the time. I couldn't imagine allowing that much negative energy into my life. I might not have been into auras and that sort of thing, but I believe that every person has an energy about them that comes from how they see the world and what they put out into it.

It was sad, I thought, that someone who appeared to have so much to give was so angry at life. I almost wished that I did believe that I could make him a tea or a salve that would open his eyes to the beauty of the world and all it had to offer.

I sighed and flipped my sign back to *open* before returning to my work. I had enough on my mind with this new shop and my parents being here. I didn't need to take on the burden of someone I didn't even know.

SEVEN

BLAKE

Rannell's Feed was my last stop on my way home, and I was glad to get there. I had enough in the way of supplies to keep me for at least a few weeks, which meant I wouldn't have to interact with anyone but Shane and Annie until I ran out. I rarely even saw the delivery people since I spent so much of my time in my workshop and at the forge. That much peace and isolation was exactly what I needed after the time I'd spent in Boston, and after my interaction with my new neighbors.

I placed my order with the cashier and then headed out to pull my truck around back to be loaded. Rannell's had changed their insurance last year, and now I couldn't load up my own feed bags either. Marcel opened the back of the truck and started loading the bags of feed into the back. I stayed in the driver's seat, checking my email and mentally preparing for what I had to do when I got back to my place.

A knock at my window startled me, but when I looked up, what I saw kept me from snapping. The woman was tall, slender, and probably in her early twenties. She had honey-blonde hair and blue eyes, the sort of features that a model would have envied.

Where the hell had she come from?

I rolled down my window. "Can I help you?"

"Hi, I'm Mindy." She smiled, dimples forming at the corners of her mouth.

"Blake."

She paused, apparently waiting for me to say something, but when I didn't, she put her hand on my door and leaned forward slightly. "I'm here visiting my brother, Desmond, and I've been bored out of my mind. Today's my last day before I head back home, and I was looking for something...memorable. You look memorable."

"Where's home?"

I wasn't making small talk. I needed to know if 'home' was close by. I didn't want to risk her being close enough to come back if she wanted more than what she was angling for right now.

"Miami. You actually live here?"

I gave her a slow, lingering look that ran from the top of her head down to her knees, which was as far as I could see without getting out of the truck. When I reached her eyes again, she tapped the top of my door with one manicured nail.

"Like what you see?"

"I do." It'd been a while since I'd been with anyone. I hadn't really been looking, but she was here, and if she was willing, I wasn't going to turn her down.

"Are you interested in being my only fun memory of Wyoming?" She winked at me.

Just to be on the safe side, I asked, "How old are you?"

She laughed. "Twenty-five. And, no, I'm not looking for a relationship or romance or anything like that. I'm not married. I don't have any kids. I just want a good, hard fuck. Does that hit all your questions?"

I shrugged. "Good enough for me."

She walked around the front of the truck and got into the passenger's side. I saw Marcel give her a look when he came around to tell me I was good, but I ignored it.

She, on the other hand, waved at him. "Nice to see you again, Marcel."

"Damn. That girl don't change a bit," Marcel muttered. He looked at me. "Be careful, Blake. That girl could chew you up and spit you out."

That was good to know. Meant she could take what I dished out.

I nodded at him, and we pulled away from the store.

"You got a place in town?" she asked.

"Nope." I took the next right.

There was another long pause between us where I knew she was waiting for me to say something more.

"You don't talk much, do you?"

"Nope." I took another right.

"Okay then," she said. She slid across the seat and put her hand on my thigh. When I didn't protest, it moved higher, and by the time she had it on my crotch, I was half-hard. I should've told her to wait until we stopped somewhere, but I let her unbuckle my pants and pull down the zipper.

"Commando," she said. "Should've guessed."

She sounded pleased, but all I cared about was the hand wrapped around my cock. Two firm strokes and then her mouth was there, hot and wet around the tip before moving farther down. Holy fuck, her mouth was scorching. And the suction...fuck!

I jerked the wheel to the left a little harder than necessary, but I figured it was better to get someplace where we could get down to it than to crash because a stranger was sucking my brain out through my dick.

I pulled into the train yard and made my way behind a

series of cars that were parked on one of the rails. I slammed on the brakes and put the truck into park, the vibrations from her laughter making me curse.

I grabbed her hair and tugged, far from gentle. She was still laughing as she came up. "I thought you'd like it rough. Good. Me too."

I gave her a hard look, needing to see if she was telling the truth. She ran her tongue along her bottom lip, the challenge in her eyes clear.

"Get out."

The smile faded. "What?"

"Get out. Drop the pants."

She grinned again and moved away, opening the passenger door. I figured she would go around the back, climb up into the bed of the truck where I had a couple blankets tied over my supplies. Instead, she went to the front of the truck. By the time I was out and over to where she was, she had her pants around her knees, and she was bent over the hood.

I pulled a condom out of my wallet and rolled it on. "Tell me if it's too much."

She looked over her shoulder at me. "Fuck me."

I grabbed her hips and drove into her hard and deep. She let out a yelp as she went up on her toes, those fancy nails scratching at my hood. Good thing I hadn't taken her face to face. She would've torn the shit out of my back and shoulders.

And probably deafened me.

"Yes! Yes! *Fuck*, yes! Harder!"

I reached around and slapped my hand over her mouth. The last thing I needed was someone at the train yard hearing us and thinking some woman was in trouble. I didn't need to add pervert to my reputation as a recluse, and public indecency was almost as bad as the rough sex I liked.

Mindy's body bucked and writhed, the gush of liquid and

spasming muscles telling me she was coming. Two more strokes and I came too, forgetting for several white-hot seconds about everything else but how good I felt.

EIGHT
BREA

I HAD TO ADMIT, MY PARENTS HAD CHOSEN A BEAUTIFUL place to build their retreat. The house was big, but still had room to expand if they wanted to add on. Trees had been planted around the property, offering areas of shade where benches and rock gardens had been set up. They'd gone all out with landscaping and interior decorating, more than I would've expected.

They'd put a decent amount of thought into this, which made me wonder if, for the first time, they'd make it a year or two before taking off again. I had to admit, I didn't hate the idea.

"What do you think?" Blair asked as she followed me around the space they'd designed for me.

"Large windows, an open space." I turned around to face her. "It's wonderful."

"Have you ordered the display cases yet?"

"I did. And I ordered more supplies. They should get here next week."

"Is that when you think you'll be moving in here?"

The look on her face was so hopeful that I almost wanted to lie to her. "I'm not moving here. You know that, right? I'll keep some things here for any time I don't want to drive home, but I love my apartment."

Her smile dimmed a bit but didn't disappear completely. "Of course. Just know that the offer is always open. Any time you want, you can move in here and be a full-time part of the retreat."

"Thanks." I ran my hand across the counter. "I'd like to see the rest of the property. Mind if I look around?"

"Go wherever you want," she said. "You are welcome in every part of this world. Walk your path and change anything you need along the way."

I thanked her and headed outside. The weather was a bit warmer than it usually was this time of year, and the sun was shining. It was the perfect day to be outside walking around. No one else was up here, so it was just me and nature.

I'd been on a walk like this one when I'd realized that I wanted to work with plants. I'd been in New York, a few hours outside of Buffalo, tent camping with my parents and another couple they'd been involved with at the time. I'd had my own little tent, and the four of them had shared a larger one. I hadn't quite been old enough to realize what it meant that my parents always had other people sleeping in their bed, but I'd known that they were all caught up in whatever they were doing.

Since they'd mostly left me to myself, I'd gone for walks. I never went off the paths, and I always made sure I got back before dark, but I walked for hours. Walked and looked at plants and trees and flowers. I picked leaves from the trees, picked up rocks, picked flowers.

And I picked some poison ivy.

I'd ended up in the hospital with an awful allergic reaction and a desire to never do something that stupid again. When I'd told Kevin and Blair, Kevin had ordered a botany book, and I'd spent the rest of the week reading. I'd fallen in love with plants as I read, and the obsession had only grown since then.

I'd even forgiven poison ivy.

My muscles were warming to the movement now, and I realized just how long it had been since I'd been on a long, aimless walk. I walked a lot in Rawlins rather than driving, but it had been a while since I'd done it for the sheer pleasure of it. I'd always been an athletic person, though I hadn't ever done much in the way of organized sports. It wasn't until now that I realized how much I'd missed the enjoyment of physical activity.

As my walk continued, my mind wandered about before coming to rest on work. The day after my parents had talked to me about opening a small shop out here, I'd started working on inventory. I didn't keep a lot on hand because much of what I dealt in had shelf lives, which meant I needed to figure out how much to take back and forth, and how much new to order.

I'd also been toying with the idea of finding something that my parents wouldn't really have to put together but would just be able to sell. That idea was still in the back of my head when I reached a line of pine trees.

Pinus sylvestris scotica.

Pine tree resin could be used for a lot of things, particularly as a powerful antiseptic and expectorant. Many of the respiratory remedies I made used resin. The needles were a good source of vitamin C. Maybe that's what I could do. Instead of purchasing the resin and needles I used, maybe I could collect them here, work on the things I made that used those ingredients. I'd feel less like I was wasting my time here if I kept busy.

I ducked under a couple low-hanging branches and put my hand on the trunk. Most people thought tree bark was pretty much the same. Some realized there was rough and smooth bark, but not many understood that even among those two distinctions were all sorts of nuances. Things that needed to be felt with the hands to be understood.

I moved around the tree, trailing my hand across the bark,

feeling it, learning where I could harvest the resin without harming the tree. I examined the branches, the needles. Pine cones made beautiful decorations.

I was so caught up in what I was doing that I didn't realize I wasn't alone until someone spoke.

"Who the fuck are you?"

I spun around, nearly tripping. I almost didn't recognize him because I was a little distracted by the mass of tanned skin and muscle that came with a shirtless Blake Hunter.

Shit. Blake Hunter.

What the hell was he doing here?

"Are you deaf? What the hell are you doing on my property?"

NINE
BLAKE

The breeze coming in from outside was nice, but even it couldn't cancel out the blazing fire I needed to work this piece of iron. When I finished this one, I'd be able to take a break and cool down a bit. Technically, I could've paused any time I wanted since I was on schedule with the order and I was my own boss, but part of what made me successful at what I did was because I stuck with things until they were done.

I might've inherited a bit of my family's workaholic tendencies, but at least I was working at something I loved. Grandfather had always said that's what my dad had done. Instead of joining the family business, Dad had become a journalist because that had been the only thing he'd ever wanted to do. When I'd been introduced to wood-working, I'd finally understood what Grandfather had been talking about. I'd always been decent in school, and I could've gone to college if I'd wanted to but working with my hands had appealed to me in a way nothing else had. When I had a project, it consumed me; and drowned out everything else. It was the only thing that had ever been able to clear my mind so completely.

Since it was just me and Annie and Shane out here, I didn't have to worry about it taking time away from anyone else.

I inspected the intricate loops I'd just finished making. If anything was wrong with it, I'd have to go back and re-do it. I compared it to one of the other finished products, then looked at the original design. All three matched. Perfect.

The familiar sizzle of red-hot metal meeting water mixed with the roar of the fire. These were the sounds of home. Not cars and people and traffic and construction and everything else that came with living in a city. Boston hadn't been a bad place to grow up, but I preferred where I was now.

I went through the process of making sure things were in their proper places, the routine virtually automatic after all these years. The blacksmith I'd apprenticed under had told me about a farrier he'd known who'd stepped outside for something without shutting things down, thinking he'd be gone only a minute, and he'd ended up losing half a building and burned the shit out of his arm. Even if I only meant to go outside to cool off, I went through every step, just in case.

I hung up my apron and headed outside, pulling my sweat-soaked shirt over my head as I went. I closed my eyes as the cool air hit me. I loved what I did, but if I could've done it with a little less heat, I wouldn't have minded. The sun was warm today, but it was a pleasant warmth, the kind that promised spring was on its way.

I opened my eyes and refocused my mind on what else I needed to do today. The scones would sit for the day and then I'd inspect them again before taking a picture and sending it to my client. If he was satisfied, I'd box them up and ship them out. The larger project he wanted was on my list, but I wouldn't be working on that today. I had some basic stuff of my own to do. I wasn't a farrier, but I'd done a bit of training under one, enough to take care of Shane and Annie. I had a pile of other 'to fix' stuff sitting on a table in the barn. I'd gotten behind during the time I'd been in Boston, and I hadn't quite gotten caught up yet. I'd made the shoes for both horses, but that was about it.

That's when I remembered that I'd made the shoes but hadn't taken them to the barn. I often made supplies ahead of time, using extra iron or some extra time while I waited for something else to finish. Instead of keeping them in the forge, I stashed them behind the building in watertight containers. It kept them out of my way and all together in an easily accessible space.

I walked around back, compiling a mental list of the order I wanted to get things done, but before I reached the containers, I saw movement over by the pine trees that sat at the corner of my property. My mind flipped through all the possible animals it could be. I'd gotten the occasional antelope and even a coyote a time or two, but the figure didn't move like any of those. Then it came around one of the trees, and I realized it was a person.

I scowled, my temper flaring to the surface. What the fuck was wrong with people? What made them think they could come wandering onto my property like it was some public park or something? I'd never had this problem before, but two times in two weeks, I'd had people acting like they had every right to go wherever they wanted.

I stomped over, my annoyance increasing with each step. Within a few yards, I realized it was a woman, but that didn't make me any less pissed. When I was finally in hearing distance, I spoke.

"Who the fuck are you?"

Probably not the best way to approach things, but I wasn't the person at fault here. If she had a problem with me being rude, then she shouldn't have been trespassing to begin with.

She stumbled as she turned around, but caught herself, and I knew she hadn't seen me before now. She looked vaguely familiar, but I couldn't place her, and I didn't particularly care to try.

"Are you deaf? What the hell are you doing on my property?"

Her eyebrows went up, answering my half-rhetorical question about her hearing, and I had the sudden impression that I'd crossed some sort of line. I folded my arms over my chest. This wasn't on me. She wasn't supposed to be here.

"I'm not deaf." Her voice was even, no trace of annoyance at either my questions or my tone. "I'm here because I wanted to look at the pine trees."

"You wanted to – what?" I stared at her. Why would someone wander onto my property to look at pine trees?

"Pine needles are an excellent source of vitamin C," she explained. "Of course, you don't want to eat them, but they can be made into a tea that's quite palatable."

"Who are you?" I asked again, but I didn't sound angry anymore. I was too confused.

"Brea Chaise," she said, coming out from under the trees. "And you're Blake Hunter."

"At least you know whose property you're on."

Again, that raised eyebrow, this time accompanied by a quirk of her lips. "Yes, I do. And I was invited."

"I sure as hell did *not* invite you here. This is *my* property. Mine. You need to go."

If my order surprised her, she didn't show it. In fact, she didn't show anything other than her obnoxious amusement. She looked down, then from side to side, as if she was trying to find something on the ground. After a moment, she took a few steps to her right, crouched down, and moved aside a clump of tall grass. A little blue flag stuck up from the ground.

"Property line flag," she said. "Which means I was never on your property. Hence, your demand for me to leave isn't applicable."

Hence? Who the fuck said *hence?* Or *applicable* for that matter?

Suddenly, I realized why she looked familiar and where I'd heard her name before.

"You own that goofy store in town."

She went still for a moment, and her smile faded from her eyes even though it stayed on her mouth.

Now that I was looking at her mouth, I couldn't ignore how nice it was. A little fuller than average, but I liked that. In fact, the more I looked at her, the more I liked what I saw. A firm, athletic body that was both strong and feminine. One that could take anything I could dish out.

And then my eyes returned to her face, and I saw she wasn't smiling at all anymore.

Dammit.

TEN
BREA

Yes, I'd been a little distracted by the fact that Blake wasn't wearing a shirt. I was only human. He was ripped. Like Greek god ripped. I was only twenty-three, but I'd seen plenty of men who took care of their bodies. Blake looked like he beat his into shape...and it liked it.

Then he'd opened his mouth and reminded me why a guy's personality had always meant more to me than his appearance. I might drool over someone who looked like Blake, but it'd never go beyond that. Especially if he was as much of an asshole as this.

I'd managed to keep myself smiling and polite...until he said, "You own that goofy store in town."

That goofy store.

I stood up, smoothing down my skirt so my hands had something to do that wasn't slapping Blake for insulting my store when, as far as I knew, he'd never even stepped foot inside it. I rarely found myself wanting to commit violence, but he'd managed to get me close to it with just a short conversation. That alone should have made me walk away.

One of my personality qualities, however, was a bit of a

stubborn streak. Sometimes, it was a positive thing. Like when things at work were tough. When finances were tight. It wouldn't be hard to shut things down and join my parents, especially now that they had this place. The one thing that the three of us had never been weird about was money. They'd never acted like my trust was the only money I had access to. If I needed it, all I had to do was ask.

But, being stubborn wasn't always a good thing, and I had a feeling this was going to be one of those times. Because I wasn't going anywhere. I'd come out here to look around, and I wasn't done. No wealthy jerk was going to chase me away from my parents' place, and I wasn't going to give him an explanation. It wasn't any of his business.

I went back to the trees, trying to refocus on what I'd been thinking about before he'd so rudely interrupted me.

When it came time to harvest from things that needed to stay living, it had to be done carefully. All the book research I'd done had helped, but there'd been no substitute for actually doing the work myself. Even though I usually bought my herbs rather than gathering them myself – not everything was available in Wyoming – I'd wanted to know the best way to do the work if I had to. I'd learned as much as possible from each person who'd trained me, and because of that, I knew I could get what I needed from the pines without hurting them.

I pulled down a branch and ran my fingers over the needles, feeling how tightly they clung to the branch, how firm they were. I loved the smell of pine. It always made me think of Christmas. My parents hadn't really been into celebrating 'traditional' holidays, but they'd compromised when it came to me. For each holiday, Blair and Kevin had put their own twist on things, but we'd always had a tree at Christmas.

"What are you doing?"

I frowned but didn't turn to face him. The last thing I needed was to let him see he was getting to me. I knew guys like him. They thrived on that sort of conflict. He wanted me to react. I was sure he was used to intimidating people with his money and size and that gruff, growly man thing he had going on.

He might think I was some flaky tree-hugger, but he had no idea who I was. If he kept pushing me, though, he was going to find out.

"I'm examining the tree," I said matter-of-factly.

"I can see that. I'm not blind."

He sounded closer, and I glanced over my shoulder to see that he was standing next to the blue flag. And he was glowering at me like I was supposed to tell him more.

I, however, went back to the tree. Maybe it was a little petty of me that I was making things so hard on him, but his comment about my store had pissed me off.

"Why are you examining the tree? Is there something wrong with it?"

"Not that I can see," I said, going to another branch. "I'm just making sure they're healthy enough for me to harvest resin and needles."

"Harvest...what the fuck?"

I finally looked at him. "You really like that question."

He scowled at me, but there was a strange light in those clear blue eyes of his. Something that didn't quite mesh with the way his mouth was twisting. It was a sensual mouth, more so than I would have imagined on such a rugged man.

"If you'd answered it the first time, I wouldn't have had to ask it again."

Good point.

"You clearly must know the sorts of things I sell in my *goofy store*, which means you know I use things such as pine needles and resin in my salves and teas." I said the words with a smile, pleased when I saw him have the decency to look embarrassed.

Unfortunately, embarrassment for him translated into him behaving like an ass.

"You can't just come in here and take what you want," he said, passing the flag and coming on to what I knew was my parents' land.

I didn't call him on it though. I waited to see what he would do next. Most men like this, I would've dismissed immediately, but there was something about him that made me wonder *why* he was like this. As if his behavior was more of an armor than the man he truly was.

"I don't give a damn about your store or what you're looking for out here. This is *my* place, and I don't want you fucking around on it."

I was tempted to tell him that if I was fucking around on his land, he would've stopped and watched, but I didn't. I didn't say anything. I turned my attention back to the tree and snapped off a small branch. I'd need to take a closer look at it before I decided these trees were the best. Before I went home, I'd take a few samples from some of the other trees I'd seen.

"What the fuck did I just say?!"

"The word *fuck*, I believe," I said mildly. "You say it a lot." I paused, then added, "I assume that means you like to do it a lot too."

I couldn't resist sneaking a peek to see how he reacted. I was glad I did though because seeing him standing there with his jaw dropped was well worth it. That seemed like a great note to walk out on, so I plucked one additional small branch and turned to walk away.

"Hey!" he shouted.

I ignored him.

"Hey!" He grabbed my wrist, and I stopped.

I turned around without pulling away. I'd give him a chance to figure out that he was crossing a line, and if he didn't, the self-defense classes I took as a teenager would give him something else to think about.

"Yes?"

"You need to listen to me," he insisted, looking down at me. "I'm serious about this."

He was even bigger close up. I wasn't a huge woman, but I was enough over average height, and not delicate, that I rarely felt small. He managed to make me feel it.

And *damn* did he smell good.

I'd never been the sort of woman who liked fancy smelling chemicals. Give me plain soap, work sweat, and natural pheromones any day. He had those in spades, making my stomach clench in a way it hadn't done in a long time.

"I bought this place because it was private. I don't invite people out here because I don't want people out here. I don't know you. I don't want to know you. I want you to leave me alone."

I considered telling him that I wasn't here for him. That I didn't want to know him either. That this land belonged to my parents and if he wanted to be alone, he should get his ass off their land and leave me alone.

After all this shit, however, I felt like poking the bear just for the hell of it.

I looked down at the hand still grasping my wrist, then back up at him. "And?"

ELEVEN
BLAKE

WHY COULDN'T I LEAVE HER ALONE?

She'd been walking away, and all she'd taken with her were two little twigs off a couple of pines that I wasn't even sure belonged to me. Why had I gone after her? Why was I talking more to her than I had to anyone in years?

Was it just because she'd fired back with that *fuck* comment? She'd caught me off guard, sure, but that shouldn't have been enough to get me to do something so out of character.

Except that comment had made me think about fucking. Not what's-her-name from Miami. No, I was thinking about fucking the beautiful dark-haired woman whose feathers I couldn't seem to ruffle.

Except I had. That comment about her store had ruffled her. That stupid, thoughtless comment that I never should have said and didn't really mean. I'd always hated it when people made assumptions about me based on what they thought they knew about me and about my family, but that hadn't stopped me from doing the same thing to her. She should have called me out on it. Sworn at me. Called me every name in the book. Instead, she'd gotten a little snarky, but I'd deserved more than snark.

Then she'd started testing me, and I knew she was doing it on purpose. No one provoked me intentionally, especially not someone who most likely knew my reputation for not liking people. But that hadn't stopped her. In fact, the more annoyed I got, the more it seemed to amuse her.

Why the fuck couldn't I leave her alone?

I hadn't meant to grab her arm, not really. I'd just wanted her to stop walking away from me. I kept telling her to go, but I didn't actually want her to go. I wanted her to keep sparring with me. I wanted to see how far I could push her.

Then my hand was wrapped around her wrist, and she was close enough for me to see into the depths of those deep brown eyes of hers. Close enough to know that she didn't wear perfume, but rather that she smelled like herbs and other plants...and pine.

"I bought this place because it was private. I don't invite people out here because I don't want people out here. I don't know you. I don't want to know you. I want you to leave me alone." The words came rushing out, but not all of them were true. Or, rather, they weren't all completely true. The things I'd always wanted were at odds with what she made me want.

Want. Maybe that's all this was. I wanted her. She was strong, and not only physically. She didn't freak out or act like she was frightened of me, not even when I'd yelled, which made me wonder if she was the sort of woman who could listen to what I wanted without judging, who was strong enough to not only take it but give as good as she got.

"And?"

For a moment, I thought she was starting a sentence, but then I realized that was all she was going to say. Any other woman would've slapped me, yelled at me, done something to make sure I understood how far out of line I was. Not her. She didn't even pull away from me. But one look in her eyes and I could tell that she wasn't holding back because she feared me. I could see she wasn't happy with me, but there was no fear.

My gaze dropped from her eyes to her lips, and for the second time in the last few minutes, I wondered what they would feel like against my mouth, my skin, my cock.

Fuck.

Just the thought was enough to get me half-hard, but it wasn't enough to make me step back.

That should have been my first warning to stay away. Any time I thought a woman could possibly mean more to me than sex, I walked away. I didn't fuck women I found obnoxious, but I also didn't fuck women I thought were fascinating either, and that if there was a single word to describe how I felt about Brea at that moment, it was *fascinated*.

I wanted to shake sense into her, but I also wanted to kiss her breathless. I wanted to leave her gasping and wanting more. Would she melt against me, her mouth soft and pliant? Or would she try to take control of the kiss? What would she sound like if I kissed her, if I bit her lip? Would she even let me kiss her or would she stop me before I could get that far? Would she tell me no or push me away? Either way, I'd respect her decision.

And that was when I realized that I still had ahold of her arm.

I released it, guilt flooding me. "Sorry," I muttered. "I wasn't thinking."

"Apology accepted," she said, straightening her sleeve.

She was going to walk away, and I couldn't let her go with that being my last impression. I didn't know why, but I didn't want her to think I was the sort of asshole who'd hurt her. An asshole who yelled and snarled like a child throwing a temper tantrum, yeah, but I couldn't stand it if she thought I was an abusive asshole.

Of course, instead of politely offering to walk her to her car, or telling her she was welcome to come back, I thought it was a great idea to ask her to dinner. And I couldn't even get that right.

"Have dinner with me tonight."

I'd meant to make it a request, but of course, it came out as a demand. I'd never been charming like my brother Slade, but this was simply pathetic. What made it even worse is that I didn't even know why I wanted to have dinner with her. I didn't really do the whole 'take a woman on a date' thing. It was always sex, nothing more.

Apologies came in the form of flowers or cards, and that would've been fine. An offer to look around my property might've put me in a better light.

Dinner? Dinner was a date, and I didn't date.

Her head was tilted to the side, her expression somber, like she was studying me, seeing deeper inside me than anyone else ever had.

"All right," she said. She took a step toward me, then moved up on her toes so she could kiss my cheek. "I'll be at your place at six. I'm a vegetarian, but I don't mind if you eat meat."

And with that, she turned and walked away, leaving me staring after her and wondering just what the hell, had just happened.

TWELVE
BREA

While I'd never been an overly cautious person, I didn't generally consider myself impulsive either. I was structured and careful when it came to work, and I'd always made sure that I played things safe when it came to dating.

First dates were always in public, and often the next couple as well. I took my time to get to know the men I went out with before things progressed to spending time alone. I considered myself a good judge of character but also knew that even the wisest and most perceptive person could be wrong.

Which was why I couldn't quite believe that I was going to Blake's house for dinner only a few hours after he'd emphatically told me to get off his property. More than once.

I knew why I was doing it though. I'd seen something in his eyes when he'd grabbed my arm. He hadn't been trying to hurt me. He was hurting, whether he acknowledged it or not. The same thing that kept him so isolated also kept him telling me to leave, even though I could see that it wasn't what he really wanted. He wanted a connection. He might not be the sort of man who liked crowds, but there was a part of him that didn't want to be alone.

However, I'd have been lying to myself if I didn't admit the physical aspect of it all. I'd never had such a visceral reaction to a man. Ever.

Which explained the extra care I'd taken when getting dressed for this evening. I'd selected one of my favorite dresses, a long, flowing one that reached nearly to my ankles. A rich burnt orange color, it did for my coloring what the cut did for my figure. Since it was sleeveless, I took along a warm wool shawl that looked better with it than a coat would have. Even though snow wasn't entirely out of the realm of possibility, I risked my flats because they were the most comfortable shoes I owned. I had a feeling I would want to be as sure of myself as possible and being comfortable was the best way to accomplish that.

As I pulled up the long driveway, I found myself admiring the sprawling ranch from a distance and then more closely. It was gorgeous, and while I didn't know much about architecture, I was confident that he hadn't done much in the way of changes. This was the sort of place that I would've seen in some old Western on TV growing up and thought about how much fun it would be to live there. As an adult, I understood how much work must come with a ranch like this, but I still thought it looked like fun.

It wasn't until I was parking behind his truck that a thought hit me, and I frowned.

Based on the gossip I'd heard around town, he didn't have any kids, and I didn't think he'd ever been married. He did some sort of carpentry or something like that, and I'd never heard anything about him having any employees who lived out here. I didn't think he even had any friends. What, then, was the point of him having a house that size? The land I understood, but why would anyone want such a massive house if he didn't intend to have it filled with people?

There was a lot I didn't understand about Blake Hunter. This was just one more thing to add to the list I'd been making for the past few hours. The biggest question, however, was whether he would answer any of them, or if I would leave in a couple hours without any more knowledge than I had right now.

Only one way to find out, I supposed.

I was still a couple yards from the door when it opened, and Blake stepped outside. My feet kept moving even though my brain had ceased telling them what to do. It'd pretty much stopped completely the moment it'd registered Blake.

He wore a pair of dark pants that could have been either jeans or slacks, but the material didn't matter as much as how he looked in them. *Damn* was the only word that came to mind. His shirt was short-sleeved and just tight enough to show off all those muscles I'd seen on display earlier. His clothes, however, weren't even the best part.

He was smiling.

Sort of.

It wasn't the sort of open, full smile like the ones my parents usually wore, but more like the smile of someone who didn't do it very often.

"Hi." He shifted his weight, looking uncomfortable, whether because of his clothes, me, or the smiling, I couldn't tell.

"Hi." I smiled at him, hoping to put him at ease. "You have an absolutely beautiful home."

"Thanks."

He stepped back a bit to give me room to enter while still holding the door, and I caught a whiff of that same clean-soap smell I'd noticed before. It was tempting to linger, but I didn't want to make him regret asking me to dinner. The nerves I'd managed to avoid for the last few hours appeared all at once, making me wonder if I'd made a mistake. I usually believed in trusting my gut, but everyone made mistakes at one time or another.

I really hoped he wasn't mine.

"Want me to take that?" He pointed at my wrap, and I handed it over. He scowled at it as he tried to figure out how to get it on a hanger, but I didn't step in to help him. I had a feeling he'd rather be annoyed than feel like I had to come to his rescue in his own home.

Once he figured out how to get it to stay, he went off to his right, and I followed. After a few steps, he still hadn't said anything else, but I was more interested in the mouth-watering aroma permeating the air.

"I made stuffed peppers, breadsticks, and a fruit salad," he said finally. Even without raising his voice, the tone had a roughened quality to it. Not like he was a smoker – he didn't smell like he smoked – but more like his voice didn't get much use and he'd already gone over his limit for the day. "You said vegetarian, not vegan, right? 'Cuz the peppers have cheese in them."

"Yes," I said. "Vegetarian. Dairy is fine. Thank you."

He shrugged like it wasn't a big deal, but to me it was. If he'd really been as much of a jackass as he'd come across this afternoon, he wouldn't have cared about whether he got it right.

Honestly, I'd been expecting him to order in his favorite meal, and if it contained meat, he'd maybe make sure there were enough side dishes I could eat. I hadn't expected him to cook, and especially not a meal like that.

I was glad to know that my first impression, hadn't been all of who he was.

The kitchen was just as beautiful as the rest of the house, a wonderful combination of modern and rustic with stainless steel appliances alongside wooden counters and cabinets. A massive garden window took up a quarter of the southern wall, and a table sat up against it, matching chairs on three of the four sides. The scrollwork on the edge of the table was a lovely intricate pattern I'd never seen before.

"I thought we could eat in here," he said. "I have a dining

room, but it seemed silly to use it since there's two of us and the table in there is huge."

"This is perfect," I said honestly. "What can I do to help?"

He looked pleasantly surprised by my offer, and I wondered what sort of women he usually brought home that they wouldn't extend that common courtesy.

"I wasn't sure what you'd like to drink," he said. "I usually have a beer, but I didn't know if you'd be okay with that." He flushed, which surprised and pleased me. "I mean, I didn't know what your opinion is about alcohol. If you drink wine or whatever."

I smiled and crossed to the fridge. "I'm actually more of a beer person than a wine person."

Another look of surprise. "Really?"

"Really." I opened the fridge. "I've spent most of my life traveling, which means I've sampled alcohol all over the world, but in my mind, nothing beats an American made beer."

I took out two bottles and carried them over to the table, feeling his eyes on me as I went. I wasn't unaccustomed to men staring at me, but with Blake, it was different than anything else I'd experienced. The intensity of his gaze felt like it was boring a hole right through me, like he could see more of me than I wanted to be seen.

"Bottle opener?" I asked.

I heard a drawer open, and by the time I turned, he was right there. I tilted my head back to look up at him, and he didn't look away even as he reached around me for the beer. He opened them both, keeping his arms around me the whole time. Neither of us said anything, but I didn't think either of us needed to. The electricity between us said enough.

He went back to the food, and I tried not to be disappointed that he hadn't touched me.

"The table's beautiful. Did it come with the house?" I

congratulated myself on keeping my voice even despite how wobbly my knees had become.

"I made it."

I turned around. "Seriously?"

One corner of his mouth quirked up in a smile. "I thought you knew who I was."

I opened my mouth to respond, then realized I couldn't actually say what I'd intended to say. Not without sounding like a snob or a bitch.

"It's okay," he said. "I know my reputation."

"The only thing I've ever heard about what you do is that you work with wood. I didn't know what that meant."

He gestured toward the table. "I make furniture." He went back to putting the stuffed peppers on a pair of plates. "Among other things. I do blacksmithing too."

He said it so casually that if I hadn't known the skills it took to do either of those jobs, I wouldn't have understood how impressive it was.

"I'd love to see more of your work."

He glanced up, a pleased look in his eyes. Something told me that he didn't have the opportunity to share what he did with anyone except customers. Or maybe it wasn't that he didn't *have* opportunities, but that he purposefully kept things to himself. Either way, I was glad the idea of showing me made him happy.

"Speaking of work," he said as he brought the plates over to the table. "I need to apologize for what I said about your store. Just because I don't understand something doesn't mean I can make judgments about it."

I didn't want to dismiss his apology as unnecessary, because he had been insulting, but I also didn't want to make a big deal about it either. "Thank you," I said. "I'd be happy to explain things if you'd like."

He went back to the fridge and took out a glass bowl of

various kinds of fruit. As he brought it to the table, his eyes met mine. "I'd like that very much."

I HADN'T HAD a date like this ever. I'd explained to him about what I did in the store and how to make sure homeopathic remedies were the real thing. He told me about blacksmithing. He asked about school, and so did I, and we both talked about why we'd chosen to forgo the college option.

We steered clear of any talk of family or anything overly personal. It was only a first date, after all, and our initial meeting hadn't exactly been pleasant. Even though we didn't talk about it, my intuition told me he felt the same way I did about tonight. We were keeping it simple, not complicating it with all the things that eventually became a part of a relationship. If this became more than a first date, we'd see where to go from there.

Right now, I was happy to be standing next to him at the sink, washing the few dishes that couldn't go in the dishwasher. He was drying and putting them away since I didn't know where they went, and we didn't need to talk to do any of that.

The silence wasn't uncomfortable, but it was charged. Each time I handed something off to Blake, our hands brushed, and I felt a pleasant jolt. I'd experienced near-instant attraction, but this was beyond me simply thinking he was attractive. It was a deep, primal tug in his direction, and the longer I stayed, the greater the chance I would act on it.

After finishing the last of the dishes, I reached for the hand towel and dried my hands, but before I could ask about what we were going to do next, I felt him step up behind me. I went still, closing my eyes as I absorbed the warmth radiating from his body.

I had a choice now, I knew. I could sidestep and put some space between us, and we'd end the night on a pleasant, albeit unsatisfying note. Or, I could wait and see just how far he wanted to take things. I'd never slept with a guy on the first date, but I didn't have some internal moral code about when the right time was. I didn't go by a specific timeframe, more the way things felt.

Right now, I liked how things felt between us.

Then he put his hands on my hips, and I *really* liked how that felt.

His lips brushed the back of my neck, and I shivered. Damn. The scruff of his beard scratched my skin in a good way as he moved, and then his mouth was at my ear.

"If you want me to stop, just say the word."

I nodded, and then it became about touch and sensation, sounds but not words.

He squeezed my hips, then moved his hands up over my ribcage and then over my breasts. Another squeeze, his grip tightening until I gasped. He paused, and I knew he was giving me a moment to protest if I wanted to. Instead, I turned around and wrapped my arms around his neck.

His mouth came down on mine, and I pressed my body against his. His muscles weren't the only thing hard about him, and if what I could feel against my hip was any indication, he was large all over. His tongue slid between my lips, and his hands slid to the small of my back, and then lower. His hair was softer than I'd imagined, and I surprised myself with the realization that I had thought about it.

I moaned as he took my bottom lip between his teeth and tugged on it. He tasted as good as he smelled. Beer and peppers and pineapple. I moved my hands down his chest and around his back, tipping my head back as I slid my hands beneath his shirt. His mouth moved over my throat, the burn of his facial hair soothed by his lips and tongue, then accompanied by the sharp sting of a bite.

I'd never been so grateful that my skin didn't mark easily.

I wanted his mouth on more of me. His hands on me. I just needed him to keep touching me.

He lifted me up, putting me on the counter so I was closer to his height. His hands moved up my calves, pushing my skirt up as they went. I pulled him in for another kiss as he stepped between my legs, and my temperature skyrocketed.

What was I doing? I needed to end this before things went any further. But I didn't want to stop. I liked the way our bodies fit together, the way it felt when he touched me. His fingers flexing on my thighs felt right in a way that things hadn't ever felt right before. With other men, I'd always felt like I needed to build toward the different levels of physical intimacy, but with him, I felt like I was already there.

I whimpered as the tip of one finger traced along the crotch of my panties. It had been too long since someone else had touched me there.

"More," I breathed against his lips. My tongue tangled with his, exploring his mouth as his fingers slipped under the damp fabric.

A light brush against my clit, and then two fingers were pushing inside me. I dug my nails into his shoulders as he stretched me too far, too fast, but I didn't ask him to stop. It was like he'd found this switch inside me, and he'd flipped it, taking me to an edge I hadn't known I wanted.

"Do you want it like this?" he asked, his voice even rougher than it had been. "Do you want me to make you come on my fingers, or do you want...*more*?"

He'd do whatever I wanted, even if it meant he didn't get off, I didn't doubt that. I wasn't going to do that though. I wanted him too badly to make either of us wait. Unusual for me, yes, but I was going into this with my eyes open, which was almost all I needed.

"Do you have a condom?" That would be the only thing that could keep me from saying no.

He pulled his fingers out of me, licking them clean as he reached into his pocket. Some humor danced along the desire darkening his eyes. All of it made me hotter, more determined to follow through.

I scooted closer to the edge of the counter, hooking my legs around his thighs and pulling him toward me as he rolled on the condom. We came together hard, and all the air rushed from my lungs as spots danced behind my eyes. He was huge, filling me more completely than anyone else ever had. He wrapped his hand around my neck, his fingers curling around the base, his thumb resting against the underside of my jaw.

For a long moment, we stayed like that, bodies locked together, every cell buzzing with energy, and then he began to move the way I'd known he would: with powerful, punishing strokes that drove me relentlessly toward climax.

I came with a wordless cry, the speed of it taking my breath away. But he didn't stop or even slow down, the continued pounding building on top of my orgasm until my entire body was shaking, overwhelmed by the sensations coursing through me.

Then his arms were around me, holding me – *no*, clinging to me – as he came with a guttural groan.

Well this, was not, how I'd imagined my day ending.

THIRTEEN
BLAKE

"Fuck!" I tossed a piece of wood across the room, glaring at it as it bounced off the wall.

For the past two days, I'd been trying to build the boat I'd been hired to build, but I hadn't gotten beyond the basic shell. None of the extras I'd been commissioned to do were coming out right. I could see what I wanted to do in my head, but it wasn't reaching my hands.

I didn't get it. I'd always been able to create what I saw, whether it was with wood or metal. The first time I'd picked up a knife and a piece of wood, I'd known it was what I was meant to do. To create. My brothers had skills in academic areas, but my abilities were in the way my hands could make what I thought up. It was the only thing I'd really been good at, and if I didn't have it, I didn't know who I was.

I sighed as I walked across the room to pick up the wood. I did get it actually. It wasn't hard to figure out that I'd started having issues yesterday afternoon when I'd tried to work on the scrollwork. Unlike on Sunday when I'd been caught in the rhythmic monotony of sanding, my brain couldn't turn off with scrollwork. Which meant the distractions were more noticeable.

One distraction actually. Named Brea Chaise.

What had I been thinking, asking her over for dinner? Acting like we were on a date? Fucking her on my kitchen counter?

We hadn't really talked after we'd finished. We'd cleaned up, then she'd thanked me for 'a wonderful evening,' and then she'd left. She seemed fine, but maybe I wasn't the best judge of that since I didn't usually talk to women much after sex. I was the one who generally left after a thank you.

She was beautiful, and sex with her had been as good as I'd imagined it when I'd first seen her, but neither of those things explained why I couldn't get her out of my head. I'd never had a problem with it before. I met someone, we fucked, we went our own separate ways, and I was good until the itch struck again. That's how it went.

Then again, it wasn't like things had progressed normally from moment one with us. We'd started with conflict, then progressed to a date, then sex. Why that should've made her stick in my head, I didn't know.

Thinking about her in the shower while I was beating off, that made sense. Why would I want to think about some nameless, faceless woman when I could remember what it'd been like inside her? Waking up with a hard-on after dreaming about her, that made sense too.

But why was I thinking about how she'd made me smile? Or how it'd been nice to eat with someone instead of by myself?

Usually, when I was around someone else, I couldn't wait for them to be gone, but with Brea, I hadn't wanted her to go. Even after we'd had sex, I'd been tempted to ask her to stay longer. Sure, I'd wanted to fuck her again, but it hadn't been just about sex. It'd been about how being around her had made me feel.

Only now, I wasn't sure I wanted it anymore.

I liked keeping things simple. Even when my work was intricate, it didn't complicate my life. I took the jobs I wanted to take, set my own deadlines. I could work extra if I wanted or take a day off – not that I did that often. If I invited someone into my life, it would mean having to work around them and their needs, because I wouldn't want to do anything half-assed. Feelings would have to be taken into consideration. Then there was what would happen if things went wrong. All those negative emotions.

I'd lost enough people in my life. I didn't need to add another to the list. I'd been able to avoid romantic entanglements for twenty-eight years. One night with Brea wasn't going to change that.

Except I couldn't stop thinking about her, which meant I couldn't concentrate on my work, and that was unacceptable.

I needed to get her out of my head, or I'd never get my work done.

I didn't have a choice.

I was sweaty and frustrated, which was probably not the best way to be doing this, but I couldn't wait. I pulled into the parking spot closest to the front door and went inside. A quick look around told me that Brea was the only person in the store, and she was staring at me, eyes wide, mouth open. I locked the door and flipped the sign over to *closed*.

"Blake?"

I crossed the space between us in only a few strides, not giving her the chance to say anything else before I was kissing her. I tasted honey on her tongue, but I knew that wasn't the only reason the kiss was sweet. It was her, plain and simple.

I felt her sigh, and then her hands clutched the front of my shirt, telling me that I wasn't the only one who hadn't been able to get the other night out of their head. After a minute, I broke the kiss and looked down at her. She must have read the question in my eyes because she answered me without needing me to ask it.

"Back here." She took my hand and pulled me after her through another door.

I had a moment to register that we were in some sort of workroom, and then she was kissing me again. Her hands tugged at my shirt, nails scratching at my skin, and I knew that she wanted me naked. I wanted her naked too, and I wasn't feeling any more patient today than I had been the other night.

I yanked open her shirt, scattering buttons, and then pulled down her bra. I bent my head to suck on one of her nipples, and she cursed, her back arching. I could've spent hours sucking and biting her, listening to all the sounds she'd make. I wanted to go down on her until she begged for relief.

But we didn't have the time.

I straightened and spun her around, bending her over the nearby table. I pulled up the back of her skirt and tugged down her underwear. She shifted her legs, allowing the panties to fall to her feet, then parted her legs. I rolled on a condom, put my hand on the small of her back, and paused.

"Say the word."

She didn't even hesitate. "Yes."

I wanted to slam into her, but she wasn't ready for that. We'd had less foreplay now than we had at my house, and she'd been almost painfully tight then. There was a difference between some pain to increase pleasure, and real pain caused by impatience.

I eased the tip inside, reaching beneath her to find her clit. Her head dropped as I pushed forward, my fingers quickly moving back and forth across that little bundle of nerves. By the time I was all the way inside her, she was slick with arousal and pushing back against me. I gave her a few seconds, and then my weak self-control broke. If she told me to stop, I would, but without that, I wasn't going to hold back.

I drove into her, going from almost completely withdrawn to balls deep, and I knew I wasn't going to last very long. She was too hot, too perfect, like her pussy had been made just for me. Like she was mine, and all I needed to do was claim her. She tightened around me, moaning my name, begging for more. With other women, I might've wondered if they were acting, but with Brea, I knew it was real. There was nothing fake about her.

A drop of sweat trickled down my temple, but I didn't wipe it away. I didn't want to let go of the grip I had on her hips, didn't want to lose the pace that was rushing me toward release. I needed this. I had to get her out of my head, and this was the only way to do it. The only way I'd be able to get back to normal. And I needed things to be normal.

Damn, she was gorgeous. Smooth skin. Strong. Confident. Self-aware. I'd been with beautiful women before, but Brea was in a class all on her own.

One of her hands moved off the table to grab one of her breasts. She pinched the nipple before I could knock her hand away. There was something better than grabbing her hips, and I had it in the palm of my hand right now. I rolled her nipple between my finger and thumb.

"*Mine*," I growled, pinching the sensitive flesh. She let out a small cry, arching her back to push her breast deeper into my hand. "Got that? *Mine*."

She nodded, "Yes. Yes. Yours. Please."

I flicked my thumb across her nipple, knowing that the callouses on my hands had to be rough against her sensitive skin. Judging by her "yes, yes, fuck, yes" that she kept repeating, she liked it all. The way I was pounding into her, how tightly I held her with one hand, how the other played with her breast.

The pressure was building in me too much, too fast, and I couldn't stop it. My heart thudded loudly in my ears, drowning out everything, isolating me in a world that narrowed down to what my body was doing to hers. My hips jerked as I slammed into her once, twice, and then stayed, coming so hard that my vision went white.

I must've stayed there, curled over her back, cock still inside her, for a good half minute before I realized that she hadn't come.

"Shit," I said as I straightened. "You didn't come."

She started saying something about how it didn't matter, but I was already moving to fix it. I went to my knees even as I pulled off the condom and set it on the floor. I'd take care of it as soon as I'd gotten her off. I was positioning myself between her and the table before she realized what I was doing.

"Blake, you don't need–ahh!"

Whatever words she'd intended to use to finish that sentence disappeared into a strangled yell when I buried my face between her legs. I kept a firm grasp on her ass and put my tongue to work. While I'd never been more than a one-night stand kind of guy, I wasn't always about the quickie. I couldn't drag this out, but I didn't need to. She was close. I could hear her panting, feel her muscles trembling.

I slid a finger into her pussy, getting it nice and wet, then moved it out and up until I found the other entrance. We hadn't talked about it, but I didn't doubt for a moment that she'd tell me no if she didn't want it. As the tip of my finger traced that muscle, not only did she not tell me to stop, but she gasped out two words.

"Fuck yes."

I latched onto her clit and pushed my finger into her ass, and that was all it took for her to explode with a scream.

I kept her there until her knees gave out, and then I caught her and lowered her to the floor next to me, pulling her over to lean against me.

After a strangely comfortable stretch of silence, she spoke, "A bit of warning next time."

I shifted so we could look at each other. I really hoped she wasn't regretting what we'd done or felt like I'd pushed her into it. "What do you mean?"

"That was amazing," she said, smiling at me, "but I'd really like to make it to a bed sometime. Or at least a couch."

She wasn't asking for a commitment, or even another date, but talking about there being a next time brought it all rushing back to me. I'd done this to get her out of my system, but I still wanted more.

My plan had backfired. Wonderful.

FOURTEEN
BREA

I was working at the retreat shop today, but I hadn't been able to really get excited about it or even focus on it as much as I should have. It was Thursday morning, which meant it'd been more than a full twenty-four hours since I'd last spoken to Blake.

Not that we'd done much talking if I was honest about it. Most of it had been the sort of rambling nonsense that happened when a person's brain was paying more attention to sex than speaking. At the end, however, I'd asked him to give me a head's up the next time he decided to go all caveman on me and drag me into a back room and bend me over a table. The sex had been amazing, and I didn't dislike spontaneity, but I meant what I'd said to him about maybe using a bed.

Plus, there was the whole 'sex at work' thing. I didn't necessarily mind a break like that, and it wasn't like I'd had customers at the time, but it didn't mean that'd be appropriate behavior to repeat. Besides, all either of us needed was for someone to see him coming out of the shop when the closed sign had been up a while. I wasn't reclusive like he was, but I did value my privacy when it came to matters like this.

"Is this all the inventory you have, dear?" Blair asked as she made her way through the shop.

This stuff with Blake had my head all messed up. "No, I just brought some of my more popular things to see how they'd fill in the shelves. I'll bring more stuff in tomorrow. Besides I don't want to stock things up here if they don't sell."

"Why wouldn't they sell?" Kevin asked as he picked up a tin of my most popular tea blend. "You said things have been going well."

"They have," I said, pushing down my impatience. I'd already explained this to them, but they'd clearly been caught up in their own project. "Most of my sales are online, and I always take that into account when I'm stocking the store in town."

I put another box on the counter and started unpacking some of the new tools I'd gotten. I hadn't wanted to risk taking things back and forth between the two stores because I knew I'd end up forgetting something at some point, most likely when I really needed it.

"Those are lovely," Blair said as she came over to me. She picked up my new mortar bowl and pestle. "Is this marble?"

I nodded. "I know you like marble, so I figured it'd go well with the whole feel of the place."

"I do," she said with a smile. "It's such a cool, tranquil stone. It will encourage the atmosphere we want here. Obviously, it doesn't fit the rustic aura here, but we've used it in every place it's appropriate."

"Have you finished all of the remodeling?" I put things away as I talked, preferring to keep my hands busy.

"We still have a few things to finish on one of the cabins," Kevin said. "It had some damage to its roof that took a little more time than we thought."

"Are you waiting until it's done to officially open?" I knew better than to ask outright if they had a specific opening date.

My parents tended to be the sort of people who scheduled things by *feel* rather than anything else, which meant they did very little planning ahead.

"We put out the word to people in some of Kevin's old social circles and decided that we would let fate determine when we officially opened."

Blair's answer was pretty much what I'd thought she'd say.

"And it just so happens that we have a set of brothers coming in this weekend. A prestigious family who we're confident will spread the word," Kevin said. He put his arm around Blair and kissed the top of her head. "You'll be able to be here, right, Brea? We don't know if they're the sort of people who'd enjoy the bounties of nature, but we want them to be able to see everything we have to offer."

I scanned my mental calendar. "I can do that."

I'd need to juggle a few things, but I could make it work. Besides, I wanted to make sure my parents knew they had my support one hundred percent. When they got bored and went on to the next thing, at least we'd all have spent quality time together. If my business in town didn't suffer, I was willing to be flexible about working here.

"What did you say the family did?" Blair asked, looking up at Kevin.

"Business acquisitions and liquidations," he said.

"What does that mean?"

Once he started talking business, I tuned him out. I loved my father dearly, but he tended to drone on a bit when he explained things. Blair was certain he'd been a professor in a past life.

I set a box of willow bark on the counter, but just as I was ready to turn away, a thought struck me. I usually used tins for my teas, but on occasion, I did sell things in wooden boxes. They'd always been simple but well-made containers I purchased in bulk, but as I ran my thumb over the front of the lid, I couldn't help but wonder if there was a better way of doing business.

Making a table and chairs wasn't the same as making a box, but I'd seen how delicate the scrollwork was on the furniture. I had no doubt that Blake could do it. I just wasn't sure if he'd be comfortable with me asking. I wouldn't expect it for free, of course, or even a discount, but I knew some people were reluctant to mix business with pleasure.

My stomach twisted, and I felt the need to press my thighs together. We'd definitely enjoyed the pleasure.

I only wished I knew what it meant.

The way things kept happening between us was strange. We'd both been aware of each other for a while, then had a rather rude introduction. A date, during which we'd had sex on his kitchen counter. Then nothing for two days until he showed up at my store and we'd gone at it like some horny high schoolers. And I hadn't heard from him since.

Even though it wasn't my usual way of doing things, I could've written this off as a fling. A one-night stand and then a quickie to get each other out of our respective systems. Except something in my gut told me that it was more.

I put the willow bark on one of the shelves and adjusted the sign next to it. I despised price tags and preferred hand-written, hand-decorated signs that gave the name and price of each item. Granted, it took a lot of time, but I'd always found something soothing about doing each one.

I didn't understand why it would be more with Blake. Not only was this not how I usually conducted my romantic life, but he wasn't even my type. I'd always prided myself on not having a physical type, but when it came to personality and other of those sorts of characteristics, I had a specific type of man in whom I'd always been interested.

Intelligent, though not necessarily book smart. Articulate, more in the ability to communicate than an overabundance of words. Compassionate, but not a pushover. Strong, but not overbearing. An ability to smile and laugh while also knowing there was a time to be serious as well.

Some people might've called me picky, but that wasn't really a list of standards as much as it was the actual qualities of the men I'd dated in the past. All of them should have been the men of my dreams, but there'd been enough missing from each relationship that it had ended.

Blake might've had some of those qualities, but he was as far from like the men from my past as I was sure I was from the women he'd dated before. My boyfriends had been...*delicate* wasn't the right word, but they'd been the sort of men who never would have looked at home on a ranch. Blake was rugged and masculine in what should have felt like a stereotypical way, but I didn't get the impression from him that he thought of himself as being some sort of macho manly man. This was just who he was.

"Brea?"

I blinked, snapping back from where my mind had taken me. Blair was giving me a curious look that told me she'd said my name more than once.

"Everything okay?"

"Fine," I said, forcing a smile. "Just thinking."

I didn't tell her what – *who* – I'd been thinking about, and she didn't ask. If I would've thought I could get some advice from her, I would've shared, but I'd learned a long time ago that my parents weren't really the people I wanted to talk to about relationships. I was all for consenting adults doing whatever it was that worked for them, but I didn't want what they had.

I wanted the white picket fence and a husband and kids. A dog. That sort of thing. And I couldn't help but wonder if Blake wanted any of that too.

FIFTEEN
BLAKE

I FINISHED THE FINAL CUT AND BREATHED A SIGH OF relief. The intricate rose pattern I'd been carving into one of the boat's seats had been some of my most challenging work, but not because it was more complex than anything else I'd done. No, it was because I'd been holding myself to a higher standard than usual. Considering that I'd always demanded perfection from myself, that was saying something.

This time, however, I hadn't been thinking about how it looked to my eye, but how it would've looked to someone else's eye. Even though Brea would most likely never see this boat, I'd spent the entire time thinking about what she'd think about it.

After I put everything away, I headed back to the house to clean up and go through the mail I'd put off since the beginning of the week. My bills were all on auto-pay, so I'd gotten into the bad habit of letting my mail pile up rather than going through it each day.

Nearly an hour later, I was clean but aggravated as I weeded through the last of the junk mail. I'd always thought email was supposed to have killed the postal service, but no one would ever know that by looking at how much shit came through each day.

My phone rang, and for once I was grateful for the distraction. For a moment, I found myself hoping that it was Brea, but then I remembered that I was supposed to be over her.

Could I get over someone I wasn't really involved with?

Before I could take that thought any further, I saw my brother's name on my screen. The last time Jax called, it'd been to tell me that Grandfather was dying, and I needed to come back to Boston as soon as possible. What had happened now?

"What's wrong?"

"Nothing's wrong," he said. "But we do need to talk. All of us."

I closed my eyes. "If you're talking about that bullshit Grandfather put in his will, I don't give a damn about it. The three of you can talk and work it all out and split my inheritance. I've got my own money. I don't need his."

"It's about more than the money."

I scowled. "When has it ever been about more than the money?"

Jax's voice was even, patient. "All three of us are going to be in your area tomorrow, and we want to meet."

"I live near Rawlins, Wyoming. Population just over nine thousand people. No one is ever just 'in the area.'"

"Well, we're going to be there to talk to you. To each other. All four of us are going to sit down and actually talk to each other."

I bristled at the command in his voice. "And if I don't want to?"

A little voice in the back of my head told me that I did want to. I ignored it.

"Please, Blake. A lot has happened, and we need to talk about it. Make amends."

I wanted to tell him that I wasn't the one who needed to

make amends. I'd been a fucking kid, and they'd abandoned me for whatever had captured their attention at the time. At least they had memories of our parents and Aimee. I didn't have anything except a giant hole where my family used to be.

"Give us tomorrow," he continued. "We'll go someplace neutral and talk. If it turns out we can't manage it, you can walk away, and we won't bother you again."

That was what I wanted. What I *should* have wanted. A clean break where I'd never need to think about any of them again. Grandfather had been the last thing holding us together, and now that he was gone, we didn't need to pretend that we cared about each other.

Despite everything I told myself, however, a part of me still wanted my brothers. I wanted us to make up for all those years apart, to become a family again. We'd never be like it should have been, with all of us, but we could have more than what we had now. I just hadn't acknowledged that part of me until this moment.

"Okay," I said. "Tomorrow."

"Excellent," Jax said briskly. "We'll be at your place first thing in the morning, and then we'll go to that neutral ground."

He hung up before I could argue, and I frowned at my phone. One of these days, Jax wasn't going to get everything he wanted, and I hoped I was there to gloat.

I tossed my phone onto the seat next to me and picked up the next envelope. I might as well finish this and then find something else to do. I doubted I'd be getting much in the way of sleep tonight.

SIXTEEN
BREA

I was bored out of my mind and couldn't figure out the best way to make my escape. It was nearing evening, and I'd already finished everything I could possibly do in my shop, plus helped Blair and Kevin get the rooms ready for tomorrow. They planned on using the bunkhouses for company retreats, while groups like this one coming in tomorrow would be put up in a suite of rooms on the second floor. The contractors they'd hired had done amazing work, putting rooms together so that guests would have up to four bedrooms and a main sitting area with a small kitchenette, giving them plenty of options about what they wanted to do.

Now that all the work here was done however, Blair and Kevin were getting into one of their aura cleansing moods. I didn't begrudge them their beliefs, but it wasn't exactly the most fun thing to watch if you'd seen it a hundred times growing up. I'd agreed to spend the night in the room they'd set up for me since that meant I wouldn't have to get up early to be here before the guests, but now I was wondering if that was a mistake. If I'd been going home, I could've listed a hundred things I needed to do when I got there and left early, but because they knew I was staying, any excuse to leave would mean I didn't want to be out here with them. They'd always given me my space to do my own thing, but I couldn't help feeling guilty for wanting to get away after not having seen them in so long.

When my phone rang, I grabbed for it, hurrying out of the room as I answered, "Hello?"

I hadn't even thought to look at the Caller ID. A telemarketer would've been welcome at this point.

"Brea?"

There was no mistaking that voice. "Blake?"

"Yeah. Are you busy?"

"No." I wasn't busy, but I was curious.

"Can you come over?"

The question sounded casual, but there was something under the words that I couldn't put my finger on. Something that made me think that he'd called me because I was the only one who could give him what he needed.

"I'll be there in a few."

We were going to have sex; that wasn't even a question in my mind. Whether or not he'd share the real reason he'd called me, I didn't know, but I'd be there for him either way.

First, however, I was going to take a quick shower, during which I'd come up with a valid, but not entirely honest, reason to give my parents for why I was leaving.

I'D DRESSED CASUALLY this time. I didn't exactly know what this was, but I was pretty sure it wasn't a date. I didn't think it was even a 'booty call' either. I didn't have much experience with those sorts of things, but it didn't really feel like that to me. It felt like something was wrong, and he needed me.

I had my hand up to knock when the door opened, and

Blake caught my wrist, pulling me to him. I had a moment to register my own surprise, and then his mouth was on mine, hard and urgent. His hands moved over my back and down to my ass, squeezing it, and then sliding his hands under the back of my shirt. I made a sound in the back of my throat as his work-roughened fingers slid across my skin.

He kicked the door closed and then pressed me back against it, his body firm against mine. His teeth worried at my bottom lip, tongue soothing it before plundering my mouth again. I wrapped my arms around his neck, burying my fingers in his hair, letting my body say what I didn't have words for.

His hand worked its way into my pants, under the elastic waistband of my panties, fingers probing and parting flesh, finding my clit. He wasn't gentle, making circles back and forth as he swallowed my whimpers and cries, but I didn't push him away. He needed to make me come even more than I wanted it.

The pressure building inside me quickly reached the boiling point, and I came on his hand, shuddering and shaking with the intensity of my climax. I broke the kiss to drop my forehead onto his shoulder, his strength the only thing keeping me on my feet.

I reached for his pants, but he caught my hands. I raised my head and found him looking at me.

"Not here, not like this."

I brushed my lips across his. "Well, that was one hell of a welcome."

His mouth twitched, but I didn't see any humor in his eyes.

Something was very wrong. "Are you okay?"

He straightened, keeping one arm around my waist. "I don't want to talk about it."

"Okay." I lightly touched the side of his face. "I won't push. Just know I'll listen."

He nodded once, a shadow crossing his face. "And if *listening* isn't what I called you over here for?"

I ran my hands over his chest, pleased to see desire flaring in his eyes. Some people might think that talking out problems was the only solution, but there was something to be said for distractions too.

"Lead the way."

He took my hand, our eyes locking as he kissed my knuckles. We headed straight for the stairs, and I followed him up, admiring the way his tight ass moved in his jeans. Just because this wasn't a date didn't mean I couldn't enjoy the view.

The room he took me into looked like a guest room rather than his bedroom, but I wasn't insulted. A bedroom was a very personal space, and even in the short time I'd known him, I could tell he wasn't someone who allowed people close very often. Maybe, one day, we'd get there. Maybe not. For right now, I intended to enjoy things as they were.

"You remembered about the bed," I said lightly.

"I haven't been able to stop thinking about it," he said. He turned toward me. "I...*want* to try something with you."

"*Want* isn't what you were going to say first," I said, "is it?"

"No," he admitted.

"Then say it." I pulled my t-shirt over my head. "I'm here, with you. I'm not going anywhere."

"*Need*," he said quietly. "I was going to say that I *need* to try something with you. But I don't *need* it—"

"It's okay," I said as I took off my pants. "Tell me. I'll be honest. If it's too much, I'll say it."

When he walked over to a set of closet doors, I thought he was going to reject my offer, but instead, he opened the closet and stepped aside to let me look in.

I recognized most of the toys, though I hadn't ever used any of them. Fuzzy handcuffs. A flogger. A crop. A couple vibrators of varying sizes and shapes were on top of a shelf. Blindfolds.

Seriously, *not* a guestroom.

"It's all right if you're not interested in this sort of thing," he said. "I don't *need* it."

"Yes..." I met his gaze and held it, "you do. Maybe not all the time, but right now you need it."

I picked up one of the blindfolds. It was a soft satin mask, crimson, with delicate floral patterns sewn in. I turned to the toys and selected a smooth silicone vibrator. When I turned back to him, he was watching me, his expression unreadable.

I walked back over to him and held out the toy and the blindfold. "You're in charge."

He took them both and gestured toward the bed. "Strip."

Since I was mostly undressed, I removed my underwear and bra, setting them on top of the rest of my clothes. Then I went and sat on the edge of the bed. He came over to stand in front of me, then reached out, brushing my hair away from my face.

"Are you sure?"

I nodded. "I'll say if I want you to stop."

He slid the mask into place, effectively blocking out my vision, but it didn't bother me. I knew I could trust him. Whatever he was going to do, I was sure I'd enjoy it.

"Lie back."

I pushed myself back onto the bed and laid down, leaving myself open and exposed to him. I had butterflies in my stomach, but they were more anticipation than anxiety.

I heard a low buzzing sound and braced myself for what came next.

Except it didn't touch where I'd expected it. Instead, I felt a faint vibration against the bottom of my right breast. My hands convulsed at my sides as he circled my breast with the toy, letting the unfamiliar sensations travel across my nerves. When it touched my nipple, I gasped, arching my back. My nipple hardened into a tight little nub, and a shiver ran through me. Damn, that felt amazing. How had I not tried that before?

He repeated the process on the other side, neither of us saying a word. The only sounds I heard were my own ragged breathing and the low hum of the vibrator, but it wasn't uncomfortable or awkward. I didn't feel the need to fill the silence with other noise or tell him what I wanted him to do. It didn't matter that he wasn't touching me with his flesh. We connected in a way that I couldn't begin to describe or understand, but it was real, and that was all that mattered at this moment in time.

The vibration moved between my breasts, and then down my stomach and over my belly button.

I couldn't help it. I giggled.

"Really?"

He sounded amused, and I wondered if he was smiling.

"I'm ticklish."

He laughed. "We won't explore that tonight, but I'll file it away for possible future use."

Future use? Did that mean tonight wasn't a one-off?

I filed *that* away for my own future examination, then sucked in a breath when the vibrator moved lower. He moved it slowly, nothing like the frantic touching before, but his goal was the same.

He was determined to make me come.

When the vibrator finally touched my clit, I smacked my hands against the bed. I wanted to grab him, sink my nails into those delightful muscles of his.

But I couldn't see him, and no matter how amazing he was making me feel, I was still aware enough to know that if I tried to touch him while I was blindfolded, I'd probably end up stabbing him in the eye or something else as equally damaging and embarrassing.

I squirmed, wanting to get away from the overwhelming sensations but also never wanting them to stop.

"Stop moving."

He didn't raise his voice, but I froze anyway.

Then the vibrator was gone, and his mouth latched onto one of my throbbing nipples. I let out a wordless cry as a new rush of arousal flooded me. Using his mouth, he followed the path the vibrator had taken, licking and sucking, mixing in the occasional bite. The heat that had flushed my skin turned into a fire, burning a trail that had every cell in my body screaming for more.

By the time he reached my clit, I was already hovering on the edge. Two quick flicks with his tongue, and then he pushed two fingers inside me. My entire body jerked. There was something about not being able to see what was coming next that made it all much more intense. He curled his fingers, and I knew what he was searching for. His tongue was still moving over and around my clit when he found it.

I'd heard the expression 'seeing stars' before, but I didn't see stars when I climaxed. I saw fireworks, an explosion of colors that rocked me to my core. I'd had great orgasms in the past, but there was something deeper about this one, something more primal.

The mattress moved underneath me, but my brain was still misfiring enough that I couldn't quite register what was happening until it shifted again, and I knew Blake was getting back onto the bed. He took my hands and moved them up over my head, holding them in place with one hand. He moved again, the heat of his body and movement of the mattress telling me he was straddling my shoulders.

"Open your mouth."

I did and felt something hot and smooth trace along my bottom lip. I darted my tongue out, tasting salt and sweat and him. He made a pleased sound and then his cock was sliding into my mouth and across my tongue. He was thick and heavy, and exactly what I'd imagined.

He leaned over me, tightening his hold on my wrists as he moved deeper. I wanted to touch him even more now than I had before, not to stop him from making those shallow little thrusts into my mouth, but to feel his power beneath my hands, feel the way the muscles would bunch and flex.

"Snap your fingers if it's too much."

His voice was hoarse, and I knew he wasn't going to last long. I wanted him to go in my mouth, to feel him lose control and know that I was the one who caused it. Fortunately, I loved giving oral sex, and I'd always been someone who threw herself into everything she loved.

I did so now with enthusiasm, sucking hard as he pulled back, then using my tongue when he pushed forward. It didn't take long before his strokes became jerky and short, the grasp on my wrists tightening to the point of pain, and then he came.

Groaning my name.

SEVENTEEN
BLAKE

THIS WAS SO FUCKING FAR OVER THE LINE.

When I'd gone to bed last night, I'd been okay. Brea and I had spent more than five hours having sex. By the time we'd gotten to the last round, coming had almost hurt. I'd had encounters that had lasted almost that long in the past, but this had been different. I hadn't been able to stop touching her. Rather than the times between sex feeling like something I'd had to force myself through, I'd enjoyed them almost as much as the sex. Almost.

She'd gone home without asking to stay, or even hinting at it, really. And then I'd showered and gone to bed. I'd slept well and woken up this morning feeling like I could handle seeing my brothers again. I'd listen to what they had to say, then they would go home, and I'd be able to get back to my life.

Except I'd barely been finishing my breakfast when I'd gotten a text from Jax saying they were pulling into my driveway. I'd hoped for a bit more of a warning, but I wouldn't have been able to brush that off if it hadn't been for what happened after I'd gotten into the car they'd rented.

"We're going to a retreat," Jax announced, glancing at me in the rearview mirror.

"Seriously? I thought we were going to some restaurant for an over-priced meal while we talked."

"We thought things would go a little easier if we were all comfortable," Slade said.

I glared at him. "Then we could've done this at my place."

"We wanted something neutral," Cai said quietly.

I folded my arms and scowled. "Figures."

"What does that mean?" Jax asked.

I shrugged.

"Talk to us, Blake," Slade said. "That's why we're here."

I barked a laugh that didn't sound anything like the laugh that came from my mouth when I was with Brea. "You want me to talk to you, but you just went and decided what we were doing without bothering to ask me."

All three of them looked like they had no clue what I was talking about, but that didn't surprise me. They'd always been that way, making decisions and expecting me to tag along.

Then we were turning, and I found something else to distract me from my brothers treating me like a little kid. The only turn this close to my place was the driveway next door.

Shit. The *retreat* next door.

"You booked the retreat that's *literally* next door to my place."

"Was that a bad thing?" Slade asked.

I glared at him.

"I thought it was convenient," Jax said. "The guy who's opening it, his family used to move in the same circles as Grandfather. I happened to mention to someone that I was interested in booking a retreat, and they recommended I contact Kevin and Blair."

"Fucking nightmare," I muttered.

"It's not that bad," Slade said. "We figured you'd be more comfortable somewhere close to home."

I would've told them that if they knew me at all, they would've known exactly how shitty their idea was, but I'd learned a long time ago that it didn't do any good. They'd see me the way they wanted to see me, project all their personal shit onto me just like they always did.

"Let's check it out," Slade said. "It can't be that bad, right?"

Leave it to Slade to try to smooth things over. He'd been doing that for as long as I could remember, trying to ease tension between all of us.

I followed them inside because I knew if I kept arguing, it'd only delay the inevitable. Hopefully, once my brothers met Kevin and Blair, they'd realize they didn't want to be here either, and we could go our separate ways. If they pushed it, I'd let them say what they felt they needed to say, then I'd go home.

I hadn't been here before, but it was a nice ranch. Too bad it was going to bring a ton of people here, and then they'd end up wandering onto my property.

Slade kept talking as we walked into the retreat, and I finally noticed that he seemed...happier. Like for real, happy rather than the forced charm I'd seen so much of growing up. Something had changed. Considering all three of my brothers were here, I suspected it wasn't only Slade who had something new going on.

All of that flew out of my head, however, when Kevin and Blair came in, both beaming. They weren't the reason my stomach was knotting. That honor belonged to the dark-haired woman behind them.

Brea.

She looked as startled as I felt but recovered quicker. My brain was still scrambling when she started moving toward me.

"What the–" What I was going to say cut off when she grabbed my arm and pulled me off to the side. I could feel the others watching me, but I couldn't bring myself to care. Now that the shock was wearing off, I was getting pissed.

"You're my parents' first group?" She kept her voice down, but it didn't take away from the intensity I could see on her face. "A little warning would've been nice."

"Are you fucking with me?" I lowered my voice too, but that was more because I didn't want my brothers knowing what was going on.

How could I have been such an idiot, to think that someone like Brea would just show up out of the blue and want to be with me?

"Why didn't you tell me they were your parents?"

"I assumed you figured it out when they told me they'd met you. Kevin and I have the same last name, and I was on their property when we first met."

I briefly registered that she called her father by his first name, but that wasn't important. I was so stupid. How could I have missed it? I should have known even if Kevin hadn't given me his last name when we'd first met.

A horrible thought hit me.

"Did they ask you to come over and seduce me to smooth things over about the retreat?"

Her eyes widened, and I caught a flash of hurt before her face went blank.

"If that's what you think of me, then it must be true." She gave me a brittle smile. "If you'll excuse me, I need to open my shop. Don't bother checking it out. It's the same *goofy* stuff I sell in town. Nothing to interest you."

She walked away, and I let her. A heavy hand on my shoulder reminded me that I wasn't alone.

"Nice to see you're charming the ladies same as always." Slade grinned at me, but there was something in his eyes that looked a lot like concern. "Come on. We're not here to get laid. Let's check out our suite."

No, I could with certainty say, I wasn't going to be getting laid any time soon.

EIGHTEEN
BREA

I hadn't paid much attention to the direction I'd gone to get away from Blake, so I was in the kitchen before I realized that I had to go the other way to get to my shop. I was stuck now. I couldn't go back through there and see him again. Not until I had myself under control.

My pulse raced, and I could taste the sour tang of adrenaline on the back of my tongue. It had dumped into my body the moment I'd seen Blake and realized that he was one of the brothers who would be spending the weekend here. I hadn't even known he had brothers.

Because we weren't a couple. Had *never* been a couple. We'd had one date and a lot of sex. That was it. That's all we were to each other. It was my own fault for placing more importance on what we'd been doing than I should have.

Not a mistake I'd make again.

Even though I didn't necessarily *need* tea, I could use a cup. I went to the cabinet where I'd stored my tea and took out my favorite mint blend. The motions should've been comforting, but even they couldn't quiet the chaos my mind had become.

While I waited for the water to boil, I took my cell phone

out and called the shop. It was only Lamb's second time at the store by herself. She could need me to come back for something. My parents had agreed that what I did here wouldn't hurt my store in town, which meant I could leave if I had to.

"*Grow 'n Heal,* Lamb Woodall speaking."

Better than when I'd called yesterday. She'd stumbled over the words until she'd barely been able to speak. I'd tried to tell her that she needed to relax, that I'd rather she simply answered with a 'hello' if she couldn't get the whole thing out, but she'd insisted that she could do it.

"Hi," I said, wincing at how falsely bright my voice sounded. "It's Brea."

"Hi!" She somehow managed to sound happy and nervous at the same time. "Did I get it right?"

"You did," I said. "How are things going?"

"I sold some tea and willow bark to a couple tourists a few minutes ago."

"Tourists? Rawlins doesn't get tourists."

"That's what I said." She laughed. "And do you know what they said? 'Well, it was Grandma's turn to throw the dart, and she was aiming for Vancouver.'"

I opened my mouth, but there was nothing I could say to that. Could anyone have said, *anything* to that?

"Apparently, three weeks ago, this family of five piled into an RV, put a giant map of North America on a wall and chose where to go by throwing darts at it. Each person had a chance to throw one, and then they'd drive to wherever that was."

Any other day, that story would have delighted me. I would've been laughing about it for days, telling my parents about it, daydreaming about doing something similar for vacation someday. Right now, however, I was laughing, but my heart wasn't in it. I couldn't quit thinking about what had happened with Blake.

The asshole.

No. I couldn't go there. He'd handled things badly, but it wasn't all on him. If I'd truly been thinking of my time with him as having fun without expectations, I wouldn't have been so hurt when he'd gone off on me earlier. I could've just written it off as him behaving like a child and left it at that. He'd go back to his life, and I'd go back to mine. We'd spent plenty of time in the same town without running into each other. We could do it again.

We *would* do it again because I was going to make sure that I didn't waste another second of my time and energy on Blake Hunter.

NINETEEN
BLAKE

IF ANYTHING COULD'VE MADE ME MORE PISSED AT MY brothers, it was watching Brea walk away and feeling guilty about it. I didn't have any reason to feel guilty. I hadn't done anything wrong. She should have told me that her parents were the crazy people next door. The fact that she hadn't, made me think she was hiding something. If it wasn't about her parents and the retreat, it was about something else, and I didn't need that shit.

"Not bad," Jax said as he came out of the bedroom he'd claimed. "But there are only two bathrooms for the four of us, so we're sharing."

"It can't be as bad as sharing one with a curious four-year-old," Slade said, shaking his head. "At least none of you will peek at me while I'm in the shower and ask me if your penis will grow to be like mine."

That statement pretty much stopped everyone in the room.

He grinned. "My girlfriend has custody of her four-year-old brother. I love the kid to death, but that question threw me for a loop."

"Your what?" I stared at him.

"Girlfriend." He sat down on the couch and kicked his feet up on the table in front of him. "Cheyenne Lamont. Austin's the kid. You'll love them."

I'd intended to spend the next few hours pretending to listen to them while they said whatever the hell it was they felt like they needed to say, and then I'd go home. Trying was more than I usually did anyway.

Except Slade had a girlfriend with a brother who was a kid and he was around enough that he'd shared a bathroom with them. And he was acting like I was going to meet them. I hadn't met any of Slade's girlfriends since Lizann. Hell, I didn't even know if he'd *had* girlfriends since Lizann.

"I know, I know," Slade said. "Me with a kid. I never would've thought it either. I mean, I never had anything against kids, but I hadn't exactly been thinking about having a ready-made family."

A sharp stab of something went through me, and Brea's face flashed through my mind. "And now you are?"

The smile that settled on my brother's face was different from the ones I'd seen before. It was softer, somehow, but not weaker. "Yes."

I glanced at Jax and Cai, both of whom had taken seats in the empty chairs across from Slade and me. They looked different too. What the hell was going on with them?

"I know what you mean," Jax said. "I never even considered settling down, but when I met Syll, I knew she had to be mine."

"And now you're engaged," Slade said.

Jax nodded. "I didn't see any point in waiting to ask. You know how it is. You see something you want and delaying the inevitable is pointless."

"You do have to admit what you want first," Cai said, the corner of his mouth curving up.

"I think all of us have learned that over the last few months," Jax said ruefully.

"How are things going with the move?" Slade asked Cai.

"Good," Cai said. "We'd thought about just getting someplace small to start, but after talking about it, Addison and I decided to wait until we found somewhere perfect."

"I can have my realtor make some calls," Jax offered. "She's amazing."

I'd started to tune them out when Jax's statement made me snap back to attention. The only way it would've made sense for Jax's realtor to get involved would be if Cai was looking in Boston. The last time I'd spoken to him, he'd still been at the CDC in Atlanta.

No one offered an explanation, and I didn't ask. They'd fallen into their usual thing of where they'd talk about the things in their lives and ignore me. Usually, I didn't give a shit, but something was going on. Besides, why the fuck was I here if they weren't going to talk to me?

And that wasn't the only weird thing. It used to be all about work with Jax. Slade would make jokes or talk about work. Cai occasionally said something, but it was usually work related as well. That had always been the way my brothers had related as adults. Work.

But now, there was some work talk, but more of it was about their...*women*. Syll. Addison. Cheyenne.

"What about you, Blake?" Jax asked, surprising me. "What's going on with you?"

I shrugged. "Nothing."

All three of them stared at me like they didn't believe me, and I couldn't really blame them. They'd seen me with Brea, and there was no way anyone could've mistaken us for being strangers. They wanted me to say something, to share about her the way they'd been doing about their own personal lives, but it wasn't like that for me. She and I weren't a couple. We'd fucked. That was all. And it was done.

"I still don't get why we had to come here," I grumbled.

"Because it's away from the rest of the world," Jax said.

"So's my place."

"Just give it a try," Slade said. "Grandfather wanted us to work things out."

Right. That was why we were here. Not because they really wanted to change, or because they *cared* about what I was doing in my life. They were here because Grandfather had wanted us to reconcile.

I shook my head. "I need some air."

TWENTY
BREA

I was glad that Lamb had sold a few things to some tourists, but the real relief came when I heard a crash, followed by one of Lamb's unique curses.

"Fudge and caramel fiddlesticks!"

The first time I'd heard her say that, I'd burst out laughing, and it really hadn't gotten any less entertaining, but at this moment, I chose to focus on the fact that I might have a legitimate excuse to leave.

"What happened?" I asked, hoping she couldn't hear how eager I was.

"I bumped into one of the display cases, and it fell." She sounded near tears. "I'm so sorry, Brea. Everything's a mess, and it's all my fault."

"It's okay," I said automatically. "I want you to go ahead and close the shop for a bit. I'll be there soon, and we'll see what needs to be done."

"You don't have to do that," she said, an edge of panic creeping into her voice. "I can clean it up myself. I'll figure out what's missing and order replacements. You can take it out of my paycheck. Or I'll pay for the supplies myself if you don't mind me switching the card–"

"Lamb," I interrupted. "It's okay. We'll figure it all out when I get there. Just flip the sign and lock the door."

"I'm so sorry, Brea. I know how much you were relying on me to be able to do this."

"It'll be all right," I insisted, keeping my voice nice and calm. "Just hold on. I'll be right there."

I told myself that I would send a brief text to my parents rather than speaking to them in person because I didn't want to interrupt if they were in the middle of conducting a tour, but I couldn't lie to myself that well. I couldn't handle seeing Blake again. Not yet. After things were taken care of in town, I'd be settled enough to come back and act professionally.

That lie I believed.

I locked everything down and put out my "Be Back In–" sign. I didn't bother pulling down the gate though. I doubted I needed to worry about Blake or his brothers stealing my dandelion roots.

As if thinking his name had conjured him, the moment I stepped out of the shop, I saw him. It was only out of the corner of my eye, and only for a few seconds before he disappeared through the doors that led to the back of the property. I didn't think he'd seen me, but I told myself that it wouldn't have mattered if he had. The accusation he'd hurled at me wasn't something I could overlook simply because the sex was great.

And that's all it'd been between us. Sex. We'd gotten along fine, and I'd read too much into it. What I'd thought had been a real connection had only been physical attraction. I should have known better. After all, he'd shown me his temper and tendency toward assumptions when we first met.

It didn't matter anymore, I told myself as I headed for the front door. I could've handled that if he'd been an adult about it. Casual sex wasn't really my thing, but the misunderstanding was on me. I refused to take responsibility for how he'd talked to me though. We were done. Sex. Talking. Dinner. Distraction. I wasn't going there again.

The drive into Rawlins was what I needed to clear my head. Now that I'd made my decision, I would choose not to think about it anymore. I would focus on my business and my time with my parents before they left again.

Lamb was standing in the middle of the store, wringing her hands when I walked inside. I wondered if she'd been doing that since we'd gotten off the phone, but I didn't ask. The distress on her face told me everything I needed to know about how awful she felt, and I didn't need to add to that. One of us feeling like shit today was enough.

"I'm so sorry, Brea," she started apologizing again.

I held up a hand. "Accidents happen. Let's clean it up, and we'll see what we need to do after that, okay?"

She nodded. "I didn't touch anything here, but I did get out the broom and dustpan, and made up some soapy water."

"Thank you." I turned my attention to the mess next to her, grateful for a problem I could solve.

The display had been one of the many odds and ends I'd found left here by the previous owner, so I wasn't out any money for it. Unfortunately, it was old enough that it had been made up of regular glass rather than safety glass, which meant Lamb and I were going to need to be careful when we cleaned up. It also meant that anything not in a tightly sealed container would have to be thrown out.

"We're going to need gloves," I said. "We'll take this slow and careful. I'd rather keep the shop closed the rest of the day than risk someone getting hurt because we rushed and missed something."

Once she realized that I was serious about not being mad at her, she relaxed and followed my instructions. After a few minutes of working in silence, she started to chatter, and I let her. Usually, I was engaged during a conversation, but now I was glad to have her going from one subject to the next, barely pausing to take a breath. I let her words fill my head, and they crowded out anything that wasn't already focused on what we were doing.

It took us well into the evening to make sure that things were perfect, so I didn't bother opening the store back up. The chances of getting another group of tourists was slim, and the only out-of-towners that I knew for certain were nearby were the Hunter brothers, and I sure as hell didn't want them walking into my store.

Blake's brothers might not have been the jerk that he was, but I didn't want them asking about the two of us. Let him explain what was going on. I didn't even care if he acted like I was the villain. I just wanted him out of my life. Him and anything that reminded me of him.

"Thank you again," Lamb said as she gathered her coat and purse. "I thought for sure I was fired."

"Just try to be more aware of your surroundings." I gave her a tired smile.

She opened the door, then paused and looked back at me. "My nephew from Cheyenne came in this week for a visit. I think the two of you would hit it off; if you want to meet him."

I wasn't really the sort of person who liked being set up on dates, but I could tell Lamb felt like she needed to do something nice for me to make up for what had happened. Besides, the best way to get one guy out of my head was to meet someone new. Even if things didn't work out with her nephew, it'd be a pleasant distraction. One that I hoped would keep Blake out of my head for good.

"Sure," I said. "That would be great. If you have his number, I'll give him a call."

"That won't be necessary," Lamb said with a wide smile. "I

told Steve about you yesterday, and he said he'd love to take you to dinner."

For a moment, I wondered what, exactly, she'd told Steve about me, but then I remembered that it didn't matter. If we were meant to be, we'd click. If we weren't, then we wouldn't.

Something simple was exactly what I needed right now.

TWENTY-ONE
BLAKE

I wasn't sure if group therapy without a therapist was better than it would've been with a shrink involved, but I did know I could think of a million different things that would be better than sitting here and listening to my brothers talk about their feelings.

A root canal, for example. Being covered in honey and tied to an ant hill. Going to the opera.

It didn't help that when I'd come back from my walk yesterday, they'd wanted to know if I'd been meeting with Brea. I'd given them a curt *no*, but they either hadn't gotten the message or didn't care about it, because they hadn't stopped wanting to know who she was and if we were together. As if their new romantic status meant I had to find a woman too.

I'd finally just locked myself in my bedroom and ignored their attempts to get me to come back out. Not surprisingly, it hadn't lasted long. Once they'd reached whatever they considered to be enough, they'd gone away and left me alone. It was what I'd wanted, but a part of me had been disappointed that they hadn't tried harder.

This morning, things had gone from bad to worse.

Instead of sitting in our suite and talking, Jax had announced we were going to use one of the retreat's 'therapy rooms.' We'd just finished up breakfast when Blair had appeared at the door, her expression far too chipper. I was tempted to tell her that we were only here because we didn't like each other, and our dead grandfather was manipulating us into working through our shit. That would've wiped the smile off her face.

I wasn't that much of an ass though, no matter what everyone thought of me.

"Right this way," she said with a sweep of her arm.

As we followed her, I found myself looking for similarities between mother and daughter. They had the same coloring, but Blair's eyes were a bit darker, and where Blair was curvy, Brea's body was leaner, stronger. I could see Brea's smile in Blair, but Brea was undeniably more grounded than her mother.

Why was I doing this to myself? Brea had played me. I'd taken her to my home – which I'd never done before – and she'd acted like she was there for me when she'd really been there for her parents. I didn't want to see her or even think about her.

Blair was talking, and I forced myself to turn my attention back to her.

"...specially equipped to facilitate communication and understanding." She pushed open the door and led the way inside. "We've removed all distractions and recommend that all electronics are put into one of our silent spaces for the duration of your time here."

She wasn't kidding about removing distractions. Pretty much the only things in the entire room were giant cushions and pillows. No chairs or couches or tables. No windows either. A single sign hung over a smallish square cut into the wall.

Silent Space. Set interior timer to unlock space.

"We have the room set at an ideal seventy degrees, with perfect humidity. We also offer complementary scents for you to choose from. Lavender, eucalyptus, rose, vanilla, and sandalwood. It takes only a few minutes for them to dissipate and fill the room with the right atmosphere for your needs."

"No, thank you," Jax said with a polite smile. "I think we'll be fine with just the use of the room."

"If you change your mind, simply press the call button next to the door." She pointed at a small button that I hadn't noticed before. "You can set the interior locks on a timer, so you won't be disturbed, and we have an override in case of emergencies. All of the instructions are in the panel next to the button."

She really thought we were going to lock ourselves in the room? I rolled my eyes. My first impressions of Blair and Kevin were proving to be spot-on. They should've been in some free love commune somewhere with mellow seasons and sunshine. Why had they chosen to build a retreat here? I loved it here, but I thrived on isolation. They looked like the sort of people who liked to go out just to meet new people. Wyoming didn't really fit that image. Even as I thought about it, however, I knew the answer.

They'd come for Brea.

Dammit. I didn't know what that meant. Had they bought the place because she lived in Rawlins, then after she and I first met, they'd asked her to seduce me to keep me from making waves? Or had they asked around about me when they'd first gotten here and realized they'd probably need something to distract me, then contacted Brea? Or had she thought of it herself after her parents told her about the grouchy man who lived next door?

It didn't matter what had happened first or how things had unfolded. The point was that Brea had hidden who she was and if I couldn't trust that, then I couldn't trust her for anything else either.

I hadn't realized that Blair had left until Jax said my name.

All three of them were staring at me with these strange expressions on their faces. Like they were worried about me.

Fuck that.

"What?" I snapped.

"How about we sit down?" Slade said. "Might as well get comfortable before we start in on everything."

I still had no idea what we were doing here. Yeah, I knew the basic idea that we were supposed to reconcile because we wouldn't get our inheritance if we didn't, but that didn't tell me much. Like how the hell anyone expected us to have some breakthrough in a weird room when we'd barely spoken to each other since...well, ever.

I plopped down on a giant cushion that was stuck in the corner farthest from my brothers. It was comfortable, I admitted grudgingly, but it didn't make me any happier to be here. I crossed my arms, scowled, and prepared myself to listen to whatever bullshit lecture I was about to get.

"I'll start," Jax said. He looked at each of us in turn, his gaze staying on me the longest. "Since Grandfather passed, I feel like my eyes have been opened. I've been so focused on being everything I thought Grandfather wanted that I forgot what it was like to be part of a family."

I barely kept myself from rolling my eyes again. Jax hadn't stopped being a part of a family when he'd gone to work for Grandfather. None of us had been a family since Grandma Olive died, and we hadn't even been a whole one then. A fat lot of good it did any of us to whine about it though. I barely remembered our family, and I'd gotten past it and made something of myself. I didn't need a family.

Jax kept talking. "When I met Syll, I finally got it. What it was like to want something more than the life I had. The company, the family name, none of it mattered as much as the people did."

Syll. His fiancée. I still couldn't quite believe it. I hadn't thought any of us would ever get married, to tell the truth. Maybe Cai, if he looked up from his microscope long enough to propose, but not Jax. Who'd want to marry someone who'd never be around? Unless she was after his money, but I wasn't about to suggest that. I didn't have a death wish. If she was a con artist, that was on Jax. If she wasn't, whatever. He'd get his happily ever after and ride off into the sunset, or whatever shit made up his fairytale ending.

My happy ending was next door. My place. My work. My life. I didn't need anyone else acting like they knew better about what I needed or wanted.

I was happy with my life the way it fucking was.

TWENTY-TWO
BREA

I WAS GOING ON A DATE, AND IT WAS GOING TO BE A GOOD one. Dinner at a nice restaurant. Maybe a goodnight kiss at my door. Absolutely, no sex. If we hit it off, we'd get there eventually, but I wasn't going to fall head-first again. I was back to my happy medium. Wishfully romantic, but with enough realism to know that no guy was Prince Charming. I'd go into the date with an open mind, but I wasn't about to start, 'planning for the future,' before I'd even met the guy. And I wasn't going to do it after just one date either. I'd learned my lesson about being impulsive.

I'd almost worn my favorite dress, but as soon as I'd taken it from my closet, I'd remembered what it had been like, seeing Blake's reaction to me in the dress. Then came the memories of what had happened at dinner, at my store...I didn't want to be thinking about Blake when I was out with Lamb's nephew. Aside from the fact that it'd be exceptionally rude, I was done with Blake. I didn't want him taking up any more of my thoughts and time.

Which was why I now had, a new favorite dress, one that didn't have any associations with Blake. It was a pretty dress, a mint green color, and I loved the way it flattered my figure. I'd put on the simple beaded necklace that Galina had given me the last time we'd seen each other, and a dab of lip gloss, not wanting to look overly dressed-up or too casual.

I would've normally arranged to meet him at the restaurant, but Lamb had spent nearly two hours yesterday going on and on about how great her nephew, Steve was, and how much we'd get along. I'd felt more than a little obligated to go the traditional route, which was why I was currently walking to the store's entrance where my date was waiting.

My first thought when I opened the door was that Lamb's nephew was hot. He had sienna-brown curls and a pair of beautiful blue eyes full of admiration. He was tall with an athletic build and nice features. The sort of man who pretty much any woman would be grateful to date.

My second thought was that Blake could still probably break Steve in half.

I pushed it out of my head and then smiled. "Hi, you must be Steve."

He held out a hand. "I am. And you are Brea."

"I am."

He stepped to the side and held out his arm. We were only a couple feet from the parking lot, but I linked my arm through his and let him lead me over to a nice, but not overly fancy car.

"So, you're Lamb's nephew?" I knew he was, but I needed something to say. The silence was awkward, and I couldn't think of anything else to fill it.

He nodded. "She's my mom's youngest sister. We've always been close."

Then we were back to silence as he pulled out of the parking lot and started down the street.

"I haven't seen you around Rawlins before." I tried again.

"I grew up on a ranch on the other side of town," he said,

glancing at me. "The last four and a half years, though, I've been at college. I just graduated in December."

I seized the subject. "Where'd you go to school?"

"Florida State University," he said. "You?"

"I didn't go." That question used to bother me, but I'd come to peace with my decision back when I'd made it. "I wanted to study botany, but I knew the direction I wanted to go with it wasn't really something that I could go to college for. It was more the apprenticeship kind of thing."

He nodded, and the conversation stalled again. If this was the way the rest of the night was going to go, it was going to be a long night.

STEVE WAS EXACTLY the sort of guy I should have been interested in. He wasn't talkative, but he was certainly more forthcoming than Blake. He was intelligent and educated without being arrogant about it. He had a BA in education and was going back to Florida in the fall to start on his masters. He wanted to teach special needs kids. He played the cello and liked classic cars. And his family – despite his aunt's odd name – was about as far from mine as a family could be. His parents had been married for twenty-six years. He had three younger sisters he adored. They went to church on the holidays but weren't overly religious.

On paper, he was perfect.

In person he was handsome and everything I should have wanted.

Except our chemistry sucked. It wasn't even non-existent. It was like negative chemistry. I hadn't even known that was a possibility.

As we waited for our check, I wondered if Steve was as aware of how awkward this was and was too polite to say it, or if he honestly thought things were going well. I hoped it wasn't the latter, because I really didn't want to hurt him. He deserved someone who could be with him with her whole heart, and I already knew that just wasn't me.

Still, I couldn't cut things short. I wouldn't encourage him, but I wasn't going to blow him off either.

"Do you want dessert?" Steve asked.

"No, thank you." I started to reach for my glass, then remembered that it was empty. I hadn't wanted to ask for a refill, because I would've felt obligated to drink it because he was paying for it. I'd tried to say we were on separate checks, but Steve wouldn't hear of it. Which, of course, made me feel even worse about the fact that this was going nowhere.

He waved over the waiter and asked for the check. When the young man walked away, Steve turned back to me with a look of resignation on his face.

"Okay, honesty time," he said. "There's no spark here, is there?"

I breathed a sigh of relief. "No, there's not. I'm sorry. I really wanted it to be there."

"Me too."

Fortunately, we were saved from yet another awkward silence by the return of the waiter with our check. After that, it was simple enough to make small talk until we were on our way back out to the car. Somehow, knowing that this would never go anywhere took away a lot of the conversation anxiety.

"Don't worry about Aunt Lamb," he said as we started down the road. "This isn't the first time she's set me up with someone she knows, and it didn't work out. I tend to have a take it or leave it mentality when it comes to dating, but she doesn't understand how it's not the most important thing in the world for me. Besides, I'd rather wait to be in a relationship that works than rush into something that doesn't."

"Whoever you connect with is going to be a lucky woman," I said.

"The same to you." He glanced at me. "A lucky man, I mean."

Blake's face flashed in my mind, but I pushed it away. He wasn't anything to me. Sure, we'd had a great physical connection, but I needed more than that.

As we pulled up in front of my place, I dug in my purse for my keys, then cursed when I couldn't find them.

"What's wrong?"

The fact that Steve was concerned even after we'd shared an uncomfortable date and then confessed that we didn't feel anything for each other made me wish even more that we'd been right for each other.

"I left my keys inside my apartment," I said. "I must've locked the door on my way out and not thought to check for my keys."

He looked at his watch. "Scott McPherson is handy with locks, and he should still be up."

"I have a spare set out at my parents' place," I said. "I'll give them a call."

"Where do your parents live?"

I gave him the address as I pulled out my phone.

"Don't bother them," he said. "I'll take you out there."

I shook my head. "You don't need to do that. I'm sure one of them will be able to run them over. I'll wait here, and you can go ahead home."

"Nonsense," he said as he pulled back out onto the road. "I'm not going to let you stand outside in the cold for who knows how long. Just because we don't work as a couple doesn't mean I'm going to be a jerk."

I smiled and settled back into my seat. "Thank you."

"You're welcome."

The drive wasn't exactly comfortable, but now that neither

of us had any expectations about the other, it wasn't nearly as awkward as it had been before. I might not be interested in dating Steve, but I was starting to think that the two of us could be friends.

"Wow," he said as he drove up the driveway. "It looks great. The last I'd heard, the Miller family had left because they couldn't pay the mortgage, and the place had fallen apart. Did your parents do all of this?"

"I suppose they did." I hadn't known anything about the shape the place had been in when they'd bought it, but it didn't surprise me. They didn't do the whole house flipping thing, but they did like fixing things up. "I didn't see it before they bought it."

He parked the car. "Do you think they'd mind if I came inside with you? I'd love to see more of what they did."

"Sure," I said. "But I need to warn you that if we run into my parents, be careful what you ask them?"

He frowned. "Why?"

"Because they'll keep you here all night giving you a play-by-play of the restoration process."

He chuckled as we started for the door, but I didn't join in his laughter because someone was standing next to the door, glaring at us.

Shit. Blake.

TWENTY-THREE

BLAKE

After spending almost all day in that fucking room, I needed air. My brothers didn't try to stop me when I walked straight outside. They'd been talking about dinner plans, but I didn't want to be a part of that, any more than I wanted to be a part of this. I'd given in, on the whole 'talking things out' shit, but I'd had enough for the day. I needed some space.

Spring was here, but the weather hadn't been notified. It hovered in that annoying range between being cold and being warm, and now that the sun was down, the chill was winning. Still, I didn't go back inside for a jacket. I'd rather be cold and alone than risk one of my brothers deciding they wanted to walk with me. I didn't know what had gotten into all three of them, but it bugged the hell out of me that they were acting like I'd been a part of whatever had bonded them recently.

I was halfway home when I realized what I was doing. It was tempting to keep going, to lock myself in my house until things went back to normal, but I couldn't quite bring myself to do it. Better to get it over with now and send them on their way. When our little retreat was over, I'd tell them that they were welcome to my share of the inheritance and they should go back to Boston, get on with their lives.

That's all I wanted. To have my life back. To not have someone setting expectations that I couldn't reach. To not feel like I was a disappointment no matter what I did.

Why couldn't they all just leave me alone?

I walked for more than an hour, aimlessly wandering from a 'meditation bench' to a little flower garden, to one of the ranch hand cabins that was still being worked on. They'd done good work, I grudgingly admitted. The place looked great, and if they kept it up, it'd probably attract a lot of people.

Wonderful.

By the time I got back to the house, I'd cooled off literally, but that was about it. Being alone hadn't helped. I was still frustrated and fighting my temper.

I was hungry, but I wasn't going to sit down for a meal with my brothers. I wasn't sure I'd be able to bite my tongue if Jax kept going on with the whole 'we need to do what Grandfather wanted' spiel. I'd get a plate from the dining area and eat in my room. Then again, there was a good chance they hadn't even noticed that I hadn't come back.

When I reached the door, a flash of car headlights caught my attention. Someone was pulling up the driveway. Maybe my brothers had gone into town to find something to eat, but the car that stopped only a few yards away wasn't the rental they'd arrived in.

Great. New people.

Except it wasn't anyone new.

Brea got out of the passenger's side of the car, and my stomach clenched. She looked great. Where had she been that she'd needed to dress up? Who had she been with?

I didn't recognize the man who got out of the driver's side, but he was smiling and laughing with Brea, and that was enough for me to hate him. She turned toward me as the guy moved to put his hand on her back, and I saw red.

Why was he touching her? He didn't have the right to do that, but she wasn't pushing him away so maybe he did. But he couldn't. She and I had been together just two nights ago. Had she really hopped from my bed into his in just two days?

I'd brought her into my home, and she'd lied to me about who she was and why she'd slept with me. I'd told myself I was done with her, but all I could do now was stare at him touching her and try to remember that beating the shit out of him wouldn't end well for anyone involved.

"Blake." Her voice was flat. "This is Steve Geraint, my date. Steve, this is Blake Hunter. He and his brothers are staying at the retreat."

"Blake Hunter?" The guy – S*teve* – sounded impressed. "I've seen your work. You're amazing."

I grunted an inarticulate reply. I didn't give a fuck what he thought about my work. I just wanted him to stop touching Brea.

"Come on," she said, looking away from me. "I'll give you the tour on the way to my room."

Her room. She'd brought this asshole *here* to fuck him. She wanted me to know what she was doing, or she'd have gone to his place or her apartment in town. No way in hell was I going to let her do that.

I moved directly into their path and glared at Steve.

"You're not going to her room," I growled.

"Blake," she said, a warning in her voice. "This isn't any of your business."

"Like hell it isn't," I snapped, shifting from him to her. "I don't want you fucking some pretty boy when I'm right upstairs."

"Whoa, whoa." Steve held up his hands, palms out. "I don't

know what I got in the middle of, but I'm not having sex with her."

"Damn right," I said.

He looked between me and Brea. "I mean, we weren't planning on it."

I pointed at him. "Shut up."

"Stop being an ass," Brea said, her usually bright features dark and cloudy. "Get out of our way."

"No," I said, crossing my arms. "I'm not letting him anywhere near your bedroom."

Brea sighed and turned to Steve. "Thank you for dinner, and for driving me out here to get my keys. I'm sorry about the asshat who won't let us inside. I'll give you a tour some other time."

I started to take a step forward but then thought better of it.

"Are you sure you want me to leave?" Steve asked, his eyes flicking to me, then back to Brea.

I had to give him credit for not turning tail and running away, but it wasn't much credit. He was still being too friendly with Brea, and I didn't like it. I told myself it was only because they were moving too fast, but even as I said it, I knew it was hypocritical of me. After all, we'd fucked after our first date. Maybe that was normal for her. I didn't know.

"I'll be fine," she said to him. "I'll stay here tonight and have one of my parents take me to town to get my car tomorrow. You go ahead home."

He shot me one more look, then went back to his car. Brea waited until he was halfway down the drive before she turned on me, eyes flashing.

"We're having this all out," she said. "Because I'm not wasting any more of my time with this. We're not doing it out here though. Follow me."

Dammit. I'd fucked up. Again. When I'd seen that guy, I hadn't stopped to think about whether it was a good idea to say something. I hadn't been thinking of anything except the fact that I didn't want his hands on her. I should've just left her alone and kept my distance.

One of the smaller rooms across from the dining area had been changed into a library, and that was where Brea took me. She didn't say anything until she'd closed the door and turned back to me. Her usually bright expression was dark, and there was something in her eyes I didn't recognize.

"What the hell is the matter with you?" She was keeping her voice low, probably to keep from disturbing everyone else.

I folded my arms and scowled at her. "I was just looking out for you."

"Looking out for me? That's what you're going with? Really?" She made a disgusted sound. "What *exactly* were you afraid was going to happen to me that I couldn't handle?"

"He had his hands on you," I said mulishly.

"And if I hadn't wanted him to touch me, I would've told him so," she countered. "Not that it's any of your damn business."

She'd wanted him to touch her. Jealousy flared up, burning so hot that I couldn't think of anything else. "I forgot. You have no problem fucking a guy on the first date."

As soon as the words left my mouth, I knew it had been the absolute wrong thing to say.

Color flooded her face. "You bastard," she whispered.

"Brea," I started.

She didn't let me get any further. "I slept with you because I thought we had a real connection, that you were actually a decent guy under that gruff exterior. Obviously, I was mistaken, because a decent guy wouldn't have said that. He wouldn't have even thought, it."

Guilt rushed through me. She was right. A decent guy wouldn't have thought it. I was a bastard.

Even as I watched, she seemed to collect herself, and I

wondered if this was it, the moment she was going to walk away from me for good.

"Look." Her voice was calmer now. "I get that this isn't really how you usually do things, but I don't deserve to be treated the way you've treated me. You made accusations about me, questioned my character."

The more she talked, the worse I felt, but I didn't stop her. I deserved everything she was saying and more.

She took a step toward me, and I could feel the warring emotions coming off her. She was still pissed at me, but there was something else there too. Something different. "I know you have baggage. Everyone does. But you can't let it drive people away."

I clenched my jaw. I should've known she was going to go there. It was always all about the feelings and coming to terms with your past and making things right and all that shit. Why couldn't she just accept me like I was?

No. I didn't want that. I didn't want *her*. I just wanted my life back.

"I should walk away," she said. "That would be the healthier thing to do. Walk away from all of this. Focus on my work like I've been doing for years. Let you keep going on your self-destructive path."

Right. Because what she was doing was so much better.

"I don't want to do that," she said, her voice softening. "No matter how angry I am at you right now, I still think there's something between us. A connection that I can't explain. I think you feel it too."

No, I didn't. There was nothing to feel. We'd had sex. That was it. Nothing more.

"But I refuse to do this dance," she continued. "I need to know, right now, if you want something from whatever this is between us. That you're going to talk to me. For real. We're going to do more than have sex and make small talk."

Shit.

I'd expected her to be furious, to yell at me, tell me to fuck off. I hadn't expected this.

"If that's not what you want, fine," she continued, "but this is where it either begins or ends. If you walk away now, we go our separate ways for good."

The thought of never being with her again, of having to watch her with other men, made me want to hit something, but I couldn't bring myself to talk to her either. Not about the personal stuff. Besides, if she really liked me, why would she want me to be anything other than who I was?

After nearly a full minute of silence, during which I couldn't look at her, but I could feel her watching me, she stepped past me and left the library without a word.

That could have gone better.

TWENTY-FOUR
BLAKE

I waited until I got home before I sent my mother a text telling her that I'd borrowed her car. The moment I walked out of the library, I'd known that I had to leave the retreat as soon as possible. I'd planned on going back to my apartment in Rawlins anyway, but now I planned on staying until Blake had gone home.

As flakey as my parents could be, I knew I couldn't tell them what had happened. They'd be pissed at Blake, and that wouldn't be good for the business. They needed to see the Hunter brothers as guests, and that included their grumpy neighbor.

Are you sure you're okay?

I smiled, but I didn't really feel it. It was nice of Blair to be worried about me, but I wasn't much in the mood for motherly comfort. Still, I sent back, quick thanks and let her know that I'd call her tomorrow. I'd have to tell her then that I wasn't coming back until the Hunter brothers left, but at least I'd have tonight to think things through.

I set my phone down on the counter, determined not to look at it again until tomorrow. Right now, I wanted to be alone, and that included carrying on conversations with my mom or dad, or whoever else might try to contact me. It wouldn't be Blake, of course, because we were done.

I swallowed hard, my eyes burning. I wasn't going to cry over him. That wasn't really my style. Especially not the way things had gone down. When my other relationships had ended, they'd done so on good terms. There'd been some sadness when we'd parted ways, but it hadn't been something devastating because I'd already known that we wouldn't be going anywhere.

I hadn't braced myself for that with Blake. I hadn't braced myself for anything with him. What happened between us had been so abrupt, so intense, that I hadn't been able to form a complete picture of what we'd been, let alone what we could have been.

I took a shower and let the white noise help clear my head. Lavender scented body wash helped too. By the time I stepped out of my steam-filled bathroom, wrapped in a plush pale blue robe, I was feeling a bit better.

Not a lot, but enough to think things through with a clear head.

I pulled a bottle of beer out of my fridge. Beer and music were vital to 'me' time. And only one type of music would work: my favorite bad-ass violinist. Once her music was coming through my speakers, I took my beer over to my overstuffed chair and settled in to try to relax.

I probably should've just gone to bed, but I knew if I did that, I would've spent the night staring at the ceiling. At least here I had beer and music to help me go through all the shit in my head. It was the only way I'd be able to move on.

The first thing I needed to do was decide if I was going to stick with my shop at the retreat. In Rawlins, I'd managed to go for two years without speaking to Blake or seeing him face-to-face. I would be safe in my store. Out at the retreat, things wouldn't be so easy. He lived next door. Granted, there was a lot of space between the two properties, but it wasn't out of the question that I'd see him if I went out walking. That was how we first met, after all.

I wished I'd never agreed to have a shop out at the retreat. Things with Blake probably still would've fallen apart, but it wouldn't have been like this. He never would've accused me of seducing him for my parents, and he wouldn't have been there when I'd been with Steve. Hell, I probably wouldn't have gone out with Steve in the first place if I hadn't needed to get Blake out of my head.

But what could have been and what was were two different things. I couldn't go back in time and going over all the possible ways things might have gone wouldn't do anything but ruin my sleep. I needed to let it go.

Except I wouldn't be able to completely move past it right now because I'd have to eventually tell my parents why I wasn't going to be around for the next couple days. I'd already decided that I couldn't tell them everything for business reasons, but I also knew I couldn't talk to my mom about the personal side of things. She wouldn't understand. She met Kevin when she was eighteen, and they'd had an open relationship the entire time they'd been together. She'd never understood why I'd never been into casual sex or why I ever wanted to get married.

Besides, to tell her the personal side of things, I'd have to know myself how I felt about Blake, and that wasn't something I wanted to admit to anyone. Because it couldn't have been anything more than sex and small talk.

TWENTY-FIVE
BLAKE

I STOMPED BACK UPSTAIRS, NOT CARING WHO HEARD ME. It'd serve them all right if I woke them up. Kevin and Blair with their fucking retreat. My brothers and their damn control issues. If everyone would've just left me alone, things wouldn't be so fucked up. I'd be home right now, having a beer and watching TV after a long day. I'd be going over commissions to decide what to do next and checking the weather to see if it'd be safe for me to go for a ride tomorrow.

Why wouldn't people let me be? It was my fucking life.

I opened the door to the suite, fully intending to slam it behind me and hope it woke my brothers. Seeing them all sitting in the main room caught me enough off-guard that I closed the door normally. I started for my room, but Jax stopped me.

"Please sit down."

My brother never asked me to do things, so the order wasn't anything I hadn't gotten a million times growing up, but the *please* was new. A part of me wanted to blow him off like I always had before, but a bigger part was tired of all of this. Tired of acting like our childhood hadn't fucked us all up. Tired of them talking around me and over me but rarely to me.

"Why?" I asked.

"So we can talk," Jax said, not reacting to my tone.

I laughed. "You mean so you three can talk, and I can listen. I think I've heard enough about how great your lives are and how much you love your girlfriends or whatever. Let's not pretend this has anything to do with *talking*."

Jax opened his mouth to say something, but Cai put out a hand. "What do you think we're here for then, if it's not to work on making things right between us?"

I ran a hand through my hair. "Honestly, I have no fucking clue. But that's not surprising since you've never actually bothered talking to me. You showed up at my house and brought me here without asking what I wanted."

"Blake–" Slade interrupted.

Now that I'd gotten started, I wasn't about to stop, not even for the brother I'd always gotten along with best. I was just so fucking tired of all of it.

"Don't *Blake* me. I'm not a fucking child anymore. Not that any of you would've noticed anything about who I am." I glared at all three of them, enjoying the surprise on their faces. "You never have. You've all gone on with your lives and your women, and this whole reconciliation shit is just you checking one more thing off your to-do list, before you go back to your perfect lives."

"Our lives aren't perfect," Slade said, his face serious. "And we haven't moved on from what happened. It fucked us all up."

"Yeah, well, at least you guys actually remember what it was like to be a real family."

"I always thought you had it easier," Jax said quietly. "You said you didn't remember anything from before, so this was all you ever knew."

"How could you think that would be easier?" I stared at him, incredulous. "I never knew what it was like to have a mother or a father. I had Grandma Olive for a few years, and then she was gone, and it was the three of you and Grandfather telling me what I was doing wrong and how I needed to behave because I was never good enough."

"I never thought I was good enough," Cai said. He leaned forward, expression serious. "I spent my whole life in Jax's shadow, thinking that Grandfather was disappointed in me because I didn't want to follow in his footsteps like Jax."

"We all have baggage," Jax said.

Baggage. That's what Brea had said too. I gritted my teeth. No one understood. "I don't give a shit about baggage. I made my own life, my own money, and I did it all on my own because I wasn't following the path you all thought I needed to take. I've been alone my whole fucking life, and I'm tired of people acting like I need to change to fit some idea of who they think I am when they'll end up leaving just like everyone else."

I'd said too much, but it felt damn good to finally say it. I'd held back all these years because it was easier to just hold it in when I was around them, and then forget about them when I went home.

"You guys came here like all we had to do was sit around for a day and hold hands while we talked about our childhood and we'd be good again. Except we weren't good in the first place. I can't say that I want us to get back to the way things had been because I don't have a 'had been.' All I've ever had is this, and I gave up wanting more a long time ago. I've worked my ass off to do what I wanted to do. I don't give a fuck about Grandfather's money, and I don't give a fuck about 'making things right' because you guys have no idea what it would take to make things right with me."

They stared at me, not even trying to say anything. Not that there was anything they could say. I meant every word. There was nothing they could do to fix what was broken between us because there hadn't been anything there to break.

"Do whatever you want," I said, exhaustion hitting me as my adrenaline rush faded away. "I like my life the way it is."

I turned and walked away, shutting myself in my bedroom before any of them could speak again. I just wanted this weekend to be over, so I could go back to my life and not have to think about them or Brea or the way things could have been if it hadn't been for a patch of black ice and shitty tires more than two decades ago.

TWENTY-SIX
BREA

"Are you sure you don't need me to bring you anything?" Blair asked. "I have some wonderful healing crystals, and I'm sure I can find a few things in the shop that I can use to cleanse your apartment of negative energies."

"No, Mom, I don't need any of that," I said as I picked at some sticker residue on one of my glass cases. "I'm just going to take it easy today. Things are always slow on Sundays."

That was an understatement. I only opened every other Sunday, and the hours were always shorter. Today was different though. Today, I needed to pretend that I was doing something worthwhile or I'd be tempted to spend the day in my pajamas, drinking hot chocolate, and reading the same page, repeatedly. That meant I'd opened at my usual weekday time, and I planned on staying open until my weekday closing time, even though I wasn't supposed to be open at all.

"Kevin and I don't mind keeping the shop closed if you want Lamb to come back to help you," she offered. "She's a darling, but I don't think the young men here are very interested in homeopathic remedies. One of them came down to the shop while I was talking to Lamb, and he barely said a word to either of us. When I offered him some suggestions to promote relaxation and mental stimulation, he just smiled and excused himself."

For a moment, I'd thought she'd been talking about Blake, but then she'd said he smiled and I knew that wasn't the case. He hadn't come looking for me. Why would he? I'd given him a chance to put all that he'd done behind us. I would've let it all go if he'd simply opened up to me.

"I'm fine, Blair," I said. "I'd rather have her there just in case you need her for something. I'll be back out in a couple days."

As soon as I was sure the Hunter brothers were gone.

"All right," she said reluctantly. "If that's what you think is best."

I smiled. Blair had never been the mothering type, but occasionally, she'd do something that almost made our relationship seem normal. I loved her, and most of the time, I appreciated the independence I'd always had, but I still liked these little moments of normalcy.

"I promise I'll call if I need anything."

"Thank you," she said. After a moment's pause, she added, "I just sometimes worry about you, not having anyone to ease some of your burdens."

"That's why I hired Lamb." I purposefully misunderstood her. Before she could correct me, I said, "I have to go. I'll talk to you later, all right?"

"Okay."

I breathed a sigh of relief when I ended the call. Neither of my parents ever made me feel like I was defective for not being in a relationship, but they also didn't understand how I could tolerate being alone so much of the time. They'd never said anything, but I'd always suspected that part of the reason they'd never gotten married and had always kept the relationship open was because they never wanted to risk being alone. If they always had a couple people on the fringes, they'd always have someone to turn to, to spend time with.

If that's what they wanted in their lives, I supported their choice, but I could never do it. Sometimes I needed the silence, but more than that, I preferred to be alone rather than be involved in a relationship that wasn't going anywhere.

I picked up my all-natural glass cleaner and went back to cleaning off the new case Lamb had brought out from the back room. I'd completely forgotten I'd had it, but when I'd called her early this morning to ask her to cover for me at the retreat, she'd told me that she'd found something to replace the display case she'd broken. She was right. It was exactly what we needed.

If only it was that easy to replace people. Some people liked to pretend they could swap friends and lovers, but even my parents – who'd had more partners than I ever wanted to think about – didn't act like the others were interchangeable. Maybe there were people who didn't need that deep, individual connection, or they had some other way of making it so that when one person left, they had another one waiting. All I knew for certain was that I wasn't that sort of person. If I had been, I would've replaced Blake with Steve, and I wouldn't have even blinked.

But I couldn't do that.

Even worse was the fact that Blake's rejection hadn't made anything I felt go away. He'd behaved like a total and complete ass, hadn't apologized, and then he hadn't even had the courage to tell me that he didn't want me. He'd simply let the seconds drag out until I'd been the one to walk away.

I should've been pissed at him.

I *was* pissed at him.

But I couldn't stop thinking about him.

I finished wiping down the outside of the display, but my mind was remembering how it'd felt to run my hands over all that firm flesh. The cleaner made me sneeze, but all I could think about was how amazing he smelled, even when he'd been sweaty from working. When I bent over to brush away some cobwebs, I could almost imagine him coming up behind me to grab my hips, pull up my skirt, and take me right there in the middle of the store...

The light ringing of the bell above my door startled me out of my daydream. Flushed, but grateful, I turned to greet my unexpected customer.

"Welcome to *Grow 'n*..." The words died as quickly as my smile when I realized I knew the man standing in front of me.

Well, not *knew*, but I recognized him and knew his name, and that was enough. Jax Hunter. One of Blake's brothers.

I bit back a curse and waited for him to tell me why he was here.

"Brea, right?" He gave me one of those smiles that I knew was supposed to be overly charming, but I wasn't in the mood today.

"Brea Chaise," I said. "How can I help you?"

"I want to talk to you about Blake."

Yeah, that's what I'd been afraid of. I shook my head. "I don't want to talk about him."

"Let me rephrase. I *need* to talk to you about Blake." Jax's expression changed, but I couldn't doubt the sincerity I saw there. "How much do you know about my brother?"

I sighed. I needed to just get this over with. "A lot of superficial stuff that doesn't mean anything."

"Has he talked about our family?"

"No." I tried not to let myself feel the hurt that came with that honest admission.

Jax nodded like that didn't surprise him. "Blake should've been the one to tell you this, but he doesn't talk about it, and you need to know."

I didn't know why I needed to know. It wasn't like the two

of us were anything anymore. If we even had been to begin with.

"Our parents and our sister died in a car crash twenty-four years ago," he continued. "Aimee was Blake's twin."

My stomach sank. He'd been an ass, but I wouldn't wish that sort of thing on my worst enemy.

"Blake was in the car."

Fuck.

Jax leaned on the counter. "He was barely four, and he doesn't remember anything, but everything changed for us when it happened. We went to live with our grandparents, and they tried their best, but after Grandma Olive died, we fell apart. Grandfather worked all the time, and the rest of us, we were just kids. We made a lot of mistakes, and Blake, he suffered the most for them. He's felt alone all this time."

Dammit. I didn't want to feel anything for Blake. It didn't matter that he'd had a shitty childhood. He was an adult and how he behaved was a choice. I couldn't excuse him just because he'd lost everyone. Maybe that made me a horrible person, but I just couldn't do it. Not when he refused to try.

"I'm sorry for your losses," I said, struggling to keep my voice even. "But some people are alone because they want to be. I can't help him anymore. I gave him a choice, and he didn't choose me."

"You've gotten through to him," Jax said. "And if there's one thing I've learned over the last few months, it's that a good woman can always get through to a Hunter man."

"He doesn't want me," I repeated the information more bluntly. "We aren't looking for the same things. I don't want a casual fuck-buddy, and he doesn't want to talk to me."

I had a moment to regret my word choice, but then I saw that Jax was smiling. "He can positively be an ass."

"That he can," I agreed. "So, you see why none of what you've told me matters?"

"I think that's why it matters more than ever," he said, his voice softening. He reached out and put his hand on my arm. "Just tell me one thing. Are you in love with him?"

I thought about denying it, especially since it was a question I'd worked very hard to keep from asking myself. I also thought about telling him that it was none of his damn business. Except Jax had come to me because he was concerned about Blake, and he'd told me something that had to be painful to even think about. I owed him something in return. I couldn't give him what he wanted, but I could give him the truth.

"Yes," I said quietly. "I love him."

TWENTY-SEVEN
BLAKE

I scowled at the food the retreat had provided, but not because it was bad. The pancakes were great, the fruit fresh, the bacon crisp. There was plenty of it. After everything that had gone on before, this should have been the best thing to happen all weekend. But I could barely taste it.

After I'd gone back to my room last night, none of my brothers had come after me. Not surprising. After all the shit I'd put out there, I wouldn't have wanted to talk to me either. Cai and Slade had both been at the table when I finally came out of my room, and they'd given me polite enough greetings, but they hadn't tried to talk to me about any of it. They'd also ignored my question about where Jax was. I hadn't cared enough to ask it again.

I wondered how long they'd want to stay now that I'd finally said all those things. Maybe it was a good thing I'd blown up. Now they knew how I felt and that there wasn't anything to fix between us. They could go back to Boston, and I could go back to my life. We wouldn't have to see each other again. I'd talk to Miss K and let her know that they'd done what Grandfather had wanted. No need for them to get fucked over because I wanted nothing to do with them.

Finally, I pushed my plate aside and picked up a plum from the bowl. Apples, oranges, bananas – hell, even pears – I understood. Who bought plums for guests?

I leaned back in my chair and tossed the plum into the air. Cai and Slade ignored me, their attention on their phones. Judging by the idiotic expressions on their faces, they were texting their women. Girlfriends? I supposed that was a more PC term.

I remembered Slade's high school girlfriend, Lizann. I'd always thought she was pretty. Then they'd broken up while Slade was in basic training, and that had solidified my decision not to date.

The suite's door opened, but I ignored it. Once the others started talking again, I'd–

A hand darted out and caught the plum before I did.

"Hey! That's mine." I glared up at Jax.

"Mature response," he said dryly. "But after how you've behaved this weekend, not surprising."

"Bite me," I snapped. "I never said I wanted to do this, so don't blame me for getting pissed at you."

"I'm not talking about what you said to us. We deserved that." He sat down next to me, and the other guys put away their phones. "I meant how you've been treating Brea."

Heat flushed my face. "That's more of, not your damn business."

"It is when her employee goes off on me for ruining the date she'd set Brea up on. By the time I was able to convince Lamb that I wasn't the one she was pissed at, I'd learned that Brea went home last night and called Lamb this morning to cover the shop here. Apparently, Brea also apologized to Lamb for 'some asshole acting like he had the right to butt into my life.'"

He held out the plum, and I took it, but I didn't throw it again. I probably would've thrown it at his head if I had.

"You need to fix things with her," he said. "Trust me. I almost lost Syll because I was an idiot. Remember? You saw how torn up I was."

"We've all fucked up," Slade said, "but trust me when I say that if it's real, it's worth fighting for."

"It's not like that," I said. "We went on one date and fucked a couple times. That's it."

"If that's all it was, why were you so worked up when she was out with that other guy?" Cai asked.

I glared at him. It figured. Cai rarely spoke, and one of the few times he did, it was to side against me. "All right. She's hot. Great in bed. I wanted another go. You guys know how it is."

"I know the only woman I'd be jealous of is one I cared about," Slade pointed out.

I rolled my eyes. "Whatever. It doesn't matter. We're done."

I pushed back from the table and stood. I didn't know where I was going, but I wanted to be away from this conversation.

"You need to fix it," Jax said.

"I don't want to fix it, Jax." I turned to face him. "Don't you get that? All I wanted from her was sex. Sure, it would've been nice to fuck her again, but it's no big deal."

"Do you really believe the shit that's coming out of your mouth?" Slade asked, shaking his head. He pushed some dark hair away from his face. "I mean, I guess someone who didn't know you might think you were being honest, but I know better."

"Obviously, you don't know me as well as you think you do." I tossed the plum into the air and caught it, hoping the gesture came off as casual as I'd intended. "Because there's nothing for me to lie about. Brea and I are done."

"Then I'll go downstairs and tell Lamb that her nephew should give Brea a call, ask her out on another date."

I put down the fruit. I knew what Jax was doing. He was trying to get a rise out of me to prove his point, but it wasn't going to work. Because he was wrong. I didn't care. She could do whatever she wanted, go out with whoever she wanted. Touch and kiss and fuck…

My hands tightened into fists.

"Yeah, that looks like you don't want her," Slade said, raising an eyebrow. "I think you're good to go, Jax."

"I'll be back in a few minutes," he said. "It shouldn't take me too long."

My self-control lasted until he got halfway to the door. "Wait."

"Yes?" He gave me a knowing look. "Is there something you want?"

"Fuck you." I flicked up my middle finger.

"I think you'd rather fuck Brea," Slade said. "But to do that, you need to apologize for being an asshat."

"Says the king of asshats."

He gave me the same salute I'd given Jax.

"He's right," Cai said. "If you care that much about Brea, you need to fix things with her, or you're going to regret it."

He was right. They were all right. I didn't want Brea going out with that guy or any guy who wasn't me.

Dammit.

She meant something to me. I'd known it all along, but there was a huge difference between *knowing* it and *admitting* it.

"Blake, go." Jax stuck his hands in his pockets. "Take all the time you need. We can talk more when you get back."

Just because I was going to talk to Brea didn't mean I was ready to discuss shit with my brothers, but that was a conversation for another time. I had to get to Brea and tell her I was an idiot.

Like she didn't already know.

TWENTY-EIGHT
BREA

One positive thing that had come out of what happened was that I'd managed to completely clean and organize the store. I'd also put together tins of tea until I'd run out of ingredients.

That had been twenty minutes ago, and now I didn't have anything else to do. Case in point, I'd been cleaning the same spot for the past five minutes. When the bell over my door rang, I turned, relieved to have someone to distract me. I would've been happy with anyone at that moment.

A church group coming in to ask me if I wanted to give up my Wiccan ways.

A new mom wanting to know if I had something to help her baby sleep and then offering to show me hundreds of pictures of said baby sleeping.

The hot recluse I'd fucked more than once and had inadvertently fallen in love with–

Shit.

"Blake?"

Shit! Seriously? Shit!

What the *fuck* was he doing here?!

"Before you tell me that I'm an asshole and I need to get out, please let me say what I came here to say."

I'd had a million things I'd wanted to say to him, a thousand different ways I'd imagined this conversation going, but I couldn't think of one. He looked as ragged as I felt, and someplace deep inside me, I hoped it was because of me. He'd managed a complete sentence without yelling at me, so I supposed that was him trying. I might as well hear him out.

"Go ahead," I said. He locked the door and then started toward me, but I didn't walk around the counter to meet him. I needed to keep something between us until he'd finished.

At least we didn't have an audience here. No matter how this went, we'd be able to have a complete conversation. We'd get to the end of it, one way or the other. While my stomach twisted at the thought of what it could mean if things went badly, another part of me just wanted it all to be over. I just wanted it to be a clean break.

When I was nine years old, my parents and I had gone skiing. I'd insisted that I'd known what I was doing, but they'd made me take the bunny slopes. I'd been furious, and I hadn't really understood why. It hadn't really been about wanting to ski on the bigger slopes. It'd been more about the fact that I hadn't wanted anyone telling me what I could or couldn't do. Not even my parents.

Of course, that'd meant I'd had to sneak away and try one of the bigger slopes. I'd managed just fine until some bigger kid had skied into me, knocking me into a bunch of trees. I broke my tibia and fibula, but the doctor said it could've been much worse. At least it had been a clean break. Those always healed the best.

"I was an asshole."

I folded my arms. An extra bit of protection. "Go on."

"Fair enough," he said. "You were getting too close, too far under my skin. Not in a bad way. Or at least what wouldn't have been a bad way if I wasn't such a closed-off prick."

That was more honest than he'd been about anything other than wanting to fuck me.

"Your brother came to see me," I said.

"I know."

I'd guessed as much, but I knew I needed to give him something honest if I wanted him to be honest with me.

"Jax told me that he told you about what happened to my parents and sister."

He looked away, but I didn't call him on it. I couldn't imagine how painful all of that had been, still was. No matter how annoyed I could get with my parents or our untraditional family, I couldn't imagine living without them. Especially losing them at a young age...the thought alone made me want to walk around the counter and hug him.

"You should have heard it from me."

That surprised me. "I wasn't expecting you to tell me something so personal after such a short time."

"If I'd told you anything personal at all, it wouldn't even be an issue." He rubbed the back of his neck. "I'm not good with words. Never have been. And I'm definitely not good with talking about my emotions or anything real." He turned his eyes toward me, his expression earnest. "I don't want to lose you, Brea. It took my brothers calling me on my bullshit to admit that I'd made the wrong choice when you gave me the ultimatum."

I could feel my heart pounding faster with every word. This was what I'd wanted from him. Something real. Something that told me I wasn't in this alone.

"I can't promise that I'm going to be an open book from here on out, but I can promise that I'll be honest and that I will do my best to let you in." He reached across the counter, his hand open in invitation.

"Can I ask you something?" He started to pull his hand back, but I grabbed it. "Please."

He nodded, his fingers curling around mine.

"I have no problem taking things slow," I began, "but I need to know if you see this going somewhere. If it's never going to be more than casual, I need to know now, cut things off before I get any more involved."

His eyes warmed. "How involved are you now?"

I had two choices here, I knew. I could be vague and possibly save myself some embarrassment, or I could put it all out there and hope that him being here meant he felt the same.

I took a calming breath that didn't really do much in the way of calming me, and then I took the leap.

"I've fallen in love with you, you idiot." I managed a watery smile. "So, I'm in pretty deep."

He smiled, his entire face lighting up. "I am too." He came around the counter, his grip on my hand tightening. "In deep. Falling in love. All of it."

We both moved into each other, our bodies colliding even as our mouths came together. His urgency mirrored mine, desire burning through me, around me. I almost unzipped him right there, but if this was going to be our new beginning, I wanted us to do it right.

Not that I intended to send him away, so I didn't repeat the sex before a date thing. I wasn't that patient. No, we were just going to go somewhere more comfortable first.

"YOU DO REALIZE how completely unfair this is, right?" I asked as I scowled up at Blake. My question didn't do anything but make that stupid, smug grin of his grow. He'd used socks to tie my arms above my head since I didn't have ties or belts, and it should have been ridiculous, but it wasn't.

I tugged at the restraints, and his gaze dropped, eyes darkening at the way my struggles made my breasts jiggle. He was still dressed, the bastard, but I was completely naked, my body alive and humming from the attention he'd given it while getting me into this position.

"Haven't you heard?" he asked. "Life's not fair."

"Jerk," I muttered.

He laughed, and the sound turned my insides to mush. "Patience."

I wanted to point out that he was the last person who should be chastising me for lack of self-control, but he was taking off his shirt, and I got distracted. I was only human, after all, and he was all hard muscle and lickable skin. My eyes traced the defined lines down to his belly button, then followed his hands as he removed his pants. Deep v-grooves at his hips and a trail of dark hair pointed straight to a long, thick cock. It curved up toward his flat stomach, and I caught my breath as he wrapped a hand around it.

"See something you like?" he teased.

"Everything."

And I meant it. Not just his Adonis-like body, but the way he let me see how much he wanted me, the warmth in his eyes, the smiling and teasing and laughing. It made sense to me, that he'd expose his feelings here first. We'd been great together physically from moment one.

He slowly fisted his cock, running his thumb over the head to gather the moisture beaded there. My hands opened and closed, wanting something to touch, to dig my nails into. I squirmed as a rush of arousal made me wetter, then pressed my thighs together to try and give myself some relief.

"Brea." My name held a warning. "You don't get off until I say you can."

I lifted my chin defiantly and continued moving my legs. In one quick move, Blake's hands were on my ankles, and he was yanking my legs apart. I gave an undignified squawk, and that earned a chuckle, but there was no mercy in that sound. He was going to make me pay for disobeying him, and damn if that thought didn't turn me on even more.

He leaned down, bracing himself on the ankles he still held and gave me a long, slow lick that made me cry out.

"I think you deserve to be punished for that," he said as he straightened. "What do you think?"

Thoughts of spankings and whippings danced through my head, but I didn't have anything here he could use for that. Unless he decided to get creative, and I wouldn't have put that past him.

"Where are your toys?"

My face grew hot. It wasn't that I was embarrassed about my sexuality, but I'd never had someone be that blunt about it before. The guys I'd been with in the past had known I had a vibrator since I didn't exactly hide it, but it hadn't been something we'd used together. Not like Blake and I had before.

"In the top drawer of the bedside table," I said. "But I only have the one."

"We'll do some shopping together sometime," he said. "Do you have any clothespins?"

"Bathroom," I answered automatically, even as I puzzled through the request. "Bottom drawer under the sink. There's some rope in there too. I hang up my 'delicates.'"

He laughed again. "You couldn't have remembered the rope before I used socks?"

Despite how badly I wanted him right now, I couldn't help but join in the laughter. "I wasn't exactly thinking laundry when you said you wanted to tie me up."

He walked out of my bedroom, giving me a mouth-watering view of his perfect, tight ass. I tried my best to not be shallow, but Blake had the most magnificent body. The things I wanted to do to it...

"These will do." He came back into the bedroom with two plain clothespins. "I think we'll start with just a couple minutes. Don't want to damage anything."

I had a pretty good idea of what he intended to do with those things, but that didn't calm the butterflies in my stomach much. He climbed on the bed, settling between my legs. I hadn't realized until that moment that I hadn't closed them, but little things like that didn't matter when he was leaning over me and taking one of my nipples between his lips.

He didn't ease me into it, immediately sucking hard on the sensitive flesh. My body jerked, back arching, but he put a hand on my waist, holding me in place. His teeth worried at my nipple, holding on just a bit too tight, pulling on it. I cursed at the sharp jolt of pain that went through me but didn't ask him to stop. Finally, when my nipple was tight and hard, he raised his head.

"Two minutes," he said. "Just two minutes."

Two minutes wasn't that long. I didn't know why he felt the need to reassure me. I gasped as he fastened one clothespin to my nipple, but after the initial shock wore off, it was far from the most painful thing I'd ever experienced.

He lowered his head to my other nipple, repeating the process. Except by the time he was ready to put on the other clothespin, I felt like my entire breast was on fire. I squirmed, but the motion only made things worse. It should have been time to take it off. We had to be way over two minutes.

"Almost there," Blake said. He ran his hand over my stomach, letting his thumb tease across the curls I kept neatly trimmed.

I wanted his fingers lower, but I didn't think I could manage an articulate request at this moment. My other nipple was starting to hurt now, the pain traveling down my breasts and into the tight coil of pleasure that sat low in my belly. Instead of chasing the pleasure away, it mixed, mingled, and became something else. Something deeper, more intense.

Something I hadn't realized I'd wanted until now.

What we'd done before had been a little different, and I'd liked it, but part of me hadn't understood just how much I wanted this sort of thing to be an option.

"All right," he said. "One's done."

I was so focused on getting the clothespin off that I hadn't taken the time to think what it would feel like to have the pressure released.

When I was young, I'd been playing in an area where my parents had been building something, and I'd tripped. I'd fallen on a strip of sandpaper that had abraded the skin from my elbow to half-way down my forearm.

Having the first clothespin removed felt something like that.

The second was worse, making my eyes water.

"Fuck!" I writhed on the bed, no longer caring about whether I was moving toward or away from Blake. I just needed to move, to do something, anything, to distract me.

Then his tongue was there, soothing my flesh, distracting me. My breath caught in my throat, air escaping in a near-soundless whimper. His hand moved between my legs, fingers finding that slick bundle of nerves, and I lost the ability to think about anything more than how he made me feel.

"Fucking gorgeous." He pressed his mouth against my throat and slid two fingers inside me. "You smell amazing. Like...pineapples."

I would've laughed if he hadn't chosen that moment to curl his fingers and rub against that spot inside me. A lightning strike couldn't have matched the electricity that coursed through my body as I came. I screamed, and part of my mind was functioning enough for me to be grateful that I didn't have any neighbors close enough to hear.

"Damn," he growled. "That's the sexiest sound I've ever heard."

He covered my mouth with his again, his tongue plundering, exploring, claiming. He slid his body along mine, skin against skin, and I pulled on my restraints again, desperate to touch him, to mark him as mine.

Because he *was* mine.

I smiled, and he raised his head, his expression puzzled. "I'm hoping that's a 'great kiss, Blake' smile, and not a 'that's a funny kiss' smile."

"You're mine," I said.

He took my bottom lip between his teeth and gave it a tug before releasing it. "And you're mine." A shadow passed across his face. "You are, aren't you?"

"I am," I said. "I'm also getting a little chilly."

Blake lowered his body onto mine, and I shifted to get him to settle more comfortably. I loved the way our bodies fit together, not just in sex, but like this too. I already knew we were great in bed together – sometimes figuratively rather than literally – but we needed more than sex if we were going to make things work between us. This gave me hope. Lying like this, comfortable in our own skins, smiling and talking.

He brushed hair back from my face. "We don't have to go any further than this. If I can lay here tonight with you, hold you, I'll be happy."

I tried to reach for him, but my hands were still stopped short. "If we don't go any further, I'm not sure *I'll* be happy."

He laughed, and I loved the feel of it almost as much as I loved the sound. "Let's get you untied." He reached up and tugged on one sock, then the other, and they both came free easily.

My fingers tingled as the blood flow returned to normal, but

I barely noticed. I was more concerned with touching. His face, his hair, his back. The scruff on his face was rough against my palms, and I couldn't wait to feel it against other, more sensitive, parts of my body.

"Condom?" he asked.

I didn't even need to think about it. "I'm on the pill."

He kissed me hard, then went up on his knees, his cock jutting out in front of him. His hands slid from my hips down my legs to my knees, then over my calves. He lifted my legs, raising them straight until my ankles rested near his shoulders.

"Is this okay?"

I nodded. I'd feel the burn soon, but I'd always been quite flexible. What I hadn't counted on was how tight this position would make me. I was wet, but as Blake pushed inside me, my eyelids fluttered. He groaned, the sound vibrating through me, adding a whole new sensation.

"Fuck, Blake." I grabbed my blanket, twisting it in my hands. I was too full, stretched too much, but it wasn't bad. It was good. Too good. "Fuck! Fuck!"

"That's what I'm trying to do."

I opened my eyes and glared at him. "If you can talk, you're not doing—"

The word became an inarticulate shout as he leaned forward and started pounding into me. My knees were almost to my chest, and the backs of my thighs screamed in protest, but the pain was only in the background, adding to the other sensations that Blake was causing. I was dimly aware that I was begging, but I couldn't feel even a little self-conscious, not when he was saying my name over and over.

He dropped my legs, leaning down to capture my mouth. As his tongue tangled with mine, I locked my ankles around his waist, pulling myself up to meet his thrusts. Our bodies slammed together with no pretense of gentleness. We caught ragged breaths between kisses, both of us racing toward climax.

I grabbed his ass, digging my nails into the firm flesh, and he retaliated by biting my lip. Sex with him somehow felt a bit like fighting, but it was a whole different form of fighting.

A sexy one that I liked a whole lot more than the other kind.

He came first, the feeling of him emptying inside me triggering my own orgasm, and we rode the waves together, wrapped around each other until we collapsed in a sweaty pile of limbs.

I could get used to this.

TWENTY-NINE
BLAKE

I didn't want to leave. Not when I was in bed with a warm and naked Brea. And not when she was pushing back against me, hooking one leg behind her to open her up to me. I slid inside, and our bodies began to move together again.

We'd barely slept, but I felt invigorated rather than tired. We'd made love – and no matter how we did it, that's what it had been – all night, sleeping, waking, coming back together again. I was surprised I could even still come, but I would never say no to being inside her.

After we finished, Brea slipped back to sleep again, and I climbed out of bed. As much as I wanted to stay with her, I knew I needed to get back to my brothers. Brea would be here when they went back home, and I knew she'd understand.

I took a quick shower, checked on her again, then wrote her a quick note to let her know where I was going, and that I'd be back. The whole way to the retreat, I steeled myself for what I was going to do next. The fact that my brothers had put my reconciliation with Brea above what they wanted had meant something to me.

I didn't knock on the suite door since I had my key, but a

part of me suspected that they'd all be gone, tired of waiting for me to deal with my shit. But, instead, they were sitting around the table, eating breakfast, but all looked up when I came in.

Before I could fall back into my old ways, I went straight to Jax. "Thank you," I said, "for going to Brea."

"You made things, right?" Jax asked.

"I did." I sat down in the empty seat and reached for a muffin. This next part wasn't going to be nearly as much fun. "And now I want us to do the same."

"We didn't know," Slade said, "what it was like for you. That's on us. All three of us. We got caught up in our own shit and never stopped to think what things were like for you."

"You guys were kids," I said, looking at each of them. "I wanted to blame you for everything because I felt like you'd at least gotten a bit of a normal life and I never did. I was wrong."

"Grandfather should have talked to us," Cai said. "I should have spoken up more often. Jax should have been our brother instead of feeling like he had to be a parent. Slade shouldn't have felt like he needed to make peace all the time. You shouldn't have felt like you were alone in this. All of us are at fault, and none of us are. One person isn't to blame for how we reacted to a horrible situation."

I stared at my usually quiet brother. That was one of the longest speeches I'd ever heard him make. And it all made sense.

"Can we all agree that we've all done stupid shit, treated each other badly, and made basic asses of ourselves?" Slade asked. "And then can we agree to move past it?"

I looked at Jax, then at Cai. They both nodded. "I'm game if you are," I said.

I'd heard people talk about weights being lifted, but I'd never actually experienced it until now. We hadn't needed a big discussion or some sort of deep breakthrough. No crying or hugging or apologies. Just an acknowledgment of what we'd each experienced and a promise to never ignore each other again.

And it was done.

"I meant what I said before," I said. "I don't need Grandfather's money."

"None of us really do," Slade said. "I've barely touched my trust fund."

Cai shook his head. "Me either, but I think we can all agree that it'll be good to get Grandfather's estate settled. And I'm sure we can all find some uses for our portions."

We fell silent for a while, and for the first time ever, I felt like part of the group. Like a man with his three brothers, wondering how things would change from here.

"There is something else we need to talk about," Jax said. "And it's not going to be a fun conversation to have."

"Because these last couple days have been a blast," I said. I was half-joking, which surprised me, but one look at Jax's face told me that he was serious. "What's going on?"

Jax met my gaze, held it with a seriousness that made adrenaline surge through my system. "I've already talked to Cai and Slade about this. But only because–"

"It's okay," I said, holding up a hand. "I get it. They were available, and I was ignoring all of you. No hard feelings."

"Thanks." Jax smiled, but it didn't reach his eyes. He sighed and leaned back. "This is going to sound crazy at first, but the three of us have checked into things, and it looks like the truth."

"What looks like the truth?" I asked.

When Jax opened his mouth and started to tell me all about the letter Grandfather wrote and his suspicions, I almost thought it was a joke. Except Jax didn't usually joke, and he didn't joke about the accident that killed our parents and sister.

Except if he was right, it hadn't been an accident. Someone had done it intentionally.

"Dad had a couple big stories he was working on," Cai said.

"The PI involved in all this talked to another journalist who'd worked with Dad on occasion."

Slade picked it up. "A few days before the accident, they'd been talking about this new story, and it was something huge. There weren't any details out there, but it sounded like something that someone might go to some pretty drastic measures to protect."

"Let me see if I understand," I said slowly. "A cop tells Grandfather that everyone else is wrong and the accident wasn't an accident at all. Grandfather hires a private investigator, but he didn't find much of anything in the last twenty-four years. Still, Grandfather thinks someone else needs to know, so he has the PI send a letter he wrote, telling you all of this. How am I doing so far?"

"Yeah, that's accurate," Jax said. "I told you it was going to sound crazy."

"It does," I said. "But what makes you guys think that anything new will be found after this long?"

The others all exchanged looks, and I had a feeling I wasn't going to like what came next.

"Because he has access to possible leads that he didn't have before," Cai said.

"What possible leads?"

"Us," Jax said. "Grandfather wouldn't let us talk to him before, but he can talk to us now."

"What could we possibly remember?" I looked at all three of them in turn. "We were kids. It wasn't like we would've even known what to look for back then."

Jax looked uncomfortable, but I had to give him credit. He didn't back away. "Actually, it's you he thinks might know something. About that day. About the crash."

About the one day I never, *ever* wanted to remember.

THIRTY
BREA

I pulled Blake's note out and read it again even though I had it memorized.

I need to talk to my brothers, but I'd rather have stayed with you. Come back to the retreat, and I'll see you later. B

Not a declaration of love, but I understood the effort he was making. Besides, he'd said it plenty of times last night.

I smiled at the memories of all the things we'd done. My body ached, but in a good way, like every twinge was an acknowledgment that it'd really happened, that things between us had changed. Every time my bra rubbed against my sore nipples, I'd think of those clothespins. Every reflective surface had me checking how well my makeup was holding up. If I'd been in town, I wouldn't have really cared if anyone saw the marks Blake had left, but at my parents' business, with Blake's brothers here, I wanted to stay professional and discreet.

I glanced at my phone. His text had come through around two, and it'd been vague about whatever they were talking about, but he'd ended it by asking if he could come by my room even if it was late. I'd said yes.

He hadn't responded to the text I'd just sent, but that was okay. I'd only needed him to know that I was going to take a shower, but he could let himself in.

I made my shower thorough but as quick as I could, more thankful than ever that I'd cut my hair. When I emerged from the bathroom, wrapped in the new red silk robe that my parents had brought back from one of their recent trips to Japan, I was glad I'd taken a shower when I had. Blake was sitting on my bed, a shell-shocked expression on his face.

I sat next to him and put my hand on his arm. "Are you okay?"

"I-I don't know," he said. He didn't look at me, but I got the impression that he wasn't looking at anything, really.

"Do you want to talk about it?"

"We talked," he said woodenly. "My brothers and me. Made apologies. I thought everything would be good from there. We'd forget about the past and move on."

After a minute of silence, I prompted, "And that's not what happened?"

He shrugged, the movement jerky. "I guess it did. It is." He raised his head, and the pain I saw in his eyes pierced me. "My parents and sister were murdered."

I didn't know what to say to that. Who would? Then Jax's words came back to me, and I went from horrified to confused. "I thought they were in a car accident."

"Me too." He scrubbed his hands over his face. "But my grandfather thought it could be murder. He even hired a PI. Jax got a letter. They think our dad was working on a story and made the wrong people mad."

I had a million more questions, but all of them were unimportant next to taking care of Blake. He'd fill me in later. Right now, he needed me.

"What can I do to help you?" I asked, combing my fingers through his hair.

He leaned into my touch. "I need to forget. Can you help me forget?"

I pressed my lips against his cheek. "I can do that."

I slid off the bed until I was on my knees in front of him. He looked down at me as I undid his belt and then went for his pants. I pulled them down enough that I could get to what I wanted. He wasn't hard yet, but the moment I touched his cock, it twitched.

I took all of him into my mouth, enjoying the way he moaned my name as I swirled my tongue around the swelling shaft. His hand came down on my head, but he wasn't pushing me. He let me set the pace, using my hands and mouth to get him nice and hard. I'd always been amazed at the way a man's penis could be soft and hard at the same time. The silky skin and firm muscle, each erotic in their own way. Knowing that I was responsible for his body's reaction gave me a power that I liked. I'd never had issues with body image, and the men I'd dated in the past had always complimented me, but something about being this way with Blake made it...better.

As he grew, I took less and less of him in my mouth, unable to go any deeper without gagging. I had one hand around the base, moving in short quick movements as I continued to work my way around the rest of him. The hair on his thighs was rough against the palm of my hand, against my cheeks, but I didn't mind. I wanted every part of him. I dropped my hand down to cup his balls. I rolled them between my fingers, explored every inch of them.

His hips started to jerk, pushing him deeper into my mouth, and he pulled on my hair.

"I'm going to—"

I sucked harder, turning his statement into a curse, and a moment later, he came. I swallowed, then used my tongue to clean him up before raising my head and sitting back on my heels.

He leaned forward and cupped my cheek, his thumb brushing over my bottom lip. "Thank you."

I licked the tip of his thumb, arousal tightening inside me at the heated look on Blake's face. I stood and moved between his legs, so I was only inches from him. He wrapped his arms around me, his head resting on my stomach. I ran my fingers through his hair, massaging his scalp, appreciating the soft strands of hair as they moved between my fingers.

"Better?" I asked after several minutes of silence.

"Better." His hands slid down my back to my ass.

"But you want more." I made it a statement rather than a question.

"I know you're probably sore from last night," he said. "I wasn't exactly gentle."

I smiled. "I think I gave almost as good as I got. How scratched up are you?"

He laughed. Not the big, full laugh that I loved, but it was still a laugh. I counted it as a win.

I took a step back, and he let me go. When he raised his head to look at me, I untied the belt to my robe and let the silk fall naturally, framing my body. I held out the hand with the belt and waited for him to decide if this was what he wanted.

He toed off his shoes, then pulled his shirt over his head. After he removed the rest of his clothing, he stood. He took the belt and looked around the room, finally walking over to my closet and looking inside.

"How sturdy is that bar?" he asked.

I shrugged. "No clue. I've barely used it the past couple weeks. Why?"

"Let's try it out."

Less than ten minutes later, my robe was on the floor, and my hands were tied to the bar in the closet. Blake stood behind me, and I could see his reflection in the closet door's mirror to my left. He was holding his belt. Unlike my silk one, his was leather, and when he snapped it, the sound made my mouth go dry.

"Give me a word you'll say if you need me to stop."

"Um." It wasn't easy thinking in this position. "Butterfly?"

He chuckled. "Seriously?"

"It's the first word that came to mind," I said. "Now, are you going to stand there all night, or are you going to do someth–fuck!!"

I'd barely processed his reflection moving before the leather came down on my ass with a loud crack. The pain spider-webbed across my skin like fractures in glass. I cursed again, pulling against my restraints. The silk dug into my skin, a new element of discomfort to work into everything my body was feeling. A second blow with the belt drove away the hurt in my wrists.

"Dammit, Blake!" I shouted. I looked over my shoulder to see him moving his hand over his half-erect cock. "You're enjoying this a little too much."

"Do you want me to stop?"

He'd do it, I knew, stop if I asked him to. But this wasn't about me. This was about him and what he needed. And he needed this.

"No," I said. "I trust you to make me feel good."

"Then close your eyes and let yourself feel it."

I faced front again and let my head fall forward. I closed my eyes and waited. The anticipation was almost worse than the belt.

A third strike, this time along the bottom of my ass.

Almost.

I focused on breathing, on feeling it all.

In. Out. In. Out. Crack. In. Out. Crack. In. Out. In. Out...

I lost count. I lost everything that wasn't the near-agony of the belt and the throbbing need that had settled between my legs. I vaguely heard the cries I made and had only enough reasoning to hope that no one could hear us. I couldn't hold on to the steady breathing I'd done, and now air rasped in and out of my lungs.

I jerked when Blake's hand touched me, but I didn't pull away. I whimpered as he lightly traced the marks he'd made, new pinpricks of pain shooting across my already frazzled nerves. Then his fingers were between my legs, slipping between my lips, inside me, back out, up, circling my clit, giving me just enough pressure to ache for more, but not enough to satisfy me.

"You're so fucking wet," he said. "Did you get this wet from going down on me, or from the belt?"

"Both," I answered without embarrassment or shame. What we were doing was pure and good, no matter what other people might think. We were two consenting adults, satisfying the needs of someone we loved. It didn't get any purer than that.

"Damn." He kissed my shoulder. "I don't think I can go slow."

"Don't then."

A moment later, he was buried inside me, and my knees threatened to give out. He didn't take his time, slamming into me while all the pain and pleasure twisted and knotted together until I couldn't tell one from the other. My legs were weak, but he held me up, his fingers bruising my hips as he raced toward the finish.

Words mixed with primal grunts, neither of them forming anything coherent alone, but together telling me exactly how he felt about me.

"Good...fucking hot...shit...Brea...love...love...need...want...need you...never stop..."

He came with my name on his lips, his thrusts becoming

short and jerky. Still, he had the presence of mind to reach down and find my clit. It didn't take much to send me over the edge, and a part of me thought that if he'd kept talking, I would've come even without his touch.

Damn, I loved him.

THIRTY-ONE

BLAKE

"Mom! Aimee poking me!"

Little sisters were 'noying.

"Am not!"

"Kids, if you keep this up, there'll be no dessert tonight." Mom gave us her scary look.

"Yes, Mom," Aimee and I said it together.

I wanted apple pie for dessert. Dad let me put i'scream on it.

The car turned, and I got dizzy. Mom screamed, and we slid like we were on ice. Dad said some bad words, but Mom didn't yell at him. The car flipped, and I hit my head. My stomach went upside-down, and I felt like throwing up. My head hurt lots, and I started crying.

Everything went black.

Everything shifted.

I was back at the car, but I wasn't in it. And I wasn't a kid. I was an adult, and I was looking at the crash that had killed my parents and sister. The crash that had almost killed me.

I knew I was dreaming, just like I knew I hadn't actually seen the wreck from this perspective, but it was still too real. I didn't want to be here. But I needed to be here. I couldn't remember why, only that I had to be here because there was something I needed to know.

And to do that, I needed to face my fears.

I crouched down next to the back window and looked inside.

It was me. I was so little, but I could see the man I'd become in the boy pressed up against the window. I was unconscious, but I thought I'd be coming out of it soon.

On the other side of me was Aimee.

It'd been so long since I'd seen her, so long since I'd even thought of her. It hurt to think about her. About all the things she hadn't gotten to do. The woman she hadn't gotten to be.

She was facing away from me, and I was glad. Her head was at an awkward angle, her neck broken, but at least I didn't have to see her face. I could remember her the way she had been. Looking like the happy little girl she'd been.

I couldn't see Mom either. Only her hair. It was dark like Slade's. I didn't know how Mom died, but I must've seen Aimee this way. Or my brain was just making it up, but I didn't think that was the case. Something in my gut said that part was real.

Dad was awake.

No one had told me that. And my instincts told me it had to be a memory.

"Abigail? Abby? Sweetheart?" Dad's voice broke. "Aimee? Blake? Kids?"

I wanted to wake up. I didn't want to hear him when he realized everyone but me was dead. It would be awful, and I didn't think I'd be able to handle it. But something told me to stay a little longer.

Then I heard it. Another car. I never knew who'd found us, but the guy walking toward me wasn't who I'd pictured, mostly because the guy didn't really have a face. He wasn't like creepy faceless, but rather just blurry features that I couldn't really distinguish.

As he came over to the car, I realized he wasn't freaking out, and he wasn't calling anyone.

Everything shifted again, and I was in the car now. A kid. But I wasn't thinking like a kid. Not really that important. What was important was that I could see the guy's boots outside the window. Nice boots. Expensive boots.

"Stay away from my family!" Dad yelled.

What? Why was Dad yelling at someone who could save us?

Dad was cursing now, and the guy still wasn't leaving.

He reached inside, and Dad yelled again, and my head was hurting, and the guy was shaking him, and I heard crying, and it was me and...

I jerked awake, my heart pounding, my skin drenched with sweat. For a moment, I didn't know where I was, then I smelled something familiar. Lavender.

Brea.

I was with Brea. At the retreat. With my brothers. Well, not exactly *with* them right now.

"Hey." Brea blinked up at me. "What time is it?"

I looked over at the clock on the bedside table. "A little after midnight."

She pushed herself up, pulling the sheet up around herself. "Are you okay?" She put her hand on my shoulder, and I caught another whiff of lavender mixed with the scent of her.

I started to say that I was fine, but I wasn't fine, and I didn't want to lie to Brea about it. "I remembered."

She put her arms around me, and I leaned into her, grateful for the comfort she offered. "You don't have to talk about it if you don't want to."

"I need to," I admitted. "I've never talked about it before. I've never *remembered* it before."

I wrapped my arms around her and pulled her onto my lap. We were both naked, but right now, all I needed was the feel of her skin against mine and the warmth of her body.

"I was in the car, fighting with Aimee – with my sister. Mom yelled at us. Something happened, and the car flipped. I must've blacked out. Then I was outside of the car, and I saw... Aimee. I couldn't see my mom, but I knew she was gone. Dad was alive though. And awake."

"Oh, Blake." She kissed my shoulder.

"That wasn't all." I forced myself to keep going. As I spoke, I remembered more, things that I knew were true and not part of the dream. "Someone came to the car. I couldn't see his face, but I could see out the window. I didn't say anything because Dad was yelling again, telling the man with the boots to leave us alone."

"The man with the boots?"

I nodded. "There was a man outside the car. I could see his boots. And then he bent over and reached into the car. He and Dad struggled, like he was trying to take something, and Dad didn't want to let him."

"You saw this in a dream?"

"Sort of." I brushed back a curl. "It started as a dream, but I remember now. Real memories."

She ran her fingers across my collarbone, and if I hadn't been certain this memory was important, I would have had her under me and panting by now. I caught her hand and brought it to my mouth, kissing her knuckles as another part of my memory came forward.

"He took something from my dad. One of those old computer disks." I frowned. "There was a picture on it. Three interlocking rings with something at the center."

"What something?" Brea's question had a strange note to it. I looked down at her. "Was it a...plant of some kind?"

The picture solidified in my head.

"A four-leaf clover."

"Shit."

Okay, not the reaction I was expecting.

"Brea?"

She sat up, all traces of comfort and warmth gone. She was all business now, but I didn't know what had caused the transformation.

"We need to talk to Kevin." She climbed out of bed.

"Now?"

"Now," she said, her face a tight mask. "I know that logo."

THIRTY-TWO
BREA

I'd thought about meeting Blake's brothers, but this was not how I'd thought I'd be doing it.

"Okay, we're all down here at the asscrack of dawn," Slade grumbled. "Someone want to finally tell me why?"

"Slade," Cai chided, "language."

Slade scowled at his older brother. "She's dating Blake. Bad language can't bother her."

"I brought coffee." Kevin came in pushing a drinks tray. "I didn't know what everyone liked, so I figured black coffee with lots of options."

"Please tell me that's not decaf." Jax reached for the pot.

"I wouldn't dream of it," Kevin said with a smile.

I knew he didn't like thinking about the life he'd left behind, but he hadn't even blinked when I'd told him what we needed. Blake and I had already heard what he had to say, but now the other brothers needed to hear it.

"All right," Jax said as he sat down. "What's going on? All Blake said was that we needed to talk."

I reached over and took Blake's hand. This would be the

third time he told his story, and I knew it wasn't getting any easier with repetition. Still, he didn't hesitate.

"Everything we talked about must've knocked something loose in my head," he began. "Because I had a dream that turned into a memory."

I squeezed his hand, offering him the strength to get through this again. It felt a little intrusive to be here while Blake told his brothers what he remembered, but he'd insisted that my dad and I stay. By the time he was done, his brothers all wore the same shell-shocked look I'd seen on Blake's face when I'd come out of the shower last night.

"Wow." Slade broke the moment. "I don't even – I mean, wow."

"This is what your PI was hoping for," Blake said. "That I'd remember something that could help us figure out what really happened."

"And you're sure it was more than a dream?" Jax asked.

Blake stiffened, and I put a hand on his arm. He relaxed as he answered, "I am."

"Okay then," Cai said. "What do we do with it? I doubt the cops are going to reopen a twenty-four-year-old closed case because of a memory from someone who was four years old at the time."

"It's not all we have," Blake said. He looked at me. "The logo on that disk is real."

"What do you mean *real*?" Jax asked.

"Three intersecting circles with a four-leaf clover was the original logo for Greene Leaf Pharmaceuticals." I entered the conversation. "It was changed almost twenty-four years ago."

"How do you know that?" Jax asked. His gaze was searching, but I didn't sense any hostility.

"Because of me." Kevin smiled as all eyes turned to him, but it was a polite smile, without any real light to it. "In another life, I lived in New York City, part of a fairly prominent family.

After years of doing what everyone expected of me, I quit it all." He waved a hand. "But that's not really important beyond how it relates to GLP. My family has known the Greene family for generations. Andre Greene is a couple years older than me and was determined that GLP would finally get his family the spotlight he'd always wanted."

I'd met Andre once, basically by accident. He'd been vacationing near where we'd been staying in Maine and had run into us at a store. I'd only been eight or nine, but I'd been able to tell that Kevin didn't like him. Now, I understood why.

"There were rumors, even back then, that he cut corners, but it's never easy to know what's real and what's just gossip. I left before your family was killed, but I still knew enough people in the business to know who your dad was. And that he'd been working on a story about corruptions in the pharmaceutical industry. Specifically, at GLP."

I watched as the realization sank into each of the brothers. I'd seen Blake get it too, and it hurt watching the others almost as much as it had hurt watching him. It had to be difficult, going from a possibility to something that was much more certain.

"Do you think there would've been anything for our dad to find?" Jax asked.

"I do," Kevin said, his expression grim. "I never saw Andre do anything illegal, but there was one instance before he'd taken his father's place. He'd had a little too much to drink. He started talking about how he was going to do things differently when he was the CEO, including what safety measures he wanted to cut. When I brought up the legal angle, he just laughed and said that's why he'd spend some extra on a great lawyer."

"There's a big difference between cutting corners and murder," Slade said.

"Not if you think of cutting corners in terms of money," Cai said. "How many times do you see people killed for money, for encroaching on territory?"

"Good point," Slade said.

Jax turned our way. "Blake, are you willing to come back to Boston and talk to the police? We could do it by phone if you want, but I think it'd go over better if you were there in person."

"I'll go," Blake said. "I owe them that much. Mom. Dad. Aimee."

I leaned against him, wishing I could take away the pain I heard in his voice. I'd go with him if he wanted me to, or I'd stay here and let him do it with his brothers. Whatever he needed, I'd do. He wasn't going to go through this alone.

"Do you really think it's going to make a difference?" Slade asked. "Isn't this what they call circumstantial evidence?"

"I might be able to help with that," Kevin said. "I don't keep in touch with many people from my old life but let me make a couple calls. If Andre did do this, he believes that he's gotten away with it for all these years, and that means he hasn't stopped. There might be some evidence now that can help prove what he did back then."

The brothers all had the same eyes, different shades of blue, but the same shape and intelligence. Now, I saw something else in them that was the same.

Hope that they might finally have a reason.

Fear that they might never get justice.

THIRTY-THREE
BLAKE

I WAS BACK IN BOSTON, AND THIS TIME IT WAS COMPLETELY voluntary. We'd all left together yesterday afternoon, thanks to the company jet, then spent the rest of the day making phone calls.

Now, it was just past nine o'clock on Wednesday morning, and my brothers and I were standing outside a house in Midtown, hoping this woman really did have what she said she did.

The door opened, and an older woman with silvery-blue hair stood there. She gave us each a cool look and then stepped aside, motioning for us to come in. She might've been in her seventies, but she looked like she could handle herself, which was probably why she wasn't afraid to invite four strange men into her home.

"Mrs. Hilly," Slade said, "thank you for seeing us so quickly."

"I've been waiting for fifteen years for someone strong enough to take down Andre Greene." She pointed to an ancient-looking sofa. "Sit."

We obeyed immediately. As I sat, I wondered if she'd been a

drill sergeant in a previous life. Either that or a teacher. She had that sort of natural authority.

"Would any of you like tea?" She eyed each of us as if daring us to ask for anything else.

We all politely declined. As much as we appreciated what she was doing for us, none of us wanted to spend any longer here than we had to. We'd waited far too long to see justice done as it was.

"My late husband, Rudy, worked for GLP back when Horace Greene ran it. Believe it or not, he started in the mailroom right out of high school and worked his way up to department head. He spent eight years taking night classes to get his accounting degree, using GLP's continuing education scholarships to pay for most of it." Mrs. Hilly walked over to a bookshelf and pulled out what looked like a journal. "Rudy worked under Horace's son as well, and then Andre Greene took over. Andre was nothing like his father or grandfather."

The tone of her voice told us all which of the Greenes she'd admired, and which she hadn't. It seemed that Andre hadn't made many friends anywhere.

"Rudy headed the financial department," she said, holding the book out to Jax. "Within a week of taking over, Andre fired sixteen people, and then hired three new ones. Usually, Rudy did the hiring for his department, but Andre hadn't given him the chance. It became a habit over the years, Andre getting rid of people Rudy had hired and replacing them with workers who reported directly to Andre."

The more I heard about this guy, the less I liked him. Even if he wasn't responsible for the crash, I hoped we could find something to put him away.

"One evening fifteen years ago, Rudy came home upset. At first, I thought he'd gotten fired, but that wasn't it. He said he'd started to notice that things weren't adding up in a few places. They seemed to be simple mistakes at first. Inventory for janitors and maintenance not matching money spent. He began looking into things – doing his job, mind you – and that's when he found bigger discrepancies."

How could something from fifteen years ago help us with what had happened twenty-four years ago? I wanted to rush her along to get to the point, but my gut told me to be patient. We'd get there. Better to get things right than get them fast.

"Most of the companies GLP had worked with in the past to double-check findings and to do quality assurance had been changed to businesses Rudy had never heard of. There was more like that. Inspectors he didn't know. The deeper he dug, the more he uncovered." Mrs. Hilly sat down in the chair across from us and twisted her fingers in her lap. "He went back nearly thirty years and found lump sum payments to people and businesses that didn't exist. He still felt too loyal to the company to go to the police right away, but he refused to look the other way too."

She paused, lost in her thoughts of the past. Slade, as always, knew the right thing to say. "He sounds like a great man."

She gave Slade a wobbly smile. "He was."

I made a mental note to ask Slade how he did that. I had a feeling my relationship with Brea was going to be full of times when I stuck my foot in my mouth. It'd be nice to know how to smooth things over.

"The long and the short of it is that Rudy managed to track down a few important facts, including a memo from around twenty-five years ago that advised all staff that they weren't allowed to speak with Chester Hunter, that he was a reporter determined to slander GLP's good name. Since he had a name, Rudy decided to track Chester down, but he found out that he was too late. Later that night, after he told me about the accident, he said that he'd checked the dates of the memo and the accident against the financial records he'd copied. A large payment had gone out to one of those fake names, and he thought Andre might have hired someone to take care of the journalist."

Even with what I remembered and the things my brothers had already found out, a part of me still hadn't completely believed that the crash hadn't been an accident. Those doubts were gone now.

"Rudy knew he'd gone as far as he could, and the police needed to take matters from there, but before he could find someone he trusted enough to give them the evidence, he had a heart attack. We'd known about his heart for years, but I still hadn't been ready for it." She gave us a sad smile. "He hung on long enough for me to say goodbye, and for him to tell me to hold on to everything. It would be my protection if Andre ever found out."

"What made you decide you could trust us to do the right thing?" I asked.

"Because I've been watching you boys for years. I didn't know how much you knew about what had happened, so I never approached you, but I did leave instructions with my attorney that he personally hand you the information if I died before you asked for it."

"Thank you," Jax said. He looked down at the journal he held and then back up at Mrs. Hilly. "We really appreciate all you've done, but there's one more favor I need to ask of you."

"Tell the police that I'm available to make a statement at any time," she said matter-of-factly. She stood. "Now, if you'll excuse me, I have some baking to do. I take fresh bread and cookies to the elderly every Thursday morning."

As we left the house and walked toward Jax's car, Slade said what I knew we were all feeling.

"It's time to hand this over."

"I'll call Bartholomew and have him meet us at the station," Jax said.

This was it. Once we gave the police what we had, it would be on them to follow-up. There was always the possibility that these detectives would get the same sort of pressure as the ones had in the past, but we had something now that they didn't then. Brothers who didn't give a damn about making them look bad or pissing off people in high places. Brothers who had friends in all sorts of places. We would do whatever it took to get justice for our family. Even if I had to move back to Boston to do it.

THIRTY-FOUR
BLAKE

I didn't think I'd ever prefer a city over the open space that I called home, but I had to admit, I was enjoying my time back in Boston. Brea and I had flown out two weeks ago, and I'd loved being able to show her all the places I'd gone when I was a kid. Even if that had been the only reason for being here, it would've been worth it, but there were two important reasons we'd joined my brothers and their significant others.

Andre Greene had been sentenced yesterday.

The information we'd provided the police had given them enough to lead them to a man named Darius Mclean. The man with the black boots. The one who'd messed with our car and caused it to crash. The one who'd walked over to the car, not caring about any of us inside, and stolen a disk from my dying father.

He'd made a plea deal in exchange for the possibility of parole. The word of a murderer wouldn't have been good enough alone, but Darius had been smart enough to know that his business would most likely lead to jail. He'd kept all correspondence, as well as a copy of the disk. It was all the cops needed to arrest Andre.

The trial had lasted seven days, and the jury had taken less than ninety minutes to convict Andre of hiring someone to kill my father, and for the unintentional deaths of my mother and sister. He'd also been convicted of embezzlement, reckless endangerment, and a few other crimes that had to do with his business practices. A reporter asked one of the jurors if it had been difficult to come to a unanimous vote. The juror had said that the only reason it had taken as long as it had was the paperwork involved for each of the crimes.

We'd all gone to the sentencing, but none of us had spoken when the judge had asked. Instead, we'd sat right behind Andre and held on to the pictures of our family.

Altogether, the judge sentenced him to one life sentence, plus a total of one hundred and thirty-two more years on top of that. Even with good behavior, he wouldn't be up for parole until he was well over ninety.

It had been an intense, emotional day, which was why Jax had invited us all to the opening of *Pothos*, the BDSM club we'd invested in. Jax hadn't needed the money, but he'd wanted us to have something we were all a part of. He'd run it, of course, and the rest of us could be as involved as we wanted. With Cai and Slade having moved back to Boston, they'd probably spend more time there than I would, but I planned to visit often. I was grateful that none of them had been upset when I'd told them that I didn't want to move back to Boston. They'd all told me that I should follow my heart, and if that meant staying in Wyoming, then so be it.

"You look amazing," I said to Brea as she came out of the bathroom.

Scarlet and tight, she was going to get a lot of attention tonight. Too bad. She was mine.

Like always, that made me smile.

We were staying with Jax and Syll, and it had been strange at first to have Brea in my former bedroom, but I was glad to be here instead of at some hotel. Even if Jax did tease both of us about the amount of noise we made. It'd been worth it to see Syll smack the back of his head and tell him to behave.

"Thank you," she said, smoothing non-existent wrinkles from the clingy silk.

"I'd kiss you, but I have a feeling that if I did, I'd end up against the wall and we'd be late."

"We can't have that," she said with a smile. She stretched up to kiss my cheek.

By the time we arrived at the club, the rest of my family was there, waiting for us before they went inside. There was already a line at the front door, and I had a feeling that the boulder of a man who stood in front of it was going to earn his keep tonight.

Staff were already busy at work, making sure everything was perfect. A couple looked nervous as they glanced at Jax, but most were relaxed, chatting, clearly at ease. That was important. If the staff acted cagey, then anyone new to the life might not feel comfortable coming back. The staff was as important as the décor.

Before I could get a good look at things, the side door opened, and a couple walked in, both smiling. She was in her late twenties, with golden blonde curls and dark eyes. He was older, probably by five or six years, with dark hair and serious muscles. Both were extremely attractive, even more so when they smiled, and I wondered who they were.

"Carrie, Gavin! I'm glad you guys could make it." Jax held out his hand, and both shook. "Everyone, this is Gavin and Carrie Manning."

It took me a moment to remember why I knew those names, but by the time Jax had gone around and given all our names, I'd remembered.

They owned Club Privé, the hot BDSM club in New York that was so popular, all my brothers and I had gone to it at least once even though we'd never talked about it with each other.

It'd been that club that had given Jax the idea for *Pothos*, though he'd gone with the name of the Greek god of sexual longing, yearning, and desire for his club name.

"I love your club," Slade said with a smile. He put his arm around Cheyenne and pulled her tight against his side.

I liked her. I liked Syll and Addison too. Each of the women were different, and they were all perfect for my brothers. They balanced each other just like Brea balanced me. While I had no plans to move here, I did want to spend more time with my family.

Something I never thought I'd say.

"Carrie and Gavin's club gave Jax the idea for *Pothos*," I said to Brea.

"It's a sex club, then?" she asked.

I nodded. "A nice one too."

She raised an eyebrow. "You've been there."

I grinned at her. "I have. It's where I realized I liked this stuff."

"Carrie and Gavin both generously gave me advice on various stages of getting things up and running," Jax continued. "Something they hadn't needed to do."

"Especially since you hit on my wife the first time we all met," Gavin said mildly.

Everyone looked at Syll.

"It was before we met," Syll said, leaning against Jax. "He already told me about it."

Jax grinned, an expression I was still getting used to seeing on his face. "See, guys? Be honest with your women, and you won't end up in the doghouse."

"Your women?" Syll looked up at him.

"Uh, I think that's doghouse talk, Jax," Slade said good-naturedly.

"The place looks great," Carrie said, easily diffusing things.

"I love what you did here. A modern twist on ancient Greek culture."

That started a whole discussion between the two couples, and it wasn't really anything I was particularly interested in. Judging by the look on my other brothers' faces, they weren't either.

"I think we should grab a drink before the doors open," Slade said.

Cai tapped him on the back to get his attention and Slade winced. Cai frowned. "Seriously? I barely touched you."

"I got a new tattoo," Slade said. He looked down at Cheyenne, and all of us could see the love in his eyes. "Chey designed it just for me."

"That's romantic," Addison said with a long sigh. "I heard you're quite the artist."

"Thank you," Cheyenne said softly.

Slade looked around the group. "How about that drink?"

"Do you want a drink?" I asked Brea.

Her cheeks flushed. "No, but I'd like to take a walk around. Explore."

One look in her eyes told me she didn't want to check out the moldings and flooring. We'd been playing with toys a bit more over the last couple months, and she'd enjoyed everything we'd done so far.

She tugged on my hand, so I leaned down to make it easier for her to whisper in my ear.

"I'm not wearing anything under my dress."

Shit. I went instantly hard.

"Jax, mind if we check out one of your rooms?" I asked without taking my eyes off the beautiful woman beside me.

"Go for it," he said. "Key cards are behind the bar. Make sure you lock the door if you don't want anyone watching...or joining in."

I looked down at Brea, and the thought of anyone seeing her

naked, seeing her flush, seeing the look on her face when she came...fuck no. "I'll lock the door."

A few minutes later, I was doing just that.

"Wow." Brea stood in the center of the room and slowly turned, taking it all in. "That's a lot of toys. You don't have this many."

"That's because I'm the only one using them. This room is for lots of different people who like different things." I walked over to the wall and gestured to a huge strap-on. "Like this, for example."

Her lips quirked up. "Does that mean you're not into anal?"

I nearly choked on a laugh, and then the sound died in my throat when I realized it was a serious question.

I swallowed hard. "You want to...fuck me?"

She laughed and shook her head. "Not like that. Well, not unless you want me to."

I crossed over to where she was standing and slid my hands over her hips and up to her breasts. "Not something I'm into...for myself anyway."

She licked her lips. "Does that mean you're interested in fucking my ass?"

My hands dropped to said body part. "Are you serious?"

"Yes."

I didn't even have to think about it. "There's a bench to your right. Bend over it."

She moved to obey, anticipation crackling around her. Any doubts I'd had about her wanting to do this disappeared.

I moved over to the dresser and opened the top drawer. Sandalwood scented lube. Who knew.

I picked it up and moved over to where Brea was waiting. "Do you have any idea how beautiful you are?"

"You don't need to try so hard," she teased. "I'm a sure thing."

I flipped her skirt up, and I saw that she'd been telling the truth about not wearing underwear. I went down on my knees and palmed her ass, squeezing the firm globes, massaging with my thumbs as I pulled them apart.

"If you change your mind, just say *butterfly*, and I'll stop."

She nodded. "I'll remember, but I won't need it. This wasn't some impulsive decision. I've been planning this for a while."

"Really?"

She looked back at me. "You're not the only one who likes to try new things."

Fuck. I loved this woman.

"If that's the case..." I leaned forward and licked her from clitoris to anus, grinning when she gasped. "Stay still. I've got to make sure you're nice and wet."

She tried – she really did – but I had a talented tongue, and I put it to good use. I teased her clit until she was on the edge, then moved to her pussy, licking around and inside. When I went back to her ass, she tensed up, but she didn't stop me. I probed the muscle with the tip of my tongue, then pushed inside.

"Fuck..." she moaned. "Never thought..."

"Relax." I bit her right cheek hard enough to leave little red indents in her skin. She yelped but didn't pull away. "Good girl."

I turned my attention back to the hole I'd be breaching tonight. I wasn't one to be caught up in counting or obsessing over past sexual partners, but some primal part of me loved the idea of being the first person to take her in this sensitive way.

I continued working my tongue into her ass as I pushed two fingers into her pussy, earning another one of those erotic moans. I worked them together, coaxing her toward orgasm. When she finally came, she did it with a shout, her pussy tightening around my fingers.

She was still trembling as I replaced my tongue with my index finger, sinking it to the first knuckle easily. I stood and squirted some lube on my finger as I worked it in and out. She hissed out a breath, her head falling as I added a second finger.

"Fuck, Blake, fuck fuck..."

"You okay?"

She nodded. "It...burns...but good...ohhhh..."

I decided to take that as a positive thing. I twisted my fingers, and she pushed back against my hand. I did it a couple more times as my free hand managed to get my pants open and down. She was as ready as she could be, and my cock was so hard that I knew I'd have to work to keep from coming right away.

I removed my fingers and was rewarded with a growl. "Easy, babe. I'll give you something better."

I slicked my cock with lube before lining up and pushing forward. I kept it slow but steady, the searing heat and vice-like grip just painful enough to keep me from coming.

Brea let out a stream of curses, and I echoed her, my legs barely able to keep me up. Her entire body quivered around and underneath me. I slid my hands underneath her, squeezing her breasts through her dress, rubbing her slit. There was nothing gentle about my touch, and nothing had been calculated to bring her pleasure. It was all about touching her, feeling her. Being with her.

"Blake, please," she whimpered.

I bit the back of her neck, then straightened. Grabbing her hips, I pulled back, leaving just the tip inside before driving back into her. She cried out, her body shaking.

"Touch yourself," I demanded. "Touch yourself and don't stop, not even if you come. Don't stop until I come."

She nodded, balancing herself on one hand while she moved the other underneath her, fingers taking over the space my own fingers had just been. She jerked as she found her clit swollen and sensitive, but she began to rub it anyway. I'd barely made two thrusts before she was coming around me.

"Fuck, Brea," I grunted.

I tried to think of something else, anything that would force my body back under my control, but nothing could distract me from the way she'd tightened around me. I pounded into her, and she kept coming, one wave after another until she was sobbing my name, begging me to finish.

"Please! Come in my ass! Please, Blake! Come! Come! Fuck! Too much! Too much! Come in my ass! Please! Please! Fuck!"

Every inch of me was on fire, and it was all because of this woman. I loved her, and that meant more than any physical sensation ever could. And it was that thought that finally did it for me.

"Fuck! Brea!"

As we went to the floor together, I wrapped my arms around her. "Love you," I murmured. "So much."

"Me too." She put her arms around my neck, pressing her face against my chest. "Love you too."

I'd never imagined life could be like this, and I never wanted to go back to the way it had been.

THIRTY-FIVE
BREA

Boston in October was stunning.

I loved Wyoming, and I'd been to some amazing places growing up, but Boston in autumn was something else. The fact that it was Jax and Syll's wedding only made it even more beautiful.

The last five months had been amazing. I'd moved in with Blake after our trip here back in May, but I'd also kept my apartment in Rawlins too. We both wanted to spend more time with his family here, but neither of us wanted to leave Wyoming, so he'd purchased a small private plane to make it easier to travel back and forth. We'd also come up with an additional solution but hadn't told his family yet. We didn't want to get their hopes up while we still had a lot to do. Find a place in Boston that had a place for Blake to do his work. Find a space where I could open another store. Find people I trusted even when I wasn't there. Once we had all the logistics in place, we'd make the announcement.

I smiled at my reflection as I made sure the jeweled butterflies in my hair were secure. Syll had asked Cheyenne, Addison, and me to be bridesmaids, and all three of us, plus Syll's friend Gilly, had gotten different accessories that matched each of our personalities. I looked forward to seeing Blake's face when he saw my hair. Though I hadn't ever used our safe word, it was still *butterfly*.

"You're gorgeous," Addison said as she came into the room. "Blake is going to lose it when he sees you. I mean, you're beautiful all the time, but that dress and your hair and your makeup. I can never manage to get my makeup like that, and my hair does what it wants half the time–"

"You look beautiful too," I said, stopping Addison's babbling. She was almost as nervous as Syll, but more because she wasn't the sort of person who liked being in front of a lot of people. I loved her. I was certain that, one day, I'd have three amazing sisters-in-law, and the more time I spent with them, the happier I was about it.

"Thanks." She beamed.

"Everything okay, Chey?" I asked as Cheyenne came in, looking a little frazzled.

"It's fine," she said, stopping in front of the full-length mirror to straighten her hair. "Someone just gave Austin a couple cookies when Estrada was in the bathroom. I'm pretty sure it was Slade. He has a hard time saying no to Austin sometimes."

Her tone made me think that she usually thought it was charming how much Slade loved her brother, but today wasn't the best day for a sugar-high five-year-old. Not for the first time this week, I wondered what sort of father Blake would be. We hadn't really talked about kids specifically, but we'd said enough to know that we both wanted more than one. Maybe Austin would prompt a natural conversation.

"How's Estrada doing now that Austin's in kindergarten?" I asked.

"Good," Cheyenne said. "I was worried that once she didn't have him all day, she'd feel like moving here was a mistake, but she's really settled in and is happy here."

"Once Jax and Syll get back from their honeymoon, we'll have to discuss the holidays," Addison said. "Do you think you and Blake will be able to come back for Thanksgiving and Christmas? Or we could all go out to you. Your parents' retreat would have enough rooms for all of us."

"It would," I agreed. "I'll tell Blake we'll need to discuss plans then."

Thinking of traditional holidays with this great big extended family brought another smile to my face. I loved them all as much as I loved my parents. Maybe they could even join the Hunters for Christmas, have something normal for once.

But first, a wedding.

"THAT WAS A BEAUTIFUL CEREMONY," I said as Blake pulled me closer. We didn't dance a lot, but when we did, it was always slow songs, and he always held me as tightly as possible, as if he was worried I'd slip away.

"It was," he agreed. "And I've never seen Jax look that happy before."

"They're really good together," I said.

He nodded in agreement, then fell silent. We danced through the end of the song, and another one started.

I'd meant to wait until we were back home, but I couldn't keep my news from him any longer. Not because this was a perfect moment, but because it wasn't the timing that mattered. I just wanted to be able to share something important with my best friend.

"Blake, I have something to tell you."

He looked down at me, all his attention focused on me.

"I've known for a couple days, but I wasn't sure when would be the best time to tell you," I began. "I don't want to wait anymore though. I want to share it with you." I smiled. "I'm pregnant."

His eyes widened, but he didn't miss a step. "You're sure?"

I nodded, searching his face for some response to the news.

"That's amazing!" He didn't raise his voice, but he did kiss me, and that was better than a huge announcement. It was a sweet, passionate kiss, full of promises.

"I know we hadn't talked about having kids, but this came out of nowhere. I believe we can make it work."

He smiled at me, then brushed his lips across mine. "Your timing is actually perfect."

"It is?"

He cupped my chin and ran his thumb along my bottom lip. "Yes. Because I want to marry you."

"What?" I stopped dancing. I'd hoped we'd get there eventually, but I hadn't expected it like this, not so soon.

"Marry me, Brea." He reached into his pocket and pulled out a small box. "Even if it's just so I don't have to carry this around anymore."

He opened it, and I found myself looking at a beautifully crafted gold ring. Diamond chips glittered in the metal. It wasn't a traditional engagement ring, and that made me love it even more.

"Yes," I said, emotion making the words a whisper. "I would love to marry you."

He kissed me hard, not caring about anyone around us. It was just the two of us, celebrating the new life ahead of us. Then I heard the cheers behind us, and as we ended our kiss, I saw that we were surrounded by family. They might not have heard my news, but they knew what it meant to see a man with a ring box in hand. And they were happy for us. This wasn't only Blake and me and the baby on the way. It was all of us, because we were all family.

THE END

Turn the page for a free preview of my upcoming series, *New Pleasures*.

PREVIEW: NEW PLEASURES

ONE

My heart pounded as I ran through the darkened hallway. He was coming, and if he caught me, I'd die. My hands were slick with blood, but I didn't think it was mine. My sides hurt from running, and my feet were cold, but I wasn't injured. Not yet. If he caught me though, I'd be worse than injured. I'd be dead.

Had he killed someone else? It certainly seemed possible.

I passed a mirror and my reflection caught my eye. I missed a step. Something was wrong. I stopped and went over to the mirror. This couldn't be me. I was a grown-up, but the girl in the mirror wasn't a grown-up. She was tall, but not as tall as I knew I'd be someday. The ash blonde hair and china blue eyes were the same, but the face was too round, too young. The hair too long.

If I knew I was older, did that mean that he didn't kill me?

"Get back here, you little brat!"

Ice flooded my veins. He was close, and he was angry. He'd been angry for almost a year now. Every day, even if it was a good day. He found something to be angry about.

"Don't you go hiding now! That's just going to make this worse!"

He was right. Hiding just made him madder, but I was scared of what he'd do if he found me. I'd been protected before, but not anymore.

I looked down at my hands, at the blood soaking my clothes. It was her *blood. He'd hurt her. Killed her. She was gone, and no one would protect me anymore.*

But I didn't need someone else to protect me. I was an adult. I could protect myself. Besides, this wasn't real. It was a dream.

The trees around me began to sway, bending low, reaching for me with their branches. I pushed them away, thin needles like razors that sliced my skin, mixing her *blood with mine. I barely registered the pain. Pines. The smell of pines filled my nose. My chest tightened, and it was hard to breathe. I needed to get away.*

I started running again, rocks cutting into my bare feet, bruising them, but I couldn't care about that. Not when I could hear him behind me, breaking things. I slammed the door behind me and then looked around, trying to find something I could put in front of it.

But it was glass. Even if I did manage to block it, he could just break through.

But I couldn't just wait here, unprotected either.

I spotted a rock. Not like a little stone or even some medium-sized flowerbed edging rock. This was huge. The kind of thing people put in their yards with their house numbers on them.

I went over to it and put my hands on it. It was rough, like sandstone, but at least my hands wouldn't slip. The blood was tacky now, clinging to the rock as I braced my feet and pushed.

A blow shook the door and my muscles screamed as I put more force into it. I needed to get this in front of the door. He was going to get inside.

Crying. Someone was crying.
An animal?
No, a kid. I was sure it was a kid.

He was screaming now. Not words. Just sound. So loud that people had to hear him.

No, wait, there were words. Bad words. Words that I wasn't allowed to repeat.

The rock didn't move, and the glass cracked. Fear dumped even more adrenaline into my body and I could taste it in the back of my mouth. I was going to be sick.

I dropped to my knees and buried my face in my hands. The smell of blood filled my nose. It was sharp and metallic and made my stomach hurt.

I made a pained sound. My eyes started watering.

This was more than just an upset stomach. It felt like fire was inside me, and I was being pulled apart. I retched, and it just made things worse. My head hurt, and I felt like I was going to pass out.

How could I pass out in a dream?

This had to be a dream. If it wasn't, it would be too horrible to consider.

The crying got worse. Why wouldn't someone shut him up? Why was he crying when I was the one who was hurting?

The glass cracked, and a dog started barking far away.

I screamed and someone else screamed and the dog barked, and the kid cried and the door broke and–

I jerked away, another scream dying in my throat. My heart was racing, my breathing ragged, and I leaned over to turn on the bedside light. Soft white light flooded the room and I looked away to give my eyes a moment to adjust.

"Just a dream." I said the words out-loud, as if that would make it all just magically disappear.

I shivered, the sweat on my body rapidly drying now that I was awake. My breathing and pulse were beginning to return to normal too. If this had been just a normal nightmare, I'd get up, maybe get some water, then climb back in bed.

I'd had these sorts of nightmares before.

Falling off a bridge. Spiders. Monkeys. Spider monkeys. Not actual spider monkeys but a creature that looked like a cross between a spider and a monkey.

Typical monsters that nightmares are made of.

This hadn't been one of those nightmares, the ones that were easy to shake off because they were ridiculous in the light of day, which meant that I wasn't going to be getting back to sleep anytime soon, if at all. I knew myself well enough to know that it'd be pointless to try.

I ran my hand over my hair, thankful for the short haircut that didn't require a lot of maintenance. I leaned back against my pillows and stared up at the ceiling. I needed to figure out what I was going to do now. I had hours before I had to be anywhere, and I wasn't going to be able to concentrate enough to read. I could've watched some tv, but the walls here were pretty thin and I didn't want to bother anyone else. Besides, if I couldn't sleep, I could at least find something worthwhile to do.

I got out of bed and turned on my overhead light before turning off the lamp. I wasn't quite ready to be in the dark again. By the time I stepped outside, however, I was comfortable enough to appreciate the stars speckled across the rich, deep blue sky. I was too close to the city for it to be completely pitch black, so that helped too.

I'd already stretched, so once I hit the cool early morning air, I didn't have to stand around before jogging a few feet. I was just glad that it was May and not January.

I started off down the path, gradually moving from jogging to running. I wasn't doing a flat-out sprint, but I was moving at a pretty good clip when I turned onto the sidewalk and made my way deeper into the city.

Virginia and Indiana weren't really that similar in weather or terrain, but I had the strangest feeling of déjà vu as I ran. My nightmares – the really bad ones – did that to me sometimes. Made me feel like I was a kid again. It made sense that I'd feel that now. I'd loved to run as a kid too, and I'd been good at it. I'd actually done track in high school and made it to state a couple times.

One of the main reasons I'd always loved running was that it emptied my mind. I didn't have to think about anything but putting one foot in front of the other. Some people liked music when they ran, but I didn't. I preferred to hear what was going on around me. Birds. Traffic. People. Some of it was because I liked those sounds, but I knew that most of it was because I always wanted to be aware of my surroundings, even while my head was empty.

I'd made it a couple miles when I realized where I was. The hotel was nice enough, not too high end, but not too tacky either. It was perfect for businesses, especially ones who had guests staying for more than a few nights, and that was exactly why I'd ended up here, even if it hadn't been a conscious decision.

I headed inside without second-guessing myself. If I wasn't wanted, I'd go back, maybe go to the weight room until breakfast. But if I was wanted...well, that was going to be vastly more fun.

I waved at the man at the front desk and he wiggled his fingers at me. I'd seen Hal a couple times over the last few weeks and as long as he didn't get any complaints about me, he had no problem letting me walk right past. Unless someone high up found about my clandestine visits, no one was going to say anything, and I didn't intend for anyone to find out. If it looked like that would happen, I had no problem walking away.

Right now, however, I intended to wipe my mind of everything that had been in it tonight. Give myself something better to think about. More enjoyable anyway.

I knocked on the door twice, and then waited.

TWO

THE MAN WHO ANSWERED THE DOOR TO THE SUITE WAS thirty-three to my twenty-two years, but he was as fit as any field agent in his twenties. A fact that I could currently see since he wasn't wearing a shirt. I took a moment to appreciate the view, from his unruly dark brown hair to the blue-gray eyes that were still muddled with sleep, all the way down his chest to the trail of dark hair that disappeared under the waistband of his pants.

"Agent Kurth." I gave Clay a snappy little salute.

"Rona?" He rubbed the back of his neck as he looked behind him. "It's three in the morning."

I raised an eyebrow. "Are you going to invite me in?"

We didn't need to do the dance about why I was here so early. He'd known me for years, and he knew about my nightmares. He didn't know exactly what they were about since the subject had always been off-limits, but he knew they often resulted in insomnia. When he'd showed back up in my life seven weeks ago, I'd been glad to see him, but things hadn't become sexual until one night a few weeks later when I'd had the nightmare and I'd gone for a run. Like tonight, I'd found myself outside his hotel room door, and one thing had led to another. We hadn't really talked about it since, but it'd become a thing between us, our friendship adding some 'benefits.' We could walk away at any time, opt out whenever we didn't feel like hooking up.

It was just sex between friends. That was all.

For a moment, I thought he was going to turn me away. It was early in the morning, after all, and he had to work early. We both did. Just because I couldn't sleep didn't mean he had to lose sleep too.

He didn't opt out though. He gestured for me to come in, then shut the door behind me.

"I wish you'd see someone about that nightmare," he said as he stepped past me and walked into the little kitchenette.

I kicked off my shoes and yanked down my pants, kicking them aside. "And I wish you'd stop talking and start working on distracting."

His eyes slid over my body, and heat followed his gaze. I hadn't worn anything sexy, but he never cared about that. It wasn't about what I was wearing, but what he was thinking about doing to me. I'd had a couple partners over the years, some of them bad, some good. Clay was better than good, *and* he was...inventive. It was a combination that kept me coming back for more, but not one that would get us past being friends who fucked.

"Come here."

When I reached him, he motioned toward the counter and I lifted myself onto it. At two inches under six feet and an athlete's build, I wasn't the sort of woman who got literally picked up by guys. I didn't mind though. I wasn't sure I'd ever met someone I trusted enough to let him manhandle me. If Clay didn't fit that particular qualification, I doubted anyone else would.

"Do you ever stop thinking?" Clay asked as he put his hands on my knees.

"What do you think?" I countered, wrapping my legs around his waist and pulling him closer.

Instead of answering, he captured my mouth in deep, hot kiss, his tongue plundering, exploring. I ran my hands over his chest, his dark hair rough against my palms. He made a sound in the back of his throat when I rubbed my thumbs over his nipples. I used my nails then, blunt as they were, scraping them over the darker flesh, and he dug his fingers into my thighs.

"Damn, Rona," he groaned, tearing his mouth away from mine.

I flicked my tongue against one nipple, then the other. One hand moved under my shirt and I stiffened for a moment, then relaxed, his signal that he could continue. We'd established boundaries the first time we were together. He could touch my breasts over my bra, but the shirt stayed on and he didn't go anywhere else. I knew he'd felt some scar tissue a time or two, but he'd been careful to stay away from it.

And to never ask questions.

His free hand dropped between our bodies and his thumb pressed against the damp fabric between my legs. I made a low sound, my eyes closing. My head fell forward onto his shoulder and I ran my hands up his back and then down to his ass. As his thumb pushed the material between my lips, he found that bundle of nerves and pressed against it. I slid my fingers under the waistband of his boxers, dipping my fingers into the two little dimples at the base of his spine.

Soft kisses trailed up my jawline, and then he took my earlobe between his teeth. Mouth and fingers worked together, stoking the fire low in my belly. For all the banter we'd had, when we finally got down to business, there was no waiting around, no dragging things out. This wasn't making love. It was having sex. Fucking. Physical pleasure and stress relief with a friend.

I squeezed my eyes closed, muscles tensing in anticipation

of the relief that was only seconds away. He rubbed my clit harder, faster, and I came with a cry. I turned my face into the place where his shoulder and neck met, panting. He gave me a moment to come down, and then he was taking a step back. I let him go, raising my head in time to see him drop his boxers. His cock was average length, but a little thicker than most, which meant it rubbed against a lot of nice places.

He fisted his cock as he opened a drawer and rummaged through it for a moment before pulling out a condom.

"You have them in every drawer here?" I laughed as the feeling returned to my legs. I could usually get myself off pretty well, but sometimes it was nice to have someone else involved.

Clay shrugged and gave me that cocky grin of his. I'd masturbated to that smile plenty of times since I'd first met him, and it still turned me on. He was one of those pretty-boy sorts that people usually underestimated, but I'd always seen the intelligence in his eyes, and that just made him sexier in my opinion.

"Down," he ordered as he rolled on the condom.

I slid off the counter and took a moment to drop my panties before turning around and leaning over. I spread my legs and heard an appreciative sound from behind me.

"You have an amazing ass," he said as he ran his hands over both cheeks before dropping one hand down between my legs. "Damn, you're wet."

I nodded and braced myself on my forearms. He shoved two fingers inside me and I let out a shaky breath. His fingers pumped in and out of me, twisting on every other thrust until he could add a third finger.

"Fuck!" I slapped the countertop. "Just get on with it!"

He chuckled and pulled his fingers out. "All right."

A moment later, he was pushing his way inside me, an inch at a time. I let out a long groan as my body stretched and molded itself around him. When he was finally inside, he reached under me and put his hands over my breasts, squeezing them for a moment before moving his hands back to my hips. He set a brutal pace, knowing that I'd tell him if he was being too rough. He hadn't gotten to that point yet. If anything, a part of me wished he'd push just a little bit further.

I wasn't going to complain though. Each snap of his hips sent a ripple of painful pleasure through me, driving me toward another orgasm. Though it wouldn't come soon enough to catch him if I didn't help it along, so I reached underneath me and pressed my fingers against my clit. I made short, brisk circles – the best way to get me off after I'd already come once – and just as Clay's rhythm started faltering, I came again.

"Yes, yes, yes," I chanted as white-hot pleasure exploded through my body.

Clay was talking too, but I didn't pay much attention to what he was saying. All I cared about was that the tension in my body had faded. I'd done what I'd come here to do.

After a couple seconds, he pulled out and moved away to take care of the condom. I rested a few moments longer and then straightened. I glanced at the clock. Dammit. Not enough time to attempt to go back to sleep.

I bent over to pick up my underwear, and then went to the door for my pants. "I'm heading back," I called. He was in the bathroom, but I knew he could hear me.

"You want a ride?"

"No," I said. "I still have time to run back, shower, and get to class on time."

"I'll see you there then."

I heard the shower turn on as I pulled on my shoes. We both knew he only offered me a ride to be polite. No one at Quantico could know that Clay and I had been sleeping together. He wasn't my supervisor, but I doubted anyone would make that much of a distinction. I was eleven weeks into FBI training and he was a guest lecturer. Not exactly kosher, even if we had known each other before.

It didn't matter though, I thought as I left the hotel. Once training was over, I'd be off to wherever I was assigned, and Clay would be off to the next lecture. We'd keep in touch, cross paths, maybe fuck. It'd never be anything more than that.

THREE

A QUICK, BUT THOROUGH, SHOWER AND A CUP OF COFFEE with a bagel were enough to wake me up completely. I might be flagging by the end of the day, but right now, I was good. My first class would be with Clay, and it didn't matter how long he'd known me or the fact that we were sleeping together, he'd call on me if he thought I was dozing. It was one of his favorite things to do to trainees. It didn't matter if he was lecturing in a full auditorium or doing a more casual class where he was in front of only a dozen people. He demanded attention. The thing that kept him from being a total asshole was that it was always about making sure people were learning what they needed to, so they'd do the best job possible. Sometimes, that meant embarrassing the hell out of someone. I sure as hell didn't want it to be me.

As I walked in the building, he was there. I barely glanced at him, but I felt his eyes on me as I walked past him and into the classroom. Today's lecture was about family annihilators and what made their psychopathy different from mass murderers or serial killers. We wouldn't be dealing with those sorts of cases much here in the FBI, but a family hostage taker could be an annihilator and we'd need to know how to handle it differently than, say, someone who wanted something.

I couldn't say I was looking forward to it, but I'd deal with it the same way I'd dealt with everything else in my life. Besides, if I couldn't handle hearing about it, I'd be no good if I was called to a scene where it was the issue. As an Intelligence Analyst, that wouldn't be my usual case, but I believed in being prepared. Besides, there was no guarantee I'd actually make it in the field I'd chosen. Best to plan for all possible contingencies.

I usually sat in the first couple rows, but before I'd gone more than a few steps, the door opened behind me.

"Quick!"

I turned around, the movement automatic the moment I heard the familiar bark of Martin Edwards, one of the senior agents at Quantico. He wasn't the very top guy, but he was up there pretty far, and he scared the shit out of pretty much every trainee here. Not me, but I wasn't exactly the best judge when it came to fear. Not many people intimidated me. I couldn't think of a single one off the top of my head.

"Yes, Sir?" I gave what I hoped was a polite, but not too cheery, smile.

He scowled at me and my heart sank.

"Come with me."

Shit. Had someone figured out about Clay and me? Shit, *shit*! We could deny it, I supposed. The fact that we'd known each other before could be a believable reason for me visiting him at his hotel. He'd been my uncle's friend, after all.

When I was almost at the door, he walked away, and I hurried to keep up with him. He clearly didn't want to walk and talk, but I was fine with that. If he was about to chew me out for fooling around with Clay, I definitely didn't want to do it with an audience.

We made it all the way to his office without a single word

being said, but as soon as he opened the door he snapped at me, "Sit."

My stomach twisted. This was worse than I thought. I sat.

He settled in his chair and folded his hands in front of him. His face was back to being expressionless, but that didn't necessarily mean I was off the hook. Especially when he didn't start talking right away. I vaguely remembered hearing somewhere that he'd been one of the agency's top interrogators, and I finally admitted that I was in extremely deep shit.

"Rona Quick."

"Yes, Sir?"

He gave me a look that said he hadn't wanted a response from me. He'd let me know if I was supposed to speak.

"Rona Elizabeth Quick." He reached forward and picked up a file folder from his desk. "That's the name you submitted on your application."

Fuck. It wasn't about Clay.

"Mother, Dana Quick, father unknown. Birthplace, Carmel, Indiana."

My pulse raced but I didn't interrupt him as I tried to figure out exactly how bad this was going to be.

"Do I need to keep reading?" he asked, clearly expecting an answer this time.

"No, sir," I said quietly.

"You were asked if you were known by another name, and you said *no*. At the end of the application, you were asked, as was every applicant, if the contents of the application were true to the best of your knowledge. You checked the 'I agree' box and signed underneath it. In doing so, you also accepted that lying on the form would be a federal offense."

I was going to be sick.

"We would normally have weeded out any discrepancies fairly early on, but you came with a letter of recommendation from one of our own–"

Shit. Clay.

"He didn't know," I whispered.

Edwards continued as if I hadn't even spoken. "Once we started looking, however, we found that you'd lied about several different things, including your name, your parentage, and the fact that a close family member had been convicted of a felony."

I'd known it was coming. If they'd found one lie, they'd found all of them, because they were all connected. Pick at a single thread long enough and everything would unravel.

"I assume all of what we found is true, and not more fabrication."

I picked up the folder and glanced inside. I didn't need to read the details to know what it said. "It is."

"Did you really think that you could get away with it?" He seemed more curious now, than angry.

I didn't want to look at him when I answered, but I forced myself to do exactly that. I'd known the risks and the consequences, and I'd made the decision anyway. "I didn't know, but I thought it was worth trying."

He tossed the folder back onto the desk. "Why didn't you fill it out truthfully?"

"I thought about it," I said, "but I knew if I did, it would all be there in my permanent file, where anyone could find it if they wanted to look hard enough."

"Your past wasn't *erased*, Miss Quick. It can still be found."

"You know all of it then," I said. When he nodded, I continued, "I didn't want anyone thinking I had a weakness that could be exploited, that I wasn't strong enough to handle what someone might throw at me because of it. I didn't want instructors using it as a reason why I wouldn't make it. And I didn't want it to be all anyone saw when they looked at me."

Maybe the lengthy explanation wasn't really necessary, but I wanted it out there. I hadn't done it on a whim, or without understanding how serious it was. Other people might not get it

– hell, I was pretty sure *no one* would get it – but I stood by my decision, even now.

Oh well. Nothing I could do about it now. Might as well get along with it.

"What happens now?" I asked.

"I need to know who knew about this," he said.

"No one."

He gave me a skeptical look.

"By the time I met Dr. Kurth, I'd already had my name legally changed," I said. "As for the rest of it, we didn't talk about it. Ever."

"And you believe that your uncle never told Agent Kurth anything?"

"He wouldn't have," I said. "Believe me, it was the last thing either of us ever wanted to talk about."

"What about when he talked to you about joining the agency?"

"I didn't say anything," I repeated. "He still doesn't know."

Edwards gave me a hard, searching look and I suddenly understood what it must have been to sit across from him in an interrogation room. As strong and stubborn as I usually considered myself, I couldn't imagine lasting very long against him.

"This isn't something that can be excused," he said, "no matter your reasoning. You have fifteen minutes to clean out your room and any other possessions you may have on the premises. Your clearance is revoked, and you'll be escorted from the grounds."

It could have been worse, I supposed. I could've ended up with a fine or jail time. Instead, I was only being kicked out the FBI academy, bringing all of the plans I'd had for the future to a screeching halt. No Intelligence Analysis. No FBI. No solving cases or protecting people. From the first moment Clay had suggested the FBI to me, I'd been determined to make that my life.

I nodded, not trusting myself to speak. I waited until he called for someone to follow me to the dorms, and then hurried away, desperate to leave before anyone realized how humiliated I was. I heard Clay calling my name, but I refused to even look at him. It was better this way. Once he realized that I'd been lying to him for years, he wouldn't ever want to speak to me again, no matter what our history.

Yet one more thing to add to the list of ways I'd fucked things up, simply so I wouldn't have to remember the past.

Continues in *New Pleasures*, the exciting spin-off to M.S. Parker's USA Today Bestselling series, The Pleasure Series.

ALSO BY M. S. PARKER

His Obsession

His Control

His Hunger

His Secret

Sex Coach

Big O's (Sex Coach 2)

Pleasure Island (Sex Coach 3)

Rescued by the Woodsman

The Billionaire's Muse

Bound

One Night Only

Damage Control

Take Me, Sir

Make Me Yours

The Billionaire's Sub

The Billionaire's Mistress

Con Man Box Set

HERO Box Set

A Legal Affair Box Set

The Client

Indecent Encounter

Dom X Box Set

Unlawful Attraction Box Set

Chasing Perfection Box Set

Blindfold Box Set

Club Prive Box Set

The Pleasure Series Box Set

Exotic Desires Box Set

Casual Encounter Box Set

Sinful Desires Box Set

Twisted Affair Box Set

Serving HIM Box Set

Pure Lust Box Set

ABOUT THE AUTHOR

M. S. Parker is a USA Today Bestselling author and the author of over fifty spicy romance series and novels.

Living part-time in Las Vegas, part-time on Maui, she enjoys sitting by the pool with her laptop writing her next spicy romance.

Growing up all she wanted to be was a dancer, actor and author. So far only the latter has come true but M. S. Parker hasn't retired her dancing shoes just yet. She is still waiting for the call to appear on Dancing With The Stars.

When M. S. isn't writing, she can usually be found reading–oops, scratch that! She is always writing.

For more information:
www.msparker.com
msparkerbooks@gmail.com

facebook.com/msparkerauthor

twitter.com/msparkerauthor

ACKNOWLEDGMENTS

First, I would like to thank all of my readers. Without you, my books would not exist. I truly appreciate each and every one of you.

A big THANK YOU goes out to all the Facebook fans, street team, beta readers, and advanced reviewers. You are a HUGE part of the success of all my series.

Also thank you to my editor Lynette, my proofreader Nancy, and my wonderful cover designer, Sinisa. You make my ideas and writing look so good.

Printed in Great Britain
by Amazon